BLACK FLAME

Book Two of the Daughters of Salem

Kellie O'Neill

ISBN: 979-8-9892443-7-9

www.KellieOneillBooks.com

For Mom, miss you.

A Spell for an Untraceable Death

(For an undetectable poison resulting in immediate death)

Ingredients:

The Root of a Snakeroot Plant Eight Snakeroot Leaves
Extra Virgin Olive Oil Moon Water One Garnet Stone

Instructions:

Boil the snakeroot leaves, mince the roots. Strain, boil again with garnet at the center of your caldron. Add one teaspoon of olive oil and one tablespoon of moon water. Mix elixir counter clockwise while reciting the incantation.

Incantation:

My silent poison in the night,
No sign you'll see, no cause for fright,
It steals your breath, no final plea,
Unbeknownst down it goes so stealthily.
Death's quiet hand, no one will ever see,
La Narine, cursed ye be.

PROLOGUE
The Hunt Is On

My phone levitates from the bed into my open palm. I swipe my thumb, and the time lights up on the screen. *Crap.* I type out a quick text.

Running late! Sorry!

While I cinch the laces on my Converse high-tops, my phone dings. It's from Jack. *My* Jack. The ends of my love struck lips curl up.

It's ok. Just gassing up. See you soon.

My bedroom door swings open.

"Mom told me to come tell you to stay in your room," Maggie says while licking a ruby red popsicle. She's wearing a swimsuit and cutoffs, like she's a walking reminder that we technically still have a few days of summer left.

I roll my eyes and groan. "What? No. My two months are up, I'm not grounded anymore."

Maggie shrugs. "Maybe she extended it."

"If Helen had any sense, she'd make it permanent," says the incessant British voice in my head. Blue leaps from the windowsill onto the bed and stares at me.

I snuck out to save Jack's life, I send back to the cat. *It's not like I ran away to Woodstock.*

"Talking to your cat again?" Maggie asks. I always forget how awkward it must seem when someone stops talking to you so they can have a telepathic conversation with their familiar.

"I'm going to talk to her," I say defiantly. Maggie takes a casual step to the side as I pass, then follows me down the tower steps to the second landing, still licking her popsicle. Before I reach the main stairs, Blue pounces in front of me.

"Don't!" He warns.

I frown at him, ready with a rebuttal, but a sound from downstairs makes my ears perk up. My mother and aunts are speaking with someone. Maggie and I crane our heads and peer through the spindles of the spiral staircase. "That is very troubling. Are you certain?" Mom asks. She's perched on the edge of the sofa with her sisters on either side of her. Across from them stands Mercy Wicklow, head of the North American Witches Committee. Even in our home, Mercy commands the room with the authority of an ardent general, like she owns the place. Mom's fearful eyes drift to the stairs, but they don't focus on anything. I don't think she spots us.

"Yes," Mercy replies with a sober intensity. "We've detected Nefari activity all over the city. It's unmistakable now; we haven't felt their influence like this since the sixties. Which is why, Helen," Mercy squares her shoulders and lifts her chin, "we formally offer you a seat on the Committee. It was discussed at length in our last meeting, and we are all in agreement."

Mom looks to Marie, who nods a silent confirmation.

Mercy continues, "We scheduled your induction ceremony for the next new moon. You have exceptional power, Helen, and an equally powerful reputation to boot. With your assistance, we will bring the Nefari to their knees…"

Maggie tepidly turns her head toward me. "Aren't you a Nefari?" she whispers.

CHAPTER ONE
The Glamours

My phone balances precariously between my cheek and shoulder as I shove my textbooks into my locker. Jack is describing his favorite professor while I try to conceal how annoyed I am at myself. It's only three weeks into my senior year and somehow, I'm already behind.

"I had my doubts about Dr. Lockheed when he applauded Oaks Gleason, you know that kid with the sugar sculptures, especially after Oaks said his favorite artist was Banksy," Jack says. "Apparently the applause was ironic." My violin case wobbles in my arms when I take it from the locker, nearly dropping to the floor. "I still think you're too harsh about 'Balloon Girl'," I say, having spent the summer reading up on the art world, from renaissance to modern.

Maggie strolls down the hall surrounded by giggling girls and drooling boys hanging on her every word. It's only her freshman year at Griggs and she already owns the place. No surprise there. She slows her pace as she comes near. She dismisses her new posse with a wave. *Ready to go?* she mouths, tugging at the collar of her stiff uniform. She peers down at her outfit in disdain.

I nod and stick my Latin textbook in my bag.

"Are you still coming up next weekend?" Jack asks.

"No, you're coming down here, remember? My sister's rehearsal dinner is that Friday. Then the ceremony's on Saturday."

He groans. "Right, sorry. I've got my days all messed up. My last class on Friday is at three, so I'll be running late."

Even when giving me bad news, his voice still makes me smile. I miss feeling his arms around me. "It's okay, talk later tonight?" I look to Maggie and nod toward the parking lot. She falls in step with me as she scrolls through her phone.

Jack's breath catches before he responds. "I'll try. I might not be available until late."

I swallow back my anxiety. *He's in college,* I remind myself. *There's nothing to worry about.* But Sally's cautionary tale echoes in the back of my mind. I was sitting in the living room, love drunk, catching my breath after Jack had just left for the night. Sally sauntered in through the front door, her lipstick conspicuously smeared off her lips.

"Abe again?" I asked while she kicked off her spiked heels.

Sally hung her head back, sighing. "I forgot what a great kisser he is." I moved from the couch and leaned on the doorframe next to her.

"This is, what? The twelfth date this month? Seems to be getting serious," I said with a playfully suspicious tone.

She shrugged her boney shoulders. "I don't know. He dreamt of me too early. He was too young. *We* were too young. Who knows what will happen."

I straightened up, all playfulness having evaporated. "But that means something, Sal. He dreamed of you. You two are destined."

Sally stared into my eyes, suddenly more serious than I'm used to from my kooky, wildly inappropriate aunt. "Not all soulmates end up together, Eleanor. Abe Fuller is a wonderful man, but at the midnight hour, we still have our free will. He and I have chosen to go our separate ways several times. Who's to say we won't choose to be apart once more, this time permanently? Some of us still end up alone…"

The sudden dead air between Jack and I is nauseating. "Everything alright?" I ask as I fish the keys from my bag. Maggie peeks at me from the corner of her eyes as we slide into Marie's van.

He's silent, save for the sound of his breathing.

Why couldn't reading minds have been my gift?

"Yeah," he says. "Overwhelmed with schoolwork, I guess. I have to rebuild my entire portfolio." His voice is distant and hollow, and entirely unconvincing. "But I'm really looking forward to seeing you, Eleanor. I miss you." A sweetness in his voice fills the emptiness that had been there only a moment prior.

I turn the key in the ignition. "I miss you too. Call me later, even if it's late," I say, my voice still reedy with nerves.

"I love you," he says before hanging up.

I slump back in the driver's seat. *He didn't actually say he'd call me. Am I being too clingy?* I run my hands down my face. *This isn't me.*

"You okay?" Maggie asks, pocketing her phone. I roll my lips in between my teeth and nod.

She nudges my arm. "Look, I know Jack is like, uber-hot, like it's his superpower, but I was stuck with you two all summer. Always making googly eyes, playing footsie every time we watched a movie, you guys were never *not* touching. No way he's suddenly lost interest."

I shrug. "Maybe I'm just reading into it."

The gears grind as we pull out of the student parking lot. Maggie hides her face behind her hand. "Can you at least use a glamour, make this stupid van look cool or something?"

I shake my head. "No, that's how I wound up with that dented fender. If I don't get the measurements practically perfect, the car behind us will misjudge the distance and rear-end us," I say, referring to the first day of school when I let her convince me to change the van into a Rolls Royce. Case in point, the dented fender.

Maggie rolls her minty-colored eyes and mumbles something barely audible in response. She flicks on the radio and plays with the antique dials. "…the trials of James Andersen and his son, Nickolas Andersen were postponed today as the defendants appear to have accepted the State's plea deal…"

Maggie jams the radio dial with the base of her fist, silencing the news report. "Sorry."

I wave her off. "It's fine. I'm used to it by now."

The media frenzy surrounding the Woods family only lasted a few weeks. Jack's grandparents pulled a few strings and greased a few palms, and then the news trucks camping outside their gates inexplicably disappeared. Even the Director of the FBI decided that, given Allen's demise, there was no need to further investigate his affairs. In some small way, that was Allen having the last laugh.

For the rest of Allen's echelon, the onslaught of indictments was never-ending: bribery, drug trafficking, racketeering, money laundering, and even human trafficking. Most of the Noble Hunter's senior members managed to escape murder charges by staying off camera during their branding and slaying ceremonies.

Their offspring, however, were far less circumspect. They brazenly took credit for every crime; some even removed their hoods and bragged directly into the camera. Every sadistic act of shooting, stabbing, strangling, drowning, and, of course, branding had been recorded.

The prosecutors couldn't have dreamt up a better case. Their motives? Chalked up to everything from ritualistic brainwashing, drugs, revenge, violent movies, to my personal favorite: the generational trauma of privilege they never worked through. The victims were, for the most part, assumed to be chosen at random. Weapons, selected for convenience. "Run Rabbit Run," that innocently upbeat tune underscoring each murderous video, purely for theatrics. Well, at least the media finally got one thing right.

My mother is desperate to move on, to put some distance between my branding and the present, so listening to anything related to the trials has been unequivocally forbidden in the house.

"Does Massachusetts have the death penalty?" Maggie mumbles. "Or maybe Aunt Sal's boyfriend can sneak us into the prison so we can brand *them*…"

I wince every time I think of that omega seared between my shoulder blades; it burns, as if the iron is again being pressed against my flesh.

"Here we go…" Maggie whispers. The van bumps along the snaking dirt road, like a submarine descending into the dark depths of the forest. Thick branches fan over the unmarked road, enveloping us in midday twilight, the trees eager to swallow us whole.

As the canopy tapers, dapples of sunlight break through the thick brush overhead. The leafy curtain is pulled back, and the azure sky bursts into view. Sunlight embraces us once again.

I crane my neck and peer toward the end of the dirt road where a once dilapidated Victorian home resides in all its restored historical glory—my mother's passion project over the summer. It's now pearly white with gray shingles and a functioning porch swing. I squint, narrowing my eyes on the driveway.

"Do you see her car?" I ask Maggie.

Maggie shakes her head. "No. Besides, mom always sends a text if Mercy is going to be here."

I release a sigh of relief and settle back down in my seat, easing my grip on the fuzzy steering wheel. There had been too many close encounters this summer. An experienced witch can sense a subtle vibration when another witch uses magic nearby, and Mercy Wicklow, leader of the North American Committee, could sense even the slightest ripple from a mile away. So, whenever she dropped by unannounced, I'd have to wear an outrageous glamour, that way the magic I used to change my eye color would be lost among the rest of my altered appearance.

My lavender eyes intensified after Allen Woods's death. Before, they could pass as blue with the right eyeshadow and eyeliner; but now, there's no disputing it. My irises are the color of Scottish heather and freshly picked lilac. The vibrant hue of my eyes is so intense now, they nearly shine through colored contacts. Achieving a strong enough glamour to sheath the nefarious lavender has become increasingly more difficult. I know I'm on borrowed time. One of these days, Mercy will visit, and I won't be able to snap a disguise into place quickly enough. I'll be found out—and destroyed.

"Yes, and I can only think of one person to blame. Can you guess who it is?" Blue sends as I put the van in park.

Is it me? I telepathically question, sarcastically sounding excited like I'm on a game show.

"Yes, it is, actually."

Oh goody, what do I win?

"An obliterated soul if you're not careful, child. Did you practice your drills?"

I sigh with a roll of my eyes as I unbuckle. *I'm sorry, I forgot. I was a little preoccupied.*

"Why do I even bother?"

Maggie and I pad our way up the porch noting how the steps no longer moan beneath our feet.

"We're home," Maggie calls out. We discard our shoes and bags in the entryway. Phoenix springs off the couch to greet his redheaded ward. She scoops him up and snuggles his little orange head with her cheek.

Our mother is speaking to someone on the phone from inside the greenhouse. Based on her shrill tone, she's probably arguing with the catering company about Shannyn's upcoming nuptials.

A tea kettle whistles from the kitchen and the scent of chamomile and mint fills the air. Teacups clink as they float out of the cupboards. Mewling cats drift about the living room. Candles glow from shelves. A leather tome whizzes from the hallway bookcase into the kitchen, and the grandfather clock on the second-floor chimes in the hour.

I place my hand on the now sturdy railing of the grand spiral staircase. I swirl my finger around the newel post inhaling the comforting familiarity of the rhythm in the house.

Maggie strolls down the hall to the kitchen to gossip about the latest high school drama with an overly excited Sally.

I clomp up the two flights of stairs to my tower bedroom to change for work. Laying on his side, Blue rests in the middle of my bed, his spindly tail sweeping back and forth.

His eyes narrow on me. *"Waist-length blonde hair, green eyes, three distinct moles on your face, extensive orthodontia work."*

"Not now, Blue," I say, still deflated after my conversation with

Jack. I unbuckle my skirt and toss it onto my desk chair along with the starchy top. I shimmy into my black trousers and long sleeve black turtleneck.

Blue's eyes roll to the ceiling as he strains for patience. *"Eleanor…"* he stresses. *"Is it a death wish or just flat out insipid teenage rebellion? Why listen to me? I'm just the old tosser trying to keep you alive. Sod it all."*

I throw him a pointed look while I slip on my shoes. "You didn't listen to a word of that video I showed you about healthy communication."

He fixes me with a deeply sarcastic look. *"You were serious about that? I thought you were just taking the piss out of me. I don't believe we should take relationship advice from someone in spandex trousers."*

I roll my eyes, switching my phone and wallet into my purse. "Whatever. You could be nicer to me, Blue."

"I reckon trying to keep you alive is very nice…" He grumbles.

With my hand on the doorknob, I pivot on my heels to face my irritable familiar. *Oculi Tempe.* I imagine my eyes shifting from lavender to a soft mossy green, then blonde wavy hair sprouting from my scalp and cascading down to my thin leather belt. Moles above my eyebrow, middle of my left cheek, and chin, pop out on my face. I pull back my lips revealing metal braces with pink bands stretching across my shiny teeth.

I wiggle my shoulders and shake out my hair. "See," I say, flatly, turning to leave.

He hung his head, dismayed. *"Bollocks."*

"What?" I spin around confused.

"Your eyes," he sends, nearly seething, *"They were green for just a moment, then immediately turned back."*

I sigh, my shoulders sag with the added weight of failing the most important part of the glamour. "There's nothing I can do about it now, Blue. I'm going to be late."

"Just focus on changing your eye color then. While you work," he orders, even though that's what I've been doing since my first day there. He nods his small black head, satisfied but his expression is still troubled. *"I still haven't had word from Elspeth,"* he states.

I exhale, my eyes rolling to the ceiling. "Yep, just like all summer. I've got to go." *Oculi Tempe.* I envision brown irises with hazel strands. I imagine blinking, long stares, closing them, opening them, rolling, glaring, up, down, and side to side.

"It's probable that she's planning something. Something…big."

"Well, she knows where to find me," I mutter. Stomping down the steps I holler out that I'm leaving for work and head out to the van. *I really miss the Mercedes.* My aunts have no plans to replace it after the Noble Hunters set it ablaze on prom night. Flashes of that night play in my mind. The woods. The song. The pain. The omega brand between my shoulder blades starts to burn.

CHAPTER TWO
Molly & Polly's

I've been working evenings at Molly & Polly's Apothecary since August. Mom not only loved that it kept me from constantly asking for gas money to get to Rhode Island, but it also meant I'd be out of the house more. And since the leader of the Committee has her own greenhouse, no Committee member dares step foot in here for fear of ruffling Mercy's feathers. It makes this a great place to stay hidden.

I pull around to the back of the shop just as Zoey Gallo, the owners' niece, is taking the trash out to the dumpster. She looks like a scorch mark against the white stone of the shop, dressed in the standard issued black and a wispy black pixie haircut.

She nods to me as she adjusts her long portrait necklace of the Italian Goddess Minerva. Zoey was part of Trixie's group of witch friends. Where Trixie was a tall elfin beauty, or wood nymph full of sunshine, grace, with angular, regal features, Zoey is a short olive-toned sprite with a turned-up nose, rounded chin, and pixie-like features.

She and her two younger sisters are orphans being raised by her aunts. Losing a parent is a pain we both share. But I'm still lucky enough to have my mom. Zoey knows my father passed away from a car accident, whereas her parents' demise is still unknown to me, and I'll never ask for fear of drudging up old wounds.

"Hope you brought homework," she says, dusting off her hands on her black jeans as I approach. "It's a morgue in there. We haven't had a single customer since two o'clock," she complains as we stride through the back door together. Even with her thick combat boots giving her an extra three inches, the top of her head just brushes under my nose.

The Clash's "Guns of Brixton" blasts from the speakers poised in each corner of the shop. Zoey likes any music that could rattle your skull. Since July we've gone through the entire catalog of The Ramones, Dead Kennedys, Bad Religion, The Pixies, ACDC, and now we are on The Clash. Only when her aunts would drop in did she quickly switch back to the harp and piano melodies that were mandatory.

I shake my head, disappointed I hadn't thought of bringing homework with me as I'm totally buried with it. "I wish I'd have known; I've got a Latin test *and* my Russian lit test tomorrow." I plop down on a stool next to her behind the counter.

She cocks a brow at me. "How? Didn't school just start? Wait did you just say you're taking three language courses?" Zoey asks skeptically. She doodles on a notepad using her magic as she rests her head in her hands.

"No, French is my language requirement. But they recommend Latin for seniors if you want to go Ivy league, plus it's Russian literature, not the language." I shudder picturing the amount of homework that class would incur. "Anyway, I had summer assignments," I mumble, wishing I had actually done them to completion. But instead, I've let a boy distract me. I try to conjure up regret but frankly I have none. I smile to myself thinking about that time we made out at the harbor after the 4th of July.

Zoey shakes her head, chuckling darkly. "With half the senior class getting arrested at the end of the semester last year, I'm shocked Griggs is still in business."

I shrug. "Some institutions are impervious to bad press." Jack's maternal grandparents made a rather large endowment, and not just at Griggs. All over Salem, parks were being cleaned up, restoration projects, a new hospital wing and voila the Woods dirty deeds have been relegated to page four and the Godspeed's humanitarian work got top billing. Evelyn is even the face of a new nonprofit start up, searching for missing children. *If that isn't ironic.* I scroll through different class syllabuses on my phone, taking screenshots of due dates and tests.

Zoey peers over my shoulder. "I'm sorry, but is that fencing I see on your schedule?"

I smile. The one fun class I allowed myself.

She scoffs, crossing her arms over her chest playfully pouting. "I'm so jealous. I was only ever homeschooled. I wish I was at Griggs; I even got my aunts to consider it until all those kids turned out to be *murderers*. I can't imagine going to school with them. It's seriously insane," Zoey complains, her eyes wide imagining all those students who had been destined for Ivy League schools this fall, only to be suited for an orange jumpsuit instead.

I nod along with her. "Yeah, it was…wild." With several podcasts dedicated to following the various trials, and the myriad of social media accounts following Vivienne's wardrobe in court, most of my conversations with Zoey ultimately circle back to the hottest form of entertainment at the moment. I would prefer it if I never had to think about the Noble Hunters ever again.

The shop itself always reminded me of a turn of the century carnival with all its colorfully painted, wooden signs, even the walls are striped in rusted reds and bygone beiges.

Zoey passively nods along to "White Riot" as she chews on her fingernails. Something catches her dark brown eyes, and she tilts her head to the side. "Betty, don't you dare," she threatens. Her familiar, Betty, a sphinx cat, whips her head back at Zoey as she has one paw raised to whack an open-mouthed Venus Fly Trap. The plant turns its head toward Zoey as she speaks.

Betty's ears are wide like a bat's, and when the light hits them just right, you can practically see through them, each vein spidering beneath the delicate skin. She retracts her sharp claws, lowers her small paw, and slinks her thin, wrinkly, hairless body down the brown-and-taupe checkered aisle, disappearing behind the rows of plants.

Zoey rolls her eyes over to me. "I love my familiar, I mean she's my familiar, but sometimes I swear—"

I lift my hands in the air palms out, "Oh you don't have to explain it to me. I'm trying to get mine to watch these marriage counseling videos because most of the time he's a total cockwomble. He doesn't know how to communicate without belittling me every time he speaks."

"Ha! Cockwomble? I'm so stealing that," she chimes, scrunching her olive toned face in a gleeful, impish grin. "Betty just has crazy ideas, mostly conspiracy theories. Plus, she has way more followers than me on our socials." I laugh, rolling my eyes as we slough off our stools and finally get to work. We spend the next three hours watering the plants, sweeping, mopping, pruning, and organizing and cataloging the elixirs we keep in locked cabinets, desperately trying to keep ourselves busy to pass the time. All the while I keep glancing at my phone, hoping I would receive a text from Jack. There were several times I even heard a phantom chime indicating such, only to be sorely disappointed.

"Betty!" Zoey screeched looking about as she reaches down, plucking a Venus Flytrap's head off the floor, having been assassinated by her familiar. "I don't care if it offended your sensibilities," she argues audibly. "Oh my gosh Betty, it's not a plant. Ugh, you know what I mean; it isn't spying on us and reporting back to someone." With her magic she zips it away across the shop and into the bin for fallen plants now used for pressing and juicing.

Listlessly, I relabel the ingredients to the pain reliever to help alleviate period cramps as the label has been smudged. I accidentally wrote down raspberry leaf twice. I growl as I snatch a new label and start over for the second time. I can't seem to focus on anything but my stupid phone and the fact that I *know* Jack won't be calling.

I can't keep living like this; I need to do something drastic. I'm not myself anymore. I'm anxious, I'm not sleeping. Every missed call puts another inch of distance between us. A noticeable fissure formed between us after Allen's funeral, but it was manageable while Jack lived in Salem. Now, with him living two hours away, that fissure has rippled into an ocean filled with missed phone calls and unanswered text messages.

"Hey, Zoey," I say, slipping my phone back into my pocket, strolling up the aisle toward the counters. "I need a favor and it's a pretty big one," I begin.

Zoey spins around on her swivel stool excitedly, she tosses her quill to the side, eager to hear more. "Yes?" she asks devilishly.

"I nee—want to visit Jack this weekend…and stay the night. Could you cover for me? If I tell my mom I'm staying with you this weekend, can you cover for me if anyone asks?" I inquire nervously as I've never pulled this classic ruse before. I step up onto the platform and amble around the counter to sit next to her behind the brass cash register.

Zoey giggles and claps her small hands together. For a moment I'm spellbound by the memory of Trixie and her sweet, girlish mannerisms that Zoey mimics practically to perfection. "Absolutely! Life has gotten pretty dull around here. Anella and Fia are still in Rome with Aunt Molly. I still don't understand why an eleven and nine-year-old got to accompany her this time," she mumbles under her breath, "but I could use a distraction. Consider yourself covered."

My fluttering heart settles in my chest. I thought I'd have to beg or at the very least offer a quid pro quo, perhaps I don't know Zoey as well as I thought. The bell above the door chimes as someone comes in. A man in a motorcycle jacket and sunglasses strolls in.

"Welcome," Zoey calls, still facing me. The gentleman ignores her greeting and wanders up and down the aisles disappearing from our sight. Zoey shakes her head at me. "Just remember, you owe your night of passion to me," she teases with a wink.

My face practically sets fire. "On no, it won't be like that," I say, shrinking back on my stool. I'm not entirely sure why my cheeks burn and why I suddenly can't look up from my shoes. Is it because Zoey thought I was trying to jump Jack's bones? Or the fact I secretly, desperately want to but *know* we can't. *However, I'm in an apothecary shop…* My face now burns for a whole new reason, a hope that maybe this weekend can be exactly what Zoey thinks it is.

A grin slowly unfurls across her pixie face, staring at me. "Man, how dirty is this weekend going to be…?" she trails off, her dark brown eyes slide over to the thin, tall man climbing the wooden ladder to reach a plant on the top shelf that has sharp triangle leaves and small, white blossoms. "Oy! Dude, you don't want that," she hollers. "That's White Snakeroot. Not named after fun hair metal. It's *extremely* poisonous."

He pulls the small clay pot with the blooming plant from the shelf and holds it to his chest as he climbs down.

Zoey and I exchange an uneasy glance as we both straighten up. Typically, customers don't purchase the plants on display, they just want the elixirs we make from them.

Betty leaps onto the tabletop and sits in front of Zoey. She extends her claws and dips her head low at the man. Zoey's eyes keep flashing to her familiar, obviously communicating telepathically. "Don't do anything to his carotid," Zoey hisses quietly to Betty.

The man strides up the three steps to the counter we sit behind and reaches into his jacket pocket retrieving a money clip. He holds the plant away from us, never putting it down as if we might retrieve it. His jaw is like steel as it's clamped shut, and his cheeks cave inward giving his cheekbones a razor edge. His aviator glasses are snug on his hawkish nose, the mirror lenses reflecting the image of us sitting stone still behind the cash register.

Zoey folds her arms across her chest. "You do know how poisonous this is, right? Abraham Lincoln's mother was killed by just drinking the milk of a cow that had eaten it."

His face is unfazed, as if Zoey never spoke.

She glances at me awkwardly, then tarries on. "If you're looking for its anti-inflammatory stuff, we've got a topical ointment over by the window you can purchase. Or we have tablets."

The stranger removes his sunglasses, revealing purple eyes the shade of a polished amethyst. He levels us with an unwavering stare. "I know what I'm purchasing," he declares, his voice even. "Are you telling me it's not for sale?"

Zoey, no longer full of bluster and steam shrinks beneath his gaze. "No, technically you can purchase it. Just usually we don't…"

He extends a hundred-dollar bill to me. "Consider it sold." I should take the bill, but I'm paralyzed, frozen in place by his eyes.

Zoey reaches across me to retrieve the cash. When she takes the bill, her hand grazes his, just for a moment. Her breath catches in her throat.

The stranger keeps a steady eye on me. He smirks. "Nice eyes, miss…" He turns on his heel and strides out the door without another word.

Zoey gulps. Her hands shake. "Did you see his eyes, Eleanor? They were purple…"

I force myself to appear casual despite my trembling fingers. I swallow and steady my breath. "Yeah, that was weird, right?" I say. "Odd choice for colored contacts."

Zoey shakes her. "No. Anyone coming into this store would know better."

I shrug nonchalantly, though my heart still pounds. "He's probably just on his way to a party. Either that or he's desperate for attention. What do they call that, 'peacocking'?" I frown, pretending to ponder that phrase.

Zoey's face falls. Her mouth forms a hard line. "That's not the kind of attention you want," she says in the most serious tone I've ever heard from her. "Do you know what Mercy would have done if she had been here? She would have *destroyed* him. Not just killed him, I mean she would have destroyed his very soul. Erased him from existence. She wouldn't have even asked him a question first. Mercy is very anti-trial. Puts the puritans to shame, really."

Oh, I'm very aware of what Mercy can do. Goosebumps cover my skin, and my neck prickles in perspiration. I try to think of something to say, some way to diffuse the situation or at least change the subject, but nothing comes to mind. My heart drills against my ribcage, like a prisoner desperately trying to escape.

Zoey continues, "He's planning something bad with that plant. I felt it when I touched him. That was a mistake, I shouldn't have sold him that." Her voice is dripping with dread.

She tilts her head toward me. "Eleanor?"

She takes an anxious step forward, turning me to face her. Betty releases a high-pitched hiss making my ears ring.

"Eleanor, your eyes. They're purple, just like his…"

CHAPTER THREE
No Good Deed Goes Unpunished

My hands still tremble as I pull into the driveway. When Zoey saw the true color of my eyes, I told her it was just a glamour, saying the man's eyes were too cool and mysterious not to try at least once. I'm not sure she was convinced. She advised I not try it again. Ever.

"Eleanor! Come settle this debate!" Sally shouts from the dining room. I step out of my shoes in the entryway and trudge down the hall. *Who was that man? He had to have been a Nefari, right? But then, why reveal himself like that? Was it because he saw his eyes matched mine? Although, his were a much deeper shade of violet.*

"Had an encounter with a Nefari this evening, I take it?" Blue questions after hearing my thoughts.

Possibly. I'm not sure, I send, walking into the brightly lit dining room. Seated around the walnut table are Mom, Maggie, Marie, Sally, and Deputy Abe Fuller who is slowly becoming a permanent fixture here.

"Evening, Eleanor," he says, rising slightly from his seat. He staggers a little when his utility belt catches on the edge of the table.

"Tell me everything."

I nod hello to the deputy. *Later. I don't want to freak out my mom.*

"Elle babe, settle this for us," Sally repeats. "Frankenstein's monster would be a better lay than Dracula, am I right?"

Abe's eyes roll to the ceiling. He pushes his roasted vegetables around his plate while Maggie giggles beside him.

"Marie and I are team Drac," Maggie says while pouring more cider into her glass. Her eyes twinkle with delight. Their bickering and hijinks have eased the grief that's been lingering in the house these past two months.

I pull out a free chair and load an empty plate with brisket and veggies. "So, that means Mom is on team Frankenstein, and you need a tie breaker?" I ask incredulously.

My mother shakes her head, insulted. "No, I refuse to play such a crass and childish game. Can we *please* change the subject? Eleanor, how was work?"

Sally waves her fork at her. "No, no. Not until we settle this. I can live with a tie but not defeat. Ella babe, pick. Who would be better in bed."

I chew on my lemon-peppered Brussels sprout, agreeing with my mother that a change of topic was in order. My own frustration in that department has been growing as of late. After the creepy and ominous stranger left Molly & Polly's, I never got to look for tonics that might stop my magic from attacking me when I'm happiest. With the number of times my mother walked in on Jack and me making out on the porch swing this summer, I'm beginning to doubt she's still helping with the search.

Maggie sits a little taller. "You have no good argument for picking Frankenstein. Now, *maybe* I could see the Wolfman, but not Frankenstein's monster." Maggie smiles mischievously at having made our mother blanch.

"Let's just call him Frank to make it easier," Sally says. "And here's my argument: the man is nine feet tall, and have you seen his shoe size? Case closed."

Abe's cheeks set ablaze to the tips of his ears.

Marie scoops her peas into her mouth, mulling things over. "I'm changing my answer. I think the Wolfman is dashing."

Sally groans in dramatic fashion. "Come on, he'd be too boring! He's only got the one move in bed," she counters.

Mom's eyes nearly bulge out of her head. "*Enough*! It's a draw."

"Thank you," Abe says, shifting in his seat uneasily.

"Anything interesting happen tonight, Elle?" Mom stares at me, brows arched, smile curt. Somehow, she's become even more of a prude now that Dad's gone.

"*Yes, Eleanor, anything* interesting *happen?*" Blue chimes in my head.

Those violet eyes flash in my mind, causing my fork to rattle against my plate in my quivering hand. I swallow back my anxiety. As I'm about to answer, I think about those college brochures sitting idly on the coffee table. The Sorbonne, Oxford, the Technical University of Munich, all schools at least three thousand miles from Salem and Mercy Wicklow. And all my mom's idea. She fears for my safety; I get that, but I still don't want to leave, not my family and definitely not Jack.

"Nothing really," I say. "I learned Abraham Lincoln's mother died from drinking milk from a cow that ate snakeroot, that was interesting." I take a bite of brisket so I don't have to keep talking.

My mom nods. "That's true."

Sally's eyes slide between my mother and me. "Wow, things sure get wild over at the apothecary," she mutters.

"More than I should like," Blue harumphs in my head.

"Don't forget, Mom, I'm going to be home late tomorrow, I've got cross country practice," Maggie informs as she clears her plate.

"Do you need a ride?" Mom asks as she rises to help.

"You are the *world's slowest eater. Hurry to your room, we need to speak."*

I spear a single pea on my fork, place it delicately between my teeth, and slowly pull it off.

"No, I'll get a ride with Piper," Maggie says as they stroll into the kitchen. "Oh man, did I tell you what her boyfriend did during the summer."

"No, what happened?" Sally shouts, following them in.

"Patience is definitely not one of your virtues," I mutter upon entering my bedroom after showering and brushing my teeth.

Blue lies awkwardly on his back, his legs splayed out like roadkill on my bed. *"I wonder, can I die any more than I already have?"*

Getting philosophical on me now?

"Oh no, you misunderstand, my dear. You see, I'm considering just killing you myself, since that is clearly the road you are determined to travel, but I'm curious whether your family would seek vengeance. Although, I'm fairly certain they would unanimously side with me if I explained the little stunt you pulled tonight. Truly, Eleanor, you failed your glamour and *a Nefari spotted you. I'm so irate with you, I could not help but concoct a myriad of unpleasantries I plan to execute the moment you slumber."*

I glare at him as I plop down at my desk, my hair still wrapped in a towel. "If you hide my phone again, I swear I'll rip your tail off myself." I turn back to my organic chemistry textbook. "I don't know why the glamour wore off just the moment he took off his sunglasses. I'm not saying that was a coincidence, but it certainly wasn't my fault," I counter. "I'm doing my best, Blue, but I'm exhausted. You've been running me through drills all summer. I'm not sleeping, I can't concentrate in class, and it seems the harder I try, the sooner my glamours fail. I'm sorry that I wanted to prolong my time before your lecture. I'm just done, Blue. I'm done." My body sags under the toll of constant magic.

Blue softens, crossing one paw over the other. *"I believe a departure from Salem is in order. We are playing with fire, keeping you here. And from what Persephone has alluded to, I believe Helen feels it too."*

I draw a single chemical bond, using dots to represent valence electrons. "Well, you will be relieved to know I'm heading to Rhode

Island tomorrow after school."

Blue rolls his eyes at me. *"A journey of a few hours hardly solves our problem.*

There are many covens there, and several members of the Committee…"

I point my chin up indignantly. "It won't be for a few hours; I'm going to stay the entire weekend this time."

Blue's exaggerated groan rattles my brain. Suddenly there's a scratching at my bedroom door. *Persephone?*

"Yes, she wants to give Helen a report on how your exercises are progressing."

Now *I* groan. "Why doesn't mom just talk to me herself?"

"She fears her constant inquiries would do more harm than good. I disagree, but no matter. Finish your schoolwork. When I return, I want to see a crew cut girl with a lip ring, neck tattoo, and heterochromia." He leaps from my bed and lands lithely on the rug before walking through my bedroom door without a second glance. I toss my pen aside, my untethered mind drifting from my homework.

I recall those deep violet eyes, and goosebumps prick across my skin. *Why had he shown me his eyes? And what is he planning on doing with that plant?*

I hate to admit it, even to myself, but I feel an odd kinship with him. Just because he's a Nefari, doesn't necessarily mean he's evil, right?

Zoey's trembling voice replays in my mind, saying the man was planning something bad. A knot forms in my stomach. I'll have to tell my mother, even though I know it will cause a fight. But before I embark on a journey that will end with angry words and slamming doors, I need to speak to Zoey.

I toss aside the towel from my head and scroll through my phone. I pause briefly on Jack's number, then scroll to the bottom for Zoey's. It rings three times before she picks up, but there's only silence on the other end.

"Hello? Zoey?" I fall back with a whoosh onto the goose feather comforter, waiting for Zoey to respond. "Hello?" I try again.

"Betty! Stop answering my phone!" Zoey yells from a distance. Stomping footsteps get louder until she picks up her phone, her breathing elevated. "Hello?"

I roll over and lift up onto my elbows. "Hey, it's Eleanor," I say.

"Hey, what's up?" she asks. A door closes on her end.

"I've been thinking about that guy who came into the shop tonight," I begin nervously.

Zoey growls. "Ugh, just forget about that creep. We aren't on the Committee, we don't need to report him. Besides, the more I think about it the more I feel like I was way overreacting in the shop tonight. I mean, come on, a Nefari perusing my aunts' apothecary shop so nonchalantly. I talked about it with Betty and the more she got all 'tinfoil hat' on me, the more stupid I felt for getting all freaked. So, sorry if I worried you."

"I'm not sure Zoe, he bought poison. And you have a gift, you felt something was wrong," I counter.

"I've been wrong before," she insists a little prickly. "So, don't worry about it, 'kay? For all we know, he's a poser just throwing up colored eyes to look 'edgy'."

"But—"

"Eleanor," her voice turns hard like ice, "if he were a Nefari, Mercy would already be on to him. That woman is like a Nefari bloodhound. So don't go blabbing that Nefari are coming into my aunts' shop. Okay?" she snaps.

For my sake, I hope she's wrong.

"It's just when you touched him, you sensed he was planning something bad with that plant. I'm worried… I feel kind of responsible now."

Zoey sighs, her frustration ringing clearly in her long exhale. She's usually short on patience after dealing with Betty…and now me. "My gift isn't always reliable. It's still working out the kinks, I guess. For all I know, I was leaning in that direction because he was purchasing poison. It's just a feeling I get when I have contact with someone."

I used to avoid direct contact with Zoey, worried she'd somehow sense my 'Nefari-ness', but usually she just picked up my school anxiety or my longing for Jack, for which she would tease me to no end. "But still, don't you think we should do—"

"Absolutely nothing," she cuts in. "Trixie Caldwell was my friend. I knew her all my life and now she's *gone*. She shouldn't have been digging around those stupid Noble Hunters. This isn't a game. This is real life. I'm not reporting some wacko with weird eyes only to die the next time I have a milkshake. There's nothing we can do, so just drop it. Okay? She's dead." Her voice cracks at the end.

I half expect her to add "because of you," but thankfully, she doesn't. "I'm really sorry," I say. My eyes and throat burn, desperately needing a good tear-filled sob.

Zoey sniffs. "It's fine. But if you stick your neck out, Eleanor, it's going to get whacked." She clears her throat, reining in any grief peeking through. "Take my advice. Keep your head down, and trust no one."

Wait. What? Why shouldn't I trust anyone? "Okay," I agree halfheartedly.

Zoey releases a breath of relief. "Good." She stops and yells too closely into the phone. "Dang it, Betty! Seriously? Sardine cans in my freaking *bed*?! How did you even open them?" She throws something, probably the empty can, which ricochets off the wall. "Can you send me those marriage videos on communication, please?"

A weak smile is the best I can manage. "Sure."

After saying our goodbyes, I call Jack. *Maybe he'll know what to do.* I'm lying to myself. I just want to hear his voice, but it goes straight to voicemail. I curl up on the window bench beneath the pentagram window, my back against the pane of glass. I wish Winston was still around, he would know what to do. Trixie wouldn't hesitate. She would traipse downstairs and insist on spilling everything to Mom. They both had a steadfast moral compass that always pointed due north. But like Zoey said, they're gone now because of it. Their faces flash through my mind. *Could I have done more?* I stare at the full moon glowing white against the black autumn sky.

The twisted branches of the old dead oak in the front yard sway in the cool breeze. Change is in the wind. I tuck my knees into my chest and place my head on my knees. My life has become more precarious than I can manage. If the Committee discovers what I am, they'll obliterate my very soul. At least with The Noble Hunters their torture and branding ended in death, releasing us back to Mother Brighid. With the Committee, we are unmade, completely erased from existence, stripped of any form of an afterlife. Another chill shivers up my spine.

I have no choice; I need to speak to my mom. She will know what to do.

I lean away from the window about to rise from the seat, but I hesitate. A black spider slowly descends from a silken thread between me and the window. I stare, dumbfounded. It's been months since I've seen a spider in my room. I suddenly realize why.

"Eleanor! She's coming!"

My eyes lift to the reflection behind me in the window.

Elspeth mouth curls into a devil's smile. "Hello, Daughter."

CHAPTER FOUR
Eyes in the Dark

Elspeth circles about my room, the train of her black chiffon dress trailing behind her.

"We do have a penchant for ending up in towers, don't we, Daughter?" she says, looking about. Her comment has me puzzled until I remember the last few months of her life were spent locked in a tower being tortured to death.

My fists clench with fury, but the rest of me is seized with fear, leaving me rooted to my seat. Elspeth appears to have a solid form, no longer the translucent phantom she was in my visions. Waves of auburn hair cascade down her back, shining against the ceiling light like polished brass. Elspeth is beautiful, there's no denying it, but a viciousness emanates from her lithesome body.

Noticing my stare, she stretches out her thin, alabaster arms above her head and feigns a yawn. Her long smile still plays upon her face like a stuffed, satisfied house cat.

"Didst thou miss me? Apologies for my absence." She glances at her nails as if this is some kind of casual drop in.

She flicks her hand, and the needle on my record player lowers onto the now spinning record. A melancholy tune fills the room. It's the Compositions of Nolie Hawk-Stuart, a famous female cellist my father took me to see for my thirteenth birthday. This particular symphony tells the story of a girl who loses hope as she's pursued by a demented figure. I wonder if Elspeth knows just how fitting this truly is.

Elspeth closes her eyes and sighs. "When I was fully alive, strings were not capable of such beauty." Her mouth puckers like she's tasting a decadent fruit. "As I watched the world evolve, or rather devolve, it was always through a veil. I could sense the change, but it was always muted, as if I were anchored underwater." She sways to the music, then stops. Her eyes pop open. "I think I shall eat while I'm here."

Blue bursts into the room, leaping through the closed door. His right ear gets caught on the other side leaving it behind on the landing outside my door. Elspeth giggles and shakes her head. "Pyewacket, always late to the party."

Blue's eyes dart to me. *"Are you alright?"* Yes. She hasn't said why she's here though. *"She's always been one for games."*

Does she have a body now?

"Sadly, no," Elspeth interrupts.

She can hear us?!

Elspeth smiles at me before continuing. "I'm not quite whole, at least not yet. Our tether is just stronger now, this is the most power I've had here since I was alive. All thanks to you, Daughter. Killing that human, I'm so proud of you." She extends her arms and gives me a slow, patronizing applause.

"You mean, your lover's heir?" I spit.

She shrugs, perching on the corner of my bed. "He wasn't *my* heir. How revolting a thought, to reproduce with Matthew Hopkins." Elspeth turns to me, tilting her chin downward, her crimson lips unfurling like a ribbon stretched across her face. "It's always the pious ones who have the dirtiest secrets. Oh, if you knew the ways he wanted to debauch me." She sighs, savoring her monologue.

"You have no business here, Elspeth. Go back to where you came from." Blue sends telepathically.

Her eyes snap to her former familiar. "Dear little Pyewacket, caught between my realm and Eleanor's. Pray tell, is this partially embodied state really an improvement to Purgatory?"

My hands quiver with rage. "His name isn't 'Pyewacket', it's 'Blue'. And he's only stuck between realms thanks to *you*."

"Thanks to *you*," she returns. "If you would have just done everyone a favor and died like you were supposed to, Pyewacket would have been freed to enjoy all the pleasures of Hell."

"What do you want?" I growl, tired of her little charade.

Her face turns deadly serious. "I want what is kept in the room next to yours."

I think back on that pointless room that shares a wall with mine, the one I heard angry whispering through on my first day in Salem. The aunts had declared that room forbidden.

"You want the dresses we wore to The Gathering?" I ask. "Have at it, I'm sure you and Sally are the same size."

Her icy stare cracks, the left corner of her mouth curls ever so slightly.

"You don't know what they keep in there, do you, Daughter?" She cocks her head to the side, examining me like a curious specimen.

"Stop calling me that!" I snap. "My mother is Helen O'Reilly of Clan Byrne. You are nothing to me." I try to appear confident, but my chin quivers. I don't want to be a Nefari; I want to belong in the Byrne coven, my mother's witch and my father's daughter.

"Then ask that 'mother' of yours what is kept in the room next door. There are only two in the world, one in that room and one in Leinster with your grandmother. That old hag is beyond my reach, so I must work through you." She rises from my bed and approaches slowly. Blue leaps in between us and hisses.

I lean my back against the window. Would she blow the window out like she did at school? I glance over my shoulder at the three-story drop. When I look forward again, she's inches from my face.

"I thought you were powerful now; just go in yourself."

She crosses her arms and leans away from me. "I can't. Your cursed aunts placed a spell upon it. No Nefari can enter."

"Then how am *I* supposed to?" I balk at her. "Did you forget something?" I point to my lavender eyes.

"You have a sister. Get her to do it. I've watched you together; she admires you. I bet she'd set herself on fire for you if you asked amiably enough."

My heart pounds against my ribs. I could never rope Maggie into Elspeth's twisted plans, or any member of my family. I think of the night Elspeth manipulated us with the Ouija board, how she chased us around the house with scissors. I can still recall the anguish in Maggie's eyes when we realized we weren't speaking to our father. *Will Elspeth hurt her? Can she?*

"Possibly. Let's give it a go," Elspeth threatens in my mind.

La Caeli.

The words come as naturally as breathing. The moment I think the words of the air spell, every sharp edge in my room floats into position. The X-Acto knife from my desk drawer, a pair of scissors, even pens and pencils encircle Elspeth from all angles.

Elspeth merely giggles. She lifts a finger and taps the scissors hovering near her, but they quickly right themselves. "Dost thou believe this shall hinder me, child? For I am but a shade; death hath already claimed me long ago."

"Possibly, let's give it a go," I sneer.

Her onyx eyes flick to the door.

My bedroom door creaks open. "Ella?" my mom calls.

Elspeth smiles something wicked before disappearing like

mist. My platoon of cutlery collapses to the floor.

Mom steps through the threshold. "Sweetheart, did you lift all those at the same time? I'm so proud of you." Persephone slinks in behind her and exchanges a strange glance with Blue.

I release a shaky breath. "Yeah, I've been practicing pretty hard," I answer. My heart still hammers away.

"You're doing so well, darling."

I move away from the window to the bed. "Thanks, mom," I say, still uneasy.

Mom pulls out my desk chair as two violet teacups resting on floral saucers zip into the room and hover beside us. She gently lowers herself into her seat and plucks her teacup from the air. "It's the new tea recipe I've been tinkering with. Apple, plum, violet, and chamomile. Does wonders for your skin." She takes a tentative sip, and her face relaxes into a gratified smile.

I take a large gulp. Of course, it's delicious. Everything my mother makes is delicious. "So, what's up?" I ask, finishing my cup on the second gulp.

Mom takes another sip then lets her cup and saucer hang in the air at her side. "Persephone said you needed to speak to me?"

My mother's tabby cat sits faithfully by her leg, studying me. I place the teacup and saucer on my nightstand and run my hands down my face with dread. "Yeah…I guess something did happen at the apothecary tonight," I begin.

My mother's floating cup rattles against the saucer. She takes hold of it and guides it down to my desk. She swallows and clears her throat. "And?"

"A man came in. He purchased Snakeroot. Not the dried leaves, he took the whole plant with him. Zoey brushed her hand against his—she can sense things about people—and she felt he was going harm someone with the plant." I raise my foot onto the bed and lean against my knee. "But before he left, he showed us his eyes. They were dark purple, Mom. And he commented on mine. I guess my glamour had faded by then." I frown.

"Which is weird, his eyes were a darker purple than mine."

Mom swallows with difficulty. "Not all Nefari have purple eyes; they come in a myriad of unnatural shades." Mom stops and releases a jagged breath. She looks down at her hands resting in her lap and plays with her wedding ring. "But that really isn't important right now." She takes another breath. "How accurate are Zoey's perceptions?"

I shrug. "Everything she's shared with me has been proven

right. I mean, she sensed the mayor was having an affair and literally a month later the story broke. When Sally came in supposedly looking for rosehips, Zoey felt she was looking for Ashwagandha." That day I learned it's an herbal Viagra for women; I wince at the memory. "Honestly, I can think of a dozen more examples."

"And she felt what, exactly?" Mom questions.

"Like he was going to harm someone with Snakeroot poison. But he purchased the whole plant, he could harm a lot of someones, or…" *or kill just one.*

Mom looks ill. She glances around the room like she's in peril. "Mom?" Her bottom lip trembles and her eyes gloss, but she doesn't answer.

What is happening?

Blue stares at Persephone, and something passes through them. "*Helen is conflicted. If she tells the Committee, they will be on the lookout for the Nefari. You could be caught in the crosshairs.*"

I look back at my dismayed mother. *So, she has to decide between saving an unknown number of strangers and saving me.*

"*That was never a consideration. She is in pain because her decision is final, and it could have deadly consequences for someone else…*"

My mother's eyes turn red around the edges, but she refuses to cry. "I don't want you returning to work until you can show me you've perfected your glamour. I mean it, no more risks." She points a stern, motherly finger at me.

I nod in agreement, too drained to object.

My mother bends forward, about to rise to her feet.

"Mom," I start.

She stops and settles back down.

My eyes slide to the wall that separates my room from the forbidden room. "Even since we moved in, that room next to mine's been off limits. Why is that?"

The rose-patterned teapot dances into my room and refills my mother's cup, then empties itself into mine.

Mom follows my eyes to the wall in surprise. "I don't have a clue, actually. Best guess is Sally was pulling some kind of prank. Why do you ask?"

I can't help but chuckle, since I had the same thought at first. My eyes survey her face, not finding any kind of tell. She seems weary from our conversation, but not deceptive.

"Doesn't matter. Was just curious." My mom starts to get up once more. "Mom," I say again.

She sits back down, giving me a weak but kind smile. "Yes?"

I play with the hem of my pajama shirt. "I was invited to Zoey's house for the weekend. We're going to her cabin up in Dracut," I say, trying to force the anxiety from my voice.

My mom's mouth crinkles in a half smile. "The Dracut cabin? Wow, that brings me back. The De Lucas still go there? I don't know why I thought they sold it," she muses.

I stare at her, taken aback. "You've been there before?"

She tucks her short blonde hair behind her ears and nods. "Sweetheart, you forget, I moved to Salem when I was fairly young. I grew up with Zoey's mom, Beatrice. We went to Griggs together, although she was two years younger than me. Her older sisters, Molly and Polly, are closer to Marie's age, but we all got along. The De Lucas invited us to their cabin every fourth of July. It kind of became family tradition for a while."

It stings realizing just how much I don't know about my mother's life before meeting Dad. "Did you know Zoey's dad?"

"Giovanni? Not really. I think he was on exchange from Italy, at Griggs when I was a senior and he was a freshman. But once I moved to Florida, I didn't stay in touch with anyone back home. Why do you ask?"

"They're both gone. Zoey never talks about them. I was just wondering." Something about it tugs at me. Maybe because I struggle with a similar grief. "So curious tonight," she says as she stands from her chair. She places her hand on the side of my head bending me closer so she can kiss the top of my head. "It's fine if you go to Zoey's, just wear your contacts while you're there."

I shrug. "I don't know why I bother with them. My eyes still look a little purple when I wear them."

"They're still more reliable then when you do glamours." She motions for the teacups to follow her out. "Sleep well, love. And don't worry about that man, I'll take care of it." My door closes itself behind her.

By not taking care of it.

Blue leaps onto the bed beside me. *"Some prices must be paid to keep loved ones safe. Don't go looking for trouble."*

You heard Elspeth. Trouble is here whether I like it or not. I click off my light. My room is painted in a ghostly pale light from the full moon. I crawl into bed, guilt-ridden at having lied to my mother. I turn on my side and curl up next to Blue.

I don't believe mom was lying about not knowing what's in there.

"You're right, she doesn't know. Persephone confirmed as much. Elspeth was mistaken." Could she be wrong about whatever is in there?

Something dawns on me. My grandmother, Colleen Byrne. She has an identical whatever in Wicklow, Ireland.

"Blue," I say aloud in the dark, "Mom never talks about my grandmother. Neither do my aunts. Is there a reason for that?"

"I know very little about your family beyond these walls. I can inquire about her tomorrow. But I'm weary to the bone. Let us rest."

"Being mostly dead must suck," I murmur.

"Being wedged between realms does have its difficulties, but it is better than the alternative." Hell?

"Indeed. Elspeth's actions condemned us both."

Everything inside me clenches. *And me. I'm a Nefari now, banished from paradise.* I banish the thought from my mind, but it comes creeping right back in. *If I can't go to paradise, I won't ever see my dad again. And what about Jack? We're soulmates, does that mean he's damned too? Or do I lose him after death as well?*

"Go to sleep, Eleanor. You are less than useless without a proper rest."

I kick off my blankets and swing my legs out of bed. "I need a distraction. Maybe I can pick the lock, just to see what's in there."

I march over to the door to the forbidden room and jiggle the handle. Then I close my eyes, picture the lock, and whisper the air spell in my head. *La Caeli.* I listen for the cogs inside to click and slide, but nothing happens. I shake the handle again, still nothing. So, I kneel down and squint with one eye into the keyhole. Nothing but darkness. The draft from inside, however, quickly dries out my eye. I move my head away from the door, suddenly worried something sharp might slide through and into my eye.

With both hands on the door, I stop, realizing something. Blue arrives at my side. "Elspeth *has* been in this room," I say, turning toward him. "The whispering I heard when we first arrived, that must have been her." I recall her voice how it began as a frantic whisper and grew into a manic scream, saying, "Get them, get them, now, now, now!"

"I remember that night. Elspeth wasn't in this room. She was standing directly behind you."

Ice plunges through my veins. I anxiously peer over my shoulder and hurry back into my bedroom.

Blue stretches out with his butt up in the air before he saunters back into my room, disappearing into the dark. I race after him, slam my door closed, and flick the lock.

I pull the covers over my shoulders, and Blue snuggles under them next to me. My eyes drift to the wall separating us from the room and whatever is kept there.

Chapter Five
All Rhodes Lead to RISD

I lean against my aunt Sally's teal Jeep while I gas up in Mansfield, Massachusetts. I'm only about thirty minutes from Jack's campus but I coasted into the station on fumes. I sigh, watching the numbers tick higher and higher. I growl to myself, ripping out the nozzle and placing it back into its spot.

Back on the I-95, I imagine surprising Jack in his dorm room. Maybe he's working out. Shirtless. I use my key to get in. *Hey, Jack,* I imagine myself saying casually, as if this is a totally nonchalant drop in, not planned whatsoever. He'll grin, rush up to me and crush me into his arms. I'll wrap my legs around his carved waist, my thighs resting on his sharply sculpted hip bones. My mouth waters at the thought. Our mouths will devour each other. His hands will grasp the hem of my shirt.

"No. No. No. Absolutely no more!" Blue shouts in my head. He leaps from somewhere in the backseat and into the passenger seat.

"Blue!" I shout startled. My head snaps over in his direction then back at the road as my exit is approaching.

"How naïve I was, to think watching over a modern teenage girl would be easy. Why would I possibly need to keep her thoughts in check..."

"What the hell are you doing here?!" I screech.

"Serving as your chastity belt, apparently. Truly, Eleanor, if you thought about practicing your magic half as much as you imagine undressing Mr. Jack Woods, you'd be the most powerful witch in your coven by now."

My knuckles strain white as I grip the wheel. "I can't believe you came!

You're not coming into his dorm. No pets allowed."

He grimaces at the word 'pet'. *"Dogs are pets, my dear. Cats are your equals."*

I don't care. You're not coming with me. You can stay in the car all weekend. I'll crack a window for you.

Blue narrows his eyes on me. *"You left me no choice. You were being entirely unreasonable. What do you think will happen if your,"* he shudders, *"fantasies play out? Hmm? You two will grasp each other in passionate bliss? Think again. Your magic is connected to Elspeth, meaning a part of it is trapped in Purgatory where happiness is impossible. Your magic will attack you until you have nothing left. I fear you shall be overcome with catatonia all to satisfy some childish lust."*

I grit my teeth as heat billows in my cheeks.

"It's not childish. I love him, Blue. This isn't some stupid high school crush. You yourself even admitted as much. We're soulmates. This desire for him isn't going to go away."

Although, I do feel childish, constantly thinking just how unfair this all is. Will we always have to live platonically? Will there be no honeymoon, no wedding night? Can I ask Jack to live like a monk?

"If he truly loves you…"

My eyes well up, but the tears pull back from the brim before they can fall, leaving my eyes dryer than before. My insides ache with a penetrating sadness that seeps down to my very marrow. High school, colleges, the Committee, the trials, the glamours, Elspeth… it's all too much. I've had my magic for seven months, yet it feels like seven years.

"I don't think you know what you're asking, Blue. I don't want kids now, but maybe one day, I mean I'm going to be eighteen in less than a year and you're asking me to live like a child for the rest of my life."

My heart sinks somewhere below my stomach. The worst part of all of this is I have no idea what my future holds. There's a constant nagging in the back of my mind, whispering I'm on borrowed time. If Mercy discovers what I am, the cobwebs on my virtue will be the least of my worries.

"Finally, you're seeing reason," Blue says with a breath of relief.

I think of the lacy little things I have stowed away in my overnight bag, the skimpy bralettes, and teddies. *You know, given what happens if Mercy does find me, this would be a better way to go.*

Blue releases a growl-like breath. *"Back on the trolly to crazy town, are we? Females…"*

Felines.

Butterflies flap about my stomach when I pull into the East Hall parking lot. I look around the lot, but don't see Jack's white Mustang anywhere. I'm not sure if I'm pleased about that.

I turn to Blue sitting in the seat next to me. "Please stay here. I'm not going to do anything stupid," I state, lifting a brow and staring him down.

He rolls his electric blue eyes. *"Did you forget I rode down here with you? All you have are stupid ideas."*

I shut the door and retrieve my bag from the backseat. Blue will do whatever he wants regardless of what I say. I nod to students I pass as I climb the stairs of the brown brick building. Most of the girls ignore me; two guys stop and watch me finish the trek to the third floor.

My stomach twitches the closer I get to his single room. *Just because I didn't see his car doesn't mean he's not here.* I shake out and fluff up my hair and square my shoulders, then use my contraband key (he's not allowed to make copies) to open the door.

Natural light fills his room. I first notice his twin-size bed against the wall to the left. His navy-blue comforter is tightly tucked, his pillow fluffed and propped against the wooden headboard. The white brick walls are barren, without artwork or personal effects. His school-issued wooden desk sits uncluttered, with a laptop resting open on top.

I drop my bag on his bed and plop down, taking in the space. It doesn't have Jack's classic scent of sandalwood and citrus; the air here is sterile. I glance about, uneasy. *Does Jack still live here?* His dorm looks nearly identical to when he moved in, the only time I've ever been here.

That is his laptop. I pull out his desk chair and wake his computer. The screen behind the password is a candid picture of Jack and I from the Fourth of July. I'm mid-laugh, nose scrunched, eyes squeezed shut; Jack stands behind me smiling like a model. His eyes hold such joy, I now consider his eye color to be the happiest of all the colors in the spectrum.

I purse my lips trying several different passwords. Each one fails. His birthday. My birthday. My name. His nicknames. My nicknames. *This could take forever.* My hands rest on the keyboard, and I gently close my eyes. Jack is sentimental with an incredible memory. I let my feelings for Jack fill my chest, letting that love overwhelm everything else. The day we met comes to mind. Running into him in the hall at Griggs, his lemonade spilling over me. I type in "March sixth". The screen opens to his desktop. I can't help but grin.

Blue! I thought about Jack and was able to crack his password to his computer. Is that part of our soulmate connection?

"Of course. In fact, back in 1692, the reason so many Salem witches were put to death was because they cracked their lover's passwords."

Jerk. "Dullard."

It shows Jack recently accessed his email, but he could have done that from his phone. Same with his music app. *This tells me nothing.* I grip the top of the screen about to close it when it chimes with a message.

Sam3217: Are we still on for tonight?

I frown. *Who could that be?* My heart leaps when several dots appear at the bottom of the screen. Jack is replying.

JackW: Definitely. Be there shortly.

I hold my breath, waiting for the conversation to continue, but it doesn't. I click on Sam's icon picture, a neon light against a brick wall. The profile tells me nothing.

Their conversation pops back on the screen. I type the address Sam3217 gives into a search engine, which takes me to an abandoned building outside Providence just off the highway.

Blue isn't startled when I slide into the driver's seat and roar the engine to life.

"You know what they say about those who assume…"

Yeah, yeah, I know. I put the Jeep in reverse and pull out of the parking lot, my heart thundering in my chest.

"You look like an ass."

"That's not how the saying goes," I snap aloud.

He rolls his little cat head around, stretching out his muscles. *"I amended it for this particular occasion."*

The directions on my phone take me far from campus, past the main street with your typical college hangouts. The sky fades from a washed-out denim blue to deep plum with blazing oranges at the very edge of the horizon. This isn't right. I should be sharing this with Jack, curled together in his dorm, not chasing him down in Rhode Island's seediest locale.

"You have arrived at your destination," my phone informs.

"Oh, for the love of Brighid, I hope not," Blue sends. We both crane our necks to peer out the windshield, aghast.

We've stopped in the middle of an unmarked road outside a three-story concrete building. Its gray façade is interrupted by weathered pressboards, littered with graffiti, that cover the windows.

My cheek brushes my steering wheel as I strain to get a better look at this ugly cement block standing lifeless in the dark. My mind whirls with all sorts of terrible possibilities: Jack's dropped out of school, ashamed and alone, is now doing drugs, and this is where his dealer lives.

"Oh, Blue, what if he's in trouble?" I cry, too scared to inch the car forward. "*Jack isn't the kind.*" Blue's voice sounds faraway, distracted. He places his paws on the glove compartment, hoisting himself up. "*I loathe to encourage your snooping, but I believe I see cars…and a crowd. Eleanor, look.*" He nods his small black head to the far-right side of the building.

My eyes follow his motion. I squint, seeing cars. *Well, I've come this far.* I putter my way over, flicking off my headlights hoping to be more incognito. I find a spot near the back of the lot.

Blue follows close behind as we inch our way past tightly parked cars to an opening where it looks like a side door used to be. I slip in behind a group of six or seven men and follow them down a staircase with Blue nipping at my heels.

I don't see any girls here. Is this some kind of poorly funded gentleman's club?

The sounds of cheering grow louder as we approach the bottom step. That's when the smell hits me, body odor mixed with the scent of a wet towel left on the floor. Blue and I stop. A crowd is gathered around the center of the room where a large space is illuminated by the only functioning lights in the abandoned basement. Lurking against the walls are shadowy figures flipping through dollar bills with small composition notebooks tucked under their arms.

"*I don't see Jack. Might I propose that we await his return in his dormitory?*"

He's here, Blue. I can feel him. But something is majorly wrong. A creeping darkness reaches into my chest and squeezes my heart. *Hang back by the wall. I can't guarantee you won't be stepped on, and there's no way I'll find your ear if it falls off.* "*Oh, really, Florence Nightingale? How can that be? You did such an amazing job sewing it on last time…*"

His blue eyes roll to the corner as if he can see his crooked ear holding on by a few meager threads. He dashes away and disappears into the darkness.

I right my shoulders and march forward. "Excuse me, please. Can you let me through? Excuse me." I try shouting, but my voice is barely a whisper against the cheering crowd, their bodies pressed tightly together form an impenetrable wall.

"Get the hell out, little girl." Someone shoves me to the floor, and I land hard on my backside. My tailbone immediately throbs.

That's it. No more nice witch.

"*Do not react, Eleanor. Just leave.*"

I rise to my feet, ignoring Blue entirely. *La Caeli.* A current of magic vibrates through the air. I push forward, parting through the crowd like a hot knife through butter. Two men stumble to the floor, cursing each other as I step over them. Several try to push me back; one even takes a swing, but the air spell slows their movements like they were underwater.

Something shifts in the air. My magic weakens as my concentration wanes. *No, I'm so close.* I can see the open space now. Two men are fighting in the center. I stumble forward, finally reaching the front.

The fighter nearest me is wearing only black shorts and has hair like molten gold. Jack. He's pummeling a man with green hair pulled back into a blood-soaked bun. The jeering crowd screams in frenzied delight. Jack's strong right hook connects with the man's mouth. Blood spurts from lips split open. Mr. green hair spits out two teeth and stumbles dazed into the crowd, only to get shoved back into their makeshift ring. Jack shakes out his hands, his hard eyes fixed on his target. Deep valleys snake around the bricklike muscles protruding from his taut torso. His bare knuckles are raw and bloody, and he bounces on the balls of his feet while he waits for his opponent to find his footing.

Mr. Green-bun wobbles on his feet, looking at Jack through a woozy gaze. A thick vein bisects down his forehead. His glistening skin is too tight around his showy muscles. His head bobs side to side on his corded neck.

Jack just stares like a jungle cat observing his prey before the strike. "Kill him!"

"Finish him!"

"What are you waiting for you mother—"

The crowd encircling the fighters pulses with unbridled rage. They shove and push each other, nearly tossing me to the floor again. The ravenous spectators' screaming makes my eardrums throb.

Then, suddenly, it all stops. I'm engulfed in a heavy silence. I glance about; the audience is still frothing at the mouth, hurling insults at the fighters, but I hear nothing.

Blue? I reach out. Nothing.

Blue? Are you there? Something's wrong!

"…going to kill him…" a voice rings out in my ears.

My pulse spikes. Then, like the flip of a switch, I can hear the crowd again. Their shoulders bump against mine. Their shouts are too close to my ears.

I feel naked, even violated. Something evil is here. He entered my brain and spoke to me. I recall the man from the apothecary.

Blue! Blue, are you there? "Yes, where did you go? Our connection was severed. Only for a moment, but it was unmistakable. Are you alright?"

I am, but he said he was going to kill him. I have to do something.

"Jack!" I scream as loud as I.

His eyes slide to me, then snap back.

"Eleanor?" I can read his lips but can't hear him over the roaring crowd.

Out of nowhere, a fist lands hard against Jack's temple, knocking him to the floor. Jack's out cold.

Mr. Green-bun lunges on top of him and unleashes a fury of strikes to Jack's face.

I look about frantically, waiting for some kind of ref to stop the fight but no one does.

Oh my gosh, he's going to kill him! "Eleanor, don't!"

I charge forward, flinging my arm towards Jack's assailant. *La Caeli.* The man flies across the circle and away from Jack. The audience leaps back as he sails toward them. I gather Jack in my arms, clutching his bloodied head to my chest. My shirt dampens with his blood and sweat. Out of the corner of my eye, I see the man with the green bun land hard on his neck.

The room goes silent. He doesn't move.

Oh, shit.

CHAPTER SIX
Too Soon

Blue! Blue, what do I do?!

The violent energy that so recently possessed the room has gone stagnant. A few people drop to their knees at the green-haired fighter's side. Suspicious, enraged, and confused glares surround me on all sides.

"We need to get the boy out of here," Blue sends from across the room. *"With your meager arms no one will believe you can carry him. Make a diversion. Do it now."*

I clutch Jack's bloodied and bruised head to my body. *What about the other fighter? Blue he isn't moving. What am I going to do?*

"What about the other fighter?" Blue sends, sounding more confused than callous.

Someone screams to call 911, but others silence the one voice of reason. *"Eleanor, now! Before they question you!"*

I press Jack against my body. He's limp in my arms, but I feel a steady, albeit faint heartbeat. I picture the bookie at the edge of the room, imagine the notebook tucked under his arm igniting in red and orange flames that lick at his shirt but stop before causing any real harm. *Ne Feerah.*

The man yelps and throws the notebook. The flames spread far beyond what I envisioned. Smoke wafts across the room and billows at the ceiling, triggering the sprinkler system. Chaos erupts as everyone makes a mad dash for the stairs.

Great. That was my exit.

"There's another way out. Over here, there's a tunnel."

Two bouncers lift Green Bun from the floor and carry him out. My stomach drops at the sight.

"Eleanor!"

I snap out of my daze and adjust Jack in my lap, shoving my arms under his. *La Caeli.* I hoist us both to our feet and walk us out, my magic parting what little remains of the dwindling crowd. I reach the far-left corner of the room where the bookies are still stomping out their books while several angry gamblers hover nearby.

Blue says nothing as I follow him, Jack in tow, down the dark hallway filled with the smell of rot. We turn a corner without any light.

"Blue! I can't see anything."

"Create a glowing orb with your fire spell."

I can't. I'm already using the air spell.

He roughly sighs. *"You should be able to do two spells at once by now."*

"This is not the time. You're sure there is another way out?" I can already feel my air spell waning. Jack grows heavier in my arms.

"I'm sure, now keep going straight. There's an opening on the right that'll lead to stairs. Let's hurry."

Once more I utter the air spell, and Jack and I lift into the air. I hold him close with one arm as we fly down the hall, dragging my other hand across the brick wall in search of an opening. We reach the stairs and surge upward, bursting through the metal door that breaks off its rusty hinges.

I fly higher into the air, above the shafts of light descending from the streetlamps. Jack's head lulls about, barely conscious. Thank Brighid he's coming to. More than half the parking lot has cleared out. I squint in the dark, spotting my aunt's teal Jeep. We make a large arc through the air, careful to stay out of the light. *This would be so much easier on my broom.*

"Eleanor?" Jack moans.

I tighten my grip on his slick body. "It'll be okay." I whisper. I can see Blue already in the car with his paws up on the window, watching intently as I near the Jeep. Gravel crunches beneath my feet when we land. I whip the back door open and slide Jack in.

Blue sits waiting for me in the passenger's seat. *"Well done."*

I'm too exhausted to thank him or even smile.

"Blue, I need you in the backseat keeping an eye on him." I peel out of the parking lot, desperate to get as far from the warehouse as possible.

Blue slips into the back of the Jeep.

A screaming firetruck races past us. Its flashing lights illuminate the car for a moment in bright crimson. My hands vibrate against the steering wheel. *Did I really kill that other fighter? Did I paralyze him? What have I done? No, I couldn't have. I was just trying to save Jack. I didn't want to actually hurt him. I mean what was that guy thinking going after Jack when he was knocked out cold? Isn't that against the rules? I was protecting my soulmate. No one can blame me for that.* My heart throbs and my stomach churns. *What if he is dead?*

"What are you blathering on about? You asked me to keep an eye on Jack, yet you're diverting all my attention."

My eyes glisten, blurring the river of headlights before me. "The man Jack was fighting; I threw him back, but I threw him too hard. I wasn't concentrating, I should have paid better attention. How could I have let that happen?"

"I still don't understand. I didn't feel your magic."

"What?"

"Your magic. I feel it every time you use it. If someone used magic to throw him back, it wasn't you. Now, if it's not too much trouble, I'd like to get back to your sodding soulmate here who's bleeding profusely," he sends, his voice dripping in frustration.

A car cuts me off, forcing me to slam on my breaks. "Is he going to be okay? Should I take him to the hospital?"

As if answering, Jack moans. His voice is but a dry croak.

"You brought herbal remedies with you, yes?" Blue asks, already knowing the answer. *"To the dormitories, then."*

Jack drifts in and out of consciousness, mumbling my name between agonizing groans. The East Hall dorms are teaming with students.

Jack's head lulls forward when I pull him from the backseat, then use the air spell to make it appear like he's walking.

"Oh my gosh, Jack, are you okay?" shouts a girl from her car. "Hey, what happened?" asks another girl, walking up to us. Blue hisses at the gathering female co-eds as we limp past.

Jack's feet are lumbering and clumsy, like Frankenstein's monster learning how to walk.

"Quite impressive, Eleanor."

"Thanks, but I don't think I can keep it much longer," I say through gritted teeth.

"Whoa! Should we call an ambulance?" a male student asks as we reach the top of the stairwell.

"No need," I grunt under the excursion. "His family has his personal physician coming, thanks."

"Hey, no pets! I'm allergic!" someone shouts from down the hall.

Blue slips through the doorway just before I slam it closed with my foot. No longer needing to be discreet, I whisk Jack into bed with the full gale of my magic, then flick my fingers to turn on the light switch.

At my command, my overnight bag unzips and my remedy kit levitates onto the nightstand next to Jack's head.

"Eleanor?" Jack moans numbly.

I've been trying not to see him in light, not wanting to confront the full extent of his injuries. When I finally look, my lungs constrict. Both his eyes are blue and swollen shut. His beautiful nose bends unnaturally to the right, and his lips are inflated like a botched cosmetic surgery. Across his chiseled cheek is an open laceration. His whole body is marbled with bruises.

His right hand lies lifelessly at his side. The knuckles are blood-soaked and raw. I leap to inspect his left hand, his painting hand. Held in the light, his middle and first fingers are the color of ripe raspberries three times their normal size. *Why would you do this Jack? You're an artist.*

I gently place his hand back down.

Blue leaps up onto the bed and rests at Jack's feet. His blue eyes sweep up and down Jack's broken body. "

The boy's wounds are extensive."

"Tell me what to do, please."

"*Just this once, since this is an emergency. But honestly, Eleanor, you need to work on this branch of magic on your own. You should have the basic tonic and remedies memorized.*"

"Yeah, I'll squeeze that in before SAT prep," I mumble. I reach for the witch hazel, even before Blue tells me to. All the healing tonics use witch hazel.

"*Good,*" Blue sends. "*Now three teaspoons St. John's Wort, two teaspoons of comfrey, and two pinches of nettle.*"

I silently follow Blue's direction, but my mind is a whirlwind. *What was Jack doing there? I thought he had given up boxing, not wanting to risk his hands. And if I didn't make that fighter fly off him, who the hell did?*

"*Eleanor, concentrate.*"

"Sorry," I mumble.

"*Three red clovers, preferably fresh,*" Blue continues.

The glass vials clink as I scrounge through the black leather bag. "Crap, I don't have that."

Blue nods once. "*Very well, double your nettles and add two dandelion heads. Then a pinch of turmeric, and a scoop of Reishi Mushrooms. Do you have any fish scales with you?*"

I shake my head, grinding the mixture with my pestle and mortar.

Blue rolls his eyes. "*Then hopefully this is enough. Let's set the poor boy's nose first, though. I'll walk you through it.*"

I cringe when I feel Jack's nose crack into place. Then I carefully tilt Jack's head back. "Jack, I need you to drink this, okay?"

"Don't forget to bless it."

I bring the stone bowl close to my lips. "La Narine, blessed be." I exhale on the mixture then gently coax Jack's lips open. I pour out the mixture in a slow, steady stream, careful that he doesn't choke. His Adam's apple bobs up and down with each gulp.

Placing the empty mortar on the nightstand, I fish out the small vial of wild lettuce tablets my mom and I made and place the sticky round pill under Jack's tongue. He doesn't fight it.

I brush Jack's dark molten gold locks away from his slick forehead speckled in blood and grime. *Oh Jack, why would you do this? Is this why you've been avoiding me and acting so strangely?* I continue to gaze at his face, a beautiful canvas that's been marred by the brutality of bare-knuckle boxing. I wince at his discolored jaw hanging loose on one side. My fingertips trail down his sternum while my chin quivers. I feel the familiar buzz beneath my fingers, an undeniable electricity. His skin is warm to the touch. My eyes gently fall shut. *He's punishing himself.*

Blue lifts his head from the mattress. *"Beg your pardon?"*

I span my fingers across his naked pectoral. Peach fuzz tickling my palm. *The fighting. I can feel it, Blue. He's punishing himself for what Allen did. "Then why fight back?"* Blue questions.

"Because he's also trying to vicariously kill Allen. Over and over again. Blue," I turn to my familiar resting beside my soulmate, "he's torturing himself and I don't know how to help him."

Blue's sapphire eyes fall to Jack's face. *"I believe he's past your help, my dear. Woods isn't even his real last name; he has no real identity. Though, I dare say he'd rather be beaten to death than be known as the heir of Matthew Hopkins."*

My heart clenches, a combination of sorrow and helplessness. My soul is weary as I peer down at Jack's prone form. "There must be something I can do. I can't watch him go through this. What if I hadn't been there tonight? Blue, he could have died." My jaw trembles and my shoulders quake from the sudden revelation. I love him with everything I have and am. Brighid created us together. We are just shadows without our mates. Even my mother's internal light has dimmed, same with Marie's. It's beautiful and tragic all at once that a love so powerful occupies your very spirit.

I lean my lips so close to his check they brush his skin. "I love you," I whisper. Our names are meaningless. They do not dictate who we are. They do not decide who we will become. Woods or Hopkins, O'Reilly or Byrne, even McEwen (as Elspeth loves to taunt me). Our love is deeper than trivial names. We're soulmates.

"Eleanor, the gash on the boy's cheek looks fairly serious. I would hate to have that perfect face be permanently altered," Blue sends. His voice started out sincere, only to morph into his usual brand of sarcasm by the end. *"Get out your phone, we'll need to send out for supplies. You have money to order delivery, I presume?"*

Ten minutes later, I tip the delivery boy and decline his offer of a nightcap. Jack stirs in his sleep; my elixir is taking effect. I mix together the dried Marigold flowers, honey, aloe vera, tea tree oil, and blue algae, strictly adhering to Blue exact specifications. Then I generously coat the open lacerations, destroying one of my makeup brushes.

Blue looks over my work and gives me a satisfied nod of approval. *"It'll take a few hours. Now rest, Eleanor."*

I lean against the wall under Jack's window. My limbs are heavy with exhaustion; it's as if my body is waterlogged. With Blue's offer of rest, my body falls under a hazy fog of exhaustion. My eyes flutter shut as I sink back into a deep sleep.

Suddenly I'm awake. I can't see anything, not even my own hand. *Wait, do I even have a hand.* I reach out to pat my body, but I can't. *Where am I? Jack? Blue?* I try to yell, but I don't have a mouth.

"I see you, Eleanor," a deep voice hisses. "I know what you are…"

And what am I? I ask myself.

"You are one of us." The voice feels close, like the speaker is standing right behind me but I can't turn around.

Wait, you can hear me?

"Yes."

You're that Nefari, aren't you? The one that came into the shop. Did you kill that man tonight?

"That man is inconsequential. His life, which he still has, is of no concern to you."

He's alive. Relief floods through me.

"He was going to kill your mate. I had to intervene. Even the Nefari don't kill needlessly. But the time has come, Eleanor…"

What do you want with me?

"I'll come for you. Soon. Look to the Harvest Moon." *Don't come for me. I'm not a Nefari by choice. Leave me alone.* "Soon."

CHAPTER SEVEN
Prison Break

"Eleanor?"

A hand brushes against my cheek. My head dips forward, then snaps back up, smacking the wall behind me.

"Ow," I grumble, still not entirely awake.

I wince against the light as I rub the back of my head. My neck feels like an iron rod with all the tension in my muscles and tendons.

I'm still on the floor of Jack's dorm, sleeping under the window. Jack crawls off his bed to kneel in front of me.

"Are you okay?" he questions, dipping his head to better look at me.

His eyes have gone from a deep midnight blue to something resembling a marred banana. The open split on his lip has already reconnected. His overall pallor has returned to that soft tawny glow, and his perfectly straight symmetrical nose appears as good as new.

I scramble to sit forward and cup his handsome face. "How are you feeling? Does it still hurt?"

He emits a lopsided smile as he inspects his completely recovered hands. "I'm okay. A little sore, but considering…" he trails off, alluding to the serious beating he endured.

I slide my hands from his face to his bare chest. A few coppery flecks of dried blood flake off.

He grimaces. "Yeah, I could use a shower," he says, peering down at his gruesome looking chest.

Blue lifts his head from Jack's bed giving me a look of warning as if I were about to suggest some company.

Calm down, mom. I've already given him all the medicinal cures he needs. This will be as platonic as a sibling sleepover, I grumble having read his mind before he could even think it.

I rub the inside corners of my eyes, gunky with sleep. "What time is it?" I ask, fighting back a yawn. My eyelashes roll and matte together, and I realize I fell asleep with a full face of makeup. *I must have the most unflattering raccoon eyes right now.*

"It's a little after 3:00 am," Jack answers. The apples of his cheeks flush with color and he smiles sweetly. He rises slowly to his feet, wincing in the process. "I'm fairly certain I broke something." He delicately places his hand across his ribs, then extends his other hand to help me up.

I shake my head and use his bed to push up to my feet. "Those are serious injuries, Jack. The elixir I gave you will have you feeling better in a few hours, but Jack, you could have died." It takes everything I have to keep any whine or nagging from my voice. "If I hadn't come…"

Then again, if I hadn't distracted him, Jack probably would have won the fight. But who's to say Green Bun wouldn't have fought even dirtier, or the next opponent wouldn't have been even bigger?

He nods with his eyes cast at the floor. "I'm sorry you had to witness that." He glances up at me through his lashes. "I can't remember—I might be concussed or something, so forgive me—but were we planning on seeing each other?"

I look away and play with my fingers. "I wanted to surprise you."

He nods to himself, then frowns, like something has just occurred to him. "How did you find me?"

My mouth rusts from the sudden lack of saliva. "I…um…" My eyes inadvertently slide to his computer as I rack my stupid brain for a convincing lie.

Jack follows my line of sight, landing on his open MacBook. He rolls back on his heels as his eyebrows lift incredulously. "Ah," he says.

I fold my arms, unable to look at him. "Unless you've got something to hide, it shouldn't be a big deal," I snap. "You can go through my computer or phone whenever you want." I can't help but cringe at my own petulance.

Jack releases a humorless chuckle. "Likewise. Phone and wallet are in the top drawer there," he says, pointing to his nightstand.

I still can't look at him. My eyes gloss with humiliation.

Jack crosses the room and takes hold of my waist, craning his head so far down that I have no choice but to relent and meet his eye. "Eleanor, I would never…" he trails off, his face crumpling with disgust at the mere thought of it. "There's no one else but you. There never will be anyone else but you. You believe me, don't you?" His brow knits with a pained expression, as if I've somehow betrayed him just by doubting his faithfulness.

I drop my arms from across my chest, allowing myself to be held. I go to rest my head on his chest only to pull it back and rub the dried gore from my cheek. "Come on," Jack says, "I'll show you where we can get cleaned up."

He stops by his closet for his shower caddy full of homemade soaps my aunts made him before he left for Rhode Island. I smile seeing how worn down they are.

"That'd be great." I spin around and pull my toiletries from my overnight bag.

Blue leaps off the bed and lands with a little stumble at my feet. "*Eleanor Elizabeth O'Reilly…*" He shoots me a sharp, scolding glare.

"Do you need a towel?" Jack asks, standing at the door. Blue hisses at him.

Jack's eyes drop to my stupid dead cat with a completely crooked ear. "*I knew it was crooked!*"

"Technically, I'm not allowed to have pets in here," Jack says with a cocked brow.

Blue's claws protrude from his paws. "*Eleanor, ready your medical kit…*"

I roll my eyes. "I just need a hand towel if you have one. And if he's going to be a problem, he can stay in the Jeep." I shoot Blue a quick scowl.

Jack pulls a full-length towel from his closet. "No hand towels, I'm afraid. And he's fine as long as he keeps a low profile."

"He will," I say, more so to Blue than to Jack while using my best authoritative warning voice. I stride over to Jack and place my hand in his. The brightly lit hallway is completely vacant. Sounds of gaming streams under the doors of several rooms we pass on our way to the bathroom that I notice is marked co-ed.

Placing my bag on the sink counter, I watch Jack through the mirror as he steps into the shower, still wearing his shorts. He shoots me a little playful wink before whisking the curtain closed.

His shorts flip over the top and hang from the shower rod just before water sprays from the shower head. I take a slow breath to steady myself. The bathroom steams up with the heady aroma of cardamom, fir, and rosemary. I nibble on my bottom lip, taking it in.

That's when my self-appointed chastity belt leaps onto the neighboring sink. "*A-hem. Let's get a move on it. No need to be lollygagging.*"

I scrub my face clean, then brush my teeth, all the while failing to keep my eyes from wandering back to the steamy shower reflected behind me in the mirror.

"*I think it prudent for you to avoid any more co-ed company while here.*" Blue's voice drips with disgust. "*You should return to the room soon.*"

The word "soon" sends a chill down my spine. My vision. The man from the shop, he's going to come for me. *Soon*. At this point, I should just tell him to take a number.

I leave the bathroom and make my way back to Jack's room. Blue skips past me down the hall and darts through Jack's closed door, leaving several wiry black hairs fluttering to the floor.

I roll my lips between my teeth, thinking. *I need to tell Mom about my vision. I can't deal with Elspeth* and *this new Nefari witch alone*. My heart sinks at the thought. My mother's hands developed tremors over the summer. She's been brewing tea with increasingly more Kava Kava and blessed chamomile to calm them.

Mercy never really accepted my mother's excuse for refusing to join the Committee, and her bad side is not a place you want to be. She tried everything, from playing on her grief from losing Dad to her civic duty after having been gone for so long. But in the end, Mom always said us girls needed her more.

I jump as the door next to Jack's opens. I duck my head and quicken my pace.

"Hey there," calls a sleepy-eyed boy with shaggy, amber-hued hair. He itches the top of his head, gazing at me in a blurry haze. "I know you," he says as I stride past. His thin lips part into a drowsy smile.

"I don't think so," I say trying to avoid eye-contact. As I reach for the doorknob, I spy a glance from the corner of my eye. He's in nothing but a flimsy pair of boxer shorts and a deep white V-neck that goes far too low on his sternum.

He nods and steps closer. "Yeah, yeah, you're Jack's girl. Um… Ellie… Ella…"

"Eleanor," I say, my hand resting on the doorknob.

His eyes and grin both widen, and he snaps and points his finger at me.

"That's it! Yeah. I've got Still Life 109 with Jack."

I sigh and drop my hand from the doorknob. I don't want to appear rude, just in case he and Jack are friends, but with all I have on my mind right now, the best I can do is to lean against the door and nod along.

"I'm Agustus, but everyone calls me Auggie. So, you're pretty famous around here, you know," he says. He crosses his arms over his narrow chest and takes a step closer.

I raise a dubious brow. "Famous?"

He chuckles. "Oh yeah, you're the subject of his best work." His eyes trail from my head to my feet and back up, taking no efforts to appear subtle. "And I can see why," he says smugly.

I peer at my shoes forcing a polite albeit awkward smile.

He must notice my shoulders tense and my inability to maintain eye contact, because he abruptly drops his smile. "Oh no, no, no oh damn, no that wasn't the whole male-gaze-thing," he says, waving his hands as if he could erase the last few awkward seconds. "Aw shit. I'm sorry, that was probably super creepy. Like I said, I do still life, and you," he motions toward my arms, then my legs, then my neck, "there's an elegance to long stretched lines. Elongated limbs add a sort of balance and harmony to the composition. I really didn't mean to make you uncomfortable."

He finally inches back away from me. "You're what, five-seven?" he guesses perfectly. "Tall girls make perfect art models." He closes his eyes and hangs his head as he scrunches his face. "I sound like such an ass, don't I? I'm sorry. I'm still half asleep… and might still be a little stoned. I'm really sorry."

I release my breath, dropping my shoulders from their tense position.

"It's fine. It's just been a pretty long day," I mutter.

He nods, taking a few steps back. "Maybe I'll see you around?" he says with an air of hope to his voice.

I shrug. "Yeah, maybe," I say nonchalantly, anxious to ensconce myself in Jack's dormitory.

"Okay," he agrees while backpedaling. "I'll catch you later." He turns on his heel and continues his walk down to the bathrooms at the end of the brightly lit hall.

I slip into Jack's room and close the door behind me, nearly stepping on Blue in the process. I rest my head against the door and loudly exhale. "Blue, I had a vision."

He peers up at me. *"And?"*

I push off the door, march over to my bag and dig through looking for something decent to wear to bed. Really, I just need something for my hands to do. "He—the Nefari from the apothecary—he said he's going to come for me on the harvest moon." I pull every article of clothing from my bag before shoving them back in and repeating the process. I purposely left every "decent" set of pajamas at home for a reason. I growl at myself. I should have brought a backup pair. I claw through my belongings once more and glance down at my shirt, considering wearing it to bed until I see Jack's blood stained across the chest. *Maybe I should have showered.* Heat fills my cheeks at the thought.

I settle on my lavender lace bralette and matching silk shorts, and let my jeans drop to the floor to change into them.

Blue moves to sit in front of me. *What did he say? I want to know everything, leave nothing out."*

I face the wall to remove my shirt and bra while I recount every last-minute detail of my vision to Blue. Even though he's just a cat, the fact we can have intelligent conversations makes me want to preserve my privacy around him.

"The weird thing is," I say as I finish changing and plop down on Jack's bed, "it didn't sound threatening. It's odd, but I don't think he means me harm."

"Eleanor, he is a Nefari; he's not to be trusted."

I turn to face him. "I'm a Nefari too. Am I not to be trusted?"

Blue stares at me pensively. *"Well, your charitable assumptions notwithstanding, you still must tell Helen. Don't make the childish mistake of keeping this to yourself. Tell her the moment we return, which should be in a few hours."*

"When is the harvest moon?" I ask. My body sags at the prospect of an early departure. I only just got Jack to myself.

"In a fortnight."

I breathe a sigh of relief. "Then I've got some time. Listen, this might be the last weekend I can do this in a while. I'm not leaving early." With Elspeth's return and now this stupid witch that plans on visiting, seeing Jack will soon become a luxury I can't afford.

Jack's door creaks open. Heat from the shower radiates from his half-naked body. His loose cotton pants hang low on the hips carved into his lower abdomen. A thin blonde line of hair trails from his navel down past the hem of his boxer briefs that barely peek out from under the waist of his pants.

It becomes difficult to swallow. I gaze at him standing in the doorway, his towel hitched over his shoulder, his damp sandy hair tousled. My gaze finally lifts to his face, his cheeks darken a few shades, his jaw slacked, his eyes…*hungry.*

"Oh, my giddy aunt," Blue sends.

Jack snaps from his daydream and closes the door behind him. He stays, with his back turned to me, the bands of muscle in his back tense. When he turns around, he averts his eyes from me. He hangs up his towel on a hook in his closet and stows away his shower caddy. "I've got an air mattress if you'd like. Or if you prefer the bed, of course. I'm fine with either."

He tugs out a cardboard box advertising the blow-up bed guaranteeing a perfect night's sleep and plugs in the attached air pump into the outlet. His eyes periodically slide to mine as he busies himself with sleeping preparations. I glance at my phone; it's almost 4:00 am. I'm physically exhausted and emotionally drained, and yet sleep is the last thing on my mind right now. I tap my fingers anxiously against the exposed skin of my thigh, and am suddenly aware of just how naked I am. I glance down at myself; my silk shorts are *short*, and the lacey bralette only covers an inch below my bustline, leaving the rest of me completely exposed. My long pale legs are on full display, my shoulders bare, and the opaque lace of the bralette that lets you make out certain details if you stare hard enough. And equally aware of how little Jack is wearing.

"Good grief. I'll be sleeping in the Jeep tonight." Blue trots to the door then glances over his shoulder at me. *"Do. Not. Be. Stupid. Think of your mother and how she'd react if you ended up in a coma in his dormitory. Or perhaps imagine her having to bury you next to your father."*

Thanks, Blue. And the mood was already dead—you didn't have to twist the knife by mentioning my parents.

Blue rolls his sapphire eyes and passes through the closed door.

With my familiar gone, I let out a sigh of relief. I lift my hair off my neck and pull it up into a messy bun.

Jack eyes my exposed neck and shoulders before going back to the now fully inflated mattress.

I tuck my smile away, having enjoyed his gaze a little too much for my own good. I can't stand still anymore; I need to move. "Do you keep bedding in here?" I ask, using my magic to open the closet doors. On the top shelf are plain folded blankets and sheets.

Jack scrambles to his feet to help, but he winces when he lifts his arm above his head.

My hand lightly rests on his bicep, stopping him from reaching further. Touching him probably wasn't the best idea.

"You're still healing, Jack. Allow me." I look to the folded linens on the top shelf. *La Caeli.*

The sheet and blankets lift out of the closet, unfold themselves in the air, and wrap themselves around the air mattress. The pillow on the top corner somersaults down and settles at the head of the bed.

A grin plays at the corners of Jack's lips. "I doubt I'll ever stop thinking how cool that is."

"Oh, it's no big deal." I roll my eyes at him with a playful air of false modesty.

He shakes his head at me with a chuckle, and I giggle when he impishly snags my waist and tugs me close until our hips are pressed together.

"You think you're so clever," he teases. He gently tickles my sides, and I squirm in his embrace. Peals of laughter escape me, and a wide grin expands on his face as I fail to break away from his grasp. Not that I actually want to, of course. Jack's hands slide from my sides to the small of my back where my bare skin is covered in goosebumps. Our smiles recede as we peer into each other's eyes. I realize we're both breathing a little heavy.

My palms lay flat on his chest. My fingers tremble at the touch of his warm skin. Jack dips his head, brushing his forehead against mine. Our noses caress. Our breath mingles, our lips parting only inches from each other. My entire body pulses. Our eyes are locked together.

Jack's lips graze mine. A delicate caress at first, then a gentle kiss. When my mouth opens to his, a fire ignites. Our mouths move in tandem while his hand glides from the small of my back to cradling the back of my head. I roll my head back as his lips tenderly press just below my ear, then slides to the hollow of my neck.

I exhale a whimpering moan as his lips skim across my clavicle. My entire body melts, becoming soft and pliant in his arms. Everything inside me pleads for more.

He gently lowers our bodies as one onto the freshly made bed while my hands run wild through his hair. His mouth explores my neck and jawline, lightly dragging his teeth across my skin. My body is tender, malleable to his touch. Every nerve ending tingles. Every touch leaves me hungering for more. His hand trails down my sternum, triggering an arch in my back pressing me further into him.

That's when I feel it, beginning in the corner of my left shoulder where he pulled the strap down. A sting, like the prickling of a hundred undulating needles. The sensation intensifies, and it spreads like wildfire from my shoulder into my entire chest. My entire body turns ramrod straight, bracing against the pain that now engulfs every inch of me. I can even feel it under my eyelids. Jack notices my abrupt change and immediately rolls off, positioning himself at my side with his knees on the floor. "Eleanor?" he asks nervously, still catching his breath.

Unable to answer without releasing an ear-splitting shriek that would shake the whole dormitory, I instead clamp down hard on my lips. *This will pass. It always does.*

Jack scans the room for my medical bag and practically leaps for it. He pulls out one vial after another, reading the carefully scripted labels on each one before moving to the next. He's making use of the hours upon hours he spent listening to my mother's herbal remedy lectures, all at his request. By the end of August, he had completely filled two composition notebooks on the subject. With each vial, he shakes his head until he finds the little tin of blessed wild lettuce capsules. With two in his hand, he scoops up my head with his free hand and cradles it.

"You need to take these, Eleanor. They'll help with the pain."

I shake my head, knowing if I open my mouth, I'll scream. Someone in the dorm might call the police.

He rests his forehead against mine. "Please. It'll be okay." He places the tablets on my lips and gently wedges them in.

I release my jaw just enough to suck them back. The moment the pills hit my tongue, they dissolve with the flavor of celery dipped in sugar. My skin immediately begins to cool against the hot poking needles, but only slightly. I keep my eyes squeezed shut and wait for the agony to cease, grateful for even the tiniest reprieve in the meantime.

"Are we having fun, my dear Eleanor? Happiness can be such a bitch?" Elspeth giggles in my mind. *"Gee, good thing you didn't consummate, or you'd be dead right now. There's nothing Purgatory hates worse than a woman satisfied."*

But I'm not in Purgatory. You are. My jaw remains clamped shut as I ride out the pain. Jack keeps our foreheads pressed together, completely unaware of the conversation happening in my mind.

"Your magic is born of death as much as it is of life; Purgatory is the in between. You weren't designed for happiness."

I writhe in pain. *I wasn't made for anything. I was a mistake.*

"Precisely, my Daughter. Now you're getting it. You were a horrible mistake, a cruel twist of fate. I cast a rare, forbidden spell to bring me back to life, and instead a new life is created in you. But no matter—mistakes can always be corrected. You and Jack may have been doomed from the start, but if you stop fighting me, get back to the house, get me what I want, I can give you what you want."

There's jolt in the back of my mind, like the dramatic sweep of a door being opened and slammed shut. The weight of Elspeth's presence evaporates.

Jack presses a cool sponge dripping with soothing witch hazel across my decolletage. My joints stop seething, my skin is quenched, and my body relaxes. All that remains is a dull throbbing headache.

"I'm so sorry, Eleanor. I'm so sorry. I'm so sorry," Jack repeats over and over. "I don't know what I was thinking. I wasn't thinking."

I unclench my jaw and release a breath through parted lips. My eyes drift open and closed with sleepy hooded lids, peering at Jack through small slits. "It's okay," I whisper. I reach over to him with a feeble hand and rest it on his arm.

He shakes his head, eyes downcast. "I'm sorry I grabbed you."

"Please," I whisper. "We'll figure this out. We've got time." I'm not sure which of us I'm trying to reassure. "I'm already feeling better. I just…" I take another shallow breath, "need to rest. I'm so tired."

Jack rises to his feet and flicks off the light before crawling into his own bed, sandwiched between the air mattress and the wall.

I stretch my limbs as best I can, letting my joints loosen. With the blankets pulled up to my chin, I roll over to face Jack. He's lying on his back staring up at the ceiling.

"Jack?" I whisper in the dark. A dull glow fills the room, cast by the pale light of the lampposts in the parking lot.

"Jack?" I say a little louder. My voice still sounds small in the vast quiet. "I think you should go home today," Jack states.

"What?" Exhaustion gives way to adrenaline. I blink my eyes open wide. "What are you talking about?"

"I can't keep hurting you. That's all I do," he says, his voice strained. His hands roll into fists at his side.

"Jack, that's not true." I reach for him, but he pulls away. I grapple with what to say, desperate to change his mind. This fissure between us will soon be a dark chasm we can't come back from.

"It is!" he counters, his voice somehow both a yell and a whisper. He sits up now, staring at me with a steady, unrelenting gaze. "That's all I've ever done. All my family has ever done. For centuries! Eleanor, you still have a brand on your back that my own father put there." His fists tremble, his knuckles straining white. "You don't deserve to be in this pain." His jaw clicks tightly shut. "You don't, but I do," he says through clenched teeth.

I crawl onto his bed so I'm sitting next to him and cup his face. "*You* didn't brand me, so *you* don't deserve any pain, especially not the pain you're unleashing on yourself in the seedy parts of town."

He shakes his head at me as if I'm talking nonsense.

"We belong together. You are my soulmate. When we are apart, we are only half of who we are. Don't you get that?"

He takes my wrists and gently yet firmly removes my hands from his face.

"If you and I are one, then that person is a masochist. I'm done with that." My eyes burn with tears that will never fall. "What are you saying?"

He shakes his head, perhaps only now realizing the implications of what he's saying. "I-I don't know. Maybe we need some distance…"

I fold my arms across my chest. "You live two hours away, isn't that enough distance?" A thought, dark and vicious, clouds my mind. "Jack, are you… breaking up with me?" I feel like I'm falling, and I know nothing will be there to catch me.

Jack shakes his head, his eyes swimming with apologies. "No. It's just—I don't know how to be with you and not put you in pain."

I roll my lips in between my teeth to keep my jaw from trembling. If my body was capable, rivers would be streaming down each cheek. I get back into my own bed and curl up on my side with my back to Jack and my legs tucked in close under the covers.

I can hear Jack sigh. His bed squeaks as he shifts his weight. He pauses, hesitating, then lies back down.

To hell with this. If I want to be with him, I'm going to be. From the moment Jack and I collided, literally, my universe shifted.

I close my eyes and reach out into the void. *Blue? Are you there?*

A low-pitched growl of annoyance sounds in my head. *"Well, look who is no longer in pain. You irresponsible—"*

Stop. I don't have time for that. You can make a list of insults and give it to me later. Blue, I feel pain when I'm happy because my spirit was created in Purgatory, correct?

He sighs. *"No one can give you a definitive answer to that question, but I am convinced it's because your magic is connected to Elspeth's, and she is in Purgatory."*

I bite down on my bottom lip thinking. *But she doesn't want to be right? Like her ultimate goal is life?*

"Yes. To have a body of her own. Bodies are a gift all mortals take for granted.

Witches and humans alike."

So, whatever is in the forbidden room will most likely help with that?

"Perhaps…" he answers skeptically, not liking where this is going. I nod to myself against the pillow. *Then I'm going to help her.*

Blue releases a high-pitched hiss that rings my mind's ears. *"You can't be— All so you can dither with your Jack?"*

It goes so far beyond that, and you know you feel it too. That pain is strongest with Jack, but it's not only with him. When I laugh with Maggie, I feel a deep, breath-stealing pinch in my chest. My head pulses when I cook with Mom. Hell, my stomach even twists when I learn a new concerto on my freaking violin! I can't live like this! No one could! Happiness is supposed to be what gives life meaning, but my happiness is literally killing me. One of these days, I'm going to be working in the greenhouse with my mom and aunts, just feeling content, and will just keel over.

"Helen is working on a cure, she'll—"

Mom isn't going to find a cure. All she can do is abate the symptoms. This isn't getting better.

"So, what are you saying?"

You know what I'm saying, Blue. I need to break Elspeth out of Purgatory.

CHAPTER EIGHT
Congratulations Are In Order

I keep glancing at my rearview mirror, plagued by regret, wondering if I should turn around and hightail it back to RISD. The events of our conversation and its aftermath replay in my mind on repeat. We slept until noon the next morning, then shared an awkward lunch out on the quad surrounded by other students. We barely touched our food; each of us just pushed it around with our forks pretending everything was fine.

Everyone could see it wasn't.

If I had thought Jack was distant before this visit, then I hadn't truly known what distance was. Jack was like a robot as he walked me to my Jeep, hands in his pockets, eyes straight ahead.

"Hey," I said, trying to get his attention. It still took him a second to look at me. I cupped his face as we leaned against the driver's side door. "It's going to be okay. We're going to work this out. I promise." I considered telling him about my plan right there and then, but decided against it. When I kissed him, he was reserved, even cold, careful not to let any passion seep into it. I guess I should be grateful he at least kissed me back.

Unfortunately, he was the first to break from it.

"I love you," I whispered as I stared down at my shoes, unsure if he even heard me.

"I love you too," he replied. He looked in pain as he said it. And that was the end of our romantic weekend together.

"I don't care if he's given up on us," I tell Blue. He trudges to the backseat, tired of hearing me vent for the past hour and a half. "We're soulmates. If he thinks I'm just going to walk away from that, he's wrong. He's not his father. In fact, he couldn't be more different." I stomp on the brakes almost rear-ending the minivan in front of me. "Even if we weren't meant to be, I still choose to be with him. I love him." I growl, knowing Blue is tuning me out. "Oh, and another thing—"

"There's no possible way Purgatory is worse than this…"

Blue continues to mumble over me every time I try to speak

about Jack. He finally pipes up when we see the Salem city limits sign come into view. *"Alright, let's give it a rest. I've tried desperately to drown out the sound of you regurgitating Jack's name ad nauseum, but enough. You have far bigger fish to fry at the moment. Is there not a Nefari coming for you in fourteen days?"*

I coast to a stop at a red light and hang my head against the headrest. Blue's right. I hate it, but he is. Since turning seventeen, nothing has been the way it should. I wish the only thing I had to worry about was boyfriend trouble. I try to keep the words "it's not fair" out of my thoughts whenever I start to wish that the SATs or my college applications were my biggest hurdles. Why can't I just be an ordinary teenager who happens to have magic? *"Witches were not created to be ordinary. In fact, desiring to be such demonstrates a lack of courage and wisdom,"* Blue chides.

My grip on the steering wheel tightens, but I say nothing.

Low-hanging branches claw against the car as I drive toward the house. When the thicket clears, I slow my speed to a crawl and check that the coast is clear. The only cars in the gravel driveway are the usual ones. After parking behind my mother's car, I kill the engine and rest my head against the steering wheel. I close my eyes and breathe *I can't keep doing this Blue. I'm so tired. I've barely had time to process losing Trixie, Winston, and my…dad. I can't keep fighting.*

Blue leaps onto the passenger seat and stretches out his claws. *"Unfortunately, you have no choice. You have to fight, but you must fight intelligently. Assisting Elspeth to escape Purgatory is worse than a fool's errand, it would be catastrophic. She's a vile witch, even by Nefari standards."*

I have to do something, Blue. She threatened my family. I don't know—we don't know what she's capable of. Maybe if I help her escape, we can sic Mercy and the rest of the Committee on her. A corner of my mouth pulls up in a tired smile, delighted at the thought but too weary to fully express it.

I hook my bag over my shoulder and hop up the steps into the house, eager to collapse onto my bed.

Blue trots beside me. *"Perhaps I can peruse some grimoires, see if you have an ancestor with a gift of veil reach."*

"What's that?" I ask, as I open the front door. The house smells of dried apples, cinnamon, nutmeg, and ginger. *Another tea mom must be brewing.* Marie is giggling in the living room. My mom emits her polite chuckle, and there are a few other voices I don't recognize. I kick off my shoes in the entryway and drop my bag to the floor. I can unpack it later; the last thing I want is to see all the silky, lacey, pathetic lingerie I hauled down there only to make an idiot of myself. *Gosh, this weekend sucked. I imagined it going so differently.*

Blue rolls his eyes and steps out into the hall, then halts. *"Eleanor, stop."*

He stares into the living room while the laughter trails off into sighs. "Now, who's familiar is that?" Mercy questions. Her voice cuts through the women settling down from their giggling fit.

The wooden beam beneath my left foot creaks. I freeze.

"You know what happens if she sees you like this," Blue warns.

"Oh," my mother says, sounding surprised. "That's my daughter's. I suppose she's home early." Her voice is high and squeaky, that only happens when she's afraid. "Eleanor, you're back from camping? Why don't you go upstairs and shower, I can smell you from here."

"Good idea," I answer back, still hidden behind the wall in the entryway. "Nonsense, this is fortuitous timing. Come here, child. You must congratulate your lovely sister," Mercy croons. Her voice drips with saccharine tones as if trying to come off like an old friend we've always rubbed elbows with instead of a newcomer trying to wedge herself in. I hear shuffling of feet and rattling of cups resting in delicate saucers.

I imagine my eyes blue. *Oculi Tempe.*

"Not enough. Do more. Bright makeup, glitter, the works."

High heels click against the wooden floorboards. Mercy emerges from the living room into the hall. Her short black bob is sleek and tucked behind her ears, putting the mother-of-pearl earrings in each lobe on full display. She wears a sleeveless black turtleneck with tweed trousers that end just above her dainty ankles. One would guess she was the editor-in-chief at Vogue, which is actually a less prestigious position than the leading witch of the North American Witch's Committee. She scarcely looks at me before snatching my hand and ruefully tugging me into the living room. I barely have time to add sparkly green shadow to each eye and maroon-painted lips.

Mom sits on the far sofa sandwiched between her sisters. Shannyn, with her perfect posture, ankles crossed, cup and saucer in her lap, sits directly across from me in the tufted leather armchair. Seated next to her is a girl I don't recognize; she has curly black hair and a golden-brown complexion. Then relaxing on the floral sofa beneath the window is a short, almost shriveled gentleman with salt and pepper hair nestled under a fedora and neatly wrapped in a velvet waistcoat. He gives me a tight smile as he brings his porcelain cup to his lips.

Mercy wraps a slender arm around my shoulders. "Your sister, Shannyn, has just been inducted into the newly formed Junior Committee," she squeals, edging on disingenuous. She gives my shoulders a little squeeze.

"We're all very excited," the gentleman croons. I'm unsure if he's being sarcastic or not.

My mother's smile is tight and controlled, while her eyes are too wide to be natural. Sally slurps her tea, looking every which way, while Marie busies herself collecting finger sandwiches from a silver serving tray perched on the ottoman.

The curly-haired girl smiles at my sister with twinkling eyes as she gives a quiet little clap using only the tips of her fingers. Shannyn chuckles at her friend, sharing some kind of inside joke.

"An impossibly lovely creature, Shannyn will be an excellent addition. I daresay I couldn't have asked for a better witch," Mercy says through a forced smile.

"Talia here was the first recruit. She's going to show me the ropes," Shannyn says graciously. She reaches over and pats Talia on her knee. "She mastered all five branches only a month into her training," my sister brags on her friend's behalf.

"Yes, she is indeed gifted, as are you. Another Byrne will be a delightful edition," the short man murmurs before dunking his shortbread cookie into his tea. He takes a tentative bite, and everything in his tone and demeanor screams he is far above all this Junior Committee nonsense.

"O'Reilly," Shannyn politely corrects.

"Whatever, dear. In the witch world, you're a Byrne even *after* you become a Burroughs next weekend. Hello, bloodlines are everything," he says with another dramatic roll of his eyes. "That's why killing certain Nefari is more fun than others," he says before peering down at his perfectly manicured cuticles.

"Horace!" Marie hisses at him.

"Please, Marie. These girls will soon know the indescribable high that only comes from destroying a Nefari's soul." He examines a cuticle more closely. "She might get an opportunity to do just that this evening."

Mom gasps.

The air in the room suddenly shifts. Mercy whips her arm off my shoulder and snaps in front of her. My mother's teacup had tumbled off its saucer, certainly due to shaking hands, but now it levitates upside down, the tea itself floating in the air just above the carpet. With a twirl of Mercy's finger, the delicate cup returns to the saucer still in my mother's hand, and a river of tea flows back into it. It all happens in seconds, leaving no trace it ever happened at all.

"Oh, thank you, Mercy," my mother says.

A smattering of applause rises from the other guests.

"Oh, it was nothing," Mercy says, feigning modesty. She waves a hand to silence everyone's tepid applause.

Mercy turns to me, takes hold of my shoulders, and looks me directly in the eye. Her eyebrows leap at the garish makeup I'm sporting, but she quickly recovers with a generous smile. "You know, Eleanor," she says, tilting her head toward me, "when you've turned twenty, you too can be invited to join." She looks over her shoulder at my sister who beams at her in return.

Mercy then notices Blue. She takes a step back as her hand flutters to her chest. "My dear, is your familiar having a stroke?" She shakes her head in disbelief and lifts her hand to her lips. "Something about him is not…right."

"Up yours, you old crone."

I scoop Blue up off the floor and tuck him into my chest. The rank smell of his fur sizzles in my nostrils. *It's okay, Blue, you do kind of smell.*

"Let's bury you in the backyard and see how you smell after a few centuries."

You just need more of mom's serum.

"Sorry, Mercy, we both probably need to wash up." I answer, walking back toward the stairs.

"He needs more than a bath, my dear." Mercy then pivots toward my mother who's rising off the couch. "Helen, you must have a tonic somewhere that might…aid the poor cat in his…peculiar condition." Mercy whips back toward me. "You know, Eleanor, you can be cited if your familiar isn't being properly tended." She wags a finger at me.

"Eleanor, just go. Your color is—"

Blue abruptly stops short just as a Burmese cat, lean and muscular with a beige and tan body and brown face, comes slinking in from the living room to join Mercy in the hall. It sits at her feet, its tail swishing back and forth. Its yellow eyes follow Blue and I inching up the stairs.

Blue? What's wrong?

"Hex," Blue sends to this new cat in a very dry, very cold greeting.

I can't hear the cat's response, only Blue's end of the

conversation, but it's clear Blue isn't liking what he's hearing.

Blue turns his head to look up at me. *"We should freshen up,"* he sends, his eyes urging me upstairs.

"Congratulations, Shannyn!" I call before dashing up the stairs and slamming my door. I flick the lock and fall back against the door. My jaw drops open taking in my bedroom. Every drawer in both my dresser and my desk have been thrown open. Books thrown. Pages ripped out. Clothes droop from their hangers. My blankets are on the floor, even the satin canopy over my bed has been torn from the walnut bedposts. It's like my wardrobe exploded and its contents flew out like shrapnel. Even my dirty clothes hamper has been turned upside down.

I tiptoe around the carnage, assessing the damage. "Blue…" I utter, still taking in the horror. Someone took a knife to my pillows; the fluff lies across my bed and the floor. "Who would do this? Could it be…?" I can't say her name. Not now. Not when I'm home. She's even more real to me here and saying her name feels like a summons. I haven't even begun to think of a plan to spring her from Purgatory yet.

Blue carefully steps over a broken lamp. *"No, I don't feel her in this."* His azure eyes shift about, never settling on any one thing. He's not gathering information. He's afraid. Deeply. Afraid.

Blue mutters darkly in his head, uttering what I can only guess are Shakespearean cusses.

I can barely swallow. "What is it?"

"Hex. He's always known I'm a dead cat, but he was unaware I had a ward. Now he knows it's you."

I sit down on the corner of my bed, afraid to take up too much space in my frightened state, instead just wanting to collapse into myself. "How do you know him?"

Blue continues pacing. *"I'm more or less acquainted with all the familiars here in Salem. The majority are aware of my…state. Most find it bewildering, some refuse to believe it. Hex has always been weary of me. Kept his distance. Which to be perfectly frank, I didn't mind. That cat's always been a prig. But now he knows the dead cat is a familiar to one of the Byrne girls. The last thing we need is to draw more attention to you. He won't let this go. He'll demand Mercy investigate."*

"I'm in even more danger now, aren't I?" I ask rhetorically.

I hear the front door open. Out my window, I see Mercy, Talia, and Horace walk out, accompanied by their three feline familiars. They pick up their wooden brooms off the veranda and mount them with their cats. Before their feet even lift from the veranda they blink out of sight, going completely transparent. There's a rustle through the forest canopy as they whiz past like the wind.

Stomping footsteps storm up the stairs. My door shakes furiously. The knob tries to turn but is locked.

La Caeli. I flip the lock open.

The door bangs against the wall as my mom barges in, red-faced and shaking. "What are you doing home?! Why didn't you call?!" She doesn't even notice the disaster about me.

I shake my head. "I'm sorry. We got into a fight and ended the weekend short. I'm sorry, I should have called."

Mom's brow stays furrowed, still angry but now concerned as well.

"What did you two fight about?"

"Our relationship. We're trying to work things out, but I don't know…"

I stare down at the scattered pillow fluff on my bed.

"You and Zoey fought about your relationship?" she questions.

I blanch. "Oh, ah…" *Crap! I said I'd be with Zoey at their lake house.* "Kind of, things are complicated…"

My mother nods listening, then her eyes frantically slide about taking in my ransacked bedroom. "What in the world? What happened here?" she lifts her feet, realizing she's standing on ripped textbook paper. "Eleanor, did you leave it like this?"

"Are you seriously asking me if I destroyed my bedroom and all my belongings?" I now see my violin next to my wardrobe, the neck snapped in two. My heart shatters.

Mom shakes her head. "No, I'm asking if you saw this and then left without saying anything because you knew I would never have let you go with your room looking like this."

"No, Mom. I got home and found it like this. You guys didn't hear anything?"

"No." Mom then gasps. She picks up a shattered picture frame with a photograph of me, my sisters, and Dad at the beach. Mom was snapping the pic. Tears fill her eyes as she holds the broken frame in her quivering hands. Shannyn appears in the doorway. "Whoa, what the hell happened here?"

I cross the room to help my mom rise to her feet. "Like you care," I accuse. Shannyn's shocked eyes turn hard when they snap from my disheveled room to me. I ignore her and help my mom to my bed to sit down as she continues to hold the broken frame.

"Excuse me?" She steps closer, broken glass crunching under her brown leather boot.

I grip my hips, readying myself for an overdue argument. "Excited to kill some Nefari, Ms. Junior Committee member?"

Shannyn crosses her arms indignantly. "How dare you ask me that?"

I take a step closer. "How dare *I*? You've always been focused on being 'Shannyn the Perfect'! I'm shocked you didn't ask to be inducted into the *real* Committee. How long did it take you to accept?! Three seconds! You know, when I'm found out, Mercy will probably make *you* be the one to destroy me!" Fury brews inside me like a churning cauldron. Anger about this failed weekend. Anger about Mercy. The Committee. The Nefari. Elspeth. And now my sister. I want to hurl my broken belongings across the room.

Shannyn's eyes are glass, her mouth a firm, hard line. "You don't know the first thing about me, Eleanor. You never wanted to. You've always acted like I enjoy being so isolated, like *I* made that choice. I didn't join for *me*. I. Joined. For. You." She says the last four words like she's grinding concrete in her mouth.

"Bullshit!"

"Eleanor!"

Shannyn blinks, taking a step back like she's experienced a physical blow. She looks at me aghast, then recovers, showing no weakness.

"Girls, enough," Mom says, stepping between us. "The last thing we need is for you two to fight. You are sisters."

"Yeah, and one of us is pretty unhappy about that." She turns on her heel and marches from my bedroom.

Yeah, which one, sis…

"She is, you know, joining for you. She thinks having me be on the Committee will give Mercy too much access to the family, but Shannyn can be our mole and help Marie throw Mercy off your trail." Mom uses her magic to slide over my waste basket and levitates in the broken glass from the floor.

"Whatever," I say, picking up my books and placing them on my desk. I know I'm being childish and pigheaded, but I can't help myself. My magic pulsates inside me, enjoying my anger, egging me to throw an even bigger fit. "Who could have done this?" my mother asks, picking up more broken items off the floor.

While helping her clean, I finally notice my headboard. I take a stumbling step back. A message is carved in ugly jagged letters.

Soon

CHAPTER NINE
The Attic

It took my mom, Sally, and I so many hours of throwing things away (broken glass, torn paper), repairing (my violin, my desk drawers, the hinges on my wardrobe), sewing (torn clothes and the canopy), and replacing items beyond repair (my pillows and shredded comforter) that by the time I was crawling into bed, the sky was shifting from inky black to the murky gray. Marie busied herself tending to Blue, fixing his cockeyed ear, ironing out his three whiskers, and whipping up a tonic to treat his mange and, of course, his smell.

"I'm beat," Sally says through a yawn. She stretches her arms high above her head, cracking her spine as she moves. "I'm heading to Abe's. He owes me a massage." She rolls her head from side to side before traipsing out of the room on her high heels that act more like stilts.

"Thanks for your help, Sal," I call, fluffing my pillows.

Sally pops her head back in. "We'll get the bastard, El. Promise." There's a clack with each step of her heels as she descends the stairs.

I wiggle in my bed trying to find a comfortable position with my new pillow. This one's lumpy and smells nothing like home.

"Soon?" My mom questions, looking intently at my headboard.

I groan, pulling my blanket that still smells of its plastic packaging. "We've talked about the Nefari witch for the last *nine* hours; I told you, he said he was coming *soon*."

Mom's jaw clicks shut, her lips pursed. She waves her hand at my intricate headboard as if batting away a gnat. There's a quiet vibration of magic in the room, and the etched word disappears. "Tomorrow, I'll pick up some wood putty and we'll actually get that fixed. Right as rain," she assures with faux confidence and a nod of her head.

I nod with a yawn. "Okay, thanks."

Mom lingers at the door after flicking off my light. Her features are hidden by the yellow light of the landing behind her, just a dark silhouette gazing at me in silence. Her presence is indescribably heavy. Even with my eyes shut, I feel a pressure beneath her stare. But when I open them again, she's gone.

"I'll be sleeping in the bathtub tonight. May we both enjoy our solitude."

I roll onto my left side, then my right. Somehow my body has managed to be simultaneously exhausted and restless. I roll my shoulders and shake out my legs. *Why hasn't Jack called? Or at least texted. And how could I have been so wrong about the Nefari? It didn't seem like he wanted to harm me, so why destroy my room? Was he looking for something?* My veins suddenly fill with ice. *Could it be the same thing Elspeth wants? The thing inside the forbidden room…?*

Every few minutes, I check the time on my phone. Seconds. Minutes. Hours. I watch them tick by, unable to silence the steady stream of anxious thoughts. *What if he comes for me today? What if he comes and my family gets in the way?*

Sunday night isn't any better. When a cat brushed my leg at the dinner table, I nearly shrieked.

Maggie rolled her eyes at me. "How many cats live here, and you're still scared?"

Every night that followed was the same. The house whistled and whined every time the wind would slip through a crack, and I'd shoot up in bed. The pipes moaned, and my eyes burst open. Not even chamomile tea with belladonna or a soak in Himalayan salt and lavender could calm my nerves enough to let me sleep. By Friday, I was dead on my feet and barely reacted when the bells chimed at school.

"Brah, is your sister on drugs or something?" asks one of Maggie's friends as they pass me in the hall. I'm leaning lethargically against my locker, my eyes hazy and unfocused.

Maggie elbows her in the side. "Just shut up, Melanie." I drag myself to class and collapse in my chair.

"Eleanor, come speak with me," Mr. Sullivan says only a second after the end-of-class bell.

I gather my belongings and haul myself to the back of the room where old Mr. Sullivan sits behind his new age metal desk. He's in his ergonomic chair that makes him growl every time he swivels in it. He inherited this room from the previous teacher who was "mysteriously" let go…right around the time all Noble Hunters were arrested. Mr. Sullivan curses while struggling to open a bottom drawer.

I cover my mouth while I yawn, and my eyes flutter close.

La Caeli.

The drawer finally dislodges, and he swallows back his grumblings. Mr. Sullivan retrieves the source of his ire and slides it across the desk. My name and the title of my research paper are printed at the top next to a big C-minus circled angrily in red. If I weren't so tired, I'd probably laugh. A year ago, that would have devastated me. I used to like school and would never have shied away from an academic challenge. But that was the old Eleanor, the pre-magic, pre-murderous witch hunting clan, pre-dead friends, and pre-dead dad Eleanor.

"What do you have to say for yourself?" Mr. Sullivan folds his arms across his chest, thankfully covering some of the hideous pattern on his sweater vest.

I stare idly at the crimson C. I'm so exhausted. "C is for cookie" is the only thing that comes to mind, but I'm 90% sure that's not the answer he's looking for. I decide to just stay silent. It doesn't use any energy to stay silent. He jabs at my paper with his forefinger.

"Your section on functional groups and nomenclature is riddled with inaccuracies and misspellings. Not to mention your structure and bonding examples were incomplete. The only reason this isn't a *failing* paper is because your understanding of molecular geometry goes beyond the requirements of this course. But this is your first and *only* warning. Do better or I'm dropping you from the class. Now get out of here." He nods his stodgy head toward the door where a group of students are huddled waiting to enter, then adds, "And I'm not writing you a tardy note, either. Consider it your punishment."

The juvenile students salaciously "oohh" as I pass by, but I'm too tired to be embarrassed. As I make my way to the student parking lot, deciding to skip senior seminar, I text Maggie that she needs to ride home with a friend after school.

Back at home, the house is abuzz with wedding preparations, so no one even notices me amble through the front door—except for the cats, who scatter around me like shrapnel as I crash onto the living room sofa face down.

"No, the cake needs to arrive *before* the ceremony," mom insists to someone on the phone. After a brief pause, she adds "But the bride wants to see it for approval first." Another pause. The sound of her footsteps keep shifting from one side of the dining room to the other. "The tasting was a disaster; the samples came three hours late. Yes. Yes. No, no, don't return any deposits. Look, is Tallulah there? Can I speak to her?"

The clock in the hall chimes. Cats mewl about the living room, meowing, rubbing on furniture, scratching on their posts. Blue is nowhere to be found. *Good, I don't need another lecture about cutting class.*

My mother's shrill voice rises several octaves. I'm not sure whose nerves are more fried. Probably hers, if I'm being honest with myself.

I turn my head to gulp in some air with less cat hair. I close my eyes, waiting for that velvety darkness of sleep to envelope me, sealing me away from reality. The seconds tick away so slowly it's excruciating. My eyes fall open like one of those old baby dolls that you tilt to open and close their eyes. I stare out at nothing in particular. *Is this what he wanted? To drive me mad with waiting?*

The doorbell chimes. Marie thumps down the spiral staircase out of breath, her long black skirt trailing behind her. "Hello?" she says as cheerfully as she can manage. I don't have to see her to know she has on her cutesy smile that scrunches her face and her eyes disappear into slits above the protruding apples of her cheeks.

"Oh goodness," she says, surprised and a little dismayed by the person at the door.

"Flower delivery," a voice at the door announces.

"Oh, I can see that dear, but those were to arrive tomorrow. Tonight is the rehearsal dinner, and this isn't even the venue. Goodness gracious, how many of you are delivering flowers? Those are seven vans in the drive. Ah… Helen, you need to come here. I'm so sorry, boys. It appears there's been a teensy little mistake."

"We have over two thousand peonies, ma'am. And four thousand pink roses," he says dryly.

"Oh yes, it's going to be a beautiful ceremony," Marie gushes. "You boys should really stop by; it'll be simply lovely."

Mom stomps down the hall, clutching her cellphone down at her side. She stops, sticking her head into the living room. "Eleanor, what are you doing home from school?"

"I can't sleep. I can't be at school right now," I mumble numbly against the cushion.

"Ell," she starts softly, her eyes side to the door and does a double take. "Are those the flowers?! No no no, they aren't supposed to be delivered *here* nor *today*! This is the billing address not the delivery address!" Mom takes a deep breath, holds it, then releases through her nose. "Okay, pack everything up. You'll all follow me to the venue. We're going to Crane Estate in Ipswich."

She then claps her hands together, snapping the rest of the family present to attention. "Come everyone, let's get a move on it.

I still have a rehearsal dinner to get ready for, and don't worry, none of the high-ranking Committee members will be there. Tonight is exclusively for close family and friends." She walks away, then stops. "Eleanor, are you calling off your shift at Molly and Polly's tonight?"

I'm glad she said something, otherwise I would have completely forgotten I was scheduled.

"No," I grumble back. "I should just get used to this sleepless existence.

If I'm going to be awake, might as well make money."

"Marie, I think I'm going to just stay at the venue and direct traffic. Can you please make sure the girls are both there by seven?" mom stresses. "Of course, dearie. Now you go take care of those peonies, they smell absolutely heavenly." Nothing can really keep Aunt Marie down. She can see the best in everything, in anyone, in any situation. Everyone needs an Aunt Marie.

"Ellie pumpkin, would you like me to drive you to work, sweetie? I don't think you should be driving or flying in your state." Even her worried voice is sing song-y.

I shrug, heaving myself upright. "Sure. I think I'll go in early. See if Zoey has a mallet she can bludgeon me with."

Marie giggles. "Oh goody. See if you were sleeping just fine and dandy we wouldn't get to go on this little drive together. See you in the van!"

It takes me over ten minutes to put on my black pants and black sweater. I keep needing a break and sitting down. My fingers shake as I put in my colored contacts. I slap my cheeks, but it doesn't help.

"I'm coming with you," Blue sends, slinking out from under my bed. *"If you should run into trouble, I highly doubt you could defend yourself in this state."*

I don't argue with him. Nor with Marie as she blasts a poppy techno beat and sings along to the innuendo-laden lyrics that all go right over her head. "Maggie's little friend Piper from soccer introduced me to her. What a talent!" Marie's frizzy curls bounce as she bobs here head to the music. "Wow, who crapped in your cauldron?" Zoey calls as I heave open the front door. She hops down from the platform in the back and skips down the three steps. "Spellbound" by Siouxsie and the Banshees blasts from the speakers around the shop.

Blue makes a beeline down the aisle farthest from the speakers near the glass elixir case. *"I can't hear myself think in this place. Must her racket always be so loud?"*

"So, I don't want to be *that* witch, but you look awful, Ell. What's going on?" Zoey questions.

"I can't sleep," I say in a deep, monotone voice. I shlepp myself to the stool behind checkout and slump onto the counter next to the register.

Zoey plonks down on the neighboring stool. She tilts her head, gazing at me with her big brown eyes. "Damn, Ell. You've got darker circles than a corpse. Is Jack keeping you up all night?" She wiggles her thick Italian eyebrows at me and ribs me with her elbow. "I've been dying for you to give me the deets about your weekend, but you kept calling off your shifts." She playfully huffs her frustration.

My jaw pops as I yawn. The corner of my mouth is crusty. *Did I brush my teeth this morning? Or last night?* "Sorry, I've been trying to sleep after school, but it's no use. Same at night." My eyes start to close on their own, and I see no reason to stop them, but I can feel Zoey watching me with a scrutinizing gaze. I peek one eye open to confirm.

Zoey shakes her head at me, then snatches her phone off the counter. "Alright, calling in reinforcements."

"Who?" I ask.

Her eyes roll to the ceiling as she waits for someone to pick up on the other end of her call. "Dotty and Ray's. We're getting takeout and closing the shop for the night. Just don't tell my aunts." She turns back to her phone growing impatient. "Hi Pete, finally," she says something indecipherable in Italian under her breath, "I need two pastrami's and all the onion rings you've got with two root beers STAT. Yup, Zoey Gallo, and *yes* this is for sure an emergency." She has one hand on her petite hip watching me while she orders.

Blue springs onto the counter and settles next to my head. *"I don't like this; you need more tea. Sally uses belladonna with blessed bone broth."*

I've tried everything, Blue. I've accepted this is how I die. Not with a bang, but a want of snoring.

"You shouldn't be flippant about this."

You're right, I'm too sleepy to be clever.

Zoey tosses her phone onto the counter and magically flips around the closed sign on the door. "Come with me into the back. Your cat stays here, though. You need a clear mind, which means no familiars." Her steely eyes narrow on my familiar next to me.

"Excuse me?"

"He's not going to like that," I mutter, sitting up.

Zoey shrugs, unfazed by Blue's glare. "Don't worry. Betty can keep him company." As if summoned, her hairless sphinx cat with enormous bat ears lands on the counter, and I could be delirious from lack of sleep, but I'm fairly certain I watched her wink at Blue while her mouth curled into a devious smile.

"Oh, bloody hell, I'd rather be skinned alive!"

Zoey snags my hand and tows me to the stockroom where she flips the lock on the heavy wooden door behind us. She pulls the dangling silver chain in the center of the room, illuminating the space. The small area is mostly floor-to-ceiling shelves with wilting plants, vacant pots, miscellaneous boxes, and empty vials. She adjusts where I'm standing until I'm positioned perfectly in the middle of the room, only inches from her.

"Clear your mind," she orders. Her voice is smooth and methodical.

My eyes fall shut and I try to picture a blank space, but instead I see the word "soon" carved into my headboard, the Nefari's violet eyes, the green-haired man pummeling Jack flying backward, glass breaking, my violin snapping. "I can't," I whimper. "It's like I'm cursed."

Zoey takes ahold of my shoulders. Her hands seem to sink deep into my flesh and grip my bones. She sucks in a startled breath and holds it. She releases it into an uneasy whine. "Eleanor, you're not cursed. You're haunted."

Elspeth.

My mind grows more alert, as if it's been pulled from sludge and dipped in a cleansing pool. "I think I know what you're talking about." I no longer feel Zoey's hands on my arms. The mossy, earthy smell of the stockroom is eclipsed by the aroma of bleach and lemon cleaner.

I open my eyes and gasp. Zoey has vanished. In fact, the entire back room is gone.

I'm standing in a darkened entryway of a small home, just inches from the front door. A light flicks on from the landing, illuminating a narrow set of stairs before me. At the top of the landing, a woman sheathed in a robe and a towel wrapped around her head strolls into the light, then disappears into the dark just as quickly.

"Zoey?" I squeak. *Is she somehow doing this? Is she forcing me to have a vision?*

I glance about, but don't see anything familiar.

I move toward the staircase and grip the wooden banister. My footsteps are light, my movement soft and fluid as I ascend the stairs. The heavy chains of insomnia that had kept me in a disillusioned fog haven't followed me here, whatever this place is. There's no rusty hamster wheel turning over in the back of my subconscious, churning out intrusive thoughts that poison my mind. I feel like myself again.

Reaching the top landing, steam billows from a darkened bathroom to my right. The door to my left opens, startling me as a woman in a cottony nightgown with little green flowers printed across it walks right through me.

I don't recognize her. She isn't one of my teachers at Griggs. Not one of Sally or Marie's friends, at least not one I'm acquainted with. I squint in the meager light coming from the bathroom door left ajar, trying to gather as much information as I can.

Hanging on the wall is a picture of Fenway with the woman holding a cup of beer next to a man clinking his glass against hers. I piece together the picture with the crown molding, the aged banister thick and grimy after too many coats of paint, and how narrow the home is. We must be in Boston.

The woman spits into the sink and tosses her toothbrush into a mason jar. Her face is shiny from some kind of serum. Her wet hair hangs by her small shoulders with thin strands of gray, although she doesn't seem older than fifty.

She brushes past me toward a bedroom across from the bathroom. I follow her in before she can close the door on me; if this is anything like previous visions, I won't be able to open the door once it's shut. I slip in and stand beside her dresser.

Her room is plain. An oval mirror hangs above her brown wicker headboard. A purse and coat hang from the hook behind the door. Her tall wicker dresser next to me just has a candle and a picture of a man, different from the one in the hall, lying without a frame next to it. Nothing is alarming or out of the ordinary. In fact, her room is so painfully boring I can't fathom why any vision would bring me here.

The woman sits down on the bed, rolling her head, stretching out the muscles in her neck. She takes several large gulps from the glass of water on her nightstand before crawling under her gray bedding, then clicks off her light.

Great, now what? Blue, can you hear me? I reach out to him but feel nothing. With a sigh, I take a seat in the wooden rocking chair next to the open window. White lace curtains ruffle in the breeze. I can't rock back in the chair, that would be influencing my surroundings. I lean on my hand glancing about. *Okay, Zoey, what was the point of this? Do you know her? Am I supposed to be doing something?*

I watch the sleeping woman's chest rise and fall, until I realize it's no longer moving. In fact, I don't think she's taken a breath in a while. I sprint to the side of the bed slip two fingers onto her neck. There isn't a pulse. I notice the half-empty glass beside her again. *Was something in there?*

The floor creaks in the hall. The air seizes in my chest.

The bedroom door creaks open. A shadowy figure, darker than the night around him, stares at me from the doorway. He steps forward into a shaft of light afforded by a skylight and the full moon. Despite the illumination, I can only make one feature: his violet eyes.

He comes toward me—not toward the woman, but me specifically— but before he can reach me, the room falls away, leaving me in a black abyss. My hands tremble as I fling them out around me, bracing for anything that might come from the darkness. My arms are visible, like I'm standing under a spotlight, which means anyone or anything in the shadows can see me too. "He-he-hello?" I stammer. Hic. "Is anyone," hic, "there?" I call out.

Silence.

A clunky clicking sound echoes, like clomping hooves walking across marble.

I swivel, ready for the attack, but my stomach is sick, like I'm on the first drop of a rollercoaster. "Who's," hic, "there?" I cry out. *Zoey, if this is you, please bring me back. Please. Don't leave me in the dark.*

A black-bearded goat with curled horns steps toward me. It peers up at me with its horizontal pill-shaped irises. I tap my foot on the floor behind me, making sure it's solid and not the edge of cliff or something. The goat turns its back to me and trots a few steps away, only to stop and look over his shoulder, as if bidding me to follow.

I tiptoe silently behind him, eager to return to the apothecary shop. In the distance is an open room sitting like it's been carved out of a house and dropped into this void. Keeping my gaze steady, the room becomes sharper, clearer. It appears to be an attic with stone walls, exposed beams, and a thatched roof. There's a woman with blonde hair rummaging through boxes, dozens of them. She kicks a box in frustration then drops to her knees and pours through another. Once she's clawed through everything in the box, she tosses it aside and moves onto an old, battered steamer trunk.

The black goat and I now stand in the corner of her attic. The air is musty and damp. My lungs ache from the dust.

BANG! BANG! BANG! BANG!

I spin toward the direction of the sound.

The attic door behind me rattles the doorframe as someone frantically pounds the door.

The woman is breathing heavily; her face is smudge with dust and dirt. Her lower jaw trembles as someone rattles the doorknob and screams on the other side.

"Colleen!" a man bellows from the other side.

Despite the violent pounding on the door, I can't tear my eyes from this woman. There's something so familiar about her. She's rail thin, frail, with a soft round face. Her wide eyes are unnaturally pink, almost magenta, and her blonde hair is streaked with white and gray, pulled back in a frizzy low ponytail. I study the fine lines at the corners of her eyes and deeply etched creases across her forehead. She looks like my mother, just heavily aged.

My jaw falls open in shock. The man called her "Colleen." As in Colleen Byrne. This is my grandmother.

She dives back into the trunk, furiously searching for something. The attic door flies off its hinges and thumps against the stone wall. My grandmother emits a scream that makes my blood run cold.

Chapter Ten
Why Do We Have to Rehearse Eating?

"No! I swear, I don't have that power, Eleanor," Zoey insists for the third time. We're on the floor behind the counter sitting cross-legged and hunched over our takeout boxes.

For the first time in… I can exactly remember, I feel rested. I feel energized, and most of all I'm *starving*. My best efforts to slow down do absolutely nothing to keep me from chomping bite after bite of my pastrami sandwich, barely remembering to take a breath as I eat.

Zoey wears a smug smile as she watches me. "Good pastrami and chicken parm can fix any ill. Trust me."

I swish back some root beer and shake my head. "It was the vision. Though Dotty and Ray's is a close second," I say, thinking of my first lunch there with Trixie. It was only last spring, but it might as well have been another lifetime. "It still doesn't any make sense, what were you trying to do to me?" I ask through a mouthful.

Zoey finishes an onion ring. "I was trying to sense if someone had hexed you, maybe with a tonic or spell. But instead, I felt a dark presence on you, like a shadow that's been following you. Eleanor," she scoots closer, "it was pretty malevolent. You need to talk to your mom or your aunts. Someone is definitely trying to hurt you."

Spit and breadcrumbs fly out mouth as I burst out laughing. I clamp a hand down over my mouth to keep the rest in, but Zoey still leans away from me, both startled and a little grossed out.

Elspeth, some Nefari witch who trashed my room, and even the Committee once they learn what I am. Honestly, the list seems endless at this point. I cough and clear my throat, trying to regain my composure. "Yeah, I think I know who's haunting me, but cursing me with insomnia doesn't seem like her style."

"Well, there's a first for everything. Can you bloody well help me?!"

"Blue?" I call out. I only now realize he hasn't been around since we left him for the storeroom.

"That bloody imbecile has me locked in a bleeding cupboard!"

I sigh and turn to Zoey. "Betty has locked Blue in a cabinet," I share as Blue continues his stream of curses and creatively elegant threats.

Zoey lets out a deep growl. "Betty!" She stands and dusts off her bottom with her hands. The chunky silver rings on her hands clink and ting against each other.

The thin sphinx slinks across the counter, head bent low and looking into Zoey's eyes.

"What the hell do you think you're doing?" Zoey snaps. Her face changes from irate to confused, then skeptical. Her eyes slide to me and back to Betty. I wish I knew what they were saying.

"Can she tell you what cupboard she has Blue trapped so I can let him out?" I ask.

"Back left corner by the door beneath the Venus flytraps. Hurry! And fetch a sack, we're killing that cat. I know a spot on the river we can…"

I skip down the steps and head straight for the small nook. "Eleanor?" Zoey calls after me.

I retrieve my work key from my pocket and unlock the latch. Blue immediately leaps out.

"Where is that demented, bald cow?" He hisses and arches his back, his hair up on end.

Why didn't you just walk through the door?

"We can't bring more attention to the fact I'm not exactly one with a pulse…"

"Eleanor?" Zoey tries again, sounding rather impatient. I straighten up and look back at her.

"Is your…and I know how crazy this sounds…but is your familiar…dead? Betty," she says her cat's name with a dubious glare, "says he's most certainly dead."

My insides clench as I stare up at my friend. Zoey and I have spent most nights together since I started working here. We always get along, but we share very little about ourselves. We've gone to the movies together, grabbed some hot chocolate from The Wolf Next Door, we've even snuck into The Witch House Museum after hours together. But did all those hours spent together sum up to trust? The kind of fragile trust that bore life and death consequences.

"He is," I answer frankly. *"Eleanor! What are you doing?"*

Zoey's head jerks back. "Wait, seriously?"

Her eyes dart between Blue and me as I walk back to the checkout counter with my undead familiar nipping at my heels. Blue gives Betty a withering stare as I take a seat on one of the stools. Betty hisses at him from atop the counter, while Zoey fumbles for words.

"How is that even *possible*? It… it isn't possible," Zoey insists. "I mean, familiars don't just crawl out of cemeteries when they're called. They're born when we are, and they can survive pretty much anything, they live until…" Her eyes grow to the size of saucers. "Holy hell! Did you die?! Were you revived somehow? This is crazy!"

"Indeed, I quite agree. Utter madness, in fact. What next? Shall we ring Mercy and piss on her doorstep? Sometimes you act like an ignorant child…"

I roll my shoulders back, feeling that sting like an acid burn between my shoulder blades. "No. I was branded and left for dead, but I didn't actually die." My eyes haze over, ignoring Blue's endless seething, and picture that forest on prom night. Allen Woods draped in his ceremonial robe alongside my ravenous classmates howling for blood. That vile novelty song telling the rabbit to run. I shake my head and clear the image from my mind.

"We aren't quite sure what happened with Blue," I explain. "But it doesn't matter, he's my familiar and I would appreciate it if Betty would respect that." I look with a cocked brow over at Betty resting beside Zoey. Zoey's face is ashen. She pushes the box of half-eaten onion rings away with the toe end of her Doc Martens and wraps her slender arms around her abdomen. "Are you okay?" I ask.

Betty turns her head to Zoey. The skeletal cat tilts her head at her ward, her grayish-blue eyes sweeping Zoey's face.

"Yeah, I'm fine," Zoey mumbles. "Anyway, Betty promises to leave Blue alone. So, what was the second part of your vision? You were telling me about the rando who died in her sleep." Her posture curls away from me, her arms still crossed defensively.

"No, she was—" a thought sends an electric chill down my spine. *Didn't Elspeth say my grandma was the only person to have an identical… whatever is in the room next to mine? That has to be what my grandma was searching through those boxes for. Is that what they were searching for in mine? Crap! If they can't get to the one in Salem, they could go after my grandmother. She's in danger.*

I leap to my feet, startling both Betty and Zoey. "I've got to go. I need to… speak to my mom before the rehearsal madness." While grabbing my belongings, I spot Zoey from the corner of my eye staring down at her feet, her eyes misty. "Hey, do you want to come to the dinner? It's buffet style so it's not like there won't be enough room." *Did I say something to make her cry?* I hesitate, debating whether I should ask what's wrong, but think better of it. Zoey lifts her head.

Tears leak from the corners of her eyes, but she swipes them away with the cuff of her ratty black sweater. "Um, okay," she sniffs. "Do you want a ride?"

I glance at the clock on the wall; Marie isn't coming to get me for another half hour. "Ah yeah, sure." I sling my purse over my shoulder.

I follow Zoey out behind the apothecary by the dumpsters. Parked next to the back door is a maroon motorcycle with cream-colored accents, chrome detailing, and a dark, glossy finish. On the right side is a low-riding sidecar. "Restored 1947 Indian Chief. This here's my baby," she says, perking up. With a flick of her fingers, a black helmet whizzes toward me.

"Oy, look alive."

I nearly drop it but manage to hang on. "I take it I'm in the sidecar?" I say, snapping the strap under my chin.

She grins, all trace of tears gone. "Hell, yeah." She straddles her bike and motions to the sidecar. Betty climbs in, placing her paws on the side. She stares pleasurably at Blue and me.

"*Oh, Fu—*"

Stop it, Blue! We've got enough to worry about.

Zoey hollers and giggles as we zip through town. At a red light on Summer Street, a few guys in a silver Corvette pull up next to us and rev their engine. Zoey leaves them in the dust mere seconds after the light turns green. I'm not entirely sure whether she used magic.

"Boys can be so silly," she calls over the roar of her bike.

I tightly grip Betty in my left hand and Blue in my right as we cruise through the forest, bumping up and down on the gravel roads. My teeth chatter the entire time, both from the rough ride and the urgency to unburden my vision on my mother. She'll know what to do about Grandma Colleen and perhaps that unknown woman.

Zoey gawks at the house after she putters to a stop. "Hot damn, this place looks different now. It's lost all its Haunted Mansion vibes. Way more HGTV now."

I snag her hand and tow her up the veranda and through the front door. "Marie, I'm back. Zoey's coming tonight," I call. Most of the lights are out. The scent of rosemary and fir wafts in the air. The living room glows with firelight.

I peek around the corner. Sally and Abe are rolling about on the couch. "Let's go upstairs and get ready," I whisper, nodding toward the spiral stairs.

Betty skips past us up the stairs and explores the landing.

"No funny business," Zoey warns as we pass her familiar on our way to my room.

"*As if she knows any other,*" Blue sends. "*Completely mental that one. I may be dead, but that one's a few pence short of a shilling.*"

"Color me jealous, this room rocks," Zoey says, throwing herself onto my bed.

I whip open my wardrobe doors and race to get ready. The sooner I get to the Crane estate, the sooner I can tell my mom about the vision of *her* mother.

It occurs to me that Zoey is at least five inches shorter than me; nothing in my closet will fit her. I shoot Maggie a quick text to bring some wardrobe options.

Maggie soon arrives with several options to pick from. They both ultimately agree the black chiffon jumpsuit with the asymmetrical neckline, with a sash and flattering bow that hangs low on the hip is the correct choice. "Here, you'll need a purse. That chain wallet attached to your pants won't cut it tonight," Maggie says, clucking her tongue at my friend. She hands Zoey a sequined envelope clutch. "I love those shoes, but Shannyn declared this a high-heel affair. None of us are spared." She passes Zoey her tallest heels, bedazzled with onyx.

"Your sister is pretty rad," Zoey says, posing in the oval mirror then strutting around my room. "And she's got a killer style. She's like a freckled redheaded fairy godmother."

Maggie returns to my room wearing emerald trousers with a matching emerald tuxedo vest, which she's styled as a shirt. Layers of gold jewelry accent her ensemble. For her purse, she carries an ornately carved wooden box attached to a long gold chain. Another of Maggie's unique purse designs. I have to agree with Zoey; my sister is *effortlessly* rad. Her long red hair is pulled up in two pigtail buns high on her head with a few rebellious strands hanging down. Somehow, she makes even a child's hairstyle elegant and chic.

"Hey, Margaret," Zoey calls, staring at her own reflection.

"You can just call me 'Maggie'," my sister answers, perching on the edge of the battered trunk at the foot of my bed.

"Any chance you'd want to go shopping? I'm on a budget, but…" Zoey pauses to check out her nicely shaped bottom in the mirror.

Maggie giggles. "Absolutely, most of my items are thrift store finds too. I prefer working with a tight budget. Makes it more interesting, like a sport," she says with a smirk.

I pull on my lavender lace pencil skirt paired with the same black turtleneck I've been wearing all evening.

Maggie's eyes roll to the back of her head. "I love my sister, but she's seriously hopeless sometimes."

Zoey's dark brown eyes flit between my sister and me, clearly unsure how to respond. "Oh yeah, totally," she finally agrees, feigning an air of confidence. Still, her cheeks color and she looks away while Maggie stomps down the tower stairs.

In a moment, Maggie returns with a gold sequined skirt and black knee-length boots. "Keep the turtleneck, but swap out the skirt for this. Then no necklace, just earrings, and put your hair up. I'll see you guys downstairs in five." She tosses me a round spherical clutch with a dangling tassel. It almost looks like a Christmas ornament.

"Are you girls coming?" Sally hollers from downstairs.

Once I finish following Maggie's instructions, Zoey and I hurry downstairs. Maggie is snapping selfies with Aunt Marie huddled by the front door while Sally adjusts Abe's tie. When we reach the entryway, Zoey holds up her black leather jacket for Maggie's approval.

My sister snaps a picture then glances over. "Oh yeah. It'll add a good texture to your look."

Having received Maggie's blessing, Zoey slips her arms into her coat. Sally smiles at Zoey's look with her approval.

Marie runs her hands down her sides, then tugs and pulls on her mustard tweed, knee-length dress. She glances at her diamond and pearl-studded brooch of a canary carrying a sprig in its talons. "I'm not sure about this dress, dearie. It's a little form-fitting, isn't it?"

Maggie's face softens at our beloved aunt. "Marie, it was in the back of *your* closet. Plus, it's a Chanel original, any woman can rock Chanel." She gives Marie a playful slug in the arm.

Marie nods, still dubious.

Sally, who's wearing a burgundy satin tea-length slip dress with a cowl neck, grins at all of us together. "Come on, ladies, we're witches. We always look good, even when we don't." She winks at Abe, who blushes in return.

We all pile into the van, which fills with a cloud of clashing perfumes while we drive into Ipswich.

* * *

The road to the Crane Estate meanders through a wildlife refuge where dense forests, rolling hills, and shimmering salt marshes stretch out like a natural tapestry. The early autumn foliage paints the countryside in a vibrant patchwork of emerald and amber, each leaf gleaming in the twilight. But it's not until we leave the main road and pass through the wrought-iron gates that the full majesty of the estate comes into view.

Atop the hill, with a breathtaking panoramic view of the Atlantic, stands the Great House, a regal and imposing edifice seemingly plucked from the pages of a storybook. The mansion is nearly a football field in length, and its brick facade is crowned by a dozen stately chimneys and even an elegant rooftop gazebo. This veritable palace, where tomorrow's ceremony will take place, would make even royalty stir with envy.

After parking behind a catering van, we join the flow of stylish guests along the footpath. The sky above us is ablaze with hues of coral and tangerine, casting a rosy golden light over the estate's sweeping lawns and marble statues. Lavender clouds lazily drift across the horizon, and the first stars, twinkling like scattered diamonds, begin to pierce the evening sky. The whole scene feels cinematic, as if we've stepped onto the set of a Regency period romance; I half expect to see Mr. Darcy emerge from around a corner.

I lean toward Marie and ask, "Is all this real?"

"What do you mean, dearie?" she replies.

"This is the mind spell, right? Like you did with the Gathering, a bunch of witches came early and cast a spell so everything would look so perfect?"

"Oh, no need, sweetie. The earth is naturally this beautiful. Sometimes nature just cooperates."

The walking path we follow goes past the Great House and toward a stone building with a green-tiled roof. As we get closer, I realize what the building is.

"Wait, we're having the reception dinner in a barn?" I ask no one in particular. "Does Shannyn know this?"

Sally just looks back at me and winks.

At the opening to the barn, Lawrence and Sariah Burroughs stand opposite of my mother graciously thanking those arriving. Mom's wearing a simple rose gold knee-length dress, and she hugs and air kisses more guests as they stride past us into the venue. I notice she's ringing her hands between greetings.

When we reach the front of the line, Mom looks each of us

over one at a time. Her eyebrows lift spotting Zoey shuffling by my side. Zoey's eyes are shifty and her head is ducked like she's sneaking in. "Zoey, welcome, are your aunts coming too?" Mom says, gathering Zoey in a hug.

"Nah, Aunt Molly is still in Italy and Polly is hosting her book club tonight." Zoey answers, still acting unsure if she's welcome.

"Oh, shit that was tonight," Sally says from behind us.

My mother's face crinkles into a soft, warm smile. "Well, I'm glad you could make it. We'll make a spot for you at our table." Mom nods to me, signaling to make it happen.

Sally kisses my mom's cheek, still clinging to Abe's elbow, then moves on to the Burroughs. Abe stumbles while getting towed behind her.

"Gabriel and Benjamin are inside looking for you," Sariah calls over to Maggie.

Sariah and Lawrence wave to me while Maggie links arms with Marie and disappears inside.

"What's with Naomi Campbell and Idris Elba over there?" Zoey whispers to me, staring starstruck at the Burroughs.

I roll my eyes with a laugh. "They're my sister's future in-laws. They're great, I've known them since I was like five. Maggie is pretty close with their two younger sons."

Zoey continues staring at them without any attempt at subtly. "She's so…beautiful. And tall, like lean and tall." She peers down at her own petite frame and diminutive stature.

I tug on the arm of her leather jacket, pulling her toward the barn. "She's pretty cool, you should talk to her when she's not so busy. She's actually a direct descendant from Tituba, and though he doesn't exactly look like it, her husband is a descendant of George Burroughs, the minister who was hanged in 1692."

Zoey's eyes bulge. "Wow, so they're like Salem royalty. I wonder why they aren't on the Committee. They'd be like the hot "it" couple."

I consider it a moment. *Why aren't they on the Committee? Did mom not know when the Burroughs moved into the neighborhood that they were witches too? She would have had to, but she shunned all things magic because of me.* I glance over my shoulder at Lennox's parents who are now giving instructions to the catering staff. *They've seen my lavender eyes, too; back when I was young, before I knew what they meant. So why hadn't they done anything?*

"This is rad," Zoey says, gazing around the rustic "barn". The walls are lined with polished terracotta tiling and string lights adorned with naked bulbs drape across the exposed beams jutting high above our heads. The glowing gold light creates a cozy, intimate atmosphere in spite of the massive space. The round tables covered in ivory silk are positioned throughout the space like shimmery pearls that fell from a severed string. Sultry jazz plays from small, discrete speakers hung in the shadowy corners of the venue.

"Wanna get some food?" Zoey asks. A small line is forming at the buffet table.

My lips part, about to answer, when I spot Shannyn laughing with her new friend from the Junior Committee. Lennox stands behind her, his arms wrapped around her waist as he chats with another guest. My fingers curl at my sides and my teeth grind. *I still can't believe she joined that freaking group. If only she had joined The Noble Hunters when she had the chance. I bet she'd have loved the elitism. Three cheers for industry and killing witches.*

"Ell?" Zoey questions.

"Who does she think she is?" I growl.

Zoey follows my glare toward my sister. "For the love of Minerva, is everyone here a damn model? Your sister looks like Aphrodite. I'm guessing the Adonis behind her is the fiancé? Clan Byrne and Clan Burroughs sure are doing well for themselves, aren't they," she says disparagingly. "They look like pure sex."

"Whatever," I mumble, redirecting my icy stare at my shoes. "She can do whatever she wants, I have bigger things to worry about." I petulantly fold my arms across my chest. *Wait, if Talia is here, then who else from Junior Committee is here?* I suddenly feel like chum in shark-infested waters. *Of course, Shannyn would want Committee members here. Anything to gain a little prestige in the witch community.* I blink several times, feeling my contacts shift. *I thought Mom said Committee members weren't coming.* I scan the venue, trying not to appear as frantic as I feel. I don't see Mercy or the others. *That's right, just the Junior Committee members.*

"Dude, what's your damage? You and your sister aren't close?" Zoey asks, her eyes falling back to the growing line at the long buffet table. Her stomach audibly grumbles, even though we ate only two hours ago.

"Let's just eat," I say, despite having no appetite.

I murder my manicotti with my fork, pushing the desecrated stuffed noodle around on my plate as I watch Shannyn flit from table to table, like she's walking on air, floating to each guest in her white Chantilly lace cocktail dress. Zoey is busy next to me talking with Maggie and Lennox's brothers. "Oh, I love Madrid," Zoey gushes. "I'm so jealous; I wish my aunts worked in Spain. Though we did a kind of pop-up apothecary shop in Milan for a summer," she shares, stuffing a wad of pasta in her mouth.

My mom enters the barn, speaking to a staff member.

"I'll be right back," I say, knowing no one is listening. They're all laughing at something Gabe said. I squeeze past gaggles of Shannyn's college friends fawning over Lennox as he shares a story, then march past Shannyn gossiping with her new in-laws' extended family.

"I need the dance floor set up tonight. The white tents are going on the east lawn," Mom explains, motioning with her hands.

"Mom, can I talk to you for a sec?" I ask.

Her back is turned to me. "Not now, Ella. I'm really busy, hon," she says over her shoulder before turning back to the staff member. "For the ceremony, let's start with the string quartet. They'll play through supper, then we have a second band for the dancing. I instructed them to set up in here."

"Mom, I had a vision of Grandma Colleen. She's in trouble," I say, deadpan.

My mother does a double take over her shoulder. Her face turns white as a ghost. Without taking her eyes off me, she asks the staff member to excuse us. She grips me by the elbow and tows me outside and around the corner toward the white catering vans parked under a lamppost. "Explain. Now," she orders.

I take a breath before diving into the details, first explaining the death of the random woman in her bed to following a black bearded goat ushering me toward her mother's attic as she furiously searched for something, then the door flying from the doorframe and grandma screaming.

Mom sucks in a horrified breath and perches on the narrow bumper of a van.

I stay silent. My mom quivers, then pinches the bridge of her nose.

I picture my grandmother's frantic movements, the fear in her eyes. *Wait…her eyes.* Chills ripple down my arms. *How could I miss such a detail?*

"Mom," I squeak, my mouth going dry, "in my vision, Grandma Colleen had…dark pink eyes. Is she…"

Mom's head snaps up, her eyes glassy and red. "Yes, but it was an accident, she didn't mean to," she stops, her chest heaving up and down. Her eyes flick back to the barn where Lawrence is offering the happy couple a toast into a microphone. "Do you have any clue what she was looking for?" she asks, dropping her voice to a whisper.

"Possibly. Elspeth wants something too, some kind of object from the room next to mine. She said there is one like it in Ireland with grandma."

Mom nods, a look of resolution in her eyes. She stands up straight and runs her hands down her dress. "I need to speak to your aunts about this. Tell no one, understand?" Mom takes a deep breath and releases it through her nose. "Okay," she says, her eyes opening, "we have a wedding to get ready for, let's get inside." She strides past, then turns and motions for me to follow. She disappears inside just as applause bursts along with clinking glasses and shouting well wishes.

A cold breath grazes down the back of my neck.

I freeze, unable to move. My nose fills with the familiar aroma of frozen mud with a dash of sulfur. Elspeth whispers into my ear.

"It's time to go into that room, Eleanor…"

CHAPTER ELEVEN
An Oncoming Storm

Elspeth circles me. "I'm tired of waiting. I want what is mine."

She lurches forward, and I flinch. Her nose is nearly pressed against mine. Her nostrils flare as she breathes, sneering at me with such vile loathing that I feel naked, completely exposed.

I grip my arms and cower. "I don't even know what you want." Her hands tremble as rage pulses through her body like a thunderstorm.

She clenches and unclenches her fists. "A candle. A very *specific* candle that lights a black flame."

"What will you do with it?" I ask, still clutching myself.

The barn doors burst open. Elspeth's head whips in the direction of the sudden noise. Party guests stream out onto the grassy field, trailing away from us just as a cacophony of sparkling color and booming percussion bursts overhead.

Elspeth wheels back to me. "What I want with my candle is none of your concern!"

"If it's yours, why do my aunts have it?" I ask. I'm emboldened by my family only a dozen yards away from me, not to mention fifty other witches who would love to have it out with the vilest of the Nefari.

"I used to believe it was fate, but no. I've heard through the lower echelons of Hell it's because of my meddling familiar, Pyewacket, that your family has what is mine. Your damned family has passed it down for generations. If you don't fetch it for me—"

I step forward. "What? What could you possibly do to me that could be worse than you getting your hands on the candle? I don't know what it does, but if you want it, it can't be good." My jaw quivers as I puff up my chest with faux bravery. My eyes fall to her throat. She's shifting between solid and translucent. Her arms and shoulders blur around the edges. "I don't think you can do anything to my family. You're not powerful enough."

Elspeth draws her thin lips into a twisted, malicious grin. Her smile pulls up one side of her face like it was carved through her flesh with a dull knife. "If you do not give it to me, I will drag you to Purgatory and keep you there until you forget who you are. I will trap you there, so by the time you manage to remember your lover, your family, friends, little Pyewacket, it'll be too late. You'll belong to the space in between. And believe me, that is a fate worse than death." She snatches my forearm, squeezing it until her fingertips press against my bones. "Perhaps you need a taste…" She pulls me into her until we are thrashing in a psychotic hug, then I'm falling flat on my face.

I gasp, the wind knocked out of me. I suck in dirty sand trying to breathe. I roll over onto my back and clutch my stomach, gulping for air. My eyes search the gray sky bereft of color. When I finally sit up, I recognize where I am. This is South Beach. I'm back in Miami, Florida. Although, the strip of shops and restaurants sandwiched together along that famous walkway are no longer painted in the bright pastels South Beach is famous for. Now they're drab and dingy, like someone dusted the entire strip in ash.

There's a tight red strap on my shoulders. I'm in a red one-piece swimsuit with a big white cross in the center of the chest along with matching terrycloth shorts. It's my junior lifeguard uniform. I run my tongue over my teeth, scraping it against my sharp metal braces. I must be in the eighth grade. This is new. *Why am I so young?*

I gaze up and down the deserted beach. Waves crash onto the shore spraying white foam into the air. In the distance, black storm clouds rumble toward the beach. Cracks of lightning flash. *My name is Eleanor. I'm thirteen.* I squeeze my eyes shut and shake my head furiously at myself. *No, I'm not, I'm seventeen. I'm seventeen, living in Salem, Massachusetts. My soulmate is Jack Woods. We're in love. I'm a senior at William Griggs Academy. I'm at my sister's rehearsal dinner. Shannyn is marrying Lennox Burrough's tomorrow.*

Blue! Blue, can you hear me?! Elspeth pulled me into Purgatory! Blue!

I turn my back to the oncoming storm tossing the entire ocean in its wake. I squint into the encroaching darkness. I can see the Clevelander Hotel from here. The art deco building is typically alive with colorful floodlights and rooftop parties with live music. Here it's quiet, dim, lifeless. A yellow light flicks on in the corner of the fourth floor. *Probably Elspeth.*

Heavy, unrelenting raindrops drill into my head like bullets. I'm immediately soaked to the bone. *Maybe she can be reasoned with. It's better than being alone in this place.* Shivering, I make my way to the legendary hotel. I leap under the awning and throw open the door, panting for air while I lean against the glass door of the empty foyer. Water streams down my face. I wonder if this is what tears feel like. I close my eyes and catch my breath.

I'm Eleanor Elizabeth O'Reilly. My parents are Will and Helen. My sisters are Shannyn and Margaret. My soulmate is Jack Woods. My aunts are Marie and Sally. I go to…something Griggs Academy. I'm— I roll my lips in thinking, the metal brackets poke painfully into my mouth. *I know this…I'm thirteen? No! No! No! I'm older…and I'm a witch. Yes. I have magical powers. Which means I have to be at least…* "Damnit!" I can't remember at what age a witch gets her magic. *I need to get out of here. Fast.*

I open my eyes and take a shaky step into the opaque foyer with art deco furniture.

DING!

The bell at the front desk chimes, and I nearly leap out of my skin. My hand flies to my chest as I slowly turn. A man in a white polo stands behind the desk, a broad, deranged smile stretches across his face. His hands are flat on the white polished desk as he stares out unblinking.

I stand statue still, not breathing, too scared to move more than my eyes.

The man stares forward, unflinching, smiling, rooted to his spot. His expression is reminiscent of those old ventriloquist dummies. Still, he doesn't move. Not even his chest.

Is he not real? Is he a mannequin?

I take a single, trembling step forward. He doesn't react. Not even a little. *Maybe he is a doll. But then who rang the bell?* My heart pounds in my chest as I tiptoe past him and into the darkened hallway toward the elevators. I press the up arrow while checking both halls. No other mannequin people lurk nearby. I keep pressing the button, hoping it will summon the elevator faster.

My name is Eleanor. I'm definitely a teenager. My parents are Will and Helen. I have two sisters and two aunts. My boyfriend is named Jack W—ilson. No, that's not right. Jack Forester. No, but it definitely starts with a "W". Damnit. What is it?!

Screw the elevator. I don't have time. I sprint to the stairwell. The air here is stale and leaves a grimy film on my tongue. I'm too winded to speak by the time I reach the fourth floor. I close my eyes trying to recall which way to run. Was it left or right? I know I saw a light on. I press my fingers to my forehead and try to conjure my view of the hotel from the beach. *It was on the right side when I was looking from the beach, which means now it's to my left.*

I jog down the hall praying no doors open with more blank faced people inside, gazing lifelessly with cheery perma-smiles plastered across their faces.

The entire hotel shudders after a bolt of lightning strikes outside. I don't slow down until I reach the last door in the hall, oceanside. The door is open just a crack, allowing the light to cut through the shadowy hall. Using my foot, I push the door open. The hinges creak while the door creeps open far enough to tap the wall behind it.

Why am I here again? Elspeth. I need to speak with her; she needs to bring me back. I'll give her the candle. I'll give her anything if it means I can get out of here. Blue, please help me. I need you. I'm Eleanor O'Reilly. Will and Helen. Two sisters. Two aunts. And a boyfriend, Jake.

"Elspeth?" I call out. I step into the whitewashed hotel room and look around. One not-quite-a-king, not-quite-a-queen size bed. Two mismatched nightstands. Three stale watercolor paintings hanging on the walls, none of them entirely straight. I forgot about this. Nothing is ever quite right in this place. It's like a never-ending social experiment to see how I'll react to everything just a *little* off-kilter. My braces, a tad too sharp. My swimsuit, a little too tight. The lights, not bright enough. The carpet, too coarse.

"Hello?" I call out again. I search for someone. Anyone. I just don't want to be alone. I'm afraid. I circle about the plain hotel room. Too small for anyone to hide. I peer out the long rectangular windows, one just an inch longer than the other. The storm is moving closer. A flash of lightning strikes the beach. *Why am I here?* I tug on my swimsuit straps that cut into my shoulders. *What am I wearing? I've got this. My name is Eleanor. I have parents. I think siblings. I'm dating someone.*

A faucet blasts from the bathroom.

Who is that? I cross the room and push open the bathroom door. I gasp and stumble back. Sitting in the bathtub is a woman dressed in a 1950s-style dress with green and red vertical stripes. Filthy water flows from the faucet, slowly filling the tub. Her poodle bob is clipped back on the sides like Lucile Ball. Her brown-painted lips are a thin straight line. Her eyes are fixed on the doorway, unblinking, unmoving.

The water reaches the lip of the tub and spills over.

My pounding heart slows. The fear drains away, leaving me empty and apathetic. My body slackens. *My name is…my name is…I can't remember.* I feel like it should bother me more than it does. *Who am I?* The hotel quivers. The storm is now upon us. Rain drivels down the windows in rivers that blur the outside world. I sit down on the floor. Water from the tub pools on the tiled floor. Thunder roars in all its bluster.

I'm sinking. *Why am I here? Who am I? Truth is, it doesn't really matter. None of it does.* There's a subtle, delicate tug inside of me, like a thread tied around my heart. A slight pull, and the line breaks. I'm adrift and alone. Sound dies. I can no longer hear the percussion of the storm nor the shriek of the faucet. All that exists is silence.

I stare at my fingers. Vacant where fingerprints should be. Devoid of identity. How strange. I run my hands over the stiff, short carpet. I can't feel the fibers. There's no sensation in my hands. I can see my clothes are damp, but I can't feel it. Not even the water dripping down the waterlogged strands of my hair. I see the water run, but I can't feel wet or cold. I'm untethering from my senses. I fall back so that my top half falls through the bathroom doorway onto the carpet. Or at least I think I do. I stare up at the water-stained ceiling. *Nobody has ever loved me. Nobody's ever known me. I'm not even real.*

There's a buzz running down my left arm. Weird.

I crane my head to see it. A cut is opening on my arm. Blood beads and rises from the skin. Another line of blood is drawn down my arm. More little red dots spring forth. *Why am I bleeding?*

My head jerks from side to side. Again. And again. And again. Each time my head jerks, something stings my cheek. Subtle at first, intensifying each time. Left. Right. Left.

My eyes bulge with exploding pressure behind them. Life returns to my body, unfurling from the center of my chest into my extremities. I shoot up right and gasp for air. The taste in my mouth is metallic; I must have bitten my tongue. My ears ring from being slapped back and forth. The cobblestones are rough, uneven, one digs into my left butt cheek. The sky lights up with dazzling pyrotechnics and I can smell the ash and gunpowder from the fireworks wafting in the breeze.

Sally and Abe are crouched beside me. Sally's arms wrap around me.

Abe's face is pale, his hand shaking that holds a pocket-knife.

I'm Eleanor Elizabeth O'Reilly. My mom is Helen Byrne O'Reilly. My dad is Will O'Reilly. He passed away eight months ago. I'm Elea—I'm El… My shoulders shake, and I crumble into my aunt, crying out like a feral wounded animal. *I was almost lost again. I can't go back there again. It was worse than last time. Blue, can you hear me?*

"S-s-sal, the blood." Abe wipes his knife on a cloth napkin.

Aunt Sally and I loosen our grip. My blood is smeared on her silk dress. She twitches her face and the stains disappear. At least for the time being. Sally pulls a handful of yarrow leaves from her beaded purse and rubs them up and down the shallow cuts on my arm.

"She might need stitches, Sal. We should take her to the hospital. Should I get Helen?" Abe asks. His forehead glistens with sweat.

Sally scoffs with a roll of her eyes. "Stop being a Nervous Nelly. Look, her cuts are already disappearing. A witch is healed by her coven, not by strangers." Sally leans in close to me. "Abe is still learning." She hoists me to my feet while her boyfriend scrambles to help.

My legs wobble beneath me. Sally and Abe each prop me up by the elbows. Zoey hovers nearby holding the cuffs of her leather jacket. She glances up at the fireworks and then back to me. Her knitted brows are a mixture of confusion and fear.

My head begins to pulse from being slapped repeatedly. "Gosh Sal, did you have to hit me so hard?" I flex my jaw and wiggle it. My skin is hot to the touch.

My aunt continues to rub yarrow up and down my arms. "It worked, didn't it? Now, I was to help with the big finale." She gestures to the fireworks behind us. "Abe, I want you to bring her home."

Abe nods, tugging at his stiff shirt collar.

"And Zoey, give my apologies to Polly. And tell her I'll drop by later with my notes for *Sultry Surrender*. And the fanfiction I wrote for it." She leans close to Zoey and says behind her ring-covered hand, "She loves my stuff. I really pack in the spice."

Zoey nods along, eyeing me warily as she speaks. "Yeah, I'll let her know. Next month's book is *Heatwaves and Heartbeats*, you might want to pick up a copy."

Sally wiggles her eyebrows in anticipation then gives me a peck on the cheek before dashing down the hill towards the gawking crowd. Shannyn and Lennox are poised in the center, holding onto one another. A surge of jealousy burbles up to the surface.

"Took a little trip, huh," Abe says awkwardly as he guides me toward the parking lot.

"Uh yeah, I guess," I mumble, leaning on him for support.

Zoey catches up with us and slings my free arm around her shoulders, which is pointless since she's too short for me to lean on. "Ragazza," she says lowly. "Does this happen a lot? This is the second time I've seen you…" she twirls her finger in a circular motion next to her ear. "Does this happen all the time?"

I shake my head, then wince. My brain sloshes around inside my skull with every movement. "Just lately."

Back home, I find Blue sitting high up in the dead oak tree up front and Betty circling the trunk like a shark. Zoey's skinny, wrinkly familiar leaps into the sidecar with an almost amused spring in her step. She bares her fangs before she and Zoey zoom off down the gravel road.

"I'll just be here," Abe assures, plopping down on the sofa and reaching for the remote. With one hand he tugs at his knotted tie, loosening it from his neck as he kicks his feet up on the coffee table.

"Thanks" I call back, heading toward the stairs. I climb into the shower and scrub my body with the loofah until my flesh is raw. It's like Purgatory had a poisonous fog that left a residue on my skin, a craggy filament marking me in its misery and filth. The cuts on my arms are completely healed and scab and scar free.

"Next time you decide to leave me with that thing, don't!" Blue drills into me when I step into my bedroom. *"I've spoken to cuckoo birds with more sense! There is something wrong with her."*

I flick off my lights and crawl into bed, anxious to sleep yet scared Elspeth will come back and pull me through to Purgatory. My heart pounds in my ears. Pulling my covers up to my chin, I press deep into my pillows. My eyes dart about, scanning my dimly lit room as it's only ghostly illuminated by the light of the moon. Shadows take on strange, distorted shapes, stretching ominously across the room. The silence is heavy, only being interrupted mentally by Blue's irate chatter.

"Blue?" I whisper.

"And another thing—"

I'm too scared to open my mouth again. *Blue, Elspeth dragged me down to Purgatory tonight. Can you stay up and watch out for her? I'm scared.* I quiver beneath my bedding.

Blue stops, jumps up onto my bed and peers at me thoughtfully. *"Go to sleep. We'll speak more tomorrow."*

Yeah, we actually have a lot to discuss.

"Sleep, Eleanor. Long day tomorrow. We'll convene after the wedding."

A spider slowly crawls across my pentagon window, stops, then continues skittering downward until it disappears into a shadow.

I clutch the blankets tighter around me and reach over to feel Blue's stiff body next to me, keeping vigil. My eyes slide back over to the window, searching for the spider.

I'm not the only Nefari in my room...

CHAPTER TWELVE
You Make Me Wanna Say I Do

Shannyn was never getting married on the cheap. My dad used to joke that her wedding would mean taking out a second mortgage. Mom would always chide him and say it'll only happen once, and if it's to whom she thinks it is, it'll be well worth it.

The Crane Estate looks even more like a fairy-tale castle with all of Shannyn's decorations. Her wedding colors—white, rose pink, and gold—have exploded over the grounds. Flowers adorn every entrance, and splashes of ribbon and cloth flank the path that herds the guests toward the giant tents for the reception. Every minute detail has been scrutinized, debated, organized, and executed with the utmost care, from the walkways carpeted in flower petals, to the very air itself, a fragrant symphony produced by thousands of pink peonies and white roses. The whole affair is the perfect blend of opulence and romance. Shannyn would have accepted nothing less.

"Ouch," I yelp.

"Eleanor, please stop moving so Esmerelda can close the dress," Mom scolds.

The elderly dressmaker, also a witch, stands on a short stepladder while fastening the hook and eye clasps of my dress. Maggie and I are both bridesmaids, dressed in identical baby pink, strapless column dresses made of delicate rosette fabric. A thin pink ribbon encircles our chest just below the bustline, like we're supposed to be ethereal bouquets floating down the aisle.

"Did someone forget I have red hair? This really clashes," Maggie complains, pointing down to her dress then back at her hair.

Even our hairstyles were meticulously chosen: curled, then loosely pinned up with a pale pink peony tucked to one side of the bun. I'm surprised she didn't ask us to color it as well. And, of course, minimal jewelry—no necklaces allowed, only round gold stud earrings and a gold charm bracelet on our left wrists. Our nails? Dainty French manicures (because, according to my sister—and despite what any influencer might say—French nails are timeless, and acrylic claws are tacky). She even picked out our perfume: rose oil, kissed only once on our pulse points. Shannyn has literally thought of everything.

"Oh, I'll take another!" Sally says in her gold chiffon dress with fluttery cap sleeves. She waves down the tailcoated waiter with a silver tray of champagne.

"Sal," Mom chides as Sally helps herself to a second flute. Mom went through eight or nine mother-of-the-bride dresses before settling on a floor-length gown of gold lace.

Aunt Sally shrugs her boney shoulders at my mother while she sips her drink.

"Please pace yourself," Shannyn calls from behind an ornate standing screen. "It's going to be a long evening."

"Yes, it will," Mom says, not quite under her breath. "I heard that," Shannyn chirps.

Marie settled on a dusty rose-pink frock with crystal beading on the sleeves. "Enough, everyone. It'll be a beautiful, wonderful day," she assures before sipping her spiked tea.

"Thank you, Marie," Shannyn says graciously. "Esmerelda could you help me with the skirt, something is wrong."

The elderly witch in half-moon glasses and hair wrapped in a silky turban examines me once more before dusting off her hands. "There is nothing wrong, the dress is perfect," she insists in an ancient, quivering voice. She clasps her hands together and waddles behind the divider.

"Eleanor, look at me." Mom commands. I slide my eyes in her direction.

Mom exhales and settles back down. "It's holding well. Your eyes really do look blue," she says, sounding delighted with a twinge of surprise.

Marie nods animatedly. "Eleanor can fully relax today, even with the full Committee in attendance." She gives a pursed smile from behind her teacup.

Marie, Sally, and Mom are tag-teaming my eyes today so no one can detect any magic energy emanating from me.

Mom gives me a soft smile that never reaches her eyes. *It'll be fine,* she mouths, more to herself than to me.

Maggie plops down at the pearlescent desk with the matching antique chair. "Come on, Shan. We haven't even seen the dress. Let's go!" she teases. Mom is peering down at her lap, her eyes fixed on her wedding ring. My dad should be the one walking Shannyn down the aisle.

"Hey, it's my day. Be patient, I'll be out in a sec," Shannyn teases back. I dig through my purse and check my phone for the tenth time today, hoping for a confirmation text from Jack that he is still coming. *Nothing.*

I give in, ending our little game of chicken. I've given him a full week of radio silence. I can't take another stupid minute.

Hey, are you still coming to
my sister's wedding today?

I miss you. I hope you're okay.

Please call me.

I flop down next to Marie and lean my elbows on my knees. I stare at my phone's screen trying to will Jack to answer. It doesn't work. I toss my phone back into my bag with a sigh. I feel…needy. *How am I so affected by him? Why are his bad days my bad days? Why is it that when he's ecstatic so am I? Is this what love is? You're no longer your own person?*

"Is it Jack, sweetie?" Marie whispers next to me.

I shrug and shake my head at the same time. "Yeah…I don't know. I hate feeling only half myself without him. This sucks."

Marie giggles and rests her hands on her stomach. "Love is giving yourself entirely to another person, allowing them to affect you and trusting it'll be okay. That's the real magic in the world, Ell. It's beautiful."

"I just wish it didn't hurt so much when he's not around," I mumble.

Marie nods, making her springy curls bounce. "We weren't designed to be solitary, my dear, even more so than humans. Every witch has their mate. We share a singular heart, each half beating in perfect harmony with the other, waiting for the moment they will unite. The heart can learn to be fine on its own, but the symphony that comes from those two hearts aligning is worth all the pain it takes to find each other, and even losing each other afterward." She pulls her mouth in a half smile, trying to be encouraging. "My heart will be okay for now, but it's also okay to acknowledge it isn't whole without Winnie. Whatever is going on with you and Jack, you two will fix it. He has in him the same celestial dust you have." She gives my hand a little pat and kisses the top of my head.

"Thanks, Marie." I lean into her and rest my head on her padded shoulder. "Alright, I'm coming out," Shannyn announces. Esmerelda steps out first and ambles over to Marie looking for a seat. Her eyes have disappeared behind thin slits from the scrunched wrinkles and folds of a satisfied smile.

There's a collective gasp when Shannyn emerges. Her platinum locks are pulled back in a tight chignon. A bejeweled golden comb holds the delicate veil that trails on the floor behind her. My sister's dress is stunning, high-necked with long sleeves that come to a V at her knuckles and a full, voluminous skirt. She gives us a twirl, showing off the cut-out that scoops from her shoulder blades down to the small of her back in thin transparent chiffon. Genuine mother-of-pearl buttons dot the back. It's simple yet dramatic, tasteful and chic. It fits my sister perfectly. She's so beautiful to behold, the ice surrounding my heart starts to thaw. On a day like today, I can put my hurt aside.

As if on cue and without prompting, we all drift toward each other, creating a circle. We dip our heads toward the center and breathe each other in, the sisterhood, our little sacred coven, and the magic we all share. When we lift our eyes, they're glassy, rimmed with tears. The remnants of heartache flicker in their colorful strands, the memory of those who should be here today but are not, but so does the resilience that carried us through it. We may bear the battle scars of loss, but we're witches; we know how to heal.

Shannyn delicately dabs her eyes. Esmerelda appears at her side with a lacy handkerchief.

Thank you, Shannyn mouths to her. None of us is quite ready to end this solemn silence just yet.

Maggie's eyes are the first to dry. She cracks a smile, glancing at each of us in turn. "Okay, if we stand here much longer our cycles are all going to sync up."

Marie tries to hold back her elevated chuckle and fails. She reaches over and gives Maggie's shoulder a little squeeze.

"Wait…we all live together, are we not synced up already?" Sally asks.

For the first time today, Mom genuinely smiles. She leans over to Shannyn and offers the crook of her arm. "I think it's time we take our places."

Walking down the flower petal strewn aisle, I recite a prayer in my head that I won't tip over in my heels. The delicate petals dance and swirl as I'm escorted by Lennox's younger brother, Gabriel.

Maggie follows behind, leaning on Benjamin in her six-inch heels (we needed to look more uniform in height for the pictures).

Mom beams at Shannyn's side, walking my sister down the aisle in my father's place. In the corner, a string quartet swoons, their music reverberating off the stone walls of the grand hall. I suspect it's been magically enhanced somehow; everything today has been too beautiful for magic not to be involved.

The backdrop of the altar is a floor-to-ceiling wall of blushing pink peonies and pink roses that give the candlelit hall a heavenly aroma.

Mercy, the only guest permitted to wear white, stands at the altar. Her gaze stays on me long after Shannyn has reached her anxious groom.

I pretend not to notice. I smile at the guests and give a little wave to Zoey and her Aunt Polly in the fourth row. My eyes scan the crowd, hoping to see Jack, all the while feeling Mercy's piercing gaze.

With everyone in place, Mercy tears her eyes from me and screws a congenial smile into place. "Family, friends, and coven members, welcome as we celebrate the union of Lennox Angel Burrough's to Shannyn Colleen O'Reilly. It is a time to celebrate this union of two souls into one." Mercy turns to my mother seated in the first row. "Your family's blade, Helen," she swivels to Sariah seated next to her husband across the aisle from my family. "Sariah, your family's blade."

A blade? What's happening? I frown at my mother, who rises from her seat holding a silver dagger etched with Celtic knots into the blade and hilt. Sariah joins my mother, holding a curved blade of dark metal attached to a handle made of bone.

"Sariah Burrough, granddaughter of our beloved Tituba, please give thy son unto his mate," Mercy instructs, motioning toward Lennox.

Lennox pushes up the sleeve of his right arm, exposing his wrist. His mother presses it against her son's flesh, creating a shallow line that barely bleeds. His face is serene as he stares into my sister's eyes.

"Helen, mighty daughter of the tribe Byrne, please give thy daughter unto her mate."

Shannyn turns her left arm out, presenting her fair and dainty wrist, never looking away from Lennox.

Just as Sariah had done, my mother drags the tip of her knife into my sister's wrist, producing a thin red line that barely bleeds at all. I try to hide my horrified expression, but I know it's still clear as day. I just hope no one is actually looking at me.

The mothers take their children's arms, placing Lennox's on top so their wounds align. Lawrence now approaches with an herbal wreath that he places over their wrists.

"You have now been joined in an unbreakable bond. Your union has no undoing, no breaking, no severing. Together, you have combined your spirits, your magic, and glory. I bless you both on your eternal journey as one."

Mercy pauses, smiling at the couple before concluding with, "Blessed be."

"Blessed be," the guests respond in chorus.

Lennox breaks from their peculiar embrace and passionately kisses his bride, twisting her around and dipping her so low she's nearly horizontal. Camera flashes explode around them. People leap to their feet with applause. Everyone cheers.

At our family's table for the reception dinner, I spear my fork into a buttery scallop with Marie seated to my left. "Okay, so seriously, Marie, what was with that ceremony? I mean, slicing their wrists open? That was a little too MCR for me," I tease.

Marie frowns at me. "What's an MCR, dearie?"

"My Chemical Romance? They're a band from… never mind. But that's not how every witch gets married, is it?"

"Oh, of course. Isn't that just the sweetest thing?" she coos. "It's a sacred tradition going back to the very first witches on earth. Brighid herself administered the rite. You know, back when witches were more accepted in society, the Celts tried to copy our ceremony. They called their version of it 'handfasting'. But the ceremony you saw today was more than symbolic. Your sister and her mate are now joined forever as one, each of them eternally incomplete without the other."

Marie gazes over at the happy couple and gushes with glee at the sight of them giggling on the dance floor. The string quartet from the ceremony was replaced by a swanky New York band with a vivacious lead singer who looks like Betty Boop in the flesh.

Sally sways on the dance floor with a red-faced Abe who is desperate to keep up with her twirling. Mom makes her rounds with the guests trying to keep Mercy from visiting the family table, leaving just Maggie, Marie, and I.

I hopelessly search for Jack.

"Hey Maggie, would you dance with me?" Benjamin asks. "Gabe doesn't think I've got any moves. What do you say we show him how it's done?" He extends his hand with irresistible self-absurdity.

My little sister laughs wholeheartedly. "Of course, but you know *Shannyn* is the dancer, right? I'm on the soccer team, so I'll do my best not to kick your shins." She pushes away her dinner plate and takes his hand.

Maggie laughs so hard she snorts when Benjamin twirls her around on the dance floor. My eyes drift to my purse where my cellphone is tucked away.

"Beautiful ceremony, wasn't it?" Mercy asks as she claims Maggie's vacant seat. She lifts her champagne flute close to her mouth, letting it hover there without taking a sip.

I straighten my back and pinch my shoulder blades together. I blink a few times, only glancing at her from the corner of my eyes. *What if my eyes go back to lavender?* I peer over at my aunt; she's speaking to Lawrence who joined our table a moment earlier. He's chewing her ear off about the Gathering in Barcelona. Sally is salsa dancing around a stationary Abe while my mother directs the bakery staff on how to position the wedding cake and other desserts.

The woman with the power to destroy my eternal soul just picked the perfect moment to have me all to herself.

"Was that your first time seeing a witch wedding?" she asks, tilting her head toward me. Her glossy black bob spills over one shoulder as she stares at me, waiting.

Crap! Are my eyes still blue? Who's supposed to be on watch right now? Mom said the power of their combined spells should be enough even without constant supervision, didn't she?

"Uh, yeah, it was." Hic. "It was kind of," hic, "strange." I answer. My fork quivers in my hand despite my best efforts to keep it steady.

Hic!

Mercy leans against the back of her gilded chair, giggling. "Yes, for a first-time observer it can be quite…unnerving." She holds her glass aloft and swirls the champagne, watching it settle like she has no intention of drinking it.

Hic.

The champagne's buttery aroma with just a hint of strawberries leaves me nauseated. Or perhaps it's the person holding it.

Hic.

"If you have any questions, I'd be happy to educate you," she says, her voice dripping in faux nonchalance.

Even as she leans back in her chair, that devious feline smile smothers me. I gulp sparkling water hoping to drown my hiccups.

Hic.

"You work at Molly and Polly's Apothecary, correct?" Her friendly air wears thin as she slowly devolves into a suspicious detective.

"Uh, yep." Hic.

Mercy repositions herself to see Zoey struggling on the dance floor with Gabriel. It's easy to find her dressed all in black amid a sea of pastels.

"For how long?"

Hic. "I started back in… um… July, I think." My fork rattles against the plate.

A tuxedoed gentleman comes marching toward us with purpose. He leans down to whisper something in Mercy's ear. Several Committee members hover nearby, watching the exchange with bated breath.

Swiveling back to me, Mercy wears a pert smile that never reaches her eyes. "Will you save my seat, Eleanor? We'll continue this in just a moment." She rises to her feet with the poise of a beauty pageant contestant and walks away with the grim-faced man.

I collapse against the back of my seat. It's not until I gasp for air that I realize I've been holding my breath. My ears are still ringing, but at least my hiccups have settled.

What was Mercy getting at?

"Excuse me," says the lead singer into the microphone. "Thank you, everyone. We are Autumn Dee," she pauses as the guests graciously applaud, "and this next song is dedicated to lovers everywhere. So, hold your soulmate close and know your journey is just beginning." She turns to her three bandmates and counts them into a slow and hauntingly dramatic rendition of *Fly Me to the Moon*. The lead waves her hand and thousands of stars twinkle above the white silk tents. The guests on the dance floor marvel audibly at the spectacle, while Shannyn and Lennox hold each other close in their own little world, blissfully unaware of anything around them.

Mercy is arguing with the man next to the dessert tables. More Committee members have slowly gravitated toward them, and the guests are taking notice. Mom glances at me, a look of worry and confusion on her face, then turns back to the Committee.

I need to get out of here.

I sneak away to the main house, up the stairs and into a bathroom to press a cool wet towel against my neck. *I can do this. I can do this.* I peer into the mirror and deep into my dishonest blue eyes. *If only they were permanent. Is eye color the only way to spot a Nefari?*

I step onto the terrace overlooking the three silk tents. Music dances through the air, and a cool breeze rustles through the treetops, but I can't enjoy any of it. Not with the Committee all here and the threat of being discovered constantly hanging over me. *I wish Jack were here…*

Footsteps fall lightly on the flagstones behind me.

I slowly turn around.

Heat blooms in my cheeks. My mouth gapes open, and my breath gets lost somehow. Jack steps out into the moonlight. He's dressed in a crisp black suit with a long black tie. I finally understand why people use the phrase "devastatingly handsome;" Jack's beauty is a joyful agony to behold. Before me stands a demigod cast from molten gold, completely unaware of the effect he has on us mere mortals. His flaxen hair is brushed back from his angular face. His cheeks are perfectly chiseled and his jawline sharp, even with the soft smile on his lips. His emerald eyes sweep over me.

"You're…" He pauses, as if he's at a loss for words, as if I can affect him the way he affects me. "Beautiful," he finishes.

"Jack," I whisper. It's the only word I can think of, like it's suddenly the only word I know. My skin is desperate to be caressed against his. At the same time, a spark of pain ignites in the center of my being. The best I can do is ignore it.

He stares at me with an ache in his eyes, an unfathomable longing that must surely be reflected in my own. "I'm sorry I'm late," he says, his voice genuine.

My heart clenches. I want to go to him, fall into his arms and beg him never to leave, but I stay rooted. I can't trust myself… or him. *What if he is here only out of obligation? To honor the promise he had made to be my date tonight… is he here to say goodbye?*

The thought turns my mouth dry. I need to escape this moment; I can't take a goodbye. Not now. Not so soon after coming back from Purgatory. Who am I kidding, I'll never be able to say goodbye to him.

He steps toward me. "I'm truly sorry, Eleanor." His hands lift slightly from his sides, as if he knows I want to bolt.

I nod, brushing his apology aside. He takes another step forward. "It's okay," I manage to say. "You told me you had a class that was going to make you late."

He shakes his head, wincing. "No, I'm sorry you haven't heard from me this week. This isn't what I wanted. Would you believe me if I told you how badly I've wanted to speak to you?"

I wilt under his words and have to lean my weight on the stone balustrade behind me. I wasn't sure he was going to address his silence. *If you wanted to talk to me so badly, all you had to do was answer my calls.* I'm not sure if I'm ready to hear why he didn't.

"Then why didn't you?" I squeak out, despite myself.

He gives me a sad, repentant smile. "I can't tell you, but—" he steps closer and takes ahold of my hips just as I'm about to protest, "I promise it's nothing bad. I hope you can trust me on this."

I peer into his endless green eyes. They're such a deep shade of gemstone green, they're *almost* unnatural. I feel myself relenting, my feelings of hurt and suspicion uncoiling. If it were anyone else, I would say "like hell, I'm trusting you." But this is Jack. He sacrificed his entire family for me. He saved generations of future witches by exposing the Noble Hunters with me. And I'm not the only one with scars. Jack's wrist will forever bear a pink scar, bubbled and thick, from where his own father filleted his skin to remove the tattoo they forced on him.

After all that, why would Jack start lying now?

"Okay," I eventually say. I just have to accept the fact I'm in too deep to hold a grudge against my mate. He is a part of me, just as I am a part of him. I know Jack would forgive me for anything, so I can forgive him for anything. Jack's eyes drift from my eyes to my lips, igniting a different thirst from the one I was feeling moments ago. He cradles the base of my cheeks in his powerful hands, and his thumb grazes my lower lip. Without thinking, I close my mouth around the tip of his finger and softly drag my teeth over his nail. When I release him, he pulls me against him, his lips pressing into mine with intense hunger. Our movements are slow and measured, mindful of the fire inside that goads us to do more.

Our mouths finally part, each of us gasping for breath as we battle a desire that threatens to break our resolve.

Jack's fingers are tight around my ribs. His grip doesn't loosen as he takes a short step back and surveys my dress. "You truly are stunning, Eleanor."

I brush off the shoulders of his coat, then grip his lapels. "You don't look so bad yourself, Jack."

He places his hand on the small of my back as we walk back to the reception. Jack leads me straight to the dance floor, his hand never leaving the small of my back as he readies us for the waltz. He is, of course, as smooth as polished crystal as he sweeps me about, guiding me with the expertise of a proper gentleman. I couldn't stop my girlish giggles even if I wanted to.

"Evelyn," Jack says.

I frown confused. "Um… what?"

"That's who we can thank that I'm not stepping on your toes all night. My mother insisted her sons be well-rounded, which meant dance classes, poetry sessions, and art exhibits. My father rued the day I took my first art class." Somehow, he's able to not only chat casually while leading the dance, but even keep me from stumbling over my own feet in the process.

"I can't imagine Marshall in a poetry class," I admit.

Jack laughs heartily. "He was kicked out after he tried his hand at slam poetry. You can imagine what a twelve-year-old slams about."

My laugh falls into a sigh as I can't stop smiling that Jack is here. My gaze drifts to Zoey, sitting next to Polly who's chatting animatedly with Sally while Abe nurses a beer mesmerized by Autumn Dee making butterflies appear and flutter about.

Holy shit! Zoey mouths to me. *He is so freaking hot!* She bites her lower lip and rolls back her eyes while pretending to fan herself.

If you think this is hot, you should see him shirtless, I think to myself, although I'm grinning too much to actually mouth anything back to her.

From the corner of my eyes, I see Mercy storm out with a posse of senior Committee members in tow, all exchanging worried glances. I lift my head from Jack's chest to get a better look. When Jack follows my gaze, he then gives me a self-assured smile.

"Ah, yes. I'm afraid our dear Lady Mercy Bishop-Wicklow has been called away," Jack states, watching them rush from the tent. "Something about a car bombing in Albany that has all the hallmarks of a violent Nefari, if I'm not mistaken."

I blanch. "What… you know about… but how… what did you?"

He leans in close to my ear. "After you told me what you are, your mom filled me about Mercy and the Committee. And I know about the explosion because I called in a favor."

"A favor?" I ask, bewildered. "How? Why?"

"Because I wanted you to enjoy the occasion. You shouldn't have to look over your shoulder all evening. I want you to feel safe. I love you, Eleanor."

"Is this what you've been working on?" I ask, still trying to wrap my head around it.

He nods. "I won't give you all the mundane details, but I may have purchased some loyalty from the covens in Manhattan and

Rhode Island." He rests his forehead against mine and whispers, "I will do whatever needs to be done to keep you safe."

I lift onto my tiptoes and kiss him as deeply as I can in the middle of a dance floor surrounded by friends and family. "I love you too, Jack."

"You know, we never made it to our prom. This was long overdue," he says as we sway.

I nod against him, feeling a singeing between my shoulder blades from the omega symbol that was branded there on prom night.

Jack pulls back, just far enough to see into my eyes, and tenderly holds me there. "Come away with me next weekend," he says.

"What do you mean?" I ask.

"My mother can't bear to close our summer home for the season," he says with a slight roll of his eyes, "so she's asked me to do it. Come with me. Stay the weekend with me on my family's island."

I blush at the thought.

"Okay, I've never been to Martha's Vineyard before."

Jack laughs a short, guttural laugh that borders on sarcastic. "Oh no, this is different. We do have the obligatory cottage in the Vineyard, but that's not our summer home. I'm talking about an unmarked island. It's far more exclusive. Just knowing about it is by invitation only." His tone is dry, making it obvious he thinks the whole thing is a farce.

Next weekend is the Harvest Moon. The Nefari can't come for me if I'm not there. I'll have to tell my family to leave town as well.

I kiss the end of his nose, making him chuckle. "I'd love to."

He rests his head on top of mine as he holds me close, and together we slip into our own little world, blissfully unaware of anything around us.

CHAPTER THIRTEEN
Paradise Island

I stare at the one-piece swimsuit in my hand, debating whether I should bring it. *It's nearly October, I'm sure it'll be too cold to swim.* I nibble my lip staring at the turquoise suit. *You know, he might have a hot tub…* I shove the suit into my suitcase. My lips roll inward trying to hide my girlish smile from my mother who sits sternly at my desk.

"I still don't think this is a good idea. We have no idea where this Nefari is, or even *who* he is. For all we know, he'll track you to that remote island and no one will be around to help. Not to mention, you're still only seventeen! You and Jack are far too young to go gallivanting away on vacation by yourselves!" Her exasperation with me is reaching a boiling point. Persephone sits stalwart by her foot, staring at me with the feline equivalent of the same lecture my mom is giving me.

Blue's eyes tick back and forth between my mother and me. *Really? Nothing?*

He examines his left paw before responding. *"This may come as a shock to you, but I believe in the present circumstance, departing Salem before harvest moon is the most prudent course of action."*

Mom wrings together her thin hands, her jaw clenching tightly. "Persephone is right. I'm going to go with you."

I stop packing and stare at her.

"Marie and Sally will protect Maggie on their holiday in New York. Shannyn will be honeymooning in Paris until the first, and Lennox won't let any harm come to her. *You* are the only one without someone to help protect. If that Nefari finds you…" Mom can't finish the thought. She rises from her chair as if her decision is final.

"Moooom!" Maggie shouts from the landing one level down. "Have you seen my lace ankle boots or my suede moccasins?!"

Our mother leans her head out the door. "Margaret, you should already be packed. Sally and Marie want to hit the road in an hour." Footsteps thunder up the stairs while I resume packing.

If Mom wants to play chaperone, I'm not going to argue. It's not like her fears are unfounded. Besides, it's a private island; I'm sure Jack and I can find our own space.

Maggie appears in my doorway. "What do you mean just Sally and Marie? Aren't you coming too?"

Mom sighs out her nose. "Unfortunately, no. I've decided to accompany Eleanor on her trip to Jack's summer home."

Maggie looks at me and snorts. "Have fun," she teases. She wiggles her eyebrows at me before turning back to Mom. "Wait, but what about your ticket?"

"Give it to Abe," Mom says with a shrug. "I'm sure he'll love Broadway."

Maggie frowns. "He says he's staying here. He wants to keep an eye on the house."

"What?!" Mom snaps. "No! Why doesn't anyone listen to me? Nefari have no qualms about killing humans. Abe's not a witch, what does he think he's going to do if one shows up? He needs to go to New York with you all." She ushers my sister out the door and downstairs.

Blue wiggles his little black shoulders smugly. *"Well, I'm quite pleased with this turn of events."* He crosses one paw over the other and rests his chin on them.

I roll my eyes. *It's fine. It's not like we were planning on doing anything…*

"Well, not now, anyway," he sends self-righteously.

I pull on my brown and white polka-dot chiffon skirt that ends just a little below my knees. My white t-shirt is a little snug and reveals just a hint of skin at my waist. Not my typical attire, to be sure, but when you're invited to a private island with your boyfriend, it's good to step out of your knit-layered comfort zone.

Slinging my duffle bag on my shoulder, I glance about my room with a prayer that everything will be intact when I return. Just to be safe, I hide my violin under my bed.

* * *

Our feline familiars follow my mom and I out of the black town car to the helipad. Jack stands next to the chopper, hands held behind his back and grinning at us. Our driver, dressed in a six-figure suit, carries out luggage behind us.

A storm of butterflies in my stomach flutters about while my heels click against the blacktop.

Jack's grin widens the closer I get to him. I try not to squeal when he pulls me, wrapping his arms around my waist, pressing my body against his. Jack gives my lips a light peck that makes my breath catch in my throat. He returns my feet to earth but keeps my hand in his.

"Mrs.—"

Mom waves Jack's formal greeting away. "'Helen', Jack. Just 'Helen'." Her smile is warm and genuine as she looks Jack over. The friendly air between them comes as naturally as an old friend.

"Helen," he amends with a little blush. "I'm glad you could come." He nods to the helicopter behind him just as the engine starts to hum. The propellers overhead slowly begin their rotation.

"Do you have kennels for your pets?" the pilot shouts, leaning his head out the open doors.

Mom and I exchange glances. Blue stiffens against my leg.

"Pets? I'm two hundred years older than that rake" Would you like me to tell him that?

"Are you mental?" He peers up at me tersely. "Because he'll certainly think you are. I ought to scratch that piddly little beard from his cheeks."

I grin with a roll of my eyes.

Jack nods at our familiars. "They're fine, John," he calls back. He offers each of us a hand onto the chopper. "Their 'pets' are very well trained."

"Trained…?"

With Blue seated firmly on my lap, I curl into Jack's side and gaze out the window at the canvas of the early autumn sky. The air, crisp and clear, begins as a vivid azure overhead, then deepens in color as it reaches the horizon. Clouds lazily drift by in thin wisps of white as the sunlight casts a golden glow over the landscape.

Jack's lips press against the top of my head. I nuzzle my head into his shoulder and grip his arm, all while trying to keep a steady stream of hiccups from bursting from my chest.

Persephone is coiled in my mother's lap, resting. Mom runs her fingers through her familiar's stripped orange coat and rubs her ears. When my mom's ocean blue eyes meet mine, her mouth forms a small, quiet smile. It's the kind of glum smile that's sheathed behind a desperate veil of encouragement. Her eyes—a deep and endless sea—hide secrets, worries, and something else. Resentment, maybe?

She doesn't resent me for having Jack. She may have lost her soulmate, but she wouldn't want any of us girls to be alone. No, it's not a resentment of being robbed of a future romance, but rather a bitterness that I wasn't meant to be her daughter in the first place. I was created by Elspeth; she just happened to be who Elspeth sent me to, and my arrival destroyed her life. Because Elspeth sent me to her, she had to avoid her family, abandon her coven, stop using her magic, and in the end, after all sacrifice, she still lost her soulmate because of me.

"*Stop.*"

I look down at my familiar who isn't as asleep as he appears to be.

What? You really think she doesn't blame me? Not even a little bit? I mean, Shannyn and Maggie could have grown up fully embracing their identity as a witch. My mother wouldn't have had to hide for the last seventeen years. And my dad would still be here.

"*Your entire line of reasoning is inane, and it is unworthy of discussion. Come back to me when you have a daughter of your own and tell me if you could ever resent her.*" Blue wiggles a little in my lap. "*My goodness, child. Have your legs always been so boney? When we arrive at this bloody island, I insist you find a pantry and raid it.*"

I roll my eyes at him.

We touch down at a small airport and switch to a private jet. After flying south for a little more than an hour, we land at a remote airstrip and transfer to a ferry. At this point, I haven't the slightest clue where we are. Somewhere between Massachusetts and the Carolinas, I assume, but can't be any more specific than that. My mother seems relieved by the complicated route were taking through remote terrain, probably thinking it will thwart the Nefari's ability to track us. No matter how powerful the witch, he still can't compete with Jack's Gulfstream. The ferry on the other hand…

"*Bloody hell! I've been on merchant vessels steadier than this…this thing! Bollocks!*" I lean my head over the metal railing and hurl crackers and soda into the gray-blue water roiling beneath the ferry. Bile disappears into the rolling waves. Blue's nails screech against the metal decking as he tries to remain still at my side. He slides away from me as the ferry tilts upwards, then skitters back as we crash into the surf.

I never get seasick! This isn't how it was supposed to go! I'm supposed to be at the bow of the ferry with Jack watching the dolphins frolicking next to us. But instead, I sent him away so he didn't see me yack.

Yup. More is coming. My stomach uncoils and bile burns its way up my throat. "Eleanor," Jack calls over the clamor of the ocean. He starts to approach, but I throw my hand up stopping him.

"Nope, nope. Stay there!" I wipe my mouth on my wrist already speckled with vomit.

Jack winces. "Can I get you anything?" I shake my head.

Jack inches closer and closer until he's close enough to place a flannel blanket over my shoulders. He gently pulls my stringy hair back from my face, then rubs my back. Cold saltwater sprays my face.

"I'm so sorry. This storm came out of nowhere," Jack yells. "We should be to the island soon." He points ahead at a dark mass in the distance.

As the bow lifts with the approaching wave, Jack places a firm hand on either side of me and braces his body against mine. At the same time, he shuffles his feet a bit, sweeping Blue in between our feet and legs.

"Hey! Hey! What does this cad think he's doing?!" Blue hisses in protest but is powerless as Jack swiftly tucks him in.

The bow peaks, then plunges down head first into the next wave. Frigid seawater covers the deck, leaving us soaked to the bone. "Are you okay?" Jack shouts.

I nod, then peek down at Blue. The poor cat is drenched and shivering, but otherwise still intact.

"I guess the boy isn't completely useless…" Blue relents.

My white shirt is completely see-through, brazenly displaying the baby pink colored bra beneath. Jack's forearms are speckled with goosebumps.

After a few more waves, the churning sea settles into a murky chop that laps in a light thumping staccato rhythm against the side of the ferry. "Come here," I say through chattering teeth. I press our bodies tightly together, aligning from our toes to our heads. With my eyes closed, I picture the water molecules vibrating from the heat, their bonds bursting apart, and the resulting vapor dissipating into the air leaving our bodies warm and our clothes dry. *Nè Feerah.*

"Whoa," Jack exclaims. Warmth envelopes our bodies, starting in our chests and spreading to our fingertips and toes. Steam rises all around us. Our clothes feel fresh from the dryer, while his blonde hair curls into corkscrews from the sea salt and heat. "That's…intense."

Jack pulls his hand back, running his fingers and thumb against each other, marveling at the buttery soft warmth of his fingertips that only seconds ago were so saturated they had started to wrinkle.

"Ah hem."

The pitiful cat remains wedged between our feet, looking both pathetic and adorable with his damp fur clinging to his gaunt frame.

"If you're not too busy," he sends curtly.

Nè Feerah.

Steam rises from his black fur, leaving him freshly groomed.

Or at least as fresh as is possible for a dead cat to look.

Mom exits the cabin with a small glass jar.

"Did you do this?" I ask, motioning toward the calming water.

Mom shakes her head. "I called Marie. She wasn't sure she could help since all I could say about our location was somewhere southeast in the Atlantic past Roanoke." She shakes an olive-green pill the shape of a gumball from the vial into her palm. "Here, for the nausea. Hold it on your tongue, it'll take a minute to melt. Then swallow it."

Jack watches with fascination as I wait for the giant pill to dissolve. "Let me guess. Ginger, peppermint, and compressed fennel, wrapped in candied chamomile leaves." Jack rattles off the ingredients like he's taking an oral exam.

Mom's smile is wide and authentic. "Excellent, Jack. I'm impressed."

The pill's honey coating has melted away now, leaving a bitter aftertaste as it shrinks on my tongue. The soothing effects, however, are immediate.

"I've been studying those books you sent me in my free time. I've also done some independent study as well. Since feverfew, or 'Tanacetum Parthenium, is in the daisy family, I think if you dried it with the common daisy, then used it as a tea rather than a capsule, the result would be far more potent."

My eyes bulge at my soulmate like I have no idea who he is.

Mom's eyebrows lift nearly to her hairline. "That's an interesting theory; however, if you go that route, you risk giving your patient mouth ulcers."

"Ah, I considered that, not if you wait until the water hits two-hundred-fifty degrees Fahrenheit before letting it cool," he counters.

Blue peers up at me with a little glimmer in his sapphire eyes. *"Now, that's interesting."*

What in the literal hell is happening right now? "Whatever it is, I like it."

Mom shakes her head. "But then it will lose its potency, even if blessed by a witch."

Jack smiles. "But that's where the daisy petals come in. The common daisy enhances the feverfew's natural healing, thus compensating for the heat. Plus, the natural wax from the petals can coat the mouth and protect it from sores, even if you don't get the water hot enough."

I gape at him. *When did Jack become a better witch than me?*

Blue nudges my leg. *"You know, you could learn a thing or two from him."* Mom chuckles. "So, daisies no matter what, is what you're saying?" Jack nods. "The common daisy, life's cure all."

Mom shakes her head with a bright grin. "You can keep him," she teases before returning to the cabin.

The pill is now wafer-thin on my tongue, finally allowing me to talk.

"Where the heck did that come from?"

"I told you. I want to learn more about you, your witchcraft, all of it." He kisses the side of my grimy face. His eyes flick up, looking past me. He pulls his lips up in a crooked grin. "Look, we're almost there." He gently spins me around.

The island is clearly in view. The shoreline is covered with palm trees, mangroves, oaks, and magnolia trees with blooms just starting to turn. A dozen yachts are tied to a dozen docks shifting in the still uneasy water. Parting the line of weathered wooden docks is a long cement platform for the ferry. The leafy, jungle-like foliage obstructs any views beyond the shoreline.

For the first time since the plane touched down, the sun peeks out from behind muted gray clouds. The captain ties off the ferry and extends a metal gangway down to the dock. Before anyone can disembark, Blue leaps down and immediately splays out like roadkill on the cement.

"Under no circumstances will I ever step a single paw back on that infernal vessel. Tell Jack I require a plane for the sojourn home. I'm not unreasonable. It can be a prop plane, private jet, I don't care. But never again will I ride that horrid excuse for a boat."

Jack and the captain unload our suitcases next to Blue lying motionless on the dock.

"What a strange cat," the captain remarks.

Jack leads us on a short walk down a well-tended jungle pathway. On either side of the path are massive trees with low-hanging branches and rippling roots that jut several feet out of the ground. Mom nudges me and points to three brilliant blue and green peacocks strutting about the village. Other birds call and tweet from their hiding places in the canopies overhead. The path soon emerges into a circular clearing that spans the whole interior of the island. Before us is a series of Grecian-style mansions of white marble and limestone, graciously spaced apart and neatly aligned in rows leading to the center of the village.

"Welcome to Eden Isle," Jack says in an almost self-deprecating manner. As we pass mansion after mansion, all of which follow a similar construction theme, it occurs to me that none of these luxurious properties have any fences around them. What's even odder is that none of the homes have doors or even glass in their windows. Everything is open, and we're able to see into each home we pass. This place feels more like a movie set than a place people actually live.

"How do they keep the bugs out?" Mom muses aloud.

Jack laughs. "It's simple, really. We don't allow bugs here. Every living creature on the island needs permission to stay. They spray for bugs every day, and an aviculturist is on staff to make sure the authorized wildlife has something to eat. Obviously, Eden has to be manufactured. And in case of storms, the staff boards up the windows and doors. But despite what you saw today, storms are surprisingly rare out here."

We stroll by a general store, a salon, a bar, and a few different eating establishments with colorful beach cruisers leaning against store fronts. All open, doorless, vacant and dark.

"Jack," mom begins, taking a step closer to him, "it's a little late to be asking this, but we're safe here, right? I assume this was a place where Noble Hunters gathered."

Jack frowns repentantly. "Noble Hunters weren't the only ones who had a home here. We had foreign nationals, dignitaries, wealthy executives. But the Noble Hunters have disbanded. Any members not facing prosecution are off somewhere in hiding, but not here." He glances around. "There are thirty homes on the island. It's late in the season, so we're the only ones here. Besides the staff, of course, who remain year-round. I would never put any of you in danger. You have my word on that."

Mom nods, having suspected as much. She adjusts her white, floppy sunhat. I extend my hand, taking my mother's and giving it a gentle squeeze. Jack returns to gracious host, explaining how his maternal grandparents designed the entire island. Just like ancient Rome, it was designed like a wagon wheel, all roads lead to the center of town and to the Woods's grand estate.

There's a general store, spa, and restaurants, but no money is exchanged.

At the center of town is a marble fountain with cherubim dancing amid cascading waterfalls fifteen feet high. Around the fountain is a shopping center with a general store, a day spa, and a myriad of restaurants. And just outside the shopping center stands the Woods Estate. Mom and I trail behind Jack as we climb up stone steps to his summer home. Like every other building, we're able to walk right in without so much as a door to slow us down.

The foyer has vaulted ceilings striped with wooden beams running the length of the room. While taking in the vastness of the room, I bump into the round oak table in the center, tipping over a large vase of orchids poised in the middle. Fortunately, Mom catches it before it hits the table.

"The rooms are upstairs," Jack says, nodding for us to follow. He doesn't seem to care that I nearly destroyed what was probably a priceless artifact. "You can have the master suite, Helen." He walks toward the heavy double doors that by now seem out of place here.

"Oh no, Jack, I wouldn't dream of it. You take it, I can share a room with Eleanor," Mom says, wrapping a protective arm around my shoulders.

I sigh.

Blue chuckles in my head.

Persephone stares at Jack waiting for him to hop to it.

"Of course. We have a guest room with two queen beds I'm sure you'll be comfortable in."

My mom beams at me, and I force a smile back at her.

The white stone walls are adorned with black and white photos that catch my eyes as we make our way down the hall. Photos of a teenage Jack with a skinny frame and goofy smile, straddling a bike alongside his siblings. Pictures of Evelyn and Honor at a card table surrounded by society women, all laughing candidly. Jack and Marshall spearfishing. A 5-year-old Jack building a sandcastle on a sandy beach with other children. A 10-year-old Jack in a polka-dot bow tie and seersucker shorts, looking perfectly glum as he slow dances with a sundress-clad Vivienne Mather at some event. My teeth grind at just the sight of her.

"Eleanor, are you coming?" Mom calls.

I rush to join them in the last room on the left. Mom is out on the balcony taking in the view of the private town and its colorful gardens. Two queen beds are positioned across from each other against the opposing walls.

Jack places our bags next to our beds. "You have a private bathroom with a jetted tub in there," he says, pointing to the wooden door. Jack shoots me a flirtatious wink before my mom turns back around.

Heat creeps into my cheeks. *I wonder if we can find any alone time this weekend…*

"Ugh. I'll be exploring the rest of the house. Do try not to get into any

trouble. " Blue saunters out the door.

"Unpack, make yourself at home," says Jack, ever the gracious host. "I'm going to see if Berty prepared supper, otherwise I'll call one of the restaurants and let the staff know we're coming." Jack kisses my cheek, and before leaving whispers, "I'll show you my room later."

Heat spreads throughout my cheeks as I watch him disappear down the hall.

Mom wanders back in and takes in the accommodations. The silk Persian rugs laid out on the floor, the Charlotte Thomas Bespoke bed linen set, to the gold foiled, To'ak chocolates resting in a Waterford crystal on the nightstand. "This is pretty lavish," she says through a poorly restrained smile. "I think I'm going to go freshen up. Why don't you and Jack go explore, have some fun." Then her smile falters. "And be safe, I mean it."

I can't help but roll my eyes. "Yeah, yeah, I will. Other than the staff, we're the only ones here. How crazy is that? It's like a fully functioning resort and we're the only guests."

Mom nods. "You know, Jack's always been upfront about his background, but I never truly understood just how charmed his upbringing must have been until now." She sighs, undoubtedly comparing the childhood she gave us girls to his.

"But I'll give him this," Mom continues, "there is something very real and sincere about him. He speaks with the diction of a well-heeled, highly educated individual, but he has an undeniable humility as well. It reminds me of your father actually. That's rare to see in someone who grew up like this." She strolls into the enormous bathroom, still taking everything in. "Oh, my goodness! There's a whole set of Korean facials in here!" Her squealing voice echoes out of the bathroom.

"I'm next in there!" I call, feeling the crunch of the dried ocean salt in my hair and the grime on my clothes. I walk out onto the terrace and place my palms flat on the stone, letting the warmth of the sun paint my face. *Even with Mom here, it's going to be a perfect weekend.*

My ears perk at a sound wafting in the air. I leave the room and skip down the stone staircase that leads into the garden. *It was just music, I'm sure of it.* I meander through the garden, unable to tell where it's coming from.

I focus on the sound; it seems to be coming from a small dwelling like a guest house behind the garden. I glide down a set of stone steps, eager to see if Jack has a surprise waiting for me. I peek my head in, but other than a single king-size bed, the guest house is empty. So, where's the music coming from?

I close my eyes, hoping to better tune my ear, and I follow the sound past Jack's yard toward his neighbor's house. Once again, no doors or windows. The music is getting louder and clearer. A record is playing with a scratch as it keeps repeating the same line, unable to play the next lyrics. It skips and repeats, going around and around. That's when I recognize it.

My heart seizes in my chest. *It can't be.* My feet move like automatons, propelling me forward against my will as dread fills my veins. I step inside the house. The lyrics are clear as day now. I know this song. I would know it anywhere. It's the soundtrack to every nightmare I've had in the last four months.

Run, rabbit. Run, rabbit. Run. Run. Run...

A foul stench hits my nose. Flies buzz about. I move farther into the house and stumble on something that nearly sends me to the floor.

Splayed out in front of a marble staircase is the body of a woman wearing a white dress with yellow printed flowers. A strand of glimmering pearls hangs loosely around her neck. Her skin is ashen and gray, and her mouth is torn open, as if frozen mid-scream. Her lips have dried and curled back displaying empty, black-pocketed gums; all her teeth are missing. In her dark eye sockets, where her eyes should be, wiggles a mass of yellow maggots that feed and feeding on the corpse.

Just as a scream rips up my throat, a firm hand clamps over my mouth.

CHAPTER FOURTEEN
Run, Hide, Escape

"Don't scream. Someone's here," Jack whispers desperately into my ear, sweeping me back behind a column. He presses me against the wall, huddled close to me, he looks around quickly.

Run, rabbit. Run, rabbit. Run. Run. Run.

My heart hammers in my chest, pulsing near the point of exploding. My hands tremble at my side. The rancid stench of rotting flesh nearly makes me retch. "Is it Noble Hunters?" I cry. "Jack, my mom can't fight them, she'd become a Nefari," I cry.

Jack shakes his head. "No, it's something else. When I went into the kitchen, I found Berty and Eunice on the floor. Their eyes and teeth were missing, but no sign of a branding. Besides, they weren't witches; someone is hunting humans." Jack peers around the corner, his face crumples as he turns back to me. "That's Francine Dorchester. She most definitely wasn't a witch. She must have been here closing up her home late this season."

I choke at the sight of her. "She seems like she's been dead…a while." A door closes upstairs.

Our heads whip in that direction.

Run, rabbit. Run, rabbit. Run. Run. Run.

He instinctively moves me behind him, placing himself between me and the source of the music. "We need to get out of here."

"Jack, if someone is here murdering humans, then I'm not the one in danger," I whisper, my eyes glossy with tears. "They're after you."

Another door opens and slams shut.

An electric fear shoots down my spine. *Okay. Think! Think! Blue! Blue, can you hear me! Blue!*

"Eleanor, something is very wrong here."

You think?! Jack and I are in danger. What can I do? Please help us! Whoever is doing this, they're in the house with us!

"You need to remain calm. Clear your mind. You need to project the mind spell, doing the rabbit illusion is far easier than just turning yourself

invisible. You need to be fast. You need to be quiet. And most importantly, Eleanor, you need to remain calm. Make it simple, picture two rabbits, now hurry."

"Jack," I cup his face and pull his head toward me. "I'm going to try something I've never done before. I need you to take deep breaths with me."

Please, help me stay focused and calm. I'm not sure if I'm praying to Brighid or begging Blue.

I close my eyes gently, as if settling in for a nap. Thumping footsteps above our heads break my concentration.

Come on, you've got this. You've done this spell before. You're a daughter of Salem.

You can turn into a rabbit. You can turn your beloved into a rabbit.

I imagine our bodies crumpling down like rumpled pieces of paper until we are small, encased in fluffy fur. I picture the same rabbit as before, a New England cottontail, tan with white speckles. Jack is a Californian white with pink eyes, long snowy ears pulled back.

That horrid song continues to play. *Run, rabbit. Run, rabbit. Run. Run. Run…*

I picture us hopping, sprinting, resting, turning, dodging, going through bushes, rushing up his stone stairs, remaining in bunny form in front of my mother. *Oculi Tempe.*

When I open my eyes, my body is transparent. So is Jack's. Resting where our feet should be are two rabbits with velveteen fur.

"Eleanor, what is happening?" Jack whispers in panic.

"Follow me. We need to get to my mother. Now." It's disorienting trying to run without seeing my body, but each time I lift my foot, the cottontail shifts in front of me.

I hear Jack's clomping footsteps behind me as he struggles even more than I do.

"Quickly," I whisper. The rabbits race through the garden toward the house.

Jack quickens his pace. "What's with the rabbits."

"I'll explain later."

My eyes dart back to the rabbit at my feet with nearly every step. Despite the glamour holding perfectly, I'm convinced our façade will dissolve at any second. Together as two bunnies, we race into Jack's house and upstairs into the guest room.

Jack whips the bedroom doors closed behind us and flicks the lock.

Before I can even call for her, my mother steps out of the

bathroom with Persephone at her side. All color has drained from her face.

Blue leaps through the closed doors. *"Helen knows everything. I told Persephone. There's also a dead maid in the courtyard. Most likely, anyone still on the island is dead."*

Mom's eyes are locked with Persephone's. *We heard movement, Blue. In the house next door. "I believe that is our killer, then."*

Mom looks intently at the rabbits near our feet. She waves her hand, and my glamour collapses, exposing our true form again. I need to learn how to do that.

Mom's lips form a quivering line while her eyes hold a faraway look. My guess is she's still talking to Persephone.

"Jack, is the ferry still at the port?" Mom finally asks. She lifts her chin, forcing her tremors away.

Jack breathes like he's been holding his breath until now. "Yes. But we need to hurry. He'll have wanted to be back before dark."

"Is there another way to the port so we don't have to parade through town?" She kicks off her slippers and steps into her sensible "mom" shoes while Jack is thinking.

Jack peers out the window, the song still drifting faintly through the salty air. "Yes. We can go through the kitchen, then to the Mather's. Daphne had a pathway paved through the tree line. You walk right past it if you didn't already know it was there."

"And that'll take us to the boat?" Mom asks.

"Not directly. It'll just take us to the shore." He stands a little taller, masking his fear with determination. "But once we hit the beach, we can walk over the rocks to the dock. The forest perimeter will keep anyone still in the village from seeing us."

I move toward my suitcase lying on the bed, suddenly grateful I never got a chance to unpack.

"Leave it," Mom orders. "We'll most likely have to make a run for it." She looks down at Persephone. "You're right," she tells her familiar. "I'll keep us invisible until we reach the trees. I doubt I'll have enough strength to do much more than that." She gazes down at her cat and nods; I wish I knew why.

Something downstairs falls to the floor and shatters.

"Jack," I squeak.

He glances over his shoulder at the closed bedroom doors. "It's locked."

Mom grabs us both by the hand and squeezes her eyes closed. Her lips move as she concentrates on her spell. Her head bobs up and down for a moment, probably feeling her magic answer her.

Her power courses through her and into us like a river floating through the air. Mom opens her eyes, then nods satisfied.

I glance down at myself, then to her and Jack. "It didn't work. I can still see all three of us," I cry. "Let me help, Mom. Two witches are stronger than one."

Mom shakes her head. "The spell worked, even on the cats. We're still visible to each other, but no one else." She snatches both of my hands, holding them tight. "Besides, I need you ready to use a defensive spell if it comes to that." Her eyes slide to Jack for just a moment. "If anything happens, I want you two to make a run for it and don't look back."

"Mom, no!"

"Shh!" Jack places a finger to his lips as a pair of feet storm up the stairs. Jack closes his eyes with his ear practically against the door. "They're going toward the master suite," he whispers.

Mom stares at the flip lock on the door intently. The gold lock silently turns, unlocking itself.

"What are you doing?" I hiss.

"If the door is locked, they'll know we're here, invisible or not."

The footsteps stop and start. Things are torn from the walls. Glass shatters. Dresser drawers are yanked from their place and thrown about.

What are they searching for? Not knowing when they'll get to this room is agony.

The footsteps stop. We all hold our breath.

The footsteps become rapid. Someone is sprinting toward us. I grip Jack's hand anxiously.

"Be ready, Eleanor. If you want to protect your mate, you need to clear your mind."

I bite my bottom lip, my mind in a tailspin. *What defensive spell could I use? Or better yet, what about an offensive? Can I really kill someone?* That's when Allen's dead eyes flash through my mind. The bullet straying from its intended target until it's drilling slowly, agonizingly into Allen's forehead. I shut my eyes, trying to will those violent images away. *I guess if it comes to saving Jack, I'll do whatever it takes. I'm already a Nefari.*

Mom pulls Jack and me back behind her a mere second before the French doors burst from their hinges and crash into the opposite wall.

All three of us Freeze in the center of the room. None of us dare to breathe.

Standing in the doorway is an impossibly tall woman with broad shoulders and a square face. Taking up her entire left cheek is a branded omega, glowing pink on her olive skin. Her irises are hazard orange. They flick about the room as a smile unfurls across her face. "I know you're in here," she says in a thick Russian accent.

The towering woman steps into the room and looks about. She spots our luggage and grins. "Come out, come out, vherever you are," she sings in a menacing tone. She tiptoes closer to us, still searching, not realizing she's mere inches from us.

Mom's arms stretch across us like a mother hen protecting her chicks. We all lean slowly away from the unkempt Nefari who sticks out her long nose, sniffing the air around us.

"Mmm…." she moans pleasurably. "I feel you, vitch. You are quite powerful." She spins away and walks toward the queen bed with my suitcase on top. With a flick of her wrist, the suitcase flies into the wall, and the woman falls back on to the bed.

Her bushy brows leap up her face in surprise, and she wiggles against the mattress, making herself comfortable. She then stares at the ceiling while she continues. "It makes me vonder, though. Are you here because you planned the same massacre, or are you vorse?" Her voice drops low with a loathsome disgust that makes my knees tremble. "A 'hore to vitch hunters, is that it? If you are one of us, then come out. Ve could use you. But if not…"

She sits up and looks about. "If not, you'd better keep hiding. For vhen ve find you," her lips curl across her cruel face, "vhat ve vill do to you vill make their torture seem like nothing. I do to you vhat vas done to my people."

She rises from the bed. Mom inches us away from her. "*Stay very calm, do not try any spells. Focus on staying invisible.*"

The woman moves about the room in a dramatic, even theatrical fashion. "I from Slovakia, you see. In small village vhere ancestors hail, the locals did not hold trials like your people did. No need for confession. Apology do nothing. Once accused, the vitch vould be taken to the town square, stripped naked, and flogged. Next, they cut out the tongues so they no more speak to devil. Then, if you be male, they remove the skin. Slowly. Inch by inch. But if you be female, they had *special* device for you." She lifts her fist in front of her and flings her fingers out like an explosion.

"*Brilliant. I've heard enough from this one. Get out. I'll meet you at the ferry,*" Blue sends.

What? What are you going to do? I peer down at him.

Blue, still invisible, extends his claws and dashes out onto the balcony.

He leaps over the edge, knocking over a terracotta pot in the process.

Blue!

The Nefari's head whips towards the balcony. It takes only three strides for her to sprint the distance and leap over the edge after him.

"Quietly now, let's move." Mom ushers us out of the room with Persephone leading the way, her little orange head darting about before we venture down the stairs.

"That way," Jack says, pointing toward the kitchen.

He takes my hand and leads us around the center island toward the back door. The smell of rotting, decomposing bodies slithers up our nostrils, goading us to vomit. Across the marble floor from the fridge is a short boxy man wearing the all-white attire of the staff. His eye sockets are gaping black pits. His jaw is unhinged, hanging to the side. His gums are gray with dark inky holes where his teeth used to be. My stomach bubbles. Nearing the back door, we find a maid lying across the open doorway, dressed and tortured the same as the man had been. Jack pulls me into him, and together we step over the poor woman's corpse and out into the vegetable garden.

The property next door is the Mather's mansion. We enter through the backdoor which leads us into a pantry and cleaning supply closet. Two plastic brooms stowed in the corner next to a sponge mop catches my eye.

"Mom, what about these?" I grab the broom and hold it up to her. Mom shakes her head. "That will never work."

"But Mom—" I start to protest.

"Eleanor, you've never flown more than a few dozen yards at a time. The mainland is miles away. I'm already using nearly all of my magic for us to stay invisible, so you and Jack would have to fly the entire way on just your magic alone. Then, if the Nefari finds us, neither of us would have any power left for defensive spells. Trust me, the boat is the only way."

I know she's right. I drop the broom and fall in line behind them.

The now-familiar stench of dead bodies fills this house just as it did the last. We race through the kitchen and down a hall toward a side door. Standing in the doorway, taking short, shallow breaths, we stare at the mere feet that separate us from the dense forest that circumscribes the entire island.

Blue, are you okay? Where are you?

"I'm on the south side of the island," Blue responds. *"I no longer*

hear that vile woman's rantings, which is not the good news you might think. I thought I heard her call out for someone, possibly a familiar or another Nefari. Be careful, Eleanor. I'm circling back to you now."

Mom turns to face us. "Once we step out, we'll be exposed. Jack, I want you to lead us down the path. I'll take up the rear. Once you get to the beach, don't stop. No matter what happens or what you hear, you get Eleanor on that boat, and you leave. Are we clear?"

Jack is speechless, his face unreadable. After a split second, he nods.

I open my mouth to object, but my mom clamps down on my mouth with her hand and shakes her head.

"Keep your footsteps light as you run. Go now." Mom steps forward with her hands held forward, ushering us to move.

My hand is held tightly in Jack's as he tows me toward the tree line, all three of us constantly looking over our shoulders. Just as we duck through into the brush, I spy a backwards glance at the Mather estate. A silhouette stands in the upstairs window.

Just how many of them are there?

Every twig that cracks under my feet sends a tremor throughout my body, fearing who else might have heard it. The stretch of dense jungle casts sinister shadows, its branches twisting outward toward us.

"We're almost there," Jack assures.

Mom and Persephone nip at my heels as I struggle to catch my breath. Thankfully, the tree canopy thins as we run, allowing sunlight to paint our path. We scramble across the boulders crowding the jagged shoreline. Jack stops at each difficult section to assist my mother and me. Mom keeps stopping and looking back at the trees, squinting to see through the glare of the sun.

The docks finally come into view.

We just might make it out of here.

We arrive at the ferry just as Blue is approaching from the opposite direction. A few patches of fur are missing from his back. *"There's at least three of them. We need to leave. Hurry!"* Blue leaps onto the ferry a step ahead of us.

The metal gangway rattles as we race up it, no longer caring how loud we are. Our chests heave, desperately trying to catch our breath. The sun grazes the horizon, sending thousands of glittering orange splashes of light across the ocean. Nature's beauty feels wrong against the cadaverous horror we just witnessed.

"Inside the cabin, all of us," Mom says. "I don't like us standing out here in the open."

Jack halts in the cabin doorway and sucks in a jagged breath. I lift onto my tiptoes to see over his shoulder. The captain's lifeless body lies in a scarlet pool of his own blood. The pool is steadily growing, meaning the blood is still flowing out of him; he couldn't have been killed more than a minute ago. I have to squeeze my eyes closed and turn away.

"Eleanor?" Mom says, coming up behind me.

I spin around. "Captain Tom's dead."

"And they destroyed the radio, along with all the control panels," Jack adds. "The ferry is useless. Unless… are you able to control the currents, Helen? Could you have us drift back to the mainland?" His voice wobbles, unsure if what he's asking is even possible.

Mom shakes her head. "I don't possess that kind of power. That would take several witches who all have the gift of water, otherwise an entire coven."

"But Marie, she calmed the waves," I point out desperately.

"She didn't affect the waves directly; she calmed the storm, and the waves stopped on their own. Besides, my phone is back in the bedroom, we have no way of reaching her."

Mom closes her eyes and pinches the bridge of her nose, thinking. "Okay," she puts her hand up, eyes still closed, "I don't see any way around it. We'll hide in the trees until nightfall, then once it's dark, we'll find brooms and fly to safety."

"But Mom, you said—"

"I know what I said. I'm going to rest while we wait for dark, and I'll drop the invisibility spell for the flight. That should allow me to fly Jack and I and still cast a defensive spell if necessary."

*"Then let's be off. We're sitting ducks out here, "*Blue sends anxiously.

We exit the boat and sprint down the docks to the jungle. Our nerves are all fried at this point. None of us can stand to look each other in the eye, not wanting to see our dread written on someone else's face as well. We crouch amongst the underbrush and wait.

Jack wraps his arms around me. Mom leans close to Jack, knowing that in spite of being the tallest and strongest of us, he's also the most vulnerable. We sit in silence—without so much as a chirping bug or buzzing fly to break it—and watch the shadows around us grow long. Soon the last remnants of sunlight dissipate. A velvety darkness covers the island.

We can just make out each other's faces under the ghostly glow of the full moon peeking through the canopy. The Harvest Moon. The same Harvest Moon I was so dearly avoiding back in Salem.

That can't be a coincidence, right? Did the Nefari follow me here? Are those servants dead because of me? But they can't be; they looked like they'd been dead for days, and we only just left Salem this morning…

Blue brushes against my bent knee. *"Did you recognize the witch?"*

No. But she could be working with the Nefari from the apothecary shop. The one who said he was coming for me. While we were running away, I saw the silhouette of a man in the window of the Mather's home. And you said there were three.

"I doubt they are here because of you. Like you said, those bodies had been dead for quite some time. You told no one outside the house where you were going. This may just be an unfortunate coincidence. Mercy told your mother and aunts that with the Noble Hunters out of the way, the Nefari have grown bolder."

No good deed goes unpunished.

Mom bends in and whispers, "It's quiet. I think we can go now. Eleanor, I want you to do the invisibility spell on yourself. I will cover Jack, myself and the cats. Jack, do you know where we can locate some brooms?" Despite her whispering, her voice is deafening after hours in a bugless forest.

"Why not use the ones in the Mather's cleaning closet?" I ask in a similar hushed tone.

"Two won't be enough, we need at least three," Mom stresses. "Plus, I'd rather not have to hike that far back if we don't have to."

Jack shakes his head. "Most residents thought storing cleaning supplies was beneath them; it was seen as a serious faux pas," he explains. "I'm not sure why the Mather's had them, but we're unlikely to find them in the other homes. The servant staff kept them, but I don't know where."

"Very well," Mom says, resigned. "Back to the Mather's house, then. We should assume they've figured out how we escaped to the beach; we probably left footprints in the sand. We'll have to stay off any paths and use trees for cover. Once we're there, Jack, is there a place you and Eleanor can hide while I search for more brooms?"

Jack looks down in thought, then after a moment, pops his head back up. "The wine cellar. The Mathers were never fans of the island's open-door policy, they didn't trust residents not to pick apart their selection while they were away, so they had the door to their wine cellar disguised as a wall. You'd never find if you didn't already know it was there."

Mom nods to herself. Her posture is returning to normal as her escape plan is coming together.

"Once we're in the cellar, you two will stay put while I search for more brooms. If I can't find two more… Jack, you'll have to ride with me. Ell, once were in the air, you don't worry about anything but keeping yourself airborne."

Jack and I exchange glances, feeling like untrained soldiers on the eve of battle.

"Persephone, I want you to stay with Jack and Eleanor," Mom states. Then she shoots her cat a warning glance. It's a look I'm all too familiar with, Persephone must have begun to protest telepathically. Mom's eyes flutter closed, and her lips move as she recites the spell. I quickly do the same, imagining myself becoming completely transparent. My magic courses through me, confirming the spell worked even though I'm still able to see myself.

Together, we dart through the dense forest back to the Mather home. Once we come to the tree line, we halt. The entire town is lit up. The gas lampposts lining the streets are aglow, as are the electric fairy lights strung across the narrow roads. Houses shine like everyone is home, and shops in the town center beam like it's the Christmas shopping season. Worst of all, "Run Rabbit Run" plays over loudspeakers.

"They're amped up for something, they know we're here," I squeak, hunched over beside my mother.

"Not for long," Mom says. "I'll meet you both back at the Mather home. Persephone, make note of how you find the cellar door so you can give me directions when I come. Now go, I'll watch out for you while you get there." Mom motions for us to move.

Jack takes my hand, and the cats dutifully slink by our sides as we trudge forward mere yards from the house. Unwanted images play a slideshow in my mind; images of my branding, finding Trixie's body, and killing Jack's father, all while that sinister song plays its happy tune like a soundtrack to my nightmare. *So run, rabbit, run, rabbit, run, run, run…* I glance back at the forest looking for my mother but am unable to locate her.

"Don't look back. Your mother is powerful. We're almost there," Blue sends.

My heart pounds wildly until we pass the threshold. Jack leads us swiftly downstairs and into a small, overstocked wine cellar.

We nestle together in the cramped corner behind some wooden crates. Blue and Persephone sit a few feet in front of us, standing guard and watching the door.

"I'm so sorry," he breathes. He lets out a few more curses under his breath. I frown at him. "Why would you think you're responsible for this?"

"You mean besides the fact I invited you to 'murder island'? Those witches are here because of what my family did to them. I saw the brand on her face. They won't stop until they've killed the heir."

He sounds so empty, even dead inside, like he's just seconds from turning himself over to them. Something in me snaps. "No, Jack, they're psychopaths. The staff here didn't deserve this. Even the oblivious wives who weren't actually Hunters didn't deserve this. Jack, this isn't justice what they're doing."

"You and your mother are in danger because of me... yet again," he mutters, leaning his head back against the stone wall behind us. "I gave her my word I wouldn't put you in danger."

I reach over and grip his arm. "Stop. Nefari are evil witches. They're agents of destruction; they don't need reason or cause. If it weren't The Noble Hunters they were after, it would be something else, believe me." I think of Elspeth; how she, a Nefari, had assisted the Hunters by creating the prods that would deliver brands that would never heal.

My burn between my shoulder blades begins to itch. Jack replies, "Just please know how sorry I am."

"And I'm sorry that my people are trying to murder us all right now." I say with a touch of levity. Jack cracks a faint smile, then rests his head on mine.

Blue, has Persephone heard from my mother?

"Yes, she's made it to the Woods's residence, but a Nefari was there, so she is currently hiding in what appears to be a billiard room."

My heart squeezes. *Is she okay? Does she need help?* My magic flickers, like sputtering lights before the current ceases and I know my spell is done. We're visible again.

"Don't you dare move. Your mother is powerful and resourceful, whereas you are... still new to this. So, STAY PUT."

Blue? "What?"

I narrow my eyes on his nearly invisible form, not from magic, but because he's a black cat in a dark cellar. *If you don't tell me my mother is in trouble and something happens, I'll never forgive you.*

"Noted."

I curl into Jack with my head resting on his shoulder. The adrenaline that's been fueling me all night finally gives out. My body, too exhausted to stay upright, melts into Jack's. Despite my best efforts to fight it, my eyes fall closed. Jack's breathing slows along with mine as we fall into the same rhythm drifting into unconsciousness.

I'm awoken by a stiff neck and numb tailbone. Or perhaps by the gray light of dawn filtering in through the narrow egress windows on the outside wall near the ceiling. It's only a few inches of light, but just enough to rouse us. Jack stirs as I yawn and stretch.

"Mom?" I croak out, assuming she made it back and decided to rest as well. I squint through the dusty light, searching for her.

"She didn't make it back," Blue sends.

"What?!"

Jack leaps at the sound of my screeching voice as I rush toward the stairs. "What, what is it?" he asks, chasing after me.

"My mom didn't come back!" I snap. I creak open the door, spying out just a glance. A clock hangs on the wall in the sitting room. It reads five-thirty. I hold my breath and listen for any noise in the house. Nothing.

"Eleanor! Get back here! You're not even invisible!"

I step out of the cellar with Jack not a step behind me. Rage is building inside me, eclipsing any fear I had before. "We need to find weapons," I say, determined to rescue my mother.

"Hello, little ones."

I whip around toward the voice. Lurking by the front doorway is a giant brute of a man. He grins, exposing his yellow teeth framed by thin lips and rough black stubble. His beady eyes have unnatural irises the color of glowing charcoal. In one hand, he holds a blood-splattered hatchet. In the other hand, he holds… something impossible.

Blue hisses.

Jack stops breathing.

What am I seeing? My mind can't make sense of it. I blink, hoping the image will change, but it doesn't. After a moment, my mind catches up, but I still can't accept it. It can't be. Tangled in the brute's fist is platinum blonde hair. Beautiful hair. Hair I know all too well. The ends are soaked in something red. I blink several more times, and my denial shatters. Hanging from the brute's monstrous fist is my mother's severed head.

CHAPTER FIFTEEN
A Deal with the Devil

No…

No, no, no.

A scream rips through my insides, a deafening, violent scream that incinerates my every last remnant of coherent thought. *My mom is dead.* A lump forms in my throat. My fists squeeze until they are white and trembling. *Mom is dead.* My magic pulses in time with my heart.

The Nefari chuckles through a wide grin that spans ear to ear. "Would you like to know her last words, little one?" He lifts my mother's head, bringing it level with his barrel chest. I can't bear to look at her, nor can I bring myself to look away.

I clamp my jaw shut, breathing through flared nostrils. My heart pounds faster. My magic is no longer pulsing; now it flows in a raging current. The tips of my fingers thrum with electricity.

Jack shifts on the soles of his feet. I can feel his mind calculating how to get the upper hand on this monster. Jack rolls onto the balls of his feet. His arms are loose, his glare deadly, like a coiled snake preparing to strike a tiger. "Do it, boy. Come at me," the Nefari challenges. He stares at Jack now, considering him to be the biggest threat. A wicked delight twinkles in his eyes.

Jack shifts his weight forward, ready to charge until I lift my hand, stopping him.

La Caeli.

A narrow gust of wind blows toward the Nefari with the precision of a blade backed by the power of a tornado. A horrible crack sounds from the man's knees, and the infernal witch releases a guttural scream as his kneecaps fracture. His legs bend backward like a flamingo's, pitching his body forward. The swirling gust of wind reforms around his writhing body, tightening until his shins are pressed against his thighs.

I take a step closer. The colossal man quivers on the floor, howling, his face twisted in agony. Even with all his strength, he is unable to escape the air that holds him down. Gone is the twinkle in his eyes from only moments prior, replaced by an existential fear. It's not enough. I raise my hand.

"Eleanor!"

Blue lunges in front of me, cutting me off from the wailing, pathetic creature on the floor. Only now do I realize he's been screaming in my head this whole time. *"Look at Persephone! Look!"* He points with his head toward my mother's familiar.

Persephone sits at Jack's side, fully alive and well.

"If your mother was truly dead, then Persephone would be also. This is just a trick of the mind spell, look!" he nods again, this time to the floor where my mother's head had fallen. The illusion has vanished.

My magic recedes, like someone turned the crank on a garden hose. What had been a surge of power diminishes to a trickle, then stops completely.

I stumble backward.

I thought...

"I know, but it wasn't real."

I collapse, but Jack catches me just before I hit the floor.

Spittle foams at the corners of the Nefari's mouth. Something sharp protrudes from his blood-soaked jeans at the spot of the unnatural bend in his knees.

Jack dashes to the cleaning closet, seizing the opportunity to snatch the broom.

What have I done? I gaze over to the man in horror as he goes into shock.

Blood drains from his face. *"You had to defend yourself."* But I... *I enjoyed it.*

"I know." Blue looks away from me.

Rage had consumed me, and when it drained away, it left an empty void in its place. I feel nothing but shame and regret now. I look at Blue. The disappointment emanating from him is almost tangible.

Bile bubbles around the Nefari's pale lips. I crawl over to him and assess the damage. His eyelids flutter; the color drains from his face. I place my hand on his cheek. It's cold and clammy. He doesn't respond to my touch, just continues shaking.

Years of conversations with my mom pass through my mind. *Come on, I know this. He's in shock. The pain is overloading his autonomic nervous system, right? Or at least I think that's what Mom said. I need to stabilize his blood pressure.*

"Eleanor?"

I whip my head toward the front door. There in a shaft of

light shining through the doorway stands my mom. She's huffing deep breaths, ignoring the dirt and leaves stuck in her hair. Her sweater is missing a sleeve, and dried blood is caked in the corner of her mouth. Her eyes fall to the quivering Nefari with his legs bent unnaturally beneath him. Jack rounds the corner holding two brooms.

"I barely got away from him," Mom says, nodding to the man.

Persephone steps around the Nefari and rubs against Mom's leg with her back arched.

Jack places a broom in my hand and reaches out to Mom with the other. "We need to go," Mom says. She takes the broom from Jack and turns to leave. "Mom," I call.

She stops and looks over her shoulder at me. "What do we do about him?" I ask meekly.

Mom doesn't even glance at him. "Leave him, we need to go." Her hand, streaked with blood across her knuckles, grips the door frame.

Jack takes hold of my elbow and helps me to my feet. "Are you okay?" he whispers.

I nod, unsure if I can speak. Together, we step over the Nefari quivering on the floor.

Out in the garden, my mother mounts her broom. "I couldn't find another broom, so Jack, we'll have to share."

"I vouldn't do that."

The imposing female witch from the guest room drops her invisibility spell, revealing herself standing next to the garden gate. Her hazard orange eyes appraise us one by one. "Come. Ve speak," she orders.

None of us move or speak. Fear has frozen us in place.

Suddenly, Persephone floats off the ground. The cat hisses and claws at the air, writhing and contorting high above our heads. The Nefari grins a wicked smile that crinkles the pink omega scar on her cheek. She releases Persephone over the garden gate, letting her helpless body fall toward the gate's decorative iron spikes. An abrupt burst of air blows beneath the orange tabby, and the current carries her to my mother's open arms.

"Do not make us vait. You come now," the Nefari orders. We're all still rooted in place. Mom's eyes are wild and wide.

"Do whatever it takes to get Jack and you off the island," Blue sends. *"Do not worry about Helen. You'll know when it's time."*

I can't leave my mother. I already lost my father, Blue. I am not leaving her.

Mom holds her head high, following the woman down the stone steps at the garden gate toward the road. Three more Nefari witches are waiting for them, a male and two females. Jack falls in line behind my mother.

A thought occurs to me. *Elspeth. Elspeth, are you there? I need you.* I imagine a phantom hand reaching out into the dark void, waiting for Elspeth to reach out and take my hand. *Elspeth, you need me. If my mother dies here, or Jack, I will never get you that candle. I'll burn down our home to the ground before I give it to you.*

"Eleanor, what are you doing?" Blue interrupts.

"Eleanor?" Mom calls over to me, her voice strained. "They want to speak to all of us."

Elspeth's voice enters my head. *"Thou hast already sworn to deliver mine candle. A bargain hath been struck."*

"Do not bargain or negotiate with her," Blue seethes. Suddenly his attention is pulled, perhaps Persephone is trying to strategize with him.

I tiptoe down the stairs, rolling my lips in between my teeth to keep my jaw from chattering. It takes all my strength to keep my expression neutral. *Only because you threatened my family. But you've never touched any of them; I don't think you can. That means you have no leverage over me.*

"How swiftly you forget the past fortnight, my child. Shall I bereave you of sleep once more, or simply drag thee back into Purgatory?"

A petite witch, perhaps twenty years old, sits on a little girl's bicycle, trilling the bell as she circles the other two. The Nefari woman from earlier stands tall, glaring at us. The man flanks her side, clearly awaiting orders. He's above average height but is still an inch or two shorter than the woman. Mom and I stand in front of Jack. He's antsy and fidgeting; it goes against every instinct he has not to stand between us and danger, but what can a human do against three witches willing to kill him?

If I try to bluff, she'll know. You can't bluff someone who can read your mind. Instead, I summon every morsel of courage I have in me and direct my thoughts at Purgatory. *Do it then, Elspeth. I can suffer whatever I have to if it means you stay where you are. But I won't let my family suffer. Helping them is the only card you have left to play.*

"You will *give me my candle, Eleanor!"*

My heart is pounding; my courage hangs by a thread. *Only if you help us now. If anything happens to my mom or Jack, the deal's off.*

"Your friend is in the house," Mom states coldly. "He'll need immediate medical attention. I don't have the proper instruments to fix a compound fracture with me." Mom places Persephone on the ground next to her feet. She grips the broom and glances at Jack, as if beckoning him to stand safely behind her. "He doesn't have long. He needs help. Now."

"You've given me little cause to trust you'll honor your deals," Elspeth finally replies. *What other option do you have?*

The tall Nefari woman shrugs, completely ignoring the petite woman giggling maniacally on her bicycle. The man glances back at the house, as if he could see up the stone steps and into the summer estate where their friend lies slowly dying.

"Who did this to Dominic?" she questions, folding her arms across her chest. The woman on the bicycle finally comes to a stop beside her.

Mom opens her mouth to speak, but I step forward. "I did," I answer.

Elspeth, it's now or never. What's it going to be? Help us escape or lose your only chance at the candle.

Mom whips me a warning glare.

Blue slinks out in front of me, putting himself between me and the feral witch. *"Eleanor, you need to clear your mind. You've proven deadly with the air spell, perhaps we must harness the air for our escape."*

"What beautiful eyes you have, little vitch. I am Simona," the tall Nefari says in her thick accent. She gestures to the man beside her. "This is Andreas." The man with eyes like mercury nods, then Simona points to the psychotic witch with Fanta orange eyes on the bicycle. "And this is Teran. I am impressed that you vere able to disarm Dominic before he could confound you with spell of mind. He vas quite talented, but also dumber than rock. Still, it is pity that he must be vasted." She turns her head to Andreas, never looking directly at him. "Go finish him, he vas a pathetic excuse for Nefari."

Our breaths hitch in our throats as Andreas casually skips up the stone steps to the Woods's summer home. For them to kill a member of their own coven, and with such cold nonchalance, means we are in greater danger than we realized.

"Join us, little Nefari vitch," Simona bids. "What?!" shrieks Teran, the Nefari on the bicycle.

Simona whips her head at Teran, silencing her with a deadly glare. The younger Nefari rolls her eyes and looks away. She's neither scared nor happy, but at least willing to hold her tongue.

I shake my head.

Simona steps forward. "Don't be a hasty vitch. Ve are more powerful in greater numbers. Ve lost many to the Committee. Join us and the blonde voman can go, along with familiars."

My heart halts, I gulp with difficulty. "And him?" I nod back toward Jack behind me.

Simona dips her head so she peers at me through a heavy brow and curly smile. "That ve cannot allow. Ve dispatch him, slowly, vorse than the others. But you two can live."

Jack takes an aggressive step forward, but I lift my arm, keeping him behind me.

"Absolutely not. He's my soulmate, you're not going to touch him." I declare with my chin in the air.

Mom's eyes slide nervously from me to Simona.

Teran hisses at the revelation. Andreas saunters down the stone steps and rejoins his coven, his face apathetic. It's only when he turns his head to his leader that I see the blood splatter across his cheek and forehead and the hatchet hovering behind him.

Simona nods to him, seeking confirmation the deed is done. Andreas offers a single nod in response.

Her vicious eyes dart back at me. "So, you vill not join us, even to allow voman to live," she glances over at my mother as she speaks.

I shake my head. Hiccups quiver up my throat, but I manage to keep them from escaping. *I will get you that candle,* I telepathically vow to Elspeth. Simona shrugs her broad shoulders. "Pity. You vould make good addition. But mark my vords, he vill not leave this island alive. Ve know who you are!" she calls over us to Jack. "Ve know vhat your family has done!"

Jack, still behind my mother and I, drops his head for a moment. "I'm deeply sorry for what my family did," he begins from over my shoulder. "I can't imagine the horrors you've faced. But I swear to you, I was never involved in that. And if I had known what was happening, I would have—"

"You would have what?!" Teran screeches. "Joined them?! Burned more witches?! We need to kill him, Simona! We need to kill him now! Let me do it! Please! Let me do it! Please! The Woods brat needs to die!"

"Teran!" shouts Andreas. "It is not your place to make requests." His hatchet rises higher in the air. My mother's eyes zero in on it, prepared to defend against it.

Elspeth finally speaks again. *"If you cross me, child, Hell awaits thee."*

Deal.

Blue hisses at me. *"Eleanor, stop! We will escape this without her."*

No, we won't. Mom is injured, I'm not powerful enough, and they are hell bent on killing Jack.

A whiff of smoke wafts through the air. If anyone else notices it, they don't let it show.

Tears streak down Teran's cheeks. Her jaw trembles, her wild orange eyes lock on Jack. "Want to see what your brother did to me?! Huh?!" she tugs down the shoulder of her moth-eaten sweater. Just above her left breast is a branded omega scar, the same as on Simona's cheek and my back. "He needs to die! Now!"

Jack winces at the sight of her branding. "I am truly sorry for what happened to you. I promise, we've done everything we can to help authorities find Marshall so he can answer for what he did."

"*We* will find him, and he will answer to us," Andreas promises darkly. The smell of trees on fire intensifies, becoming impossible to ignore. Great plumes of black smoke billow from the outer rim of the town.

Simona lifts both palms in the air, silencing her subordinates. "Vhen ve find him, he vill die. But first this one. First, ve remove his eyes, then his tongue. Next, ve take his skin in long strips before ve brand him. Then ve boil him like rabbit stew. Ve take him now."

Teran leaps off her bike, giggling for the magical blood bath about to begin. She retrieves three rabbit masks from out of her satchel using the air spell and distributes them to her small band of Nefari. The masks have faded pink noses, bristled whiskers, and dark hollow eyes. They're crude and pagan-looking, remnants of a bygone age.

Everything inside me cringes at the sight of them. No longer do these rabbits run from the farmer and his gun; now *they* are the hunters.

Simona tilts her head to the side, staring at us through her rabbit mask. With her eyes so opaque, it's hard to make out what she's gazing at. Then Jack gurgles behind us.

"Jack!" Mom screams as she whips around and dives to the ground where Jack has fallen and struggles to breathe as water gushes from his mouth, his lips turning violet.

Magic explodes inside me, a torrent of energy so powerful my knees nearly buckle. This is more power than I've ever felt.

I don't think. I don't have time to think. *La Caeli.*

The air around the Nefari begins to spin. In mere seconds, they're surrounded by a tornado ten feet in diameter, clawing the smoke out of the air above them.

"Hold steady!" Simona shouts over the raging storm.

Nearby trees bow to the wind, forcing birds to take flight.

Terracotta shingles break from the rooftops. The lights strung in zigzag patterns above the town square detach. Even Teran's discarded bike whips off the ground. *Is this all from me?*

The entire island is now encircled in billowing black smoke. The pungent plumes expand as the outer circle of houses are ablaze. Waves of heat waft toward us on the salty breeze. Mom kneels by Jack, still trying to counter whatever spell they've placed on him. If anyone can heal him right now, it's Mom; that means it's up to me to keep them safe.

Andreas flings his floating hatchet toward us. It covers half the distance to us before I lift my hand. The hatchet abruptly stops in midair, then flies off to the side and joins the rest of the swirling debris. The marble fountain in the town square begins to crack at its base; it will break free any moment now. It's clear that Elspeth's magic is flowing into my own.

With the tornado bearing down on them, Andreas and Teran spin around and extend their arms, trying to counter my air spell. Their hair and clothing flap violently in the coiling storm.

Their counterspell hinders the flow of my magic, like a boulder obstructing the current of a river. But just as a river weaves its way around the boulder, the Nefari's combined strength can't stop the tornado from spinning.

Blue and Persephone cower against the iron fence, fighting against the suction of the storm that threatens to scoop them up as well.

"Enough of this!" Simona screams. "Now no one vill leave this place alive!"

She shifts her focus from Jack to the tornado. Suddenly, all the houses around us burst into flames. The tornado inhales the flames, becoming a swirling fiery pillar. The magic of her fire spell infects the tornado, like she's trying to take over the air spell from within. By now, the spell feels more like Elspeth's than mine.

The tornado's inferno shrinks under the weight of the three Nefari's counterspell. Andreas and Teran look wilted; their strength nearly spent. Soon the tornado collapses into little more than a black wisp of swirling smoke.

"Very powerful, indeed," Simona says. "But now vitness the true power of a Nefari."

Teran howls into the blackening sky of the stormy morning. Her hands slowly rise, palms towards the sky like she's casting a levitation spell, but nothing seems to happen.

Water ceases to gush from Jack's mouth, and he sucks in his

first breath of air in minutes. That breath immediately turns into an ear-shattering scream. I fall to the ground at his side as he writhes in pain. Blood vessels burst in his eyes one by one, changing the snowy white to scarlet. *Oh Brighid, they're trying to gouge out his eyes!*

Mom shouts behind me. "Get him out of here! Now!"

I can't. I won't leave you.

"Mom, you need to fight against their air spell!" I leap to my feet and immediately turn to face them.

Elspeth help me! We need to end this. Hurry!

"A little busy, you trull. They're trying to make your dear mother burst into flames and peel your beloved's skin from his bones. But if you wish me to let them, just say the word?" Elspeth's voice is aloof, as if this is all a big game to her.

No, I growl in response. I lift my hand, ready to use the same spell I used on in the Mather's home. I imagine a swift air current as powerful as a bullet ripping through Simona and her companions. *This is the only way. They mean to kill us. La Cae—*

My brain goes blank. My hand, steady only moments ago, now quivers. The corpses, half-burnt and grotesquely disfigured, emerge from the burning homes. Their movements are slow and limping; their heads flop from side to side like possessed marionettes. Their gray skin is charred black. As they trudge closer, the smell of human rot and burnt flesh becomes nearly unbearable. The nightmarish and haunting scene leaves my body numb.

This isn't real. I can't be here. I'm just a senior in high school. What is happening? "Eleanor, they aren't really back from the dead," Blue sends. *"She's using the air spell to move them as a distraction."*

Teran. That's what she was doing when she lifted her palms. The corpses have unhinged jaws, sunken-in cheeks, and gouged-out eye sockets, black as coal and void of life. They stumble closer and closer to where we're sitting. The Nefari laugh at the dread painted across our faces, their laughter muffled by their macabre rabbit masks. Simona lifts her arms forward, her hands encircled by sparking bolts of electricity.

Before Simona can cast her electric spell, water bursts from the air around her. The force of the water knocks her to the ground while extinguishing her electric current.

I can hear my mom gasp in exhaustion from the spell.

As if in retaliation, hundreds of Spiders crawl up my legs. I cry out as their bites puncture my skin. They scurry toward my nostrils, mouth, and ears, desperately scouring for a way in. I claw and bat at my face.

"It's only in your mind, Eleanor! Stop!" Blue shouts in my head. *"Look out!"*

Every kind of household blade from kitchen knives to pruning shears float out of the houses and swivel in our direction.

I raise my arms to form a barrier in the air around us. *La Caeli!*

Knives, scissors, and needles all drop to the ground within mere feet from us. Spiders scuttle into my ears and pierce their fangs through my skin.

"Eleanor, there are other spells! Use the mind spell, confound them!" Blue shouts in my head.

Small hairless ones scramble under my eyelids. From the corner of my eye, I see one dirty trowel zip past me. I whip my head around just in time to see it carve out a valley through Jack's exposed neck.

"Jack!" I fall to his side, determined to save him, but my skills are useless against such a traumatic neck wound.

Three knives leap off the ground and fling themselves at Andreas, burrowing into his chest; he falls back, gasping. *Elspeth?* While her spell continues on Andreas, the corpses also collapse to the ground. Even the spiders dissipate, like steam disappearing into thin air. I look over at Teran; she's writhing on the ground in agony. Elspeth didn't counter Teran's spell, she just countered Teran.

Jack's eyes are wide with confusion and fear. Within seconds, his skin is deathly pale. The color recedes from his lips. Scarlet blood pulses out of his wound. His frightened eyes flutter closed.

The torrent of water on Simona ceases, and Teran is freed from whatever curse had been torturing her. The psychotic Nefari scrambles to her leader's side. "Simona! Wake up!"

Mom replaces her hand firmly around Jack's neck. She whispers the air spell, and the blood seeping through her fingers reverses course, flowing back into his neck.

"How is this miscreant still alive?" Elspeth growls. Increasingly more cutlery fling themselves at Andreas, wiggling like a worm on his back trying to survive.

I snatch the broom off the ground and hand it to Mom. "Please, Mom, you can't wait for me. Get him to the mainland and save him. Please, hurry!" My mother doesn't argue, which should be a relief, but only accentuates just how near to death Jack really is. Using her magic, they both mount the broom. Jack is deadly still. My mother glances back behind her at me. "You'll be right behind me?" she says, more of a command than a question.

I nod urgently. "Yes, now go!"

On their broom mom and Jack fly high into the air, disappearing behind the clouds.

"You need to go now. I've done all I can from here. I feel myself fading…"

"Persephone! Blue! Let's go," I shout, snagging the other broom off the ground. The plastic bristles keep smoking, but soon drip with water that extinguishes the embers. *Thank you, Elspeth. "Don't thank me, just get me that candle."*

"Don't you dare!" Teran screams fumbling to her feet. "The Woods brat is already dead! You are too late for him!"

Just as I swing one leg over the shaft of the broom, I collapse to my knees. Images flood my brain, forcing me to see Jack tortured, screaming out in a hospital bed before succumbing to his injuries. I see a white sheet pulled over his lifeless body. A lonely hole in the ground with a casket being slowly lowered down into the earth. *It's not real.* I try to force my mind to concentrate on a counterspell to hers, but I keep seeing death. After Jack, I see my mother, stabbed, beaten, drowned, burned at the stake. So overpowered are my thoughts I can't even usher in the mind spell to break this.

A light breaks through the darkness of my mind. *"Eleanor, listen to my voice, hear me, hold onto my voice. This voice is your tether in the storm."*

My familiar's voice carries through the morbid images like a life raft tugging me to calmer shores. While Blue is saving my mind, Elspeth continues to protect my life. Teran deftly resists every knife and blade hurled at her, but suddenly she's engulfed in flames. She drops to her knees, screaming.

"Leave now, Eleanor. I can't hold her for long. It's not even real fire. I wasn't strong enough…" Elspeth's tired voice trails off.

"Get on," I order. Blue and Persephone leap onto the plastic bristles. Rain begins to fall, but I don't look back. It's probably just another spell. My feet lift off the ground; soon I'm high above the burning homes. Teran's screams have ceased; either the rain put out the flames, or the torture inflicted by the mind spell killed her. Either way, I don't look back.

A Spell to Brew Witch's Gin

(For those who wish to silence their visions and nightmares)

Yields 10 servings.

Ingredients:

4 Citrus Peels* (continuously peeled in a single strand)   Teaspoon of Ground Amethyst.
Pinch of Pink Himalayan Salt.
Two Sprigs of Juniper
4 Cups of Water Bathed Under a Waxing Moon
8 Cups of Water Bathed Under a Crescent Moon.

Instructions:

Combine ingredients in cauldron, boil for six minutes, then pour mixture into glass bottles.
Bless amethyst powder separattely. Add powder and Himalayan salt.
Upon serving, blow into the mixture, create a cyclone air spell to mix, then whisper incantation.
Place the cork, and do not remove
until salt has exploded and the liquid becomes still.

Incantation:

*"In silent moments, where scars have yet to fade
I offer light, to shine where shadows stayed.
Though haunting flashes linger in the mind's eye,
Healing through dreamless sleep is found by and by."*

**Orange peels work best*

CHAPTER SIXTEEN
A Flame, Black as Night

I fly higher and higher, penetrating deep within the wispy clouds. My invisibility spell isn't the best, so hopefully the clouds will conceal me. Still, I can't help but search the sky around me for any Nefari that might be on our trail.

The air is so cold and thin up here that my hands shiver against the broom. *Ne Feerah.* A blanket of warmth surrounds the cats and I, though I can't help but worry I'm using up too much magic in the process. Then again, being invisible isn't very helpful if you freeze to death. Blue doesn't chastise me for wasting magic on a fire spell, which I take to mean he agrees with me.

It's well into the night when we finally reach the mainland.

"Land on the top level of the parking garage, Eleanor. It should be empty at this hour," Blue instructs from the back of the broom where he's crouched tightly against Persephone.

"And Persephone is sure it's this hospital?" I call out. "Their connection wasn't good an hour ago." I swear I can feel Persephone's offended glare drilling into my back.

"Yes, she's certain, now land."

My broom wobbles between my legs as we descend in a widely arched spiral. When my feet are inches from the ground, both cats leap off and stretch.

Persephone takes a moment to groom herself. Her narrow eyes occasionally glance up at me trying to regain my balance on shaky legs. When the air spell completely ceases, I nearly collapse to the concrete under the overwhelming drag of gravity.

I discard the broom next to the elevators. "Stay outside, but keep near the ER," I tell the cats as I wait for the parking garage elevator. "I'll update you as soon as I can."

I pass nurses guzzling coffee with dark shadows blooming under their eyes. A nurse behind the front desk instructs me to follow the blue line to the intensive care unit where Jack is still in surgery.

Mom stands tall in the hallway, her platinum blonde hair shining like a halo against the fluorescent lights overhead. She's seeping a bag of tea into a Styrofoam cup; her face is calm and free of any blood and bruising.

As I rush to her side, I detect a subtle buzz of magic; she's using a glamour to mask her own grizzly appearance. The moment she sees me, Mom crushes me in her arms, her tea slopping over the side of the cup. Before the droplets can even hit the floor, they've managed to reverse course and slip back into her cup.

Mom holds me, her cheek pressed hard against my head. "You got away."

"Persephone told you I had," I say through her vice grip.

She sighs, breathing me in. "I didn't quite believe it. But you're safe, you're here." She finally releases me and cups the side of my face with her free hand.

"How is he?" I ask.

Mom ushers us to a few open seats below a television bolted to the wall. The TV is useless; the few people actually in the waiting room right now are hunched over with eyes fixed on their phones. If there's any place you want to escape reality, it's an ICU waiting room.

Mom places her tea beside months-old magazines speckled with coffee stains. "He was alive when we landed."

I suck in a horrified breath. *What does she mean, "when we landed"? How long ago did they land? What's happened since?* Before I can say anything, she places her hand on my thigh and continues.

"His carotid was severed clean through; he lost a lot of blood. I made certain my air spell stayed in place until the surgeon clamped the artery and inserted the bypass. Since then, all I could do was wait. He's received several transfusions so far, and they're performing the reanastomosis now."

Mom's hands tremble in her lap. For a split second, her entire glamour blinks, exposing bloody hands and a shirt soaked through with crimson. Mom blinks, and the glamour is back in place.

"Reanastomosis," I repeat. "That's when… when they connect the two ends of a severed tube, right?" Reciting medical facts is the only way I can think of to keep the image of Jack on the surgical table out of my head.

Mom nods. I know she remembers the nights she would quiz me on medical terminology with the same fondness that I do. She manages to let a single ray of pride shine through a smile that's otherwise heavy with fear and pain.

"How did he survive the flight here with a… with his injury?"

I ask, not able to actually describe the injury aloud.

She shakes her head, mystified. "I had to keep us invisible while flying as fast as possible, all the while having enough magic left to hold the artery in place. I truly don't know how we did it. But thank Brighid, because against all odds, Jack's going to live."

Slithering out from the back of my mind is a dark, seductive chuckle. *"Let's not thank that rank cow just yet. Perhaps you should put your gratitude where it's deserved, with me."*

You helped him?

"And he would be dead right now if I hadn't. Your mother was too weak, too preoccupied about your safety. I'm the only reason he arrived with a pulse."

The revelation leaves me dumbstruck. *She really wants this candle. What infernal power could it possess that she would save my soulmate to get it?* I made a deal with the devil, and there's no backing out now.

Thank you, Elspeth.

"He's not out of the woods yet. You and that 'mother' of yours must find a way into that boy's room. He needs your blood."

Mom clears her throat, gazing down into her half-empty teacup she's clutching once more. "That Nefari, Teran…what did you…how…what happened?"

What do you mean "give him my blood"? I don't even know if we are the same blood type.

"Ugh, 'blood type'. Your pathetic world believes itself to be so learned, but you know nothing, my little dark one. You have witches blood streaming in your veins. Your simplistic classification of blood matters not when dealing with your soulmate. Your blood can heal him faster than anyone else's."

I nibble on my lip. *If you're lying to me, or even just mistaken, he could die. He would suffer organ failure, severe hemolysis—*

"Eleanor?" Mom says, reaching over to give my hand a gentle squeeze. *"Why would I work so hard to save the little mongrel only to kill him before I've obtained my prize? Think, child. I need him healed swiftly so that you will swiftly fetch me my candle. Now hurry, you can leave tonight."*

"Sweetheart, whatever you had to do, it's okay," Mom whispers. "It doesn't make you a bad witch, or a bad person. You had to defend yourself. Our laws allow for such things against Nefari."

I shake my head. "I used a little defensive magic, but I'm not really sure what happened. I just got on my broom and fled." I turn in my seat to face her. "Mom, we need to…" I pause to glance around the room. The four people scattered about the waiting room are all slumped over in their chairs either asleep or on their phones, while the nurse at the desk is clicking away on her computer. "I need to give Jack my blood."

Mom frowns at me. "Ella love, that could be incredibly dangerous. We don't know if you're even a matching blood type."

I shake my head, still glancing about to make sure we don't have any eavesdroppers. "Elspeth told me soulmates can heal each other with their blood. She said he'll be well enough to travel. Tonight."

Mom's eyebrows lift high on her forehead. "In all my research, I have never read anything like that. Not in a single healing grimoire. If that were true, don't you think someone, somewhere would have noticed and written it down?"

I shrug, exasperated. "I don't know. Perhaps no one in our line has ever done this. But Elspeth is certain."

Mom narrows her eyes on me. "Why? What's in it for her?"

Jack doesn't have time for this. "I said I'd get her a candle the aunts have in the room next to mine. I believe it's the same one Grandma Colleen has in Ireland."

"Eleanor!" Mom hisses. She grips my hand a little too tight. "You promised you'd get that for her?!" she asks through clenched teeth.

Two nurses come through the automatic glass doors. For a second, I'm back in the waiting room in Salem, seeing Mr. and Mrs. Caldwell come out to tell us Trixie is dead. I fear that's what the nurses are here to tell us, but instead they stop by the desk to speak with the nurse. A doctor exits behind the nurses in the green scrubs of a surgeon, but he approaches an elderly woman a row behind us asleep in her chair.

I'm not losing Jack.

"Mom," I dip my head close to hers. "I had no choice. We weren't getting off that island alive. She helped you and Jack get here."

Her mouth twitches as she finds her words. "You should have talked to me first."

"When?! There was literally no time!" My retort is louder than I intended.

A nurse glances over at us.

Mom leans in closer. "I don't even know what these candles are for, but whatever they are, they can't be good, especially if Elspeth wants one."

"Agreed. But I made a promise, and if I don't keep it, things could get really bad. But remember, she's in Purgatory; her power is only so strong.

Whatever she has planned, we can fight back. But Mom, we need to go to Jack. Now."

Mom nods. "Okay, follow me." Mom rises from her chair and

leads me into the bathroom. Once she ensures we're alone, her glamour disappears. In the blink of an eye, we're both invisible. "Now wait here while I fetch a transfusion kit."

After she returns with the necessary equipment, which she's also turned invisible, we wait next to the automated doors hoping to tailgate behind someone with a security badge. Once inside, we make our way to Jack in the post-op recovery room.

I nearly faint at the sight of Jack unconscious on a gurney. He has tubes looping under his nose and around his ears. His neck is completely wrapped in bandages; I shudder to think what his neck looks like underneath it all. IV bags dangle from metal poles at the side of his bed. A faint overhead light glows above him. My heavy breathing is deafening in the quiet room, where only beeping monitors punctuate the silence.

"Oh, Jack," I cry. I want to reach out and take his hand, but both his hands are taped with needles securely injected in his veins.

Mom drags a chair for me to the side of his bed and immediately goes to work securing a tourniquet around my arm. My eyes stay glued on Jack. His skin is the color of snow, and his lips are nearly the same shade. He's a ghost, a phantom resting beneath blue hospital sheets. His frail chest struggles to lift with each breath.

"Okay, here comes a pinch," Mom says, returning to her old nursing habits. With the needle in place, blood instantly fills the long tube connected to one of Jack's needles. Mom detaches one of his IV bags.

"Lean back and relax," she instructs. "And keep pumping your fist."

Once I close my eyes, my brain finally registers just how battered my body is. My jaw clicks as I give into a full yawn and lean my head back. "Ell, I need you to stay awake," Mom tells me.

"I am, Mom. I'm just resting my eyes…"

Mom snorts. "Yeah, that's what your father always said before one of his infamous 'coma naps'."

In spite of everything, the memory of Dad makes me smile.

"Fine," I say with a sigh. I open my eyes, but everything's wrong. No longer am I slumped in a hospital chair connected to Jack through a transfusion tube. Now I'm in a glossy black void, standing under a spotlight. I instinctively fling my arms out, ready for some sort of ambush.

"Hello?" I shout out. My pounding heart aches from suffering one adrenaline rush after another, my body desperate for rest.

High heels click against the glossy onyx floor. I smell

wildflowers, sea grass… and sulfur.

"When I was your age, only the nobility wore shoes with high heels.

Nothing like the delicious spikes you can procure today…"

I whip around toward the voice. Out from the shadows struts Elspeth in her usual black chiffon toga-style dress. Her coppery locks are piled high on her head like a Greek goddess. Her features, severe carved angles out of alabaster. She stops a mere foot in front of me; her dark opal eyes narrow on me. Even Medusa would wilt under Elspeth's gaze.

"Is this Purgatory?" I ask.

Elspeth shakes her head. "Your magic was giving you a vision, I interceded. You need to retrieve my candle now. I've waited far too long as it is." My blood boils with aggravation. "I told you I'd get you your stupid candle. Jack is receiving my blood right now; I can't pump it out any faster." More clacking around us, like hooves on marble. The black goat with pill-shaped eyes and curled horns steps forward, gazing at us both. Elspeth stares back at him with furrowed brow and bated breath.

"Okay seriously, what's with the goat? He appeared in my visions last year too. He never says anything, or even does anything for that matter. Doesn't help me or hinder me. Actually, I take that back, he did ram into me once." I instinctively take a nervous step back from him.

Ignore him. We'll talk here. " Elspeth sends telepathically.

Wait, do you know him? The aroma of brimstone has gotten stronger. I gag and wave my hand in front of my nose hoping to waft the smell of rotten eggs away. It doesn't help.

"It matters not. Now, about my candle."

I exhale a growl. *There is literally nothing I can do right now, I told you. Once Jack is awake and is well enough to travel, we'll go back to Salem and I'll get you your freaking candle. It's not a big deal, you can wait."*

Elspeth looks at me sideways. *"Come, my dear… don't feign ignorance with me.*

Our little Pyewacket has surely divulged the candle's secrets…"

My ears perk at the mention of our shared familiar. "Blue knows what the candle is?"

The black-bearded goat takes a step forward and bleats at us.

"Foul beast," Elspeth growls. She crosses her arms and shivers, eyeing the goat out of the corner of her eye.

I frown. "Elspeth, does Blue know what this candle is, why it's so valuable?"

Her obsidian stare slips from the goat back to me. She raises a thin red brow. "He truly hasn't told you?" Elspeth's dark lips curl up in a devious smile making her cat eyes even thinner. "Cat beag glic a' fàgail ar beag anns an dorchadas," she mumbles to herself.

I grit my teeth. "No. So why don't you enlighten me. Why do you want this candle so badly?"

Elspeth circles me with her chin held high, a cat toying with its prey. "Why do you trust little Pyewacket? He will always be my familiar before yours; that's why the ocean itself can't conceal the secrets he keeps from you."

A battering ram of betrayal hits me square in the chest. *Is Blue really keeping things from me?*

Elspeth halts directly behind me. She leans forward, her lips brushing against my hair. "It's me you should trust, child. Not him. I could even keep your magic from attacking you," she resumes her slow, theatrical circle around me, "when you feel… at your happiest."

My head snaps up. "You can do that?" I know she's manipulating me, and it's working.

She's standing directly in front of me now. "Oh, yes. Now that I have a stronger footing in your world, we are more connected than before. I could lessen that agony you feel. Perhaps even take it away entirely."

She's lying. She has to be.

"Oh, do I? If you'd like my help, I'd be willing…"

"But only for a price," I retort.

She shrugs her bony shoulders. "Perchance. Nothing is totally free. Although, do you truly *want* to be cured? Blinding pain and exquisite pleasure are so closely tied together, perhaps you'd rather indulge…"

What is wrong with this woman? "*You know I can hear you…*"

I shake my head, needing to get back to the subject. "Of course, I want to be cured, but I need to know the cost. Why do you want this candle so badly?" *And why didn't Blue tell me sooner?*

"I see no harm in telling you. The candle is a Black Flame Candle. It burns with a flame darker than midnight. It was created with Brighid's blood combined with dust from the nineth circle, possessing the extremes of light and dark magic. There were originally six in existence. Now we're down to just two…" She wiggles two fingers at me.

I manage to keep my face impassive despite the goosebumps rippling across my skin. An intuitive pinch in the back of my mind tells me I'm the reason fate delivered these rare candles into my family's hands.

"Not quite. I'm the reason, child. You just happen to be connected to me."

I hate that she can hear my thoughts.

So, you light this candle, it emits a black flame, then what? What is it supposed to do?

Elspeth turns away, but her thoughts are as plain to me as my thoughts are to her. For a split second, there's a crack in her impervious marble, her face is awash in misery.

She has no idea what the candle does.

In a blink, her face is back to its cool, collected mask.

"Why do you want it?" I ask aloud, despite the eavesdropping goat nearby. Ice drips from Elspeth's loathsome stare. She curls her thin top lip back in a sneer. "Its value is beyond measure. And I'm not the only one looking for it."

"So, what? You're going to barter with it?" I question.

Elspeth marches closer and seizes my shoulders, squeezing them without mercy. Her nails dig painfully into my flesh, and the more I wince, the more she relishes it. "What *I* do with *my* candle is *my* business. Now get back to Salem and fetch me my candle."

I blink my eyes and I'm back in the hospital.

Jack weakly opens his eyes. Color has returned to his chiseled cheeks; his full lips crinkle into a sad half-smile. "You're okay," he mutters. Relief floods his eyes.

I rise to my feet and clasp his hand. "Of course, I'm fine. You're the one who almost died." *Again.*

"I was so scared something was going to happen to you and I was powerless to stop it."

I rest my forehead against his, our noses brush together. "I'm okay. We're okay. I love you."

"I love you too," he whispers.

Behind my eyelids, I see the demonic-looking rabbit masks, the animated bodies without eyes or teeth. My mother's dismembered head. The blood. The havoc. The Nefari. It all flashes through my mind in seconds. My trembling hands cling desperately to Jack's.

CHAPTER SEVENTEEN
Fate

Jack called his mom from the rental car about the desecration of their summer home. Authorities were already alerted to the mass murder and arson. Palms were greased, statements were given, and swift exits were made. Generous settlements to the victim's families were discussed with Jack cutting in every so often, snapping at his mother with "that's not good enough" and "we can do better" and "give them more."

By the end of the thirteen-hour car ride, Jack has set up multiple scholarships and trust funds in names of various staff members. He even made a note in his calendar to visit each of the soon-to-be-grieving families. Throughout his many phone calls, I'd occasionally reach over and give his knee a supportive squeeze.

Jack finally slips his phone into his pocket and rests his head back, his face drooping with exhaustion. I run a finger down his neck, tracing the thin whisper of a scar. His neck is fully healed, and the white line is nearly invisible now. His body is covered in nearly invisible scars, his soul too. *Oh, Jack.* We keep puddle jumping from one disaster to the next.

"You'll stay with us, Jack," mom says as we enter the city limits of Salem. "I've never healed someone with soulmate blood before, I don't know how you'll react."

"You wish to keep me under observation?" Jack replies with his eyes still closed.

"Exactly," mom says, glancing back at us from the rearview mirror. "You'll get no objection from me." He slides his hand across the seat onto mine.

Blue glances back at me from the front seat he shares with Persephone.

"He won't be sleeping in your bedroom, mind you."

I don't respond. I have nothing to say to him right now. I just stare out the window naming every mundane thing we pass, hoping it will block him from reading my mind. *"Eleanor?"*

House. Tree. Tree. House. Dog walker. Powerline. Tree.

Darkness drapes over the rental car as we drive through the tunnel of trees toward the house. I nestle into Jack and place my head on his shoulder. The moment my head rests against him, I feel that familiar hum, the soft pulse of contentment. It's the feeling of home. More than any dwelling or address, state or neighborhood, when I'm with Jack, I'm whole. This is home.

"Should be rather quiet. Maggie and my sisters shouldn't be home until tomorrow," Mom says, clearing her throat. "Jack, I'll set you up in Marie's sewing room. It has one of the softest beds in the house."

Jack lifts his head, smiling. "That works perfectly, thank you."

Elspeth's voice plays from memory in the back of my mind. *"I can fix your pain…"*

Blue levels his gaze at me. *"You've been chatting with Elspeth?"*

I guess I couldn't hide my thoughts forever. *Yeah, Blue. At least, she's more forthcoming than you.*

"Have you completely lost your senses?"

You knew all about the Black Flame Candle and didn't tell me a thing. You're always keeping me in the dark. I'm sick of it.

Blue props himself up with his paws on the center console and cranes his head around the seat. *"What did she tell you?"*

Hardly anything, which is still more than you.

Mom pulls to a dusty stop on the gravel driveway. The house glows pearlescent in the milky twilight under the cotton-candy sky of the setting sun. The leaves of the surrounding trees have begun their autumn change from the emerald green to brilliant gold. We trudge up the veranda stairs, the wear of the weekend magnifying the closer we get to our warm beds.

Mom reaches for her keys only to remember her purse and belongings are still on the island. She waves her hand at the lock, then hesitates. "The door was unlocked. Everyone get behind me," she orders, even though we're already huddled behind her.

The door creaks open. Two cats skitter down the darkened hall. "Mom?" I whisper nervously.

"Sally! You're cheating!" Maggie shouts from down the hall in the dining room.

Mom flicks on the entryway light. "What on earth are they doing home?" She marches down the hall, her shoulders tense. No one jumps when she storms into the room. "Excuse me, what happened with New York?"

Sally, Marie, Abe, and Maggie are seated around the dining room table with playing cards and chips strewn in front of them.

Abe leaps to his feet and nods before taking his seat again. Sally giggles behind her deck of cards.

"It was lovely, Helly, but we had to cut the trip short because of the cats," Marie explains. She hiccups and pushes away her empty wine glass before continuing. "But rest assured, we never let our guard down. We kept this place on lock down."

"What are you talking about? The front door was unlocked!" Mom balks, pointing down the hall.

"Oh," Marie says sheepishly, while she straightens up in her seat trying to gain composure.

"I believe this is a full house! Pay up witches!" Sally lays her cards down face up. She glances up at us, then does a double take.

I suddenly realize our glamours have all worn off. My mother has a fat lip, tangled hair, and torn, blood-stained clothes. The entirety of Jack's shirt is stained a rusty red.

"Sister," Sally gapes, "what happened?"

"Mom?" Maggie says wide-eyed.

"There were Nefari on the island," Mom mutters, folding her arms across her chest. "Jack actually got the worst of it."

Everyone cranes around Mom to see Jack. "Are you sure?" Sally mutters.

"Yeah…he looks…fine," Marie states, probably more flirtatiously than she meant to.

Jack blushes.

Maggie scrambles to her feet, knocking her chair to the floor in the process, and wraps her arms around our mother's torso, crushing her in a hug.

Mom kisses the top of her copper head. "I'm okay, hon. We're all okay.

Now, what's this about the cats?"

Sally rights her shoulders, collecting the chips in the center. "Pyre and Priss stayed behind to watch over the house…what the hell? Who put Canadian change in here?"

"That would be you, sister. From last time we played. I said we shouldn't use money, because it's illegal and suggested using fake money."

"Oooh yeah! So I suggested Canadian money," Sally recalls.

"It's not technically illegal," Abe joins in. "Penal Code Chapter 23k governs gaming rights and regulations. It's allowed as long as—"

"For the love of Brighid, what about the cats?" Mom tries again. Maggie releases Mom and sits back down in her chair.

"They detected movement inside the spare room in the tower. They thought it best we come back, but we didn't notice anything amiss," Sally says. "In fact, it's been fairly quiet. Other than Maggie over here totally losing her shirt at Texas Hold 'em." Sally laughs, then adds, "Don't worry, Helly. I didn't mean that literally."

My heart sinks. I almost allowed myself to forget about that damn room and Elspeth's stupid candle. My eyes lift to the ceiling. *No rest for the Nefari.*

Mom rubs her temples, wavering ever so slightly. "Okay, I'm going to take a shower. Please make Jack feel at home and fix up Marie's sewing room for him. He'll be staying the rest of the weekend."

"Jack looks positively knackered; perhaps he would like to freshen up as well," Blue sends, uncharacteristically warm with concern.

I snap out of my daze. "Ah, yes. Sally, do you have any clothes left over from old boyfriends?" I ask.

Sally snorts. "What kind of measurements are we working with here?"

Abe fixes his eyes on the table.

I nod to Jack at my side. "Just something that'll fit him."

Jack shifts his weight awkwardly beside me.

Sally grins. "I have something that'll look marvelous on him," she says wickedly.

Abe clears his throat, staring at his cards.

"Hey, it doesn't matter who I've been with, it only matters who I end up with," she chimes, pushing up from the table.

"I'll come help, maybe we can even throw some stuff out," Abe suggests, following her out of the room.

Marie scurries off to prepare her sewing room for Jack while Sally fetches him some clothes. When she hollers from down the hall asking which quilt he would prefer, Jack plants a soft kiss at my temple before ambling after her.

Maggie offers to dish me up some takeout from the New England Soup Factory down on Washington Street. I accept with just a nod, and my sister eyes me warily while filling a bowl.

"What is it?" I ask, scooping up a mouthful of clam chowder.

Maggie raises a brow sitting across from me. "You look like serious hell. I mean, did you see Mom?"

A flash of her severed head forces its way into my mind's eye. My spoon rattles against the side of my bowl. A lump forms in my throat. "Yeah, trust me, I was there."

My sister crosses her arms over her chest and leans back in her seat with a stony look on her sun-kissed, freckled face. "What happened? You know Mom isn't going to tell me. She still thinks I'm a baby."

Being a baby's a lot easier than knowing the truth. I scoop another bite into my mouth.

"Uh, Marie, that's plenty of pillows, trust me," we hear Jack insist politely from the sewing room. "Thank you, though."

"Oh, you can never have too much! See, this one is shaped like a cat. See the button nose?" Marie coos to him.

Maggie pulls her chair closer. "Seriously, spill it. Why does mom look like she went 12 rounds with Mike Tyson?"

My stomach clenches thinking of that Nefari, writhing on the floor with his kneecaps cracked in half. I push the bowl away. *Please ask me anything else, Maggie. The truth is just too much.*

"Now isn't that interesting?" Blue sends, brushing up against my leg under the table. *"My young ward finds it difficult to be completely forthcoming with her youngest sibling. It's almost as if she is better served when discretion is used…"*

I scowl at him through the table. "We were attacked," I begin, determined not to give Blue the satisfaction. "Nefari showed up looking for vengeance against The Noble Hunters or something. They tried to kill Jack; they almost did. They hurt mom too, but we were able to get away."

I see in my mind's eye his neck sliced open, the scarlet wave drenching his shirt while his pallor turns to alabaster, Mom trying to hold back the flood while he slips away with every weakening pulse. I let my head collapse into my hands.

"Are you okay? You don't look too great either," Maggie asks, patting my shoulder.

My breathing grows heavier. Maggie wraps her arms around me, and I rest my head on her shoulder. Her sweatshirt caresses my cheek with soft cotton and the aroma of roses and bergamot.

"You smell nice," I compliment.

"Yeah, no offense, but you don't. Did you throw up?" Maggie drops her arms to the side and scrunches her nose.

I sniff my shirt and wince at the acrid stench of old bile. "Uh, yeah. Seasick."

Maggie drowns out my scent by inhaling the fragrance on her wrist. "Coach perfume. A gift from Sally to make up for canceling the trip. Stupid room. New York would have been fun."

My stomach drops. The second tower room. Again, I almost allowed myself to forget.

"Tick tock, Daughter. My candle is waiting…"

I straighten up. "Yeah, what was that all about?"

Sally comes thundering down the stairs while Abe trudges behind. "Jackie boy, I've got your pajamas! I even have brand new briefs, never been opened."

"You still haven't explained what you were doing with new, unopened boxer briefs," Abe complains.

Sally stops at the mouth of the dining room, placing her hands on her minuscule waist. "I told you it was for role playing and I dumped the bastard before we ever got that far. I thought that'd make you happy." She rolls her eyes and continues to the sewing room.

Abe retakes his seat at the table with a huff.

Maggie glances back at me and shrugs. "I'm not sure. Something about that closet next to your room or something. Miss Priss and Pyre suspected someone had broken in. Abe went first, but didn't detect a break in. Then Sally went upstairs and checked and it looked totally normal." She picks her four cards back up. "Okay, we are so finishing this round," she states, moving her chips about.

Abe chuckles. "You don't want to let the other players know you have a good hand," he chides playfully.

She shrugs one shoulder. "Maybe I'm bluffing."

Perhaps someone did break in, and they took the candle. Would my aunts know to look for it? Do they even know they have it?

"Yes, they are aware." Blue leaps on the table next to me.

Oh, are you going to tell me the truth now? You sure you don't want to leave me in the dark still? I rise from the table just as Sally and Marie return from the sewing room as Jack steps into the bathroom.

"Jack's taking a shower," Sally says with an eyebrow wiggle.

"Sal," Abe scolds.

Sally shakes her head at him. "Oh stop, he's far too young for me. I was thinking about Eleanor over there. Might as well strike while the iron's naked," she teases.

I blush from the crown of my head to the very end of my toes. "I'm going to get cleaned up myself." I dash from the room before Sally can make more crass suggestions that I secretly wanted to oblige.

Mom is already out of the shower and tucked away in her bedroom. Blue follows me into the bathroom, then turns around as I drop my clothes to the floor. The bathroom is still steamy from my mom's shower.

I promised Elspeth I would retrieve the candle for her. I had no choice, so there's literally no point in lecturing me. She was getting that candle one way or another, and at least this way she helped us escape. So, your turn. Tell me everything.

Blue releases a resigned sigh. *"Those magics are very, very old. Before recorded time, when the first witches were made."*

I use my nails on my scalp as I lather the rosemary and tea tree shampoo. "Go on," I urge.

"Some claim it was made by Mother Brighid herself, others say the devil. There were originally six, now only two remain. Both are kept in your family."

Did you do that? I ask while scrubbing away a veil of grime and gore.

"I could not have organized such a feat, though I appreciate your confidence. I suppose we must recognize the hand of fate that the candle was ultimately unearthed here in Salem, on your aunts' property no less. Though it's truly puzzling how your grandmother in Ireland came into possession of a Black Flame Candle. For that I cannot account."

I shut off the water and wrap myself in a towel. *Do you know what the candle does?* I step out of the shower, roughly tug on my robe, and tiptoe up to my bedroom.

Blue follows. *"There are rumors but no confirmation."*

But there were once six and now only two. That means four of them have been used, right? So how does no one know? Did no one write it down? I pull on some yoga pants and a lose tee.

Blue leaps up onto the trunk at the foot of my bed. *"Everyone who used one died shortly thereafter. They never had a chance to tell anyone what they saw."*

I sit at my desk and run a brush through my hair. "Then how does anyone even know it has a black flame?"

"There is but a single witness. A witch named Mary Hall who found her lifeless child in front of the lit candle; its flame was like a glistening onyx stone."

Then what happened?

"The candle melted down, whatever power it possessed was concluded."

I frown staring down at my lap. "So…it kills people?" *That seems rather… "Facile?"*

I turn and face Blue. "Yeah. This weekend proved you don't need some stupid candle to kill people with magic. We have plenty of spells for that."

Blue runs his left paw over his ear. *"I don't believe death is its intended consequence. There is darker magic at work, but as for what that magic is, we have only rumor and hearsay.*"

"You know what they say about rumors, there's always a seed of truth. What are the rumors?" I glance at the wall separating my room from the spare. In some dark corner of that room hides Elspeth's coveted candle.

Blue sighs another defeated exhale. "*The most common rumor is that it opens the gates between realms. For example, a gate between the Nineth Circle and Earth through which the Devil can better wage his war against the Sons and Daughters of God. Witches be damned.*"

The hair on the nape of my neck stands on end. "What else?" I ask while my skin breaks out in goosebumps.

"*Another rumor is that it delivers a prophesy. You light the candle, and it'll reveal divination for the end of times…or how to bring it about, and so forth…*"

My stomach clenches, stirring up the measly amount of soup I consumed. School, college, SAT scores, they're all drifting further and further out of reach. None of them seem all that important anymore.

"I can't get Elspeth that candle," I mutter.

When I had made my deal, I had no idea the kind of power it wielded. I didn't even think something like that could exist. Where does this fit in the five branches? How is any of this possible?

"Like hell you're not getting me my candle." Elspeth materializes next to the pentagon window.

Blue arches his back and hisses at her.

"Enough, Pyewacket, you fiendish turncoat!" She flicks her hand and Blue tumbles backward onto the floor.

I drop to my knees and scoop him up. My hands tremble. *I had no choice, right? Jack and my mom were going to die. I had already promised her I'd retrieve that candle.* Elspeth laughs, a cruel, malevolent sound devoid of genuine happiness.

Her eyes sparkle with sadistic wrath. "I hope a bone or two splintered. Perhaps I shall reach through his skin and feel?" she glares over at us.

"*I'm fine, child,*" Blue insists to me. He leaps out of my arms and stares at Elspeth like they were eye to eye. "*Do you really want to risk being thrust into Judecca? You may very well see yourself trapped in a far more* nefarious *prison than Purgatory.*" Blue's voice is dripping with venom. "*Perhaps Beelzebub and Leviathan could use the company. I do recall a ménage à trois of the damned is their specialty. You might just enjoy flesh hooks and fire. Remember the tower? That pain? That torture? It'll be nothing compared to what you'll endure in Judecca, where a mere second lasts a century. "*

Elspeth bites her thumb at him with a curly smile. My eyes dart between the two of them, feeling like I'm missing part of the script.

"Thou perjured cur," she hisses through a tight smile. "If you truly believed I'd be ensnared in that infernal ice, you would have lit that flame centuries ago."

Blue springs onto my bed and settles next to my pillows. "*If you recall, my spirit only returned to this realm a mere seventeen years ago. Rest assured, had I not been lurking in Purgatory beside you, I would have ignited that damn flame eons ago. But alas, your evil deeds trapped us both, and as you very well know a familiar cannot harm their ward. So, it was with the utmost joy that I was reassigned. All wagers are forfeit, my dear.*"

Elspeth folds her thin pale arms over her small chest. "Pathetic. I decry your bluff. If a Black Flame Candle could imprison me, you would not have waited these seventeen years to do it. You would not have wasted seventeen minutes. Perhaps when your new assignment was born… No…" She turns on her heel to face us both. "No, I believe you lean toward it being a key rather than a lock. But your opinion is of no consequence. Eleanor swore she would fetch me the candle, and fetch it she must." Her dark ebony eyes flick to me. "Get me that candle or be assured there will be hell to pay…"

Blue rises, his black wiry hair stands on end.

There's a knock at the door, shattering the icy tension. "Eleanor?" Jack calls. "Eleanor is something wrong?"

The glass knob turns and the door swings open. Jack gazes over at me, his perfect emerald eyes soft and full of concern. He opens his mouth to speak, but it closes when he notices Elspeth glowering next to my window seat. "Pardon, I didn't mean to interrupt…"

"*Oh, my Brighid. He can see her; she's getting more powerful. "*

I have to get her that candle, Blue. We can figure out how to keep her from using it later. We couldn't have escaped the island without her. What if she turns that power on my family?

Blue shakes his head at me. "*You gave her access to your magic. That wore her out, if you recall, trying to straddle two worlds. "*

"Hello," Jack greets Elspeth formally. He pulls his shoulders back and tugs at the hem of his monster truck rally shirt with cut off sleeves. Somehow, even in his loose forest green flannel pajama bottoms and seedy top, he still looks regal. His golden hair, still wet from the shower, glistens against my ceiling light. His eyes search her, like he knows her in some way, a bizarre recognition without explanation.

Elspeth glances at me then back at Jack. Her thin lips curl. "Tha e na thoileachas coinneachadh ribh," she says in a heavy Scottish brogue.

Jack's brow momentarily knits, then he puts on a polite smile. Keeping his eyes on Elspeth, he crosses the room and places one hand on the small of my back. He keeps one foot forward, prepared to take the brunt of any blow that could be sent my way.

Elspeth plops down on my window seat and crosses one leg over the other. She leans forward, placing her elbow on her knee and resting her head in her palm. Her long thin fingers drum against her cheek. "Most fascinating, indeed. Your soulmate perceives me; I reckon that illustrates my point far better than I ever could." She stretches and wiggles her fingers, trying to demonstrate she's fuller bodied than before, thus gaining more access to my world and power. Her eyes glide up and down him with indelible delight. "Fine figure, that Mr. Jack Woods. Much better than his great, great, great grandda. It'd be a true shame for anything to happen to him..." Her stare drills into me. "Get. Me. My. Candle. Now." In a breath, she vanishes.

Jack doesn't startle. It's as if he's more accustomed to witches evaporating than I am.

My eyes stay glued to the spot where she vanished. Try as I might, there is no fighting this. The hand of fate moves like a shadow in the dark; I never had a choice. One way or another, she was always getting that candle, and I was always going to be the one to hand it over.

CHAPTER EIGHTEEN
Shallow Grave

I rest my head on Jack's chest, his arms wrapped firmly around me. His shirt smells like the tea tree oil laundry detergent that Marie brews.

Blue?

"Yes, yes, we have a lot to discuss…"

I have no choice. I need to get her that candle.

"We could be dancing on our own graves right now." Blue saunters to the door without a backward glance.

"Was it that Elspeth you've told me about?" Jack asks.

I nod. My hands glide up the muscles of his back and rest on his broad shoulders.

"Did she actually disappear or was that an illusion from the mind spell?" Jack asks like a seasoned witch enthusiast.

"She's just a spirit, so she can pretty much come and go as she pleases." I step out of his embrace and take hold of his hand, pulling us both toward the door. We pass the spare room before trudging down the first set of stairs.

I have to look away. When we reach the landing, Jack tugs on my hand. He's stopped next to the round table with a small pumpkin and a vase with cotton branches in the center. I swivel to face him.

Jack frowns. "What is it?" I ask.

Jack releases a big gust of air through his nose. "I don't know… it's like…someone has turned gravity on full blast. It's strange, like I'm being pulled from the inside out."

My eyes dart about in the dark. *Blue! Blue! Where are you?*

Blue comes creeping down the tower steps. He was in the room next to mine.

Blue stops at our feet and peers up at us.

Blue, I think Elspeth is trying to harm Jack somehow.

Blue closes his eyes. *"I believe you're right; bring him downstairs with your aunts.*

They can protect him. It's time you and I face this deal you've made."

I grip Jack's hand, and we resume walking. "Are you any

good at poker?"

He chuckles. "I don't know why, but people always assume I am. I'm actually quite terrible. I can't bluff a bad hand to save my life."

I grin. "Well, don't start betting away your college fund, then."

The needle on the record player drops and a crackling record plays a bellowing saxophone. A jaunty piano soon joins in. It's "Hush Hush Hush" by Henry Hall echoing from the living room.

"This isn't poker music, Marie," Sally complains.

When we stroll into the dining room, Mom is at the end of the table talking quietly on her cell phone. A feather of steam rises from her white and violet patterned teacup.

Maggie studies her cards, as does Abe sitting across from her. Marie frowns at her cards, which quickly morphs into pouting. Her free hand scurries across the table toward the plate of cookies sitting on a lace doily.

Sally's eyes snap up to us hovering in the doorway. A wide grin fills her face. "Jackie boy, you look delicious! Take a seat, I'll deal you both in." Jack takes a free chair next to Maggie and peers up at me.

I shake my head. "I'll be right back, there's something I need to do real quick."

Mom hurries to the kitchen still on the phone, her free hand pressed against her other ear.

"Sally, Marie, could I have a word?" I ask. They both look up at me and I nod toward the hall. Sally rises to her feet, followed by a yawning Marie.

"What's up, toots?" Sally asks, gripping her hips.

I nibble on my lip, wishing I had rehearsed what to say. "Um, you know the room next to mine?" I ask.

Sally raises a skinny, penciled on brow. "Yes?"

Marie cocks her head to the side, her eyes searching mine.

My stomach knots. "It's locked, and I need to get in there. Do you have a key?"

Without skipping a beat, Sally turns to the bookshelf behind her and lifts the glass of a bell jar. Inside is fuzzy green moss, crystal, and a butterfly coated in wax poised on top. My aunt runs her skinny fingers under the greenery. "Ah, there we go," she says, retrieving a long brass skeleton key. She turns back to me. "This opens every door in the house."

"But why do you want to go in there, sweetie?" Marie questions, waving back Sally's outstretched hand.

I'm so freaking close. Blue, what can I possibly say?

"Not the truth." Blue tiptoes down the stairs.

"I need a wolfsbane candle. When Zoey was here, she sensed there was a stockpile of them in there."

Sally shrugs. "Who knows, it's been forever since we've cleaned that place out. I'm almost tempted to go in there myself," Sally muses.

"Sally," Jack calls, "I believe it is your turn. Do you fold?" he asks. He leans back in the dining room chair and gives me a quick wink.

Does he sense I need her to stay?

Sally laughs a devilish chuckle before tossing me the key. "Hell no, I'm not folding. I call." She takes her seat and tosses a few chips into the pot.

Marie stares at me, her brow knitted in a deep frown. "Would you like my help finding them, dearie?"

I shake my head. "No, but I'm worried I won't be able to get in unless you undo your spell."

Her frown deepens, and she tucks her chin toward her chest. "Spell?"

"Don't you have a spell keeping Nefari out?"

She chuckles humorlessly. "No. Why would we?"

"I thought… never mind. I'll get the candle and join you all in a moment." I head for the spiral staircase with a tight grip on the key.

Marie follows me to the stairs. "Are you working a spell, dear?"

I stop halfway up the first set of stairs. "Uh yeah, I'm having strange visions, can't make sense of them. I was reading in one of the mind spell grimoires that lighting multiple wolfsbane candles can help."

"Okay, let me know if you run into any trouble." She bought the lie entirely. I feel a deep stab of guilt. *I had to. I didn't have a choice.*

I hurry up the second set of stairs where Blue waits on the second landing.

"Let's get this over with." His thoughts drip with unadulterated dread. I pause at the door. *Why did Elspeth think Nefari couldn't enter?*

"Perhaps she tried and failed, then surmised that a spell was the reason. Let's not worry about that now, we need to do this."

"Are you on board now?" I mumble, not ready to enter quite yet.

He rolls his eyes at me. *"Absolutely not. But you made this cockamamie deal, and while the consequences of honoring are unclear, the consequences of double crossing her are sure to be disastrous. So, there's no time to waste."*

I pause, the key in one hand, the doorknob in the other. My fingers tremble as I slip the key in and turn. Something clicks. The door's unlocked. As I stand at the threshold, my entire body vibrates with anxiety. Once I fetch her the Black Flame Candle, there's no going back. There's a heaviness in the air around me. Whatever lies before me in this room will change the course of my life…forever.

Blue loses his already limited patience and slips through the closed door, leaving a few wiry hairs behind.

I gulp back a hiccup and push open the heavy wooden door. The hinges cry as if they're in pain. The room is painted in deep blue shadow. The air is stale and heavy, and dank with dust. A rack of period clothing, presumably once used for the Gathering, blocks further entry into the room. The wheels on the rack squeak as I push it to the side.

"Blue?" I whisper. I squint at the rafters draped in cobwebs, hoping to find some kind of pull light. There isn't one. I run my hands up and down the wooden paneling hoping to find a light switch. Nothing.

Blue creeps out of the darkness, rolling a long white candle with his nose. When it hits my toes, he drops a box of matches from his mouth beside it.

"Is that—is that it?" I stammer.

"No, but it'll provide enough light for us to search this place properly. Hurry now, this place is a pigsty. Absolutely nothing is labeled." Blue dashes away back into the shadows.

I drop to my knees and light the wick. The single candle illuminates the room more than I would have anticipated. The silver cobwebs hanging from the rafters shimmer like gossamer threads in the soft glow, giving the attic room an ethereal, otherworldly feel. I glance about, taking in the towering bookshelves that fill the space. They're crammed with weathered shoeboxes, dusty potion bottles—some empty, some full—and glass mason jars filled with contents long forgotten. The thick air coats my tongue as I breathe.

I roll my lips in as I search between tightly sandwiched bookcases. The room is cold, and it sends a damp chill that seeps through my clothes. The wooden floorboards creak with every step. I kneel beside a crate of long-stemmed candles. "Blue, I'm not even sure what I'm looking for. Do you know what it looks like?"

Blue pokes his head out from under the neighboring shelf, his cat eyes reflecting the glow of the candlelight. *"I know not the size or color, but given its power, I'm sure you'll feel the pulse of its magic.*

And I doubt the smell will be all that pleasant to inhale."

I run my fingertips over the candles, feeling nothing. *None of these are it.* A thought occurs to me. Elspeth won't accept failure. *Elspeth, if you want your candle so badly, point us in the right direction. You can come in here; there's no spell keeping Nefari out.* I wave my hands about myself as proof. I close my eyes waiting for her slithering presence to snake its way out from the back of my mind. Once again, I feel nothing. *What the hell? Do you want this thing or not…* I push the crate away and pry open an old shoe box, only to discover smelly old buckle shoes in the style of the seventeenth century. I slide them back into place and continue searching.

Hot wax drips on my fingers. I yelp and flick the fat globs to floor. Then I snatch a candle holder from the shelf and plunk the candle in.

"*Eleanor,*" Blue sends with an urgent tone.

I rise to my feet. "Where are you?"

"*Corner to your left.*"

Blue, the room's a circle. I roll my eyes.

"*Incorrect. It's the shape of a quarter moon, giving you three corners. Go to your left.*"

I step over discarded shoeboxes and crates filled with crystals. I have to step sideways to squeeze through the tightly packed bookshelves to get to the corner of the room, then carefully place the candle on the high shelf.

Blue steps aside, revealing a small wooden box, and I kneel to inspect it. The box is coated in a fuzzy blanket of dust. I brush it clear and run my fingers over the ancient wood. It feels nearly petrified. The corners are worn down and rounded. Shining against the candlelight are four nails driven into each corner of the box. I hover my hand over it and close my eyes. *La Caeli.* The nails creak against the wood as they lift from the box. One by one, they spin and topple to the floor.

I slowly raise the lid. My heart is thumping, and my breath catches in my throat. Nestled upon withered packing straw is a thick candle, the length of my forearm but far more slender. I wave the open box directly under my nose. The acidic aroma of brimstone and the coppery scent of dried blood assault my senses.

I pluck the candle from the box and hold it up to the light. Etched in the molten candle are peculiar grooves and bulges, strange symbols like I've never seen before. The writing winds its way down the candle, changing and morphing as it goes. The etching trails off near the bottom, almost as if it finished mid-sentence. "Do you know what this says?"

Blue stares intently. "*It begins in a form of ancient Proto-Elamite, then Sumerian, Egyptian, Hebrew, then Greek. I recognize the language, but I can't read it. Except the last few words, those are in Gaelic. They say, 'Let the flame grow'.*"

"So, what does it mean, is it a spell, a prophesy, warning?" I rattle off anxiously.

Blue shakes his head wearily. "*No, I believe it is merely instruction.*"

My shoulders fall. Part of me was praying Elspeth was wrong, that my aunts didn't actually have it. But it was a fool's hope. "Well, let's not keep Elspeth waiting. And here's hoping she's illiterate." I tuck the candle under my arm and rise to my feet.

Blue chuckles dourly and follows me out. As soon as I step out of the room, the door swings shut and the lock clicks. We both glance behind us.

"*Pay it no heed. Let's get to your room.*"

We waste no time as we hurry into my bedroom and shut the bedroom door behind us. I lay down on the floor and place the candle in my hand. "Blue, should we break a glass or something to help bring me back?" I ask, looking about. "Are you going to say the incantation? Oh, crap. We don't have any of the proper candles or crystals." When I move to stand up, powdery sand coats my open palms and sticks to my slick knees. *I'm back.*

The sun shines a muted mustard color. The chrome and glass skyscrapers don't glisten against the noonday sun. The white stone restaurants along the boardwalk are all lifeless gray. There is no beach teeming with life, nor a single kite fluttering against the washed-out hue of an endless sky.

Wait, where's the candle? My eyes sweep my surroundings, then my hands scramble through the sand. *Where the hell did it go?*

Concrete clouds roll across the sepia tone sky. Elspeth walks barefoot through the sand until she's standing over me. "My candle?"

"I—I don't know." I peer down at myself. I'm still in my yoga pants and t-shirt.

Elspeth's hands grip her cinched waist as she looms over me. "What do you mean you don't know?"

I circle about on my hands and knees, padding the tightly packed sand. "I don't know. I had it in my hands when you pulled me here."

Elspeth throws her hands up exasperated. She stomps around me, her eyes darting about. "Pyewacket, what did you do?"

"*The candle is still here in her hand. It doesn't have a soul, so it can't cross over.*"

I fall back onto my backside. "It's still—"

"I heard him!" She stares off into the still, subdued ocean. She closes her eyes, her face ironing out. After a moment, her lips pull back in a sneer. She spins around and looks down at me. "Go to Pyewacket's grave and place my candle inside his chest."

Wait, do what?!

She lowers herself to my level and seizes me by the shoulders, her nails bite into my skin. "How is Jack feeling? Does he feel Purgatory's pull? I won't have to kill your beloved, you know. I'll twist him, pull his mind apart. I'll inflict so much agony, he'll do the deed himself. Perhaps he'd even beg you to do it for him…" Her cruel smile widens with glee. I feel my resistance draining, my will bending to hers. I know she feels it too.

I nod. "What do you want me to do?" I ask, not entirely sure what she's asking of me.

Elspeth yanks me to my feet. "Our shared familiar exists between realms. He can act as a bridge, a vessel to bring the candle from your realm to mine. Take my candle and place it inside Pyewacket's chest cavity. Then bury it."

Before I can respond, she throws me backward.

Returning to the physical world is like falling in a dream. My mind feels it, but there's nowhere for my body to go, so it just spasms against my mattress. In a blink, I'm back in my bedroom, the Black Flame Candle discarded at my side.

My eyes meet Blue's resting at my side, knowing he heard everything. *Sorry.*

He sighs, his gaze lifts to the ceiling. *"Tis the selfsame folly for yet another day,"* he sends.

We hurry down the stairs with the candle tucked under my arm and breeze through the dining room.

"Eleanor! I'm kicking ass!" Sally squeals.

"Not surprised," I shout back, rushing past through the kitchen. I dig through the drawers in search of a knife. Blue leaps onto the counter.

"The paring knife, just there. That should do it."

I snatch the delicate blade and bolt out the kitchen's backdoor. The cool night air carries the scent of turning leaves and distant wood smoke. I dash across the cobblestone patio to where his body is buried. The moon shines its pale spotlight over the yard, giving the garden and headstone a celestial glow. From my hands and knees, I mutter the air spell and levitate a gardening spade from the shed toward me. Seeing it careen through the air, I gasp, recalling that dreadful trowel hurling toward Jack's throat. The spade falls to the ground only a few feet away. I shake off the harrowing image and crawl over to it, then finally begin to dig.

Blue tiptoes around his headstone before sitting next to the growing pile of dirt. The knees of my cotton bottoms moisten on the lawn.

"This feels weird with you watching," I mutter just as my shovel tip hits his little coffin.

"Well," he says dramatically, *"I'd hate to make you feel 'weird' while digging my grave to desecrate my poor decaying body. Perhaps I should give you two some privacy?"*

I don't understand. If your body has been buried here for over three centuries, why hasn't it decayed into dust?

"It was, until you were born. The power of life that created you also pulled me from Purgatory, but Elspeth is still an anchor on my soul, just as she is anchor to your magic."

Because I'm stuck between realms, my body only reanimated to a point, not enough to live. Thus, my spirit is only partially attached to my body.

I dust away the remaining dirt clumps before prying the top free. The trees rustle with the frigid fall breeze, as if the forest were careening closer for a better view. Blue and I both peer down into the hole. His small body lies in the coffin, looking identical to his spirit beside me, only deathly still.

I nibble on my bottom lip. "I guess I should make a small incision just below the rib?" I squint trying to see in the dim light.

"Just hurry, you never know who's watching," Blue sends, glancing about.

A twig snaps somewhere in the woods. An owl hoots, then the trill of the crickets ceases. The woods have gone silent.

Without a second to lose, I press the knife into his lifeless body.

"Hey! Be gentle!"

I pull the knife down across his little belly, about four inches. The sensation is like pulling a blade through old carpet. I cringe. *This is just a stuffed animal. This won't hurt him.* With the opening created, I carefully wedge the candle inside, trying not to think about the tiny cat organs putting up resistance. I give the candle a hard shove, feeling the obstacle collapse and break inward. I whip my head in Blue's direction. "Are you okay?"

"Well, it didn't feel quite like a hug, but don't bugger about it. Just close me up and let's get back inside."

This feels so wrong.

I place the coffin lid back into place, shovel the dirt into the hole and pat it down with my feet. The crickets have resumed chirping. "Let's get back inside."

It takes blue a bit to trot up to the house as I hold the kitchen door open.

I raise a concerned brow.

"And just how spry do you think you'd be with a candle shoved up your arse? This will take some getting used to. I do pray this will be a short-term solution."

Laughter erupts from the dining room. I idle by the door listening to the chatter while Blue ambles on, looking like it's his first day walking. Normally, I'd feel desolate, isolated from my coven, but instead I feel lighter. I gaze out the window to Blue's grave. With the Black Flame Candle out of the house and underground, I feel settled, even safe. Until now, I hadn't realized how much that candle's dark presence had shadowed the house since we arrived.

"How do you think we have all those cars in the garage? Definitely not from Marie's linguistics degree," Sally besmirches.

I rinse the mud off my hands in the sink.

"Card counting, that's quite a talent," Jack says impressed. "Vegas or Atlantic city?"

"Both, and Montecarlo, too. You wouldn't believe what I won off this one Russian aristocrat," she says devilishly.

I take a deep breath before strolling into the dining room, finding a seat next to Jack. I glance about and notice my mother is missing. Most likely resting in her bedroom.

Sally has a pile of chips in front of her the size of Everest compared to everyone else's pitiful collection. Abe doesn't seem to have a single chip to his name.

"Well, it helps if you have magic," I say, attempting to seamlessly slip into the party.

Sally leans back in her chair with folded arms. "Excuse me? I have a degree in applied mathematics from Cambridge. I don't need magic to take your money."

My eyebrows shoot up while the rest of me sits in stunned silence. Sally glances at our incredulous faces. "What? You've all seen me wearing my alma mater's apparel."

"I just thought it was an old boyfriend's shirt," Maggie mumbles. Phoenix springs up and rests in her lap.

"That's sexist," Sally chides, pointing her finger at my sister.

Maggie rolls her eyes with a chuckle.

I lean toward Jack and place my head on his shoulder. The candle is buried. The Nefari failed to find me during the harvest moon. *Can things finally go back to normal?* The prospect leaves me giddy. I kiss Jack's bare bicep, enjoying the feel of his skin.

"Okay, want us to deal you in, pumpkin?" Marie says sweetly, magically shuffling the cards in a dazzling, levitating dance. "This is going to be the last round; Jack is feeling pecked."

"Plus, I'm nearly broke," Jack says, gesturing to his dwindling pile of chips.

"Sure," I say with a shrug. Marie puts on a show while shuffling; the cards dash and dive into a complicated figure eight, reordering themselves in the process.

"Well, I guess I'm out," Abe says, sounding slightly relieved. He leans back in his chair and rests his hands on his slightly rounded abdomen.

A kettle whistles in the kitchen, two cats hiss at each other from the living room, and the grandfather clock on the second landing chimes. The typical pulse of the home is alive and well.

"Did you accomplish what you needed to?" Jack whispers to me.

I nod with my head still on his shoulder. *How did he know?*

CHAPTER NINETEEN
Witch's Gin

"Hey, Eleanor," Criss Sampson starts as she leans next to my locker, "do you have any notes from Latin? Ms. Reinyard is up my ass again." She lifts her phone, using the camera as a mirror to examine what most likely took over an hour to properly contour each cheek.

I sigh and dig through my bag.

"What do you have next?" she asks. She clearly could not care less, but she needs to keep a friendly air until I hand her over my notes.

"Fencing," I reply before snapping my locker closed. I took the class as a lark, but also thinking colleges might consider the standard P.E. credit a fluff class. Plus, Jack told me Ms. Murphy gives everyone an A.

"Sweet, thanks!" She yanks the notes from my hand before prancing down the hall. The faculty have no idea she live streams most of her classes; she's one of several contenders hoping to fill the influencer void left by Vivienne Mather.

I hurry to the girls' locker room and change into my white padded fencing clothes. My phone chimes just before I leave for the gym.

Hey, your place or mine this weekend?

I roll in my lips to keep from squealing like the stupid schoolgirl that I am. Several girls roll their eyes at me as I type out a quick reply.

Not sick of me yet?

After our disastrous weekend on the island, Jack was given a medical leave to miss classes the entire week.

Eleanor, you're one habit I couldn't break if I

tried. But stop evading me, am I going to Salem
or are you coming to me?

The knell of the class bell reverberates throughout the hall. I quickly calculate my weekend schedule in my head.

Come to Salem, the guest room is still
made up for you.

I put my phone away before Jack has time to reply. I grab my gloves and fencing mask and race through the underground tunnel that connects the locker rooms to the school's Olympic size gymnasium.

I select a sword—technically, a "foil"—from the rack and join the other students in line. The gym is divided into four sections: weightlifting, half-court basketball, gymnastics, and fencing. School legend was that the gym used to be a prison of sorts during colonial Salem. The stone walls are all whitewashed with a glittering glass mosaic of what appears to be a physician attending patients. Although, no amount of renovations can rid the gym of that eerie, grave-like feeling.

"Eleanor, you're paired with Savannah, Brooks with Preston, Lily with Esther…" Ms. Murphy continues rattling off students' names.

Savannah gives me a wink before pulling down her mask. She's a sophomore and fellow witch, although she hasn't come into her magic just yet. According to her mother, who attends the same book club as my aunt, that's not for the lack of praying to Brighid asking for it to come early.

We both take the 'en garde' position. Savannah and I shuffle back and forth, neither wanting to take the first jab. Savannah relents first. She arcs her sword and swishes it forward, giving me an obvious advantage with the kind of showmanship Ms. Murphy says is a surefire way to defeat. A simple parry and riposte would give me an easy lead, but instead, I freeze.

The sight of Savannah's sword swishing through the air too closely resembles the gardening trowel whisking toward Jack's neck. Macabre memories shuffle through my mind like a deck of cards. The blood-soaked hatchet hovering in the air, the kitchen knives, the hedge cutters, my mother's head, Trixie crying out, the face of Allen Woods as the bullet penetrated his forehead.

The gymnasium spins around me. The earth falls out from

under me. The foil tumbles from my hand. Somehow, I end up on the flat of my back, hyperventilating.

"Eleanor! Oh my gosh, I'm so sorry, are you okay?" Savannah tosses her sword aside and falls to her knees at my side. "I-I-I don't know what happened. I'm so sorry!"

My eyes can't stay still. They dart between the lights fixed to the ceiling. My heart accelerates beyond what it should be capable of. *Am I having a heart attack?* I see the army of mutilated bodies, their black pocketed gums, the gaping holes in their faces where their eyes should be. My stomach roils; bile bubbles up throat. My mother's head. I roll to the side and vomit.

"Oh gosh, I'll get Ms. Murphy!" Savannah rushes to fetch the instructor.

The clanging of swords ceases. No more dribbling of basketballs, no more weights thumping to floor. Only silence.

"You alright, O'Reilly?" Ms. Murphy asks. She sees the pile of puke next to me and wedges her fingers under her nose.

I close my eyes and nod, feeling the contacts shift across my eyes. "Yeah, I think my lunch just didn't agree with me." I roll onto my side before going on all fours. The nightmare images fade into the distance, the gymnasium stops spinning. I take a deep breath and release it slowly.

"Gonna hurl again?" Ms. Murphy asks, taking a step back.

I shake my head "Nah, I'm fine. I just need to get cleaned up." I wipe the sick from the side of my mouth with the back of my head.

"Savannah, go into my office and dial star 66. Tell the office to send a janitor down here." Ms. Murphy then orders the rest of the class back to their positions.

After showering, I put my school uniform back on and check my phone. I have a new text from Jack confirming our weekend plans, then another from Zoey proposing a girl's night this week after one of our shifts.

I lean back against the wall of lockers with my leather satchel hitched on my shoulder. My heart sinks. I was so full of hope before the island. I actually thought we could move on from everything. But it's becoming abundantly clear there is no going back.

I can't focus during senior seminar. My eyes keep drifting to the windows overlooking the courtyard. The rabbit traps have been inconspicuously removed from the grounds. The cobblestone courtyard is a brick island gulfed by a vibrant sea of green with a wrought iron fence slicing through it. I lean my head in my hand, lifting my gaze to the lonely chapel with stained glass windows. *I need a spell to deal with…everything. If Mom or the aunts don't have something, maybe Zoey will.*

A shadow drifts across a window inside the chapel. I sit up straighter and narrow my gaze. *Probably just a janitor. I'm sure it doesn't mean anything.* The hair on the back of my neck prickles. I keep staring at the window, but the shadow doesn't return. *I'm sure it's nothing. I'm just being paranoid.*

The bell trills and I head to the student parking lot alone as Maggie has cross-country practice. My aunt's van stalls a moment before turning over. The shining sun seems to be beaming in pure mockery as I drive.

"Mom?" I call as soon as I walk into the house. Cats skitter about.

The kitchen door swings open and my mom steps out wearing Marie's frilly apron. "What's going on?"

I drop my belongings in the entryway and flop down in a dining room chair.

Mom dries her hands on the apron and looks me over with a knitted brow. "More visions?"

I shake my head. "Not visions. Can a witch have PTSD?" I ask, hanging my head back and gazing at the new crown molding.

"Of course, love. Anyone would if they had gone through what you've gone through." A chair scrapes against the floor and creaks as Mom sits next to me and pats my knee.

I roll my head so I can see her from the corner of my eyes. "Got anything for that?"

Mom frowns, then her face brightens. "Yes, gin."

My eyes bulge. "Um, I think Sally is rubbing off on you."

Mom chuckles with a shake of her head. "Witches gin is different." She stands and nods to the greenhouse.

Cats parade behind us on our way into the greenhouse. Homemade cinnamon brooms line the doorway with dried apple slices dangling between the bristles. Exotic plants are suspended in birdcages above our heads.

Mom stops at the weathered open cabinet housing hundreds of mercury glass bottles, small vials, bell jars, mason jars, and the odd smudge stick idling in an abalone shell. After struggling to reach the top shelf, she places her hands on her hips and jerks her head to the side. The bottles shuffle and part to reveal a long neck clear bottle. Citrus peels and a sprig of juniper swirl inside the crystalline liquid.

She retrieves the bottle and ushers us into the kitchen.

"Persephone," she calls. Her tabby familiar hops onto the countertop. "Oh, there you are. I'll need your help." Mom dislodges the cork as I lean on the opposing counter, watching.

A wispy cyclone spins the mixture from within. Mom keeps glancing up, making eye contact with her familiar. She sprinkles in a pinch of some kind of black powder then drops in what looks like a pink Himalayan salt crystal.

Blue saunters into the kitchen and studies the commotion.

"For the nightmares you keep having, I take it?" Blue muses.

I nod, watching the liquid swirl in the bottle on the kitchen island.

"They had improved by mid-August. I was rarely roused from sleep by your incessant screaming," Blue sends, sounding mildly irritable.

I roll my eyes. *Sorry I interrupted your sleep, but they're back and with a vengeance. I keep seeing the dead staff from the island, those horrible Nefari masks. That mind spell about Mom.* I can't even think the words.

Mom nods to Persephone, then recites an incantation in verse:

"In silent moments, where scars have yet to fade
I offer light, to shine where shadows stayed.
Though haunting flashes linger in the mind's eye,
Healing through dreamless sleep
is found by and by."

With the incantation complete, she whispers, "La Narine, blessed be," close to the opening of the bottle, then blows a breath into the mixture. The salt crystal at the bottom bursts like a single firework, then disintegrates. The cyclone ceases. The solution is perfectly still.

Mom leans against the opposite counter from me. She looks up from the bottle to me. "The blessing was successful, but there's a catch. You need to know it before you drink."

I nod, waiting for what is sure to be some horrendous side effect.

"You may not have visions for a while. Your gift will be suppressed," Mom warns.

My brows lift, taken aback. *No visions? Would that be so bad?* I consider the sweet slumber of a dreamless sleep, just curled up in my bed without a care in the world when I shut my eyes. "So…this elixir…what? Makes me… apathetic, like I won't care what happened?"

Mom shakes her head and dusts off her hands. Persephone leaps off the island like she has something important to do. Blue, however, stays, staring at the liquid intently.

"No, it's not like that. It mutes some of the recall, especially while you sleep. To be honest, I was hesitant to even mention it. Your gift is still developing, and there is a slight risk to it, but with everything you went through last spring then the terror on that island, Persephone and I both believe this will be beneficial."

I walk over to the bottle and take a whiff. It smells like juniper, mint, and vanilla, with just the faintest smell of citrus fruit. I place the bottle down and my mother corks it.

"Two teaspoons before bed," Mom instructs. "You can keep the bottle in your room." She turns back to the cauldron burbling on the hearth.

What do you think Blue?

Blue cocks his little black head at me. "*To be frank, if I might, you are currently in a precarious situation. The Black Flame candle may be safely buried but Elspeth may be trying to find another way to transport it or even another buyer as we speak. Not to mention this unknown Nefari who had plans to meet with you, only to be bamboozled with your absence, and then… what? Has he given up? That seems highly unlikely. I think it ill-advised to dampen your abilities in the moment we should be enhancing them.*" I sigh, knowing he's right. "I don't think I can take this," I mumble.

Mom gives me a lopsided, understanding smile. "Well, why don't you take it, and if you feel you need it, it's there for you." She cups my cheek with her hand. There's pain woven into her endless blue eyes. I wonder if that will ever go away, or if I'm just adding to it.

I glance back at the bottle, *maybe I should take a swig, mom wouldn't have to worry about me so much.*

Blue glares at me. "*Do try to quell your female teenage desires for self-sacrifice, if it's not too much of a burden. Might I suggest we instead continue training? That would be of far better assistance to your mother than you lying catatonic in bed.*"

I place the bottle in the crook of my elbow. "Thanks, Mom." I walk around the island and plant a kiss on her cheek.

Her warm smile returns, and she threads her arm across my shoulders. "Are you hungry? I have a lamb stew brewing with some of that fabulous rosemary Zoey dropped off earlier."

"Zoey stopped by? She didn't tell me," I say, pouting. I search my skirt pocket for my phone.

Mom shrugs, taking back her arm and returning to her stew. "It was quick, just returning some of Maggie's things she borrowed and delivering a thank you gift, which we'll be eating tonight," mom says wistfully. She leans forward, inches from the steam and inhales the woodsy aroma wafting up from the symphony of vegetables.

I begin texting as I wander up to my bedroom.

Hey my mom said you stopped by,
you should have stayed.

Once I reach my bedroom, I stow the bottle at the bottom of my wardrobe. I cast off my uniform and slide into a pair of worn corduroy bellbottoms that I've been dying to wear all summer. After pulling on a maroon crew neck sweater, I plop down at my desk and retrieve the homework from my satchel.

My cursor looks bored, blinking idly on my computer screen. I stare at the blank page and toss my hair into a high ponytail. I release a big gust of air through my mouth. *Why did I have to take French? We lived in Miami; Spanish would have been far more practical.* I peer down at a small hole in the toe of my sock. If I was being honest with myself, I took French because Shannyn did.

"I don't understand you two. Is it a simple matter of envy?" Blue ventures. He sounds genuinely curious sitting in my window seat.

I shrug. "I don't know. It's complicated with her." *I turn back to my computer and growl. Okay seriously, I can't keep stalling.* I glance down at some notes I jotted down from Google translate. "L'année était 1793 et le sang s'accumulait sur les rues pavées en cette froide matinée d'octobre." I'm nodding to myself as I write. *Yeah, that sounds right, I think.*

The bathroom door swings shut downstairs. *Maggie must be home from practice.*

I jot down a few more facts about the French Revolution trying to make it sound as lyrical as Madame Cambert demands.

My phone chimes.

I grab my phone and swivel away from my essay. It's a text from Zoey.

Ciao! Uhhh…sorry! Yeah, didn't want to stay, ima be honest.

My heart speeds up. I haven't had any normal teenage friend drama in over nine months. I'm quite rusty in the average puberty hell of female friends. Trixie was always so easy going and we weren't friends long enough to have any friction.

Did I do something wrong?

I nibble on my bottom lip waiting for her to type out her reply.

"You're doing this just to get out of your studies, correct? I mean, with everything going on, you're not really going to fret over one Zoey Gallo, are you?"

I ignore Blue and try to focus on my essay, but my mind still circles back to Zoey's cryptic text. Somehow, I manage to get through three more paragraphs before Zoey gets back to me.

> Nah, it's not that. Dropped stuff over. Got weird vibes. Felt like someone didn't want me there. So I left. We good?

I frown.

> Yeah we're good. Were these your magic witchy vibes? Bc ur always welcome.

> Def witch vibes. They were strong!!! Thought maybe u mad.

Now I'm really puzzled. *That's weird. Do you think maybe she sensed Elspeth?*

Blue leaps to his feet. *"Eleanor!"*

My bedroom door crashes into the wall. Everything goes black.

CHAPTER TWENTY
Night School

My head snaps up the moment I regain consciousness. Everything is black. I can't tell how long I've been out. My head feels heavy. There's a black sack over my head, keeping my breath hot against my face with every exhale. My heart pounds in my chest so hard that I can feel my pulse thrumming in my ears. My hands are bound together and shaking. I'm tied to what feels like a wooden chair. My bindings are too tight, and the rope even wraps around my chest making it hard to breathe. My skin is slick with sweat.

Blue! Blue, tell me you're here!

"I'm here. As for identifying where 'here' is, I'm afraid I am as lost as you are."

Well, at least I'm not alone with some maniacal kidnapper. I'm alone with a maniacal kidnapper *and* my familiar.

Where are you? Are you tied up too? What's happening? Are we alone? Do they have my family? I gulp. *I'm going to kill them. Whoever they are, I'm going to!* I need to get out and I need to get out now. I picture my bindings, imagine them burning through, the flames stopping before they reach my fabric or skin. *Ne Fe—*

The black sack is ripped from my head. I squeeze my eyes shut, not ready to see the monster that took me. I'm not ready to see my mother's head again, or my sister's, or aunts. I can't. I just can't, not again.

Nothing happens. Somehow, that's even worse. My terror feeds on the unknown, amplified by the piercing silence. I can't take seeing those rabbit masks again. I don't think my heart can bear it. But I can't take not knowing, either. I slowly, hesitantly peek my eyes open. My lips tremble.

I'm alone, looking up at a slightly raised platform, a lectern, and a back wall. Hanging from the rafters high above the platform are the American flag, the Massachusetts flag, Pride flag, and the Griggs's Academy flag. The faint outline of a cross can still be seen from back when the auditorium was a working chapel. I'm at Griggs. The only light in the room is from the flood lights outside filtered through the stained-glass windows. Colorful phantoms splash against the walls. But I seem to be alone.

I squint in the sparse light. *Blue? Blue, where are you?* A black sack next to the pulpit starts to squirm and rustle.

"I can't claw or work my way out of this bloody sack. I believe I'm being confounded by magic."

I squeeze my eyes shut and imagine the sack levitating toward me. *La Caeli.* I open to see the black sack lift about three feet from the floor.

Blue hisses a high-pitched, agonizing whine as it's slammed back down to the floor.

"No magic right now," a male voice calls.

Footsteps fall in a rolling gait up the flagstone aisle behind me. *Blue, are you okay? I'm so sorry!*

Another set of footsteps approaches from my left, and the Nefari from the apothecary shop saunters into my field of view. He's even dressed in similar fashion as before: black motorcycle jacket, black jeans, blonde hair cropped short. Without his mirrored aviator glasses, his violet eyes are on full display.

"Eleanor, be careful."

"I apologize for the rough landing," he says, gesturing to Blue still tied up.

"L-l-let him go," I stutter, terrified.

A blonde woman, maybe mid-to-late twenties, joins him. She's wearing a Wesleyan sweatshirt and jeans. Her platinum blond locks are braided in two long strands that rest on her chest. Her round face looks almost…kind?

The man jerks his head back toward Blue. "You can let him out. But if he tries anything, he goes back in the bag."

The woman nods and obeys.

"My name is Silas Foster," he says with a quaint bow.

Blue leaps out of the sack and sprints to my side. His eyes dart between our abductors.

"I don't care who you are! Let me go!" I spit.

The woman steps closer to Silas, whispering into his ear.

Silas shakes his head, his eyes fixed me. "No, not yet. We aren't quite sure if we can trust her. But soon." He stretches out his arm, palm open, and a folding chair from the platform flies with impressive speed to his hand. He spins it in front of him and sits on it backwards, resting his arms on the back. "You were not at your home during the harvest moon," he admonishes with a condescending cluck of his tongue and a wagging finger.

"What an absolute prick," Blue hisses.

"Sorry, I had another engagement." My eyes slide between the two witches. The girl with the kind face has an effulgent air about her as she looks me over with tenderness.

Silas chuckles, and I return a tremulous smile.

The Nefari rides his chair as it slides closer to me. His knees press on either side of my leg while he looks deep into my eyes.

"Isolde," he calls like a master to a servant.

The female Nefari strides to his side and bends in half so that her face is close to mine.

Silas snaps his fingers. The chandeliers and wall sconces all set ablaze, illuminating the old church like it was noon day.

I wince against the sudden brightness. After a moment, I peek my eyes open, allowing them time to adjust. Isolde is so close to my face she could kiss me. I flinch back but can only move an inch. I reluctantly meet her soft hazel eyes, taking in all the brown and green flecks embedded in the ring of amber. I can even see a quiet smattering of freckles just beneath her eyes. This witch isn't a Nefari.

"Now, show her the picture," Silas commands, staring at me with such intensity I squirm under his probing gaze.

Isolde stands up straight and walks to a pew to retrieve a canvas bag. She tugs out a brown hardcover book with a year splashed across the cover. It's a high school yearbook dated seven years ago. She flips through it as she walks back to me, then thrusts the book into my face. It's opened to a senior page filled with smiling headshots.

Isolde taps the last picture on the third row of the first page. Isolde Ashford. Her hair is cropped short in a stylish pageboy cut that she pulled off like Charlize Theron. She's grinning ear to ear in an off the shoulder blouse. Her cheeks are dusted rose pink, her lips coral. And her eyes a bright, unnatural citrine yellow.

Wait.

Silas nods at me. "The picture isn't doctored or manipulated in any way. I'm sure you can find her yearbook online. Staples High School in Westport, Connecticut. We'll even let you take the book with you if you wish to have it analyzed. But as you can see, her eyes are no longer that unnatural hue." Silas puffs up his chest and rights his shoulders like a preening doctor holding out his patient for admiration.

I blink several times, glancing between Isolde and the open yearbook. "I don't believe you, it's not possible."

"I don't think we're in any danger, I believe we can remove her bindings," Isolde says with a raised brow.

Silas nods, and the painfully tight bindings tumble away from my wrists. I roll my shoulders and wiggle out my arms. *Who the hell are these witches, Blue?* Blue takes a shaky breath. "*I don't know. But I'm quite far from trusting them.*" Isolde lets me take the yearbook from her. *What do you think of the picture?* "*Do you feel any pulse of magic? Close your eyes and concentrate, can you feel the slightest pulse, the quiet buzz of power manipulating her eyes?*"

Silas and Isolde look from Blue to me and back, knowing what must be flowing between us. I peer down at the stone floors, trying to feel that subtle pulse of magic flowing from either of them. I feel nothing, like standing in the center of a still pond. There isn't a single ripple.

"You're not sensing any kind of glamour, are you? It's because she truly has been cured, ransomed from darkness, whatever you want to call it," Silas wheedles like a man who has delivered this speech many times before. "Her magic craves the light now; it obeys her perfectly."

I swallow, too scared to believe it's true. *Blue, is this possible?! Can a Nefari be cured?*

"*There is no record of a Nefari witch being healed. Ever.*"

I stare into those yellow eyes in her school picture. I run my fingers over the left then the right, dragging my fingers back.

Silas pushes to his feet and strolls about the chapel, giving me time to process. With one hand holding the other behind his back, he gazes about the stained-glass windows, the auspicious arches, and painted ceiling. "I know what you're thinking, Eleanor. It's simply impossible."

"I thought the same thing," Isolde chimes in. "I didn't even know I was a witch. My dad was a normal human, my mom was a Nefari. They divorced when I was two, she took off and my dad had no idea witchcraft even existed. Nefari, familiars, not any of it. One night while I was doing a semester abroad in Berlin, I was discovered by Committee members. They cornered me. They were about to destroy my soul before Silas stepped in. I had no idea what was happening. Silas rescued me, explained everything to me. Explained why this big ol' orange coon cat showed up and pretty much adopted my family when I was born. We named him 'Mumford'."

I fold my arms and refuse to give in, refuse to accept the bud of hope they're trying to plant in me. Then it dawns on me; they aren't the first group of Nefari to cajole me into joining them. Simona on the island offered me a place in their group as well. Both groups see me as just another Nefari to be used. I'm suddenly so very tired.

Isolde claims Silas's empty chair, turning it around to face me. "I started when I was eighteen, still a kid, but since I'm a woman, witches trusted me more. So, I would be the one to deliver the poison. The change started out as little flickers, brief moments in time where a natural hazel took over." Her eyes glaze over as she recounts her time with Silas, almost mystified by her own story. "As time went on, the hazel would last longer and longer, until one day I woke up and the hazel was permanent."

I jut my chin in Silas's direction as he examines a window of the Garden of Eden, pretending not to listen. "Is that why his eyes are still violet? You've done all the killing?" I question.

Isolde nods. "After we hypothesized that destroying Nefari was healing me, Silas stopped altogether to allow me to better test out our theory. That's when the cure became permanent."

"If you're healed, then why are you still with him?" I ask, my eyes straying back to Silas.

A wry smile plays at the corners of Isolde's lips. "There are more of us, many in fact, all working together. I want them to heal as I have."

I nod along while I nibble on my lower lip, weighing her words, turning them over, looking for any lies hiding behind her confidence. Then it hits me. Poison. The snakeroot. I whip my head around toward Silas and leap from my chair. "That's why you came to the apothecary. My vision, you killed that woman in Boston. How did you even know she was bad? She could have been like Isolde or me."

He turns on his heel; an amused smile hangs on his square face. "You mean the black widow? She was a nurse, putting insulin in her patients IV's *and* her lovers, after she's cleaned out their bank accounts." He strides toward me. "We do our due diligence before every kill. Why do you think we tossed your room. We searched for evidence that might reveal your true character. Now we want you to join us."

I turn back to Isolde. She nods.

"You don't have to stay a Nefari forever," Silas states plainly. There's an edge to his voice. His frame is tall and muscular, and when his arms cross, his fingers tap on his biceps. His calm, impassive mask is beginning to slip, revealing the tension twitching close to the surface.

I take my seat again and peer down at my knobby knees. My stomach is in knots. I shake my head ever so slightly. "I'm just not sure."

Silas rolls back on his feet and releases a breath through flared nostrils.

Isolde throws up a hand at him. She twists her body toward me, still holding Silas at bay. "Eleanor, I know this can be overwhelming. I'm twenty-nine, and I've been with Silas for eleven years, longer than anyone in our group. I know him very well, and I trust him. I've trusted him with my life. It took three years for my eyes to change, but I'm not the only one who's been healed. I'm just the only one who stayed to help others. You don't have to keep living in fear of the Committee. I know that fear; healing the mental scars of being hunted takes even longer than the eyes."

"I don't think I can kill anyone. I'm sorry, I just can't." The weight of their disappointment is as heavy as my own. I fantasize about having a natural eye color, about my magic being my own, about being pure and good. It would be like throwing off every shackle that binds me to Elspeth as well. Not to mention my family would be safe, I would be safe.

"Oh, no?" Silas cuts in. "You only kill humans, right? Allen Woods, I believe?"

I whip my head at him. "That was different, I wasn't breaking into people's home and poisoning them. It was self-defense. I was saving someone I love."

Silas laughs as he stares at the ceiling shaking his head at me.

"Eleanor," Isolde says as she sits in the chair across from me again. "We aren't killers either. Think of us more like secret police or double agents." She pauses as her eyes glisten. She swallows and blinks back tears, dropping her eyes to her sneakers. "There was this one Nefari, down in Texas. I had to get close to him…" she pauses again, her lips trembling. "If you saw all those we rescued, locked in cages in his basement, you wouldn't have wanted to use poison, it was too merciful a death. You would have wanted to use your bare hands. We execute justice on our own kind because were the only ones who can. And perhaps our eyes heal because Mother Freyja grants us absolution, because we tip the scales so far in her favor."

Isolde's eyes bear into mine as she reaches out and takes my hands in hers. "Join us."

I feel Blue lean against my leg. *What do I do, Blue?*

"I detect no malice or deceit, especially from the young woman. I believe

they're being sincere."

Even Silas?

"He seems rather…rash. I would not trust him with your safety," Blue concludes.

"Silas!" Isolde whispers in a hiss as she leaps to her feet. "Someone is coming." She points to the chapel's double doors.

"Do it!" Silas orders.

Isolde waves out her arms at us as if directing a symphony.

In mere seconds, the double doors creak open and a ruddy-faced security guard pokes his head in. His eyes slide from one side of the room to the other before he steps inside. "Hello?" he calls out. "Come on out!" he shouts, hovering next to the doors.

Isolde must be using the mind spell on him. I pick up Blue and cradle him to my chest. My familiar emits a quiet little purr as I tuck him under my chin just in case the spell didn't include him.

The security guard adjusts his belt digging into his low hanging tire. "I say this again, if anyone is in here make yourself known. You are trespassing on private property."

As I'm holding my breath, I can hear Isolde and Silas breathing normally; Isolde face is practically serene. Her eyes follow the guard strolling up and down the pews.

Silas tiptoes up behind him until he stands just a breath away from him. Isolde watches him, her calm demeanor unchanging.

Silas whispers a spell:

"Step forward, don't look behind,
All is secure, peace you'll find.
No shadows lurk, nothing to hide,
Go in grace, hearts aligned."

He finishes with, "Oculi Tempe," so quietly I strain to hear it.

The security guard huffs, spins around, and shakes his head. "Damn wires. Building is old as shit." He flicks off the lights before leaving the way he came. The chapel plunges into darkness momentarily. My eyes slowly adjust to the dark. The floodlights outside barely creep through the stained-glass windows giving just enough light that I can make out Isolde and Silas's outlines.

"What was that you were whispering?" I ask, my voice cutting through the silence the moment I felt it was safe.

"A prayer my grandmother taught me. She raised me in San Diego, a total free loving hippie that wonderful woman. We would make up all kinds of poems to go along with the mind spell." His voice is too loud against the darkness, verging on boisterous.

"She must have been a genius too, because he's taught me spells most witches never heard of," Isolde chimes.

Blue shifts uncomfortably in my arms, prompting me to place him back down on the floor. I dust my hands off and fold my arms uncomfortably. "What would 'joining' you entail?"

"You'd travel with us," Silas explains. "We traverse the globe. The bigger the threat, the bigger the reward. There's some movement here in Salem we've been investigating. But come All Hallows Eve, we're taking Isolde's family plane out of the country."

"It's *barely* my family. It's my cousin's jet. I do a little accounting work for them, so they sometimes let me use it, but only when no one else is using it," Isolde says almost defensively.

My insides clench. I can see my aunts' home in my mind's eye, practically smell the tea brewing, hearing the chiming grandfather clock, my sister laughing at something, mom cooking, aunts bickering, Jack pulling up in the driveway. I can't leave them. Salem is my home now. My heart accelerates imagining saying goodbye. Or rather, sneaking away, since Mom would never let me traipse around the world with a bunch of strangers.

"I'm sorry, I can't. I can't leave Salem. I can help you around here, but I can't leave with you." I hope to convey a finality in my words, but instead it sounds like I'm begging for their permission.

They share a glance with each other in the limited light of the chapel before looking back at me.

"We're leaving through Logan Airport," Silas says. "Midnight. In case you change your mind."

"Which would make it All Hallows Day," Isolde notes. "Because technically it would be November first."

Silas's eyeroll is nearly audible.

I ride in the backseat of a black SUV as Silas and Isolde drive me home. No one speaks the entire way. Pebbles ting inside the wheel well as the car makes its way up my driveway.

All the lights in the house are out. *Strange. I would think mom would be freaking out, maybe even sent Abe out with an APB to have all of law enforcement looking for me.* "I have no idea what I'm going to tell them."

Isolde coughs and ducks her head, sitting in the front seat.

Silas leans back, his hands on the wheel as we idle in the driveway. "I slipped some blessed belladonna into what was perhaps the best lamb stew I've ever tasted."

"What?!" I screech.

Blue arches his back staring at Silas, his hair standing on end.

Silas adjusts in his seat to turn and face me. "You sent your mother a text saying you weren't hungry but you might eat later. You said you were taking practice tests and timing yourself so you couldn't be disturbed. Everyone had dinner, then promptly went to bed feeling full and satisfied.

Not harmed, just blissfully asleep." He seems almost amused with himself. "Never do that again," I growl, popping open the back door.

"Oh, Eleanor," Silas calls, clearly delighted by my irritation. I turn around, ready to slam the car door shut.

"If you could be a doll, send me your mother's recipe. It really was delicious, my contact info is already in your phone," he says with a wide grin.

The car door slips from my hand and shuts itself, probably from Silas. "I really can't stand that guy," I say, walking into the kitchen to dispose of my mother's leftovers. I tip the large Tupperware bowl over the trashcan. My mouth waters at the smell.

"He's an interesting fellow, to be sure. But if he medicates our family again, I shall remove all his dangling appendages post haste."

You'll get no objection from me. I rinse out the bowl and place it in the drying rack before heading to the bathroom. The grandfather clock in the hall says it's already past 1:00 a.m.

"Do you think I made the right decision?" I ask, squirting toothpaste onto my toothbrush.

Blue is perched on the toilet lid. *"I find the whole affair quite vexing. The prospect of you leaving Salem, and thus beyond Mercy's reach, is rather enticing. But the hands of that man is one of the last places I wish to place your safety. Although, if his theory is true, we technically could see you cured without him."*

I freeze mid-brush and gawk at him through the mirror. *Are you serious? You want me to go off on my own as some kind of Nefari assassin?* I spit in the sink.

Blue rolls his eyes at me, swishing his tail back and forth. *"If you are dispatching the lowliest scum of this realm, then yes. You could be free, my dear. Imagine taking an easy breath."* He tries to take a deep breath himself, but ends up coughing and hacking instead. *"Damned candle."*

"You sound like a Committee member," I mumble.

"Eleanor, we hide you from the Committee because you are an innocent Nefari, what I would deem a rare anomaly. But the Committee is still

fighting a righteous and necessary war against evil. You saw those damnable witches on that island. I'm afraid they are far from unique. Most Nefari are in league with creatures far worse than the Noble Hunters, and the Committee is all that stands between them and rest of the world. Never forget that."

I nod to my bedroom as my shoulders and eyes droop. "I've got a test tomorrow. Maybe we can talk about assassinating witches later."

"Sure."

As we trudge up the stairs to my tower bedroom, a tired, a bemused smile plays at the corners of my lips. "You know, you totally purred tonight."

"Mention that again and I will sever your tongue."

CHAPTER TWENTY-ONE
Tick Tock Tick

I'm only one week into my first October in Salem, and I already understand why everyone romanticizes autumn on the eastern seaboard. The gentle breeze still carries a trace of summer's warmth, while its delicate chill heralds the coming winter. The town collectively decorates in fall colors, and it seems to have put everyone in a festive, delightful mood.

Pedestrians comment on the crunch of the leaves underfoot and ask why this season couldn't last all year. Even Masshole drivers appear to cut people off less often and keep their middle fingers level with the others. Although, from what I hear, as Halloween approaches and more tourists flock to the town, the pleasant autumn patience starts to wear painfully thin.

As Maggie and I drive home from school, beams of sunlight dapple through the trees setting the forest ablaze in shades of scarlet and tangerine. Back in Florida, you'd hardly notice the seasons change unless you checked the calendar, but here in Salem, with ruby-hued leaves on every tree, patrons dressed in cable-knit sweaters, and pumpkin spice lattes on every corner, autumn arrives like its wrapped in neon lights.

Maggie slumps in the front seat, her feet up on the dashboard, her thumbs hammering the screen of her phone. "Everything okay?" I ask.

She nods. "Just talking to Savannah and Piper. Apparently, Savannah's mom has been recruited to the Committee. Mrs. F isn't sure if she'll accept," she says, irritated.

I frown as we pull up to the house. "And… why does that bug you?" Maggie exhales through her nose. "I'm just sick of hearing about the Committee! Mercy is forming a subcommittee, and a Junior Committee, it's like she won't be freaking satisfied until every witch is some kind of pseudo member and killing their own freaking kind. It's stupid and it's shitty if you ask me."

I put the van in park. "Dude, you keep swearing and mom is going to be pissed," I say in a teasing tone.

Maggie glares at me. "I *hate* the Committee," she seethes, "maybe even more than the Noble Hunters. The Committee kills their own kind. That's freaking sick." She hauls herself out of the car and slams the door shut.

I shrug the strap of my messenger bag over my shoulder and follow after her. "I don't know," I mumble.

Maggie stops on the porch midstride. "Are *you* seriously defending them right now?" she asks, her voice an octave higher than usual.

"No, I'm not. But you weren't there on the island, Maggie. Not all Nefari are good. Some are pretty damn evil, and those deserve to be wiped out." Maggie grips her hourglass hips and marches down the steps towards me, trying to square off with me despite being several inches shorter. "Yeah? And how do they perform their little purity test? They look at your eye color, and then they destroy your soul. They don't give a shit about the rest. So do not start singing their praises when they would like nothing better than tear my family apart."

There's a tug on my heart seeing how fierce and loyal my sister can be. I throw up my hands in surrender. "Maggie, I'm not defending them, but I also understand what normal witches are up against. Trust me, I greatly prefer staying alive to the alternative."

Maggie releases the tension in her shoulders. I suddenly notice her navy blue school-issued blazer; she's added metallic gold piping along the edges and an antique brass bumble bee broach to her lapel.

"How many demerits did all that earn you?" I say, nodding to the modifications on her school uniform.

Maggie chuckles as we march up the remaining veranda steps. "Two, along with one Saturday class. The entire boys' lacrosse team is sitting in with me in protest," she says with a wide, devious grin. "Three of them, by the way, have pictures of you as their wallpaper on their phones. You should tell Jack he's got competition," she teases.

I shake my head. "No, he really doesn't."

We kick off our shoes in the entryway; Maggie's penny loafers have actual pennies wedged in each shoe. *Huh, so that's why I'm seeing those all over school.*

We both saunter down the hallway through the dining room towards the kitchen where we can hear Sally cackling. Abe is plopped down on a stool with his back to the kitchen door as he animatedly uses his hands telling a story. Sally sits on a stool across from him next to the island, her bare feet resting in his lap while

Mom leans against the counter next to the stove laughing behind her hand.

Abe pauses as Maggie pops open the fridge.

"So, the perp has his pants around his ankles with the gun still wedged—" he stops, blushing as he eyes the two minors who just entered the room. "Um, in his…"

"Ass?" Maggie finishes, head still in the refrigerator.

"Margaret Rose!" Mom scolds.

Maggie pops back out with a block of smoked gouda and places it on the island. She nods to our mother while tucking away a rueful grin. "Ell, pass me the crackers."

My magic sends the box of crackers floating over to the block of cheese along with a cheese knife from the drawer. I make it land on the corner opposite Maggie.

"Couldn't bring it closer?" she complains, standing on her tippy toes reaching over for it.

After what happened on the island, I didn't want to risk it.

"Perhaps, I'll finish the story another time," Abe says, shifting in his seat.

Sally hasn't completely stopped giggling since we walked in. "You going on a date tonight, babe?" she asks, still lounging on the stool. She reaches behind her and steals a piece of cheese from Maggie while's she distracted with the box of crackers.

I nod, gazing out the kitchen windows to the back gardens and Blue's grave. I linger on the mound of fresh dirt, matted down by two rainstorms since I buried the candle.

"Where's Jackie-boy taking you?" Sally asks.

"Turner's Seafood," I answer, monotone. Elspeth hasn't reached out with further instructions since we buried the candle. It's been a welcome reprieve, but I know she hasn't just given up. Once my mind starts conjuring up the myriad of malevolent schemes she could be up to—who's she's working with, how she's going to obtain it, and what plans she has once she has it—any relief that reprieve once offered is quickly swallowed in dread.

"One of my favorite places in town, and the first place I took your father when we visited," Mom comments from behind a steaming teacup held close to her mouth.

"Hey, where's Marie?" Maggie inquires, her mouth full of crackers and cheese.

"Committee meeting," Sally answers nonchalantly.

Maggie pauses mid-chew. She throws our mother a glance, then slams the box of crackers on the island and storms out of the room.

"Hon?" Mom calls. Even before Maggie was out of the room, Mom had set down her tea and was walking after her.

Abe pales, gaping over at Sally, gripping her feet mid-massage. "Was it something I said?"

"Yes," Sally says solemnly.

I sigh and use a dish rag to dry off my hands. *I wish there was something I could do, but there's nothing.* I think of faceless Committee hunting down innocent witches like Isolde and Silas's crew, then my brain circles back to those Nefari on the island, wrathful and deranged with vile blood lust.

"I need to get ready for my date," I mumble.

There's shouting from Maggie's bedroom as I pass by.

"No Mom! Marie and Shannyn need to quit the Committee! It's not right!" my sister yells over our mom.

With my bedroom door shut, I hurry out of my school uniform and into my black jeans, gray crew neck, knit sweater and fasten my mother's star necklace around my neck. I glance over at Blue as he lies almost lifeless on my bed. I keep staring as I struggle to pull on my ankle boots. Once they're on, I cross the room and perch next to his prone form at the foot of my bed.

"Blue?" I gently call, caressing his head.

He doesn't stir. I brush my finger across his little nose. It's cold and dry. *Crap. It's always cold and dry though, right?* I roll my lips in between my teeth staring at him, waiting for his little chest to move up and down. It doesn't. *Okay, don't panic. Maybe this is nothing. He's a heavy sleeper...* My heart begins to race. I fetch my phone from my dresser and search how to check for a cat's pulse. *Inside hind leg, high up on the thigh, femoral artery.* Lifting his leg, I use my index and middle finger to search the inside of his leg to locate his pulse. Nothing. *Crap. Crap. Crap. What does this mean?! Blue! How is this possible? You can't be dead, err whatever this is! Come on wake up! Wake up!*

I scoop up his small form, race down the stairs and out the back door, passing Abe and Sally making out against the counter.

I carefully place Blue on the ground while my magic uses the shovel to unbury his coffin. I pry open the lid, tossing it to the side. His body is still curled up on his side, the candle still stowed away in the macabre prison of flesh and bone. I turn back to Blue, still lifeless on the ground.

"Okay," I say aloud, "How does this work? Your body is still in the ground with the—"

A breeze rustles through the branches, sending brittle orange and red leaves drifting down to the ground. *Someone could be out there listening*. Everything is still. I drop to a whisper. "You're a partially embodied spirit, still somewhat connected to your body, which makes you…dammit, how does any of this work? Okay, you can't be fully dead because there's still two of you, your body and," I wave my hands about him, "but you won't wake up…" Something occurs to me.

I gaze about the garden, paranoid I'm being watched. My aunts' garden has been winterized for the fall, their flowering bushes are wrapped and tied with burlap for protection, the serpentine cobble stone pathway is sheathed beneath an autumnal blanket of fallen leaves. The sky is a dripping ombre of peachy pink that bleeds into a deep indigo the closer you look to the horizon. *I think I'm alone.*

I lean close to his ear, the one that's been sewn on more than a dozen times, "Blue if you can hear me, I'm going to pull you out of Purgatory." I turn my attention to the kitchen door and imagine the paring knife floating carefully around Sally and Abe, out the back door, and landing in my outstretched hand. *La Caeli.*

I keep my eyes closed, focusing, but I can hear the back kitchen door creak open. There's a subtle whoosh of air as a concentrated breeze drops the knife into my open hand. I let out a grateful breath.

Sorry, Blue. I press the blade into his upper arm just below his shoulder and drag down a few inches and stop. I look back at his spirit next to me. Still here, not moving. *Please, wake up.* I poise the tip below his rib and push. Nothing. "Blue!" I shout. "Come on, come back!"

The warm indigo sky fades into a deep velvet streaked with gray clouds drifting over the moon. Electric light from the kitchen windows illuminates the yard in long shafts of light. Blue still hasn't moved.

I stick the knife in, accidentally wedging it into bone. I have to wiggle it back and forth to set the blade free. My breathing is heavy, my heart pounds, and my eyes are desperate for tears. "You stupid cat that I didn't want! Or even like! Get back here!" I yell at him.

Nothing.

"Eleanor?" Jack calls from the backdoor. Footsteps descend the patio steps behind me.

I bury my face in my hands. *What am I going to do? Would Mom know? I can't reach out to Elspeth on my own, especially with Blue missing.*

Jack sinks to his knees in the grass beside me, placing a protective hand on my back. "Everything okay?" he peers over at Blue, then Blue's body with the knife in my hand. "Um…can I help?" he asks, bewildered.

Can't say I blame him. I wipe my nose on the back of my hand and shake my head. "It's Blue…I can't…" I gaze at his body, tossing the knife aside. I can't bear to stab him again, not that it would help if I could. My eyes rake over his little body I've been mutilating. I can barely see the base of the candle through the open slit. "Jack," I say, reaching into the coffin and into Blue's side to pull out the candle.

Jack watches in horror. "What the—"

I grasp the candle and whip around to face Jack placing it in his hands. "I need you to hide this in the bottom drawer of the bookshelf in the hallway. Please hurry before anyone sees you," I say with alarm.

Jack thankfully doesn't say another word before he sprints off into the house.

I turn back to Blue lying next to me. "Okay, you brought me back from Purgatory. Maybe pain maybe isn't enough. I need to perform the spell you did for me." Just as my hand slides under his neck, his head begins to turn.

"*There's no need, child.*" He sounds gruff and exhausted.

"Blue!" I pick him up and crush him to my chest. "You're back. I seriously thought you were gone," I breath into his scratchy fur.

He wiggles in my arms until he's free, then arches his back, stretching.

"*How did you know I was trapped? Could you sense it?*"

I shrug. "I honestly don't know I made a guess. But I don't understand, you were still somewhat here, in your weird half-spirit form."

"*I wasn't in Purgatory, but I wasn't here either. I was stuck in the same between realms. Elspeth believed I could function as a conduit for her candle. Suffice it to say, it did not work. Once you took the candle from my body I was released. That's why you could still see me, I hadn't crossed over. I was merely detained at the gate, if you will.*"

Blue's thoughts are weary and desperate as if he had been in Purgatory. He stretches and prances about the yard, rotating his head and cracking his bones as he moves. He halts and whips around at me. "*Where is the Black Flame Candle now?*"

I jerk my head towards the house. *Jack is placing it in the drawer with the crystals in the library.*

Blue nods his head once. "*And there it shall remain for the time being.*"

I push to my feet and brush off my knees. *This is probably a dumb suggestion, but could we, I don't know, light a bonfire, toss the candle in and run away?*

Blue stares at me, unblinking. *"You're right. That was a dumb suggestion."*

I sigh. "Good to have you back, Blue." I use the air spell to rebury his little coffin while we saunter up towards the back door.

"Welcome back Blue," Jack says while holding the door open for us.

Blue strolls past and into the house, genuinely too weary for any type of glib remark.

Jack kisses my cheek and slides his arm around my waist. "The candle is secure," he states. "Are you okay?" He tilts his head towards me, his eyes searching mine.

I nod. "There's a lot going on right now." I can't begin to think of how to explain it all, and frankly don't have the energy. "Hungry?" I ask weakly.

Jack tucks a lose strand of hair behind my ear. "I believe we missed our reservation but perhaps we can still get a table if you're interested. Or…" he says, observing my crumpled posture and drooping eyes, "I can order in, veg out here, no pressure."

I collapse in his arms, allowing him to bear my full weight as I gratefully wrap my arms around his shoulders and press my lips ardently against his.

Jack hoists me up with his hands gripping me at my jean pockets, easing my legs to wrap around his waist and dangle behind him. He pulls back from the kiss, resting his forehead against mine. "Is anyone home?"

"Only everyone. Except Marie, I guess."

Jack, resigned to our unfortunate night celibacy, walks us over to the center island and gently places me down, but stays rooted between my knees. His hands slide from my backside to rest on my thighs.

My heart flutters as I watch his muscular hands caress my legs. My knees are pressed on either side of his carved-out hips. "Why? What did you have in mind?" I ask with a coy smile.

He dips his head towards mine, pulling his mouth into a lopsided, wicked grin. "Your mom brewed some more herbs, right?"

My hands quiver on his broad shoulders as heat spreads into my neck and cheeks. "Yes…she has. But…" I stall, feeling my bravery waver.

He chuckles nodding. "Almost everyone is home."

"Hello!" Marie bellows cheerfully swinging open the front door. Jack and I chuckle from the kitchen.

"And now it's complete," he jokes, giving me a little peck. "Besides," he cups my chin, tilting my head up to meet him. "I was only half serious," he says with that easy smile that leaves me with that all-too-familiar weakness in my knees.

I slide my hands from his shoulders to his chest. "I think about you and *that* all the time."

Jack's hands stop high on my thighs, his thumbs lift on my hip bones. "So do I. But I just, I don't want to hurt you, Eleanor."

"It always hurts the first time, from what I hear," I whisper cheekily.

Unable to meet his eyes, I steal a peek at his face instead.

The apples of Jack's cheeks brighten to a rosy pink. He clears his throat. "You know what I mean, you've told me the risk. As has your mother…"

I exhale heavily. "Well, that makes this awkward."

"Hello? Isn't anyone home?" Marie shouts from the hall.

"I think everyone is upstairs," I answer, hanging my head back.

Jack tightens his hands around my waist and tugs me closer. His thumbs brush under the bottom hem of my sweater, his palms caressing the skin from my hipbones to my back.

I suck in a jagged breath. My eyes flutter closed as his fingers trace the bottom bone of my ribcage. My skin tingles at his touch. My stomach muscles contract as his hand slowly inches higher. I gasp. *For the love of Brighid, he's only touching my ribs and I'm already seeing stars.* Jack smiles dangerously at me, knowing Marie could skip down the hall at any minute. I wait for the prickling pain to seep into our moment, but it doesn't. My heart beats wildly.

I bite down on my lip as Jack brings his face closer to mine. "In pain?" Jack questions, keeping his hands still.

I shake my head, unable to speak while his fingers stroke my skin. I feel undone, a slave to his touch, and to the pleasure it fills me with. I grip his shoulders tighter as if that'll keep me from disintegrating into a puddle of nerves.

He brushes his lips against mine…a slight pulsating begins at my temples. "Well, I came home to see we had a visitor waiting outside on the veranda," Marie calls in her giggly, pleased tone.

My heart drops. *Someone from the Committee? Is Silas back?*

"I believe they're in the kitchen, dearie. You just head down the hall there," Marie instructs someone.

Jack sighs, gliding his hands out from under my sweater, taking the euphoric sensation with him. He steps back and places his hands into his pockets of his trousers.

I feel flushed, so I hop quickly down off the island.

"You're breathing heavy," Jack whispers behind me.

"I wonder why," I mumble back playfully. I brace myself against the counter, facing the kitchen door and whoever will parade through it.

Zoey, to my relief pushes through the swinging door. "Caio, Ragazza," she greets. She immediately notices Jack standing off by the back door, then back to me struggling to return to earth. Her olive toned cheeks beam in a bright tomato red. She shrinks back awkwardly. "Sorry, I hope I wasn't interrupting anything…" she trails off, unable to look at Jack.

Jack chuckles. "Hardly. You must be Zoey. Eleanor has told me a lot about you." Ever the gentleman, Jack steps forward and holds out a hand.

Zoey leans forward and places her hand in his, she glances at me from the corner of her eye. "Check out, Mr. Darcy," she mutters out the side of her mouth as if Jack can't hear her.

I smile with a roll of my eyes. "I'm glad you came inside this time," I say, leaning my elbows on the center kitchen island.

She mildly nods. "Yeah, well, I didn't feel anything this time," she says. Jack frowns, curiously.

I straighten up. "Well, we were talking about getting some food, wanna eat with us?" I ask, stealing a glance at Jack.

He smiles, as if he too were about to extend an invitation. "Either going out or vegging in. Still deciding."

Zoey taps her narrow abdomen. "Stuffing our faces here sounds perfect. Annella and Fia just returned from Italy and of course they have a cold, so if I can avoid them…"

"Aren't there tonics for that?" Jack asks.

Zoey shrugs. "Yeah, but I have to take my aunts elixirs otherwise they get all butt hurt, and theirs taste seriously awful."

Jack fetches his phone from his pocket with an easy-going smile. "Dotty and Ray's, then?"

Zoey and I both nod enthusiastically.

"One of everything?" he questions, putting the phone up to his ear. Zoey's brow wrinkles. "One of everything?" she repeats.

"I think he means on the menu," I explain. Zoey gapes at me. "I seriously love him."

I link arms with her, grinning as I tow her to the living room. "We're going to find something to watch," I shout back at him as we breeze through the kitchen doors.

"I sure the hell hope he's your soulmate," Zoey teases. "Otherwise, your actual soulmate will have some trouble filling those very large shoes. Congrats on that, by the way."

"He's my soulmate, trust me," I say as we plop down on the couch sending cats scattering. "So how was work tonight?"

Zoey tucks her legs beneath her and stares down at the coffee table, her smile slowly straightening.

"Zoey?"

She runs her hand through her short black pixie, her silver bangles clink. "Uncomfortable…" I frown. "How so?"

"The leader of the Committee came in, and I mean the leader, as in the entire north American Committee, Mercy Bishop," she mutters.

"You mean Mercy Wicklow?" I question.

Zoey shakes her head incredulously. "Oh no, Wicklow is gone. A lot of rumors spreading about that divorce. But anyways, she came in, didn't bother to buy anything, not even under the pretense of shopping."

I feel sick. "What—" Hic, "happened?"

"She asked me about our shifts, about working together. How much time we spend together. What I do with my time. And about you…"

I just cower into the sofa. *Does she know about me? If she even just suspects…* Jack joins us in the living room, informing us that essentially the restaurant's entire kitchen will be delivered soon. Zoey perks up, changing the subject from the apothecary to Betty's latest antics and misadventures, including dating a cat down at the shelter. Apparently, a very scandalous thing to do.

Dinner arrives, and the aroma brings my family trickling down one by one. Soon everyone is feasting and laughing, first at Zoey stories, then Maggie's various impersonations of teachers at Griggs.

I try to capture this moment in my mind. Jack, tucked close to me, sensing my unease and giving me occasional hand squeezes. My aunts giggling, Abe finishing the nachos and adding his own hilarious stories from law enforcement. My mom snorting behind her hand as she balances a salad in her lap. Bewitched plays in the background, adding to the simple charm of the moment. I think of Silas's offer, the escape, and possible redemption.

I try to give Jack an encouraging smile, wondering how much time I have left here…

CHAPTER TWENTY-TWO
The Uncle

Every two seconds, I have to tap the break to avoid hitting the endless stream of careless drivers cutting me off. I seriously consider just lying on the horn the entire drive. The town is bloated with tourists. They're congesting the roads, crowding restaurants, and flooding downtown.

The sweet October novelty of Salem wore off quicker than spring break in Miami. Every woman caught outside is wearing some sort of a witch's hat and the town is overrun with ghost tours. I've even seen a few tourists using EMF devices around Griggs before the headmaster shooed them off the grounds. As the days get shorter and the nights get longer, the added populace is leaving the town a tad claustrophobic.

Halloween fever has even reached the halls of the academy. Girls squeal as they send each other pictures of their recently purchased costumes. My Russian lit teacher, Dr. Klien, let his ire slip due to the frequent inane chatter surrounding the holiday. Dr. Klien slams his copy of Anna Karenina down on his desk.

"Come up front, grab a tablet and stylus; you're all taking a pop quiz. We'll open with an essay question on Levin's journey of spiritual awakening and self-discovery," he orders before turning to the whiteboard, writing out the rest of the quiz questions.

Everyone groans, dragging themselves from their desks to the front near Dr. Klien's desk where the basket of tablets and corresponding pens rest.

"And begin," Dr. Klien drops in his desk chair with a smug smirk. There's a brisk knock at the door and everyone snaps their head up.

Nicole Morgan from the front office pops her head in. "Uh, I've got a note here for Eleanor O'Reilly?"

Dr. Klien growls before dismissing me with a wave.

I tuck away my grateful smile as I gather my belongings and hurry to the door. Nicole hands me a note with no information beyond where to report to. When I enter the office, it occurs to me

I haven't spoken to the secretary since my first day here last spring.

Once again, the woman doesn't look up at me. "Eleanor O'Reilly?" she drawls.

"Yep."

"Your uncle's here to pick you up." She looks behind me and screws her mouth into a tight, pert smile. "It was nice meeting you, Mr. Foster."

I turn to follow her eyeline. In a chair against the wall sits Silas Foster wearing a respectable business suit that looks incongruous to his blonde buzz cut, sandy-colored scruff and all-around gym rat vibe.

He grins at me and winks one of his "brown" eyes as he rises from his seat. "My beloved niece," he croons, holding out his arms.

I'm so bewildered that I stay rooted in place, even remaining stiff while Silas wraps me up in a bear hug. *Is he going to kidnap me from school? What the hell?! I thought their little band of misfit Nefari was on a volunteer basis; I never volunteered! And what will he do if I resist?*

"I told you he wasn't trustworthy. There's something very underhanded about him," Blue sends.

Blue? Are you here at school?

"Shall we?" In faux gallantry, Silas sweeps the office door open wide for me. "After you my dear," he says with a broad, verging on creepy smile. I glance back at the Secretary whose nose is buried in an open file again. I release an uneasy breath, then follow Silas down the hall and out the front door towards the parking lot. Silas stops and turns on his heel so suddenly I nearly bump into him. We've stopped just outside the high arching wrought iron gate displaying the school's insignia.

A white and black cat with a merle coat pattern trots up the sidewalk towards us, and oddly enough, Blue is just a step behind. My familiar races to my side and sits down beside my feet.

"Silas came to the house. He sent his familiar, Machado, into the house to fetch me while he stayed in the woods."

And you came?

"For reasons that shall soon become apparent, t'was easier to work with them." Silas says nothing; he just loosens his green tie from around his collar. "What are you doing here? And why do you have Blue with you?" I fold my arms and glance about, worried that someone is watching us.

Silas discards the paisley tie next to his familiar sitting dutifully at his feet, which I now see are clad in scuffed Nikes clashing horribly with his disguise as the loving and responsible uncle.

"He wants to discuss a matter with you but feels it's too dangerous to speak aloud; he wants to relay messages through familiars," Blue informs.

The hair on the nape of my neck rises, which has nothing to do with the autumn chill. I pull my blazer tight around me and glance about. Griggs is a fairly secluded campus. A wrought iron gate encloses the school grounds, which house a chapel, courtyard, and the ecology class's greenhouse, then is bordered by separate parking lots for staff and students, several athletic fields, and even an Olympic-sized pool.

What does he want? My mangy black cat rights his shoulders and looks intently at Machado sitting patiently, his tail swishing behind him.

Silas folds his arms, leaning against the gate like he thinks this is a waste of time. I'm guessing this was all Isolde's idea.

"There's a rumor," Blue begins, *"that you are in possession of a Black Flame Candle…"*

I gulp. *Can Machado hear me?*

"No."

I clench my jaw so tightly I worry my teeth just might crack. *"How the hell does he know that Blue?! I mean, I haven't told anyone! Even my aunts seem oblivious, who could have started these 'rumors'?!"*

"There's a myriad of explanations; perhaps someone in his ranks can commune with spirits, or they heard whispers in the wind from someone who knows Elspeth, I can't say. Perhaps he overheard you during one of his spying sessions. I don't know and frankly don't give a damn! He knows!"

Silas lifts his eyebrows, staring at me.

What am I going to do, what should I say?!

Blue turns his attention from me to Machado. *"Eleanor may be in possession of such artifact; what business is it of your master?"*

The cats stare each other down as a conversation flows between them. I wish I could hear Machado's reply.

"Ha," Blue scoffs. *"I must say, that might be the most adorable excuse you could have conjured. Whatever is in the possession of the Byrne clan belongs to the Byrnes by right. And thus, I believe our business is concluded."* Blue rises to all fours, emphasizing this exchange is over.

Machado hops to his feet with a hiss; the hair on his back stands on end. Silas steps to his left, blocking me from returning to school. Silas wags his finger at me, even though I haven't moved.

"You don't know what you're messing with, girl." Silas curls his fists at his side, his body tense. His mouth pulls back in a snarl, but there's fear in his eyes.

I take a step closer. *Blue, ask him if he knows what the candle can do.*

Blue sighs but relays the question to Machado who can then speak to his ward. Machado and Silas exchange a strange, indecipherable look.

"It appears they are not sure. They just understand it has tremendous power. And…some significance to dark forces, perhaps even the Dark Prince himself."

A petrifying chill spreads goosebumps up and down my limbs. A flurry of leaves swirls at our feet and drifts down the sidewalk away from us. The sky is a murky pool of gray. My legs rattle in my plaid skirt. Cowardly, I wish I could have delivered Elspeth the candle even if just meant I was no longer in its charge.

"Look," I say, stepping closer to Silas, "I'm giving you the benefit of my extreme doubt, but you can trust it's in a safe place. I have no intention of using it, nor am I giving it to anyone." I set my jaw firmly and meet his gaze, unwavering. "I trust you will leave it be."

Silas shakes his head and looks away like he's deliberating. He exhales roughly and seizes my shoulders, prompting Blue to leap in front of me and hiss. Silas disregards him. "If it ever comes down to you or the candle, you better choose correctly. None of us, not even your family, or hell, even all of Salem itself, none of it matters more than keeping that candle safe. Do you understand me?" He fingers drive through my coat into my bones. "Nothing!"

"If you don't tell your man there to release my witch, I'll be forced to act, and let me tell you a few broken bones won't slow me down, boyo."

"Let go of me!" I try to shake his hands off my shoulders. My phone buzzes in my skirt pocket.

Silas hesitates, but reluctantly releases me. "Don't tell anyone where it is. Not even me." He straightens up and stretches his neck causing it to loudly crack. "The offer still stands, if you want to fight for your freedom. Logan airport. Midnight." He jerks his head towards the parking lot and Machado falls in line. The two stalk away without a backwards glance.

"I'll wait by the van; you finish your school day." Blue sprints out towards the student parking lot.

The rest of the school day goes by in a blur. I can't escape the gravity of his warning; if it comes down to it and it's my life or the candle, I must choose correctly. Translation: die to keep the candle out of Elspeth's hands.

I scarf down a quick dinner next to the kitchen sink as Mom and Marie work on replenishing brews for the medicine cabinet.

"Perhaps I should accompany you on your shift tonight, in case Mercy

drops in," Blue suggests while I get ready in my bedroom.

I shake my head as I pull on my black and gray tweed trousers. "Betty will be there, and apparently she's in heat." I glance over at Blue, practically seeing the blood drain from his face.

"On second thought, I'm sure you can handle yourself if Mercy happens to stop by, which is highly unlikely."

I fight back a smirk as I gallop down the stairs. At the front door, I announce that I'm leaving to no one in particular and hurry out to the van.

The street is lined with cars in front of the apothecary, and customers are lined up around the block waiting to come in. Some are dressed in full costumes, but most have just donned a traditional witch's hats. They bounce in their heels in the chilly evening air waiting outside.

"What the hell is happening?" I mutter as I park around back. Before I unlock the back door, I close my eyes and try to sense if anyone from the Committee is nearby. I calm my breathing but feel nothing. *Crap.* All it means is if they are in there, they aren't using their magic. Which would make sense, give how many humans are around. I release a breath and head in.

Zoey sits on the stool, bouncing her knees as she watches dozens of shoppers lifting vials, reading the ingredients aloud, touching merchandise, and playing with the display plants.

"Oy!" she yells at a group of teens. "Want me to come put my finger in your mouth? No? Then keep your damn hands out of the Fly Trap's mouth, got it?!" A teen dressed as a vampire gently sets down the ancient, tenderhearted Venus Fly Trap near the homeopathic literature section.

I slip in behind her and take the neighboring stool. "Hey," I say warily. She shakes her head, glaring out from our platform. "I freaking hate this season. Look at them," she juts her chin out at the shoppers, "our way of life is not their costume. Damn faux witches. Trixie, bless her pure heart, she loved it. She found it a hoot that the Sons and Daughters were celebrating us, buying overpriced candles and smudge sticks all in the hope they can be one of us." A flock of giggling women carry a box of crystals, a book on emotional healing, and an elixir for fighting cellulite up to the checkout counter.

Zoey screws her face into a fake smile. "Did you find everything you need?" she asks, high pitched. Her polite tone verges on menacing.

Thankfully, no one in the group picks up on it.

"Oh yes! We're from Minnesota. This shop is a scream!" the woman says as she hands over her credit card.

Zoey pauses with the card in hand, then cranes her neck around the group. "Oy! Don't make me come over there!" she yells at the same group of rowdy teens as before. She swipes the card, muttering the entire time. "Don't kill them. You can't kill them. You'll become a Nefari. Missing tourists lead to awkward questions. Don't do it." She shoves the card back to the woman who glances around her group and leans away from the counter.

I leap from my stool and intervene. "Would you like a bag?" I ask. Not waiting for an answer, I produce a brown paper bag from under the counter and place their items inside.

Zoey and I don't get another chance to talk for the rest of the hour as we rush to swipe credit cards, count out change, and mutter curses when Apple Pay keeps stalling.

I nudge Zoey who then gawks at a patron wearing green face paint, a fake nose, warts, even a long prosthetic clef chin. Their pumpkin spice lattes inexplicably tip in their hands and pour down their costumes.

Zoey snorts as she prints out a receipt.

After the last customer leaves, Zoey flips over the closed sign and we both collapse in the tuft velvet chairs poised in opposite corners of the shop. With a flick of her fingers, Zoey extinguishes the light, plunging the shop into darkness. The only light in the store trickles in from the yellow streetlights outside. In a scene straight out of Fantasia, brooms and mops begin to sweep and wash the floors. I order the feather dusters to swirl around the shelves and over the plants.

"Tomorrow is going to be worse," Zoey calls across the shop to me. My feet throb. "Would you hate me if I called out sick?"

"Don't worry about it; I already called in sick for both of us. Sent my aunts a text this morning."

I sigh. "Thank you, thank you." I close my eyes and listen to the swishing mop.

"Hey, let's get out of here tomorrow, like out of Salem. Don't you guys usually meet on the weekends? We should crash RISD," Zoey says before giggling deviously.

I smile picturing Jack's dorm room and the extra bed he keeps for me.

My gaze lazily drifts over to the front windows.

Mercy smiles.

CHAPTER TWENTY-THREE
The Rhode to Hell

My mind goes blank. My heart stops beating. A high pitch siren rings in my head. I can't move from my seat. My fingers curl around the armrests of the chair. *Don't panic. She might not know about me. This could merely be a coincidence. Blue, please say you're close enough to hear me?*

Mercy taps on the window, still smiling. "I can read the 'closed' sign, but… might I come in anyway?" she calls through the glass.

Okay, she hasn't seen me yet. I've practiced for this. I carefully slide my chair back a foot, placing a Ficus between Mercy and me.

Mercy cups her hands around her eyes trying to peer in.

"Who is it?" Zoey moans exhausted, not rousing from her seat. "It's Mercy Wick—err Bishop, or whatever. She's outside!" I hiss.

"Ugh, not again," Zoey grumbles. She pushes to her feet and moves towards the door. "Coming!"

My eyes fall shut. I take slow measured breaths, keeping my heart and mind calm. Inspired by Isolde, I picture long parted braids in two thick plaits resting down my back. I picture my eyes blue, bold lipstick, a nose piercing, and orange and black eyeshadow (to go with the season).

Zoey yanks the chain lock and turns the two deadbolts. "Hey, Ms. Bishop."

"Zoey, call me 'Mercy', please," she says in her best attempt at effete charm. Zoey just nods. "Cool, cool. So uh, the cash register is closed but you can order a curbside or delivery for tomorrow if you want." She leans against the door frame, and the streetlight shines through the excess fabric of the black lace tank top that hangs loose on her tiny frame.

"No, that's fine. Is it just you here?" she asks, rubber necking to see into the store.

"Nope. O'Reilly is around here somewhere," Zoey answers sounding as disinterested as one can possibly get.

Mercy settles back down in her heels. "Hmm," she muses, "well, I won't keep you then. Tell Eleanor I said *hello*," she says, ending the message purposefully loud so I would hear. She lingers by the door, glancing about before stepping back from the door and out of the yellow spotlight.

"Ugh…she's so slimy, like a reptile," Zoey murmurs as she slides the locks back into place.

Betty slinks up the aisle and joins Zoey at the door, peering out the glass. "Argh, whatever, reptiles can be slimy too. Fine, amphibian then. Geesh, who died and made you the expert? You can be such a know-it-all," Zoey grumbles to her cat. She strolls past, giving me a quick glance before stopping short with a staggering double take. She releases a terrified yelp, jumps back, then squints at me. "What the hell, Ragazza?! You scared the shit out of me! What's with the glamour?"

I shake my head. "Just fooling around," I mumble.

She nods at me skeptically. "Well, maybe don't do it skulking in the dark. Damn, you nearly made me wet my pants." Her glare softens into a forgiving smile. "So, Rhode Island, Saturday?" she asks, wiggling her eyebrows at me.

I weakly nod as the adrenaline rush leaves me even more exhausted than before. "Yeah, we'll need to get costumes," I say, hauling myself out of the chair. Jack mentioned Delta Phi was hosting some kind of costume party at Brown this weekend when we made plans for me to come down. Jack was hesitant about us attending; every fraternity begged, cajoled, and outright bribed him to join, but he turned them all down. But we both decided we needed to branch out when I visit so we aren't always cooped up in his dorm, so close to his bed.

Zoey uncharacteristically squeals in pure delight. She claps her tiny hands, her chunky jewelry clacking against each other. Even when we lock up and head to our vehicles, Zoey is still giggling about our upcoming weekend.

I park in the gravel driveway and stare at the house in the dark. The many windows scattered about the front façade glow a soft amber, like the home were a giant Jack-o-lantern.

"Hey," I call into the house. *Oh, and Blue, Mercy did stop by tonight, so thank you for all your help,* I send sarcastically as I kick off my shoes in the entryway. I pull my hair up into a ponytail. It's Mercy I'm really mad at, not Blue. If she just understood what my family has been through, maybe she'd back the hell off.

The scent of spiced apples and cinnamon cakes mingles with the crisp autumn air that seeps in through the open windows.

"Hey, hon," Mom calls from back in the living room.

Sally and Marie bicker in the background.

"What are you guys up to?" I ask, lumbering down the hall into the room and leaning against the door frame.

"We're decorating, what do you think? Maybe we need more pumpkins?" Marie asks. The room is filled with at least two dozen pumpkins, some carved, some left whole, all in various sizes and colors.

Using her finger to direct her magic, Mom drapes thick black and orange banners across the high ceiling. The satin shimmers under the chandelier lights. On the fireplace mantel, Marie arranges Halloween decorations circa 1960: smiling jack-o'-lanterns, grinning plaster cats wearing orange party hats and frilly collars, and white-sheeted ghosts peering through droopy black eyeholes.

Sally lounges in a high-back tufted chair, her legs dangling over the armrest. Her finger flits about directing bowls of red apples to end tables and shelves, while cinnamon brooms fasten themselves to open hooks on the walls.

I smile, deflated, wishing I could join the merriment of the holiday. But seeing Mercy tonight has soiled my mood. "Are we hosting a party or something?"

Mom swivels slowly on her heel. Her eyes are round and apologetic. "Yes, actually." She sits on the floral sofa across from the windows while the banners finish hanging themselves. "Mercy proposed that your Aunt Marie host a Halloween party for Committee members."

I nod, my eyes wide. "How nice of her to insist that someone else throw her a party," I mutter.

Mom crosses her legs at the knee and laces her hands in her lap. "It's the day after tomorrow, and I was thinking perhaps you and Blue could visit Jack this weekend. Maybe even Persephone can join you; she's never been to Rhode Island." Mom gives me a thinly veiled smile.

I roll my eyes. "Blue is enough of a chastity belt, thank you." My eyes drift about the festive decorations and my aunts pretending to be decorating still instead of eavesdropping. Granted, I wanted my mother's blessing to visit Jack, but I'm still miffed they're hosting a Committee party. *In their defense, it's not like they could have refused. Freaking Committee…*

* * *

"I hate punny costumes," Maggie says. "They're rarely all that clever. Besides you can never beat a classic." She pulls out a skeleton costume as we peruse Esmerelda's costume section.

Esmerelda's dressed in her silk bejeweled turban, asleep and drooling behind the counter. Zoey chuckles, shaking her head. "She doesn't look it, but she's like seriously, seriously old. I mean, like, crazy old."

I glance back at Esmerelda. She appears to be in her mid-to-late 80's. But once a witch turns seventeen, it takes three years for them to age as much as human does in one. So yes, she must be really, really old.

"Ah! Found my costume!" Maggie exclaims. She hops down from the wooden ladder and holds up the gown of an Elizabethan countess. The dress is rich in texture, made from ivory fabric with gold embroidery that glimmers when she waves the skirt. The tightly corseted bodice has crisscrossing ribbons down the front giving it a regal finish. Clipped to the neck is a high frilly collar adorned with glistening pearls.

"What are you going as? And to what? Mom is never letting you go to a college party," I say, fighting against my scolding-older-sister tone.

Maggie rolls her eyes. "For your information, I'm going with Piper and Savannah to the costume ball at the Hawthorne. And as far as the costume goes," she pauses to slide her head through the hanger so the dress rests against her like an apron. "I'm going as Dracula's bride. I've seen a bunch of videos how to make a really cool bite mark and blood that won't be sticky all night." Her eyes go wide with excitement, and she skips to the counter and places her dress across from the snoring Esmarelda.

Zoey peruses the costumes looking lost and crestfallen. I haven't even begun to look; all I can think about is Isolde's family plane sitting at the Logan airport waiting to fly out in seven days.

"I really don't want to look stupid," Zoey mumbles under her breath.

Maggie waltz back to us giddy with her find. "Okay, back to you guys," she says. Her eyes narrow on the costume Zoey just pulled from the rack. "What do you think?" Zoey holds up a Little Red Riding Hood costume.

My sister scrunches her button nose and shakes her head. "Uh, no. There will be like thirty girls wearing skanky variations of that. You want to stand out, not mix in." Maggie scans the costumes, and her face lights up. "Perfect!"

She holds up a white wisp of a dress like a Grecian robe. It has a gold rope around the waist and a single thick strap over the left shoulder. A wicker basket filled with golden apples is attached to the hanger as an accessory.

"Pomona, goddess of fruit, orchards, and gardens. It's cute, it's hot, unique, and works as a litmus test; only the cultured guys will know what you are," Maggie says, handing her the costume.

Zoey grins, snatches the dress, and hurries into a dressing room.

Maggie's eyes meet mine. "Okay, sour grapes. Your turn." She sticks her tongue out at me spinning back to the costumes.

We walk up and down the four aisles of costumes only to circle back twice. I turn down a scarecrow, mummy, devil, and glittering flamingo costumes.

"Maybe I don't need a costume."

Maggie growls. "Stop. As soon as Esmerelda is done hemming Zoey's costume, we'll ask her to find you something." She pulls out a mermaid costume and holds it out to me. I shake my head.

My sister mutters something under her breath and runs her finger along the hangers. She stops, and her eyes bulge. "How did I miss this? I don't care if you say no, this is it! Cinder-Eleanor," she declares with a wide, self-congratulatory grin.

I take the dress from her. It's a silvery confection, and at the right angle, the shimmery fabric has the smallest whisper of blue. The sweetheart neckline is paired with thin silk cap sleeves. "Cinderella is blonde, though." I say, running a finger down the silky, elbow-length gloves.

"Princesses come in any color, as long as you're in the iconic dress," she says.

I gaze at the dress, unsure if I like it but not in the mood to debate. I loop it over my arm and follow my sister to the checkout.

Back at home, the wind rattles my bedroom window as Maggie, Zoey, and I primp and prim. Blue quietly watches us from the window seat, periodically rolling his sapphire eyes at what he keeps referring to as our 'inane chatter'.

"I predict a storm; hopefully, Rhode Island can proffer better weather…" he sends grumpily. *"At least the trip can offer us that."*

Oh, cheer up. You're the only one who hates the tourist congestion more than Zoey, and now you'll get to escape for the weekend.

"Yes, yes, but could you please ask Margaret if she can turn down this insipid racket? My brain cells are shriveling even faster than my patience."

I chuckle, bobbing my head to the synth pop beat while brushing a clear coat of nail polish on my fingernails. I've pushed away any sullen feelings and embraced the fact that no matter what the future holds, I'll be spending the weekend with a friend and the love of my life. I turn up the song to tune out Blue's droning.

Maggie contours Zoey's face, sculpting her cheekbones sharp and alluring. She brushes gold dust over her cheeks and down her neck, then sweeps a deep crimson lipstick across her lips turning them plump and voluptuous. Zoey adjusts her metallic wreath crown and poses in my full-length mirror, running her hands down her glittering arms.

"Eleanor, hold still!" Maggie snaps. My sister snatches my chin, forcing me to sit still while she finishes mascara. My face shines with highlighter brushed along my nose and cheeks. For my lips, Maggie picks a bright baby pink, then slathers on the gloss.

Maggie's copper locks are wrapped around hair curlers as she prepares for her ball here in town later tonight. She examines my face, and her smile slowly grows as she admires her work. "One more sweep of hairspray." She shakes the industrial-size can and sprays a sticky cloud around my loose, swept-up bun.

She presses a hand to her face. "It's like a work of art!"

I carry my voluminous skirt down the stairs, the clear plastic shoes clinking against the spiral steps. Sweat has already begun to pool at the toes; apparently "glass slippers" don't breathe.

Zoey carries her duffle out to my mom's old Lexus with Betty at her side. Mom's lending us her car since no one trusts Marie's van to make it to campus and back in one piece. Plus, my mother didn't seem so keen on having such a large empty backseat.

"A regular ol' sin wagon," Sally had joked with a playful wink.

When I stop in the entryway, Mom scrunches her face in disapproval. Her eyes zero in on the extraordinarily tight bodice. Not only is it nearly impossible to breathe in this thing, but it pushes my boobs up to just below my throat; one hiccup could spell disaster. "Does it come with a jacket?" she questions anxiously.

I shake my head and tug up the hem of my gloves. "No, but don't worry, it's so tight I'll probably duck out early just so I can change and breathe again." I snag a pair of regular shoes to pack in the trunk and make my suitcase float down to me from the top of the stairs.

Mom folds her arms. "And do we need to go over the rules about drugs or drinking?" she says while raising a thin eyebrow.

I shake my head. "Nope. I promise to behave. Plus, Blue will be on me the entire time, along with Betty," I mutter, slinging my bag up over my shoulder.

Mom frowns. "Yeah, is there something wrong with that cat?"

"*You have no idea,*" Blue sends standing beside me.

The entire drive to Providence, Blue begs that I either put him in the trunk, or Betty. Preferably Betty, in a burlap sack, tied tight.

I keep smacking my skirt down as it tries to fluff up around me in a cloud of crinoline, chiffon, and silk. I tug on my black choker, wishing I had waited to dress once we arrived.

Zoey laughs at me. "I think I'm too short to see you over your dress. You're gonna steal the show tonight."

I imagine having everyone's attention and my stomach drops.

When we stop for gas, other drivers take out their phones and snap pictures of me at the gas pump. Zoey stays in the car to touch up her makeup and rearrange the gold apples in her basket for the twentieth time.

"Okay, Ragazza, we are sleeping in his dorm, right?" Zoey asks, her voice edging higher with excitement.

"Yeah, though I'm not sure how much sleep we'll get. Jack said the closer they get to midterms, the more intense the parties get. Probably blowing off steam or something," I say as if I have a clue what college students do.

Zoey presses her face to the glass looking out at students crossing the parking lot. I don't see Jack's Mustang parked anywhere.

"Okay, Blue, Betty," I call, pulling into an open spot and placing my visitor parking pass on the dashboard. "You both will stay in the car until we leave for the party. Afterwards, you'll need to sneak into the building. I can't promise we'll be able to make you two invisible."

Blue tilts his head at me. *"Excuse me? And pray tell, why will you be unable to perform such a perfunctory task which you've now mastered? Are you insinuating you'll be too inebriated?"*

Zoey sighs, "Yes, Betty, I will limit the drinks. No, I didn't bring a beer funnel. Wait, you packed one for me?"

Blue shuts his eyes as he fights to gain his composure. *"Ignore the dimwitted canker blossom next to me. You will absolutely not accept any beverages from young men. Do not go into secluded areas of said party—"*

"Blue, I don't drink, and I promise to be the most boring person at the party. Besides, Jack doesn't want to stay long, this isn't his scene."

Blue settles down on the seat, begrudgingly.

"Animal cruelty? Betty, it's 50 degrees out, you'll be fine," Zoey tells her hairless familiar. Then her eyes bulge. "Oy that is not proper Italian!"

Zoey and I haul out our suitcases from the trunk. Several students gawk at our elaborate costumes so early in the evening. *Yep. Should have waited to get dressed.*

Zoey stares at everyone wide eyed. "I want to come here," she whispers. "Everyone seems so…cool."

I fish Jack's spare key from my purse and head into the stairwell. For all the mischievous, badass persona she exudes, my petite friend is actually soft-hearted and sensitive inside. She does everything she can to disguise her vulnerability.

Blue appears at my side as we walk down the hallway. "Hey, what are you doing here?" I whisper. My eyes dart about the empty hall, hoping no one will spot a mangy-looking cat in the hall. "Wait. Blue, where's your tail?"

"Some escapes demand sacrifice."

I unlock Jack's door, but before I open, I knock, just in case. No one answers. "Welcome to Jack's dorm," I tell Zoey.

His dorm room is bathed in a soft, crosshatch pattern of fading evening light. Zoey fights against a grin, trying to play it off cool as she bustles inside. She strolls to the center of the room and spins in a slow circle, taking it in. We levitate our bags to the floor beneath the large half-moon window.

"Mind if I sit on your boyfriend's bed?" Zoey asks.

"Knock yourself out," I say as I fluff out my skirt that's bunched in the back. My eyes drift over to his open sketch book on his desk. What I see sends a chill down my spine. All over the exposed pages are drawings of a black bearded goat staring off the page…

CHAPTER TWENTY-FOUR
The Party, the Goat, the Game

Jack's sketchbook quivers in my trembling hands.

I feel eyes on me. *Elspeth?* My heart accelerates. *No, Elspeth's malevolent presence is too familiar to me now. This is new, darker. An inky black cloud trying to swallow me whole.* My eyes stay fixed on the goat, facing outward, his eyes following me.

Blue leaps onto Jack's pale wooden desk and bends his head towards the book. "*Friend of yours?*"

No. But I've been seeing that goat in my visions more frequently. It started last year. Remember, when I saw that puritan village burning then that freaking black goat rammed me off the hill? He keeps returning, never really doing or saying anything, but…why is Jack drawing him?

Zoey bounces her bum on Jack's bed, causing the springs to squeak. "Oh my Minerva, it's just like the movies."

I flip through hundreds of hasty sketches of the goat. A close-up of his menacing pill-shaped eyes, his curled horns, and then an enlarged floating head looking down at an estate of some kind. *What the hell?*

Footsteps stop outside the door.

Zoey immediately leaps up off the bed, smooths the wrinkles out of her Greek Goddess gown, and adjusts her gilded leaf crown.

I snap the sketch book closed and place it on his desk just as the door sweeps open. Zoey stands awkwardly by the bed, clutching her basket of golden apples.

The sensation of being watched vanishes.

I meet Jack's wide grin and twinkling eyes as he takes in my voluptuous skirt and painfully cinched waist. Jack tosses his backpack to the side and shuts the door behind him, gathering me in his arms and spinning me with a passionate kiss. My skirt whooshes about me, my head is awhirl as his lips move against mine.

Jack returns me to my feet but keeps his arm securely around my waist as he greets Zoey.

"Hey," she says back, doing her best to restrain her excitement for the evening.

"And Blue, good to see you as well," Jack says. He turns back Zoey with a playful smile. "Did you bring your familiar. From your stories, I'm pretty anxious to meet her."

Blue releases a gust of air. *"Just when I was warming up to the lad…"*

Zoey juts her thumb at the window. "She's in the car napping until it's safe to come up."

"What if we sprang for her own room at a local establishment? I dare say she'll be more comfortable there…"

I glance over at Blue. *The cat doth protest too much, methinks…* I quote in my head.

"I. Will. Cut. You."

Jack nods. "Well, I'm sure you can sneak her up. It's Saturday, everyone's already drinking, I doubt they'd even notice a cougar walking up the stairs." Jack kisses the side of my head, letting his lips linger for a moment. "I'll go change, then we can head to Delta Phi. Um, is he coming along?" He nods to Blue.

Blue raises a brow.

"Yeah, but he'll make himself scarce," I assure, speaking more to my familiar than to Jack.

When Jack returns from the communal bathroom, both Zoey and I gape. He's dressed as the Dread Pirate Roberts from *The Princess Bride*— one of my favorite films—exuding roguish charm in full force. His lean athletic frame is on full display in his tight black pants and billowy black top with tall leather boots. A glinting silver sword dangles from his holster.

My heart beats erratically and I struggle to swallow. Zoey blushes.

"Ready?" he asks.

I nod, not sure I could speak, and eagerly take his hand.

"Jack, do you have a brother?" Zoey questions, trailing behind us. Jack and I exchange a glance from the corner of our eyes.

"Uh…yeah," he answers awkwardly. We turn down the hall towards the stairwell. "Jack!" a jovial male voice calls out behind us.

The three of us turn towards the voice.

Jack's neighbor, Auggie, is locking his bedroom door—I remember him from my disastrous visit last month. Now he's dressed in low-hanging blue jeans, chaps, a suede vest with no shirt, a red handkerchief around his neck, and a tall Stetson on his head. When he looks up from pocketing his keys, his jaw goes slack. "Holy shit." His eyes slide from me to Zoey, back and forth, until finally he's able to close his gaping mouth.

Jack looks at him impatiently. "What's up, Auggie?"

"Uhh… are you guys going to Kappa Alpha Theta's party tonight?" He takes a step forward, noticeably unsteady on his feet, and grips his open suede vest, exposing his poorly defined chest speckled with black hair.

Jack shakes his head. "No, Brenden Whistler invited us to Delta Phi." Auggie nods.

"You're welcome to come along," Zoey invites with a small smirk. She adjusts the basket on her arm, her dark brown eyes surveying his wannabe Magic Mike costume.

"Yes," he answers, eyes bulging.

Outside the frat house, students dressed in a myriad of costumes and in varying degrees of undress dance, drink, and film each other on their phones. Girls scream and pretend to flee from mask-wearing boys chasing them through the midnight crowd. A club remix of 'Spooky, Scary, Skeletons' blasts from large speakers poised in the windows, creating a pulsating rhythm that fills the air as the bass line thumps in my chest.

Every girl we see greets Jack as we weave our way into the house. Zoey stays close to my side, and Auggie stays close to hers. Strobe lights flash and a fog machine puffs in the living room, making it nearly impossible to see more than a few feet in front of us. The smell of alcohol, weed, and fifty different perfumes fill the air.

"Something to drink?!" Jack shouts over the music to Zoey and me. I nod. "Do you think they have water?!"

Jack nods. "I'll be right back!" He glances about the opaque room, unsure if he wants to leave us.

Blue hisses at a caveman who nearly steps on him. "*Eleanor, I can't believe I'm going to say this, but I'll be waiting in the car with that mentally unstable, fur-impaired excuse for a cat. Send word if you need me.*" Blue releases another hiss at someone who nearly stomps on his head and dashes out the door.

Auggie is giving Zoey's costume a once-over for the fifth time tonight.

"Those are some good lookin' apples. Juicy," he says, clucking his tongue.

Zoey barks out a laugh and snorts. "That was so bad," she teases. Her laughter is unbridled, guttural, and childlike.

"Well, Aphrodite, wanna dance?" Auggie yells.

She motions to her costume and basket of fruit. "I'm Pomona, goddess of the fruit and orchard, but yeah!" Zoey spins around to face me. "I'll be right back!" Then she dashes four feet forward to dance with Auggie who's already lost his vest.

The song ends and a thumping remix of *The Exorcist* theme floods the room. Everyone starts jumping and hoisting their Red Solo cups into the air, splashing their drinks as they dance, and I find myself being constantly groped and shoved. I hoist up my skirt and squeeze through to the hallway. I was expecting the house to feel like a veritable mansion, like the ones you see on Greek row in the movies; instead, the ceilings are low, the hallways narrow, and the rooms compact. I feel like I'm in a rat maze as I search for Jack with no luck. I stop, aimlessly joining the serpentine line for the bathroom.

"Hey," calls a man dressed as the latest Joker iteration. He leans his elbow against the wall in front of me. "I know you, right?" His eyes slink down from my face to my chest.

I fold my arms across my chest and look away. "No, I don't think so."

"Yeah, yeah, you were at that one thing, um on the quad," he says. "No…um I don't go here."

He nods, still feigning recognition. "No, not the quad at Brown, the one at RISD. You go there, right? My friend Ben goes there. You know Ben," he says as a statement, nudging my shoulder.

His nudge nearly knocks me off balance in these stupid heels. Clearly, the power lust hits frat boys even more than usual. "No, I don't know Ben. I don't attend RISD either, I'm here with my…." I trail off as a black bearded goat worms his way through the party. My eyes follow him as he slowly trots down the hall, noticed by absolutely no one.

Three people cut in front of me and I lose sight of it.

"Hey!" I call. I turn back to the Joker. "Did you see that? That goat?"

"Goat?" he frowns and looks around us.

I nod. "Yeah, a black goat just walked by."

"Wow, my brothers really went all out for the party. But they better not expect me to help them clean up goat shit, though," he mutters, peering disappointedly into his empty red cup.

The gathered crowd naturally parts, revealing the black bearded goat at the end of the hallway. He stares at me with his insidious pill-shaped eyes. Joker drops his empty cup to the floor. "I'm Clay, and if I may, you might be the hottest girl at this party." He dips his head closer to mine and reaches for my waist with a heavy paw.

I step out of his reach and maneuver around him. The goat's

eyes have me caught in a magnetic pull. The hallway and the living room all fade into the periphery. The sharp scents of sweat and smoke, the pulsing rhythm of the house beats, and the flicker of the strobe lights all become distant and muffled as I'm beckoned forward.

My body moves on its own, drawn by a powerful, invisible force. Each step feels slow, dreamlike, as if time itself has thickened. Everything else falls away; the chaotic party is merely an echo, distant, irrelevant. The stiff carpet is replaced by pristine wood flooring. The compressed ceiling over my head soars high above me. The beige walls crumble into bright damask wallpaper. Gold and crystal chandeliers descend from the ceiling like grapes dipping down from a vine.

By the time I reach the goat, I'm standing in a great hall. Candelabras shine from every surface, and candle lit sconces adorn the walls. An ornately carved sweeping staircase dominates the entrance hall. A string quartet adjacent the staircase plays a surreal, dreamlike waltz.

I sway to the hypnotizing tune, drifting back and forth in my heels, until I realize I've lost sight of the goat. Women in dresses with fitted bodices and puffy skirts glide into the room, escorted by men in white gloves and tailcoats. Those in the center move in step with a choreographed dance. Women glance at me sideways and whisper behind paper and lace fans. *Wait—they can see me? Is this really a vision, then? Where am I?*

I attempt a curtsy here and there as I drift down the hall, desperately trying to find the stupid goat that led me here.

"Anne Tottenham!" a male voice declares from the hall. A smattering of polite applause.

I can hear ruffling skirts and solitary footsteps descending the staircase and I walk farther down the corridor. Several candles have burned out, leaving the hallway dim. Thunder roars close by. A few guests in the hall let out a nervous chuckle. And the strings kick up a boisterous tune just as a knock at the door pounds loudly against the oncoming sounds of a storm.

Blue, can you hear me? I glance around, meeting the eyes of several gossiping women and curious servants. *And I don't think I'm at a costume party.*

Hooves clomp against the wooden floorboards. I gather my skirts and rush down the corridor as the trotting hooves move away from me. I'm closing in.

I see the tail end of the animal tramping into a brightly lit room.

I skid to a halt in the doorway of a billiard room, my shoes slick with sweat. Men and women are scattered at different gaming tables. The black goat saunters around the center table and vanishes.

One of the gentlemen rises from his seat as a young woman approaches the table. The rest of the men look up from their cards and quickly jump to their feet, bumping the table in their haste. The woman looks about my age. Her features are mousy; two pipe curls dangle on either side of her temple as she meekly takes the free seat that's pulled out for her. When her soft brown eyes meet the stare of a gentleman across the table, she blushes and looks away, ducking her chin towards her chest.

I approach the table, mindful that I'm not invisible this time. All the chairs are taken, so I hover nearby.

"Miss Tottenham, have you ever played Faro?" a man asks, shuffling a deck of cards.

The demure young woman shakes her head, curling her shoulders in, while her cheeks deepen in color.

I gaze about, pretending to take in the room. Thankfully, I'm not the only woman circulating the table. Several women drink, looking over their partner's shoulders. This must be the 18th century version of girls watching their boyfriends play stupid video games for hours. The older women are poised in gilded chairs at the corners of the room, whispering and giggling to each other behind their fans.

A small black spider skitters across the card table. No one seems to notice. The men explain the game to the girl as she carefully listens, her lips repeating the instructions to herself. The dealer passes out the cards and everyone makes their bet. I sigh at the rather perfunctory and perfectly boring scene. *Maybe this isn't what I'm meant to watch.*

I wave my hand out in front of me as a fly buzzes by my face. Time might as well be ticking backwards. The guests are engrossed in their various games, oblivious to anything but the shuffle of the deck or the clinking of coins. My stomach growls. I turn about the room noticing the end tables laden with tiered pastry trays and platters of fruit and meat.

A second, more persistent fly nearly hits me in the face as it whizzes on by. I can't help but swat at it while also attempting to keep my composure.

Once I complete a full circle about the room, I begin again, hoping to eaves drop on anything pertinent.

"I find the dress enchanting…"

"That mark though, on her back, why not hide it…"

"No proper introductions? Truly uncouth."

I near the mouthwatering pastries once more, but this time they've changed. The fruit is now rotting and shriveled. Its surface teems with white, wriggling maggots. The other sugarcoated confections are now withered and fuzzy with mold. My stomach heaves with revulsion. *How did everything rot so quickly?* The room suddenly fills with a nauseating, sulfurous stench, like rotten eggs mingled with the acrid odor of burnt coal.

I spin around from the food worried I might actually retch all over myself. The air itself is heavy with grime and malice. The gossip slowly changes from petty remarks about attire to cruel observations and wishing genuine harm on other guests.

The branding on my back begins to ache—just a tingle at first, then a painful itch, and finally a searing burn. I wince and shift my shoulder blades as I stifle a whimper. My eyeline drifts to the ceiling where several spiders repel on silken threads from the chandelier.

I need to get out of here. As I turn to leave, I notice a new player at the center table playing across from Miss Tottenham. He's a towering, broad-shouldered figure in a black hood and cloak.

Miss Tottenham drops a card. She quickly apologizes and bends down to retrieve it. As she's tucked under the table, she releases a shrill, ear-splitting scream.

The new player slowly swivels in his seat, his head sheathed under the black hood slowly turns towards me.

I clap my hands over my mouth to muffle a shriek of my own. Terror seeps from every pore down to my marrow.

Inside the hood are curled horns, coiling back from the face of a black goat.

CHAPTER TWENTY-FIVE
How Much Longer Do We Wait?

I'm plunged into darkness. My limbs drag me down as if laden with lead. I blink several times, or at least, I think so. I can't tell if my eyes are open or closed. I can't even lift my arms. My heart pounds, but it's a slow, heavy, thumping rhythm. *Please, don't be taking me to Purgatory.* I struggle to breathe as the pressure is immense, like a diver descending into dangerous depths. A new sensation appears, a tugging of sorts. Not to my body. *My clothes, maybe?* There's a strange gurgling around me. *Wait, am I underwater? No, I'm breathing.* The gurgling gets louder, clearer.

They're voices. Someone, or many someones, are talking around me. More tugging. Something loosens on me, something on my shoulders and perhaps my ribs. I can breathe a little easier. I think I'm being jostled but I still can't see anything. Unexpectedly, everything stops. I can't feel anything touching or pulling.

Instead, I feel a white-hot rage. Something is boiling, spilling over. The fury is overwhelming.

Something's tingling. My fingers. I can feel them. And my toes! The unnerving, discombobulated sensation is dissipating.

Thud. Thud. Thud. Smack. Thud.

"Eleanor! Eleanor, wake up! Now! Wake up! I command thee to wake!" Blue's voice is echoing and shrill in my ears. *"Eleanor! You must stop him. He's going to kill them!"*

I take a breath and concentrate on my eyes, forcing them to open.

Plaster ceiling. Overhead fan. Obnoxious fluorescent lights. My eyes flutter several times. My ribs expand effortlessly. I peer down. My corset has been completely untied.

"Thank Brighid! Eleanor, stop him!" Blue leaps onto what I realize is a large four post bed.

I shoot up in bed to see two men, a pirate and a guy in plain clothes, lying bloodied on the floor. Jack holds a third man wearing a "Hugh Heffner" silk robe by the throat, pounding his other fist into the guy's face. Blood gushes in a thick burst from a broken nose.

"Jack!"

My soulmate's head whips around to face me, his hand still clutched around the man's throat. His face is dark, twisted with a rage I've never seen before, making him almost unrecognizable.

I scramble off the bed onto my feet, only for my legs to buckle. I catch myself in a split second by gripping the bedpost with trembling hands. "Jack, please," I cry.

His eyes are wild when they meet mine, lost in his fury, as if he doesn't even recognize me. Slowly, his features shift. With his eyes locked on mine, he lets the man crumple to the floor. Blood continues to dribble down his face in two thick torrents painting his lips and chin.

Jack rushes to my side, hoisting me up while I regain my sea legs. The room is still spinning. I hold onto his steely chest as I regain composure.

"Are you alright?" he asks.

I nod at first, then shake my head. "I-I-don't know actually."

Jack tightens his grip on me.

"*What happened?*" Blue questions, standing on the bed on all fours.

I place a hand on my temple as a headache storms inside. "I had a vision. I followed the goat down the hall and suddenly I wasn't here anymore. I was at a party in the past, at this large manor."

"Did you drink anything before hand?" Jack questions.

"You broke my effing nose! And my tooth!" silk robe guy screams, still collapsed on the floor.

My stomach drops when I peer around Jack at the two other young men on the ground not moving. Blue, following my eyeline, leaps down and tiptoes close to their mouths, lingering there for a few seconds.

"*Both are alive. Unconscious, but alive.*"

Jack glares darkly at silk robe guy. "Call an ambulance for your friends, and if I ever see any of you again, I won't hold back." Jack escorts me from the room before the man can reply.

The music is still pulsating throughout the house.

Jack keeps me tucked in close as we descend the stairs. He notices me wince as we get closer to the overpowering speakers. "It might be faster if I carry you."

I shake my head, taking the last step. "Where's Zoey?"

We forge our way to the front room where the dance party is still going strong to a remix of Day-O. Zoey stands high up on the couch above as a crowd of men on their knees repeatedly bowing.

She eyes them looking flustered and uncomfortable.

"We're not worthy, Pamela," the crowd drunkenly chants.

Zoey's eyes light up when she spots us across the room. She leaps from the couch and rushes to our side. "Things are getting seriously weird in here, let's go, quick!"

Jack is stony and silent as he helps us both into the car.

Betty pounces onto Zoey's lap the moment my friend is seated. "Yeah, yeah, I know. I thought you wanted to nap so I didn't wake you. No, I didn't bring you back anything. What the hell are party favors? Shockingly enough, no one was passing out catnip," Zoey retorts sarcastically.

Tell me everything that happened, "Blue demands after sitting in my lap.

I fill Blue in on every horrifying detail, from the putrefied food to the truly terrifying face of the man in what I can only hope was a goat mask.

Jack glances at me when we approach a red light. "Are you sure you're okay?"

"Yeah, do you know what happened?"

Jack's fists tighten around the steering wheel. "When I returned with a bottle of water, I couldn't find you. I went searching, someone mentioned that you appeared to have passed out and someone was bringing you to a room to rest." He pauses, his jaw clenches as he breathes out his nose. "I found them attempting to help you out of your dress."

I nod, grateful for his intervention. I reach over and stroke his tense knee. "I'm okay, though. You found me before they could do anything." I stop for a moment, and a thought occurs to me. "How did you find me?"

Jack's eyes dart to Blue in my lap then presses on the accelerator as the light turns green. "Blue alerted me. At first, I was just worried, but when Blue said something was wrong, I panicked. I may have broken two doorframes before I busted into the right one," he admits.

How did you know?

"Truly? You know I can hear your thoughts. You believed you were seeing that blasted goat, then your thoughts vanished entirely. Your mind must have been cloaked by the vision.

The dormitory is rather quiet; everyone must still be out partying. Jack is silent as he sets up the sleeping arrangements: Zoey on the air mattress, me on his bed, and Jack on the floor squished tightly against the closet with merely a blanket and pillow.

Jack clenches and flexes his fists, examining the scrapes opening across his knuckles. Small beads of blood dot the freshly opened cuts. "I think I'll go wash up. Zoey, the bathrooms are down the hall. There's a big sign so you won't miss it."

Betty makes herself comfortable on the air mattress. Within seconds, she's snoring. Loudly.

Zoey slips out of her dress and into pajama pants and an off-the-shoulder sweatshirt displaying a Ouija board across the front. She uses a pad soaked with blessed spring water and rose hips to clean her face. "Hey," she calls to me as I shimmy out of my ballgown that takes up nearly half the room, "here." She tosses me a small black leather bag.

I catch it with a befuddled frown.

"It's for his cuts, they look pretty nasty." She takes out her aunts' homemade dental ointment and rubs it across her teeth. She catches me staring. "I'm way too exhausted to go actually brush my teeth, Ragazza. Feel free to use it." She crawls into bed and pulls the waffle knit blanket up to her chin, then props up her phone streaming an episode of 'I Dream of Jeannie'.

Blue watches me from Jack's bed. "*We need to discuss your vision. I find it highly concerning.*"

I nod, slipping on my silky pajama shorts, then my razor back tank top and a lavender knit pullover. "Later, after I help Jack," I say before tugging on my fuzzy socks.

Blue's ocean-colored eyes drift away from me, unnerved.

Carrying Zoey's bag of tonics, I make my way to the communal bathroom where I'm greeted by a thick wave of humidity. The air is heavy with steam, immediately clinging to my skin as I venture further into the large bathroom. Condensation drips from the tiled walls. The mirrors are completely fogged.

"Jack?" I call out, treading lightly towards the shower section.

A crank turns and the soft roar of water stops. The yellow shower curtain whisks open and Jack steps out with a towel wrapped around his bottom half. He runs his hand through his glistening wet hair. "Hey, everything okay?" he asks.

Will I ever get used to this? My eyes slowly meander his tight form, droplets of water trickle down his sculpted chest and defined abdomen. The towel is slung low, revealing the lean, carved out hip bones. *Oh, I hope Blue can't hear my thoughts right now.* I hum a children's song in my head to chase away any imagination of what is hidden beneath the towel.

"Eleanor?" Jack tilts his head, his emerald eyes looking me over.

I rip my gaze away and peer into the open tote. "Uh, I brought some things to help your hand."

Jack peers down at his injured hand, an all too familiar injury. He closes the distance between us and he holds out his hand.

The wounds on his knuckles are clean from the shower, so I get to work applying the witch hazel, then garlic essence, and comfrey.

"Sorry, if it stings."

He shakes his head, watching me as I work.

My fingers graze the veins that wind beneath his skin like bifurcated rivers on the back of his square hand. My fingers linger on his skin, taking in his scars, the callouses. I think of the strength and power I've witnessed in these hands, the same ones that can hold me with such tenderness and unyielding protection. They now lay open, vulnerable before me. I bandage his hand and bestow a little kiss to the white dressing.

"I'm sorry if I scared you," Jack says softly.

"It's okay," I answer, still clasping onto his hand not ready to release the feeling of his hand in mine.

"It's just—when I saw them standing over you, one holding you up while the other tried to… I was just—it was like I blacked out. Suddenly I was punching them." He shakes his head, his jaw clenched. "The thought of them…"

I cup his face. "I'm fine. Nothing happened. It'll be okay." I kiss his cheek, forehead, and nose in little reassuring pecks. "I promise, I'm safe." I kiss his defined jawline. I feel his mouth grow in a smile when I kiss his cleft chin. I tilt my head upwards so I can reach his lips. First a quick two pecks, then a third longer one as his lips open to mine, drawing me in.

His arms seize me, lifting me up until I'm sitting on the lip of the sink, my legs dangling as he stands in between. Our lips caress in a slow, burning collision, the kind that draws time to a standstill. His mouth moves against mine, longingly, like every breath we share is vital. His hands slid down from my back to the hem of my sweater, pulling it up over my head and discarding it into the neighboring sink. There's a delicious push and pull in our kisses, an unspoken rhythm, both of us giving ourselves and taking the other in equal measure.

I cry out in pleasure as his good hand grips the back of my head, his other hand gripping, tremblingly, yet strong on my hip as his lips slide down my neck to my collarbone back to that soft, nerve sensitive spot of skin below the ear.

I can barely breathe as I run my hands wildly through his hair pulling back his lips to mine. Our mouths move in a perfect, paradoxical dance; moving against each other but always somehow in sync, as if our very souls understood the unspoken language of our unquenchable desire. The need to be one keeps building with every heartbeat and kiss.

We aren't simply "making out". Our hands grip each other's skin in desperation, but not out of pure lust. This goes far beyond physical attraction. This is our souls colliding. It's a connection. An unbreakable pull that neither of us could resist if we wanted to.

We kiss, gasp, and hold each other. In this moment, Jack is everything.

Tears fill my eyes, knowing they will never fall.

Jack lifts my tank top just enough to expose my stomach, so our skin is pressed against one another. My fingers drag down his chest until they rest on the top of his wrapped towel. My fingers quiver as I slip the tips of my fingers in, ready to pull the cloth down. I loosen the fold, keeping the towel taut.

Jack's hands glide from cupping my face to holding my wrists, stopping me. He closes his eyes, catching his breath, resting his forehead against mine. "We can't. Not until we solve—" he grapples trying to find the right words. He chuckles, exasperated. "Whatever this thing with Elspeth is."

I move my hands from his waist back to his bare chest. I can feel his heart pound beneath my palm. "Jack, this hasn't been painful." I kiss him, my lips desperate for his passionate return.

"Really?" he questions, his voice has a quiet, subtle ring of hope.

I nod, vigorously. "Yeah, I don't know why. Elspeth said she could help me with this."

"But with strings attached," he finishes, his brow raised.

I sigh. "Yeah."

He nods before gathering up my hands, cupping them in his and kissing my fingers. "If we're able to figure this out without sacrificing anything truly important, then we will. We definitely will. But you deserve better than a RISD communal bathroom," he says, his mouth forming his signature, lopsided grin that charms me to the point my insides turn into a puddle.

With less enthusiasm than before, he helps slide my sweater back on and helps me down off the sink. He steps back into the shower stall to get dressed, then we walk hand in hand to his dorm where I insist we share a bed. Jack, ever the gentleman, ardently protests, but when I tug on his arm his resistance is all but gone. He curls up behind me, wrapping his arm around my waist.

The faint lights from the parking lot drift through the half-moon windows, casting a soft, gentle glow about the room. I spot Blue, asleep in… I do a double take. It's a cat bed, monogramed with his name on it. A dark blue velvet bed with a canopy. It almost resembles my bed from home. *Oh Jack, I do love you.* I give his arm a little squeeze. Zoey and Betty snore in tandem.

I sigh, feeling Jack's breathing slow, his chest rising and falling against my back. I can't stop my smile from filling my face. I even feel it sink to my insides. This smile, this feeling of utter contentment. I snuggle deeper into Jack, so our hips are hugging tightly.

As soon as my eyes fall shut, I see the goat staring at me. That warm, serene feeling deep in my chest dries up and cracks.

I gasp and cup my mouth worried I might scream. My vision, the visitor at the gaming table. I was so consumed by his demonic goat face, I didn't register something at first. Something vital. On the table, left of the goat man, was a hefty, prominent black candle. It was burning, the flame obsidian.

CHAPTER TWENTY-SIX
All Hallow's Eve

Zoey is practically giddy the entire drive back to Salem. She giggles about the guys that followed her around the party like lost puppies. She switches to a different song every thirty seconds, jumping from dead punk rocker to dead punk rocker as she describes Jack's dormitory neighbor in vivid similes.

"And you're sure you're okay? You disappeared for a while," Zoey says skeptically.

I nod, glancing at Blue who says nothing. "Yeah went to find a quiet place to rest. The music was really getting to me," I assure.

Zoey slowly nods at me. "Okay if, you're sure."

"I am," I say, trying to force an encouraging smile and begin asking questions about the party.

"I've never really hung out with the Sons and Daughters before last night. My typical crew was Trixie, Sebastian, and the rest of the witchy bunch. I've never gotten to experience the power lust before," she says, tucking the heels of her sneakers on the seat so her knees are pressed against her chest. She scrolls through her phone, switching between social media sites. "Apparently you don't exist if you don't have these." She then shows me the newly downloaded icons on her home screen. "You know," a smile creeps across her pixie face, "I haven't given much thought to 'after' high school. I mean, I 'graduate' in December."

I suddenly remember she's homeschooled.

"I think Brown could be pretty cool," she croons.

I chuckle. "Brown isn't the only school that has a social scene. In fact, I think they all do."

She raises her brow. "Where are you applying?"

I feel my insides sink, like my heart is actually sagging in my chest. "I don't know. I used to plan on the University of Miami, or for a while I considered Duke."

"Really? So far from Jack?"

I exhale, knowing with unfathomable certainty deep in my core it's all inconsequential. I won't be attending any university next fall.

"Well, maybe we could look at colleges together, it would be fun to room together." Zoey turns off her punk rock playlist that's a fixture of our shifts at the apothecary. Now it's a club mix of Halloween music akin to the writhing, pulsating mixes we endured last night. She bobs her head to the thumping beat.

I limply smile. "That would be fun," I agree.

"I'm interested in criminology, or maybe forensics. Maybe even abnormal psychology. I think all of that would be so rad. Man, I'm just so excited! College is going to be great. Even though I graduate sooner than you, I'll wait for you and stuff." She gives me a little nudge with her elbow.

I force a smile, but it falters. Thankfully, Zoey is too caught up in her daydreaming to notice. I glance at the rearview mirror, spying Blue staring out the backseat window, ignoring Betty sniffing him.

Blue? You okay? "No."

What's going on?

"We need to get home to the candle. From this moment forward…you will sleep with it under your pillow. There's a powerful force moving towards it. Can't you feel it?"

I think for a moment, pondering all the sensations I've experienced lately. There's been a definite uptick in the feeling of dread, but I'm not entirely sure where it's coming from..I've been attributing it to the Committee. The Committee!

Why haven't I thought of it before?! Blue! the Committee, why don't we give it to them? They will be far superior in protecting it than either of us will. They will actually keep it safe from Nefari or…

"Me?" Elspeth chimes in a deadly ire. *"You hand over my candle and you'll be begging for them to destroy you. I assure you, child, that brand you bear will be nothing to what I will inflict. Did you like seeing your mother's head? I will drive you mad with visions of your dead father, your mother, aunts, sisters, your beloved soulmate. Your mind will be so twisted, you'll live out the rest of your days in solitary confinement where the walls are safely padded."*

Blue looks over at me through the mirror. *"Her threats are genuine. But I advise you to keep the candle in your possession. Not for Elspeth, but I don't necessarily trust Ms. Bishop."*

Elspeth giggles. *"Thank you, Pyewacket. Listen to my familiar, Eleanor…for now."*

I pull up to Zoey's house. Her stout Aunt Molly is hiked up on a tall wooden ladder plucking apples from their tree out front, while eleven-year-old Anella is on the porch swing reading and nine-year-old Fia is in the grass hosting a tea party on a quilt with imaginary participants.

Zoey stares out the passenger side window at them. "Or maybe Salem State could be cool, we could still get our own place, but not so far away, ya know?" she says.

Polly comes bounding out of the house carrying four carved pumpkins with grinning faces. Anyone else would be amazed by her strength and balancing prowess, but to us witches, she's clearly just using the air spell.

"Sucks that Halloween is this Wednesday; it'd be so much cooler if it were on a Friday or Saturday. We could have gone to Rhode Island again," she says with wiggling eyebrows.

I laugh. "I've created a monster."

Zoey rolls her eyes at me. "Well, we've got the Halloween shift together at least. See you Wednesday." She hauls her duffle and familiar out of the car. When I pull up to my house, several cars are parked in the gravel driveway. I don't recognize them, which means they could belong to Committee

members. "What should I do?"

Blue stares at me deadpan through the mirror. *"You're a witch, Eleanor.*

When a witch can't go through the front door, she flies to a window."

I gather up my belongings, including Blue, and whisper the air spell. We levitate up to my tower window, dipping and drifting several times. Too many times. Blue ridicules me the entire time.

I unpack with Blue nestled against my pillows, watching me. Out my window, I catch a glimpse of the partiers from last night's Halloween jamboree trickle out the front door. By the time 1:00 p.m. rolls around, the last car pulls out of the driveway and disappears into the forest.

"Everyone is gone, time to get that candle. Go now." Blue springs from my bed to the floor.

I don't argue. I put aside my homework and follow him downstairs. Sally's familiar, Pyre, is passed out on the staircase. Marie's familiar, Miss Priss, is striped black and orange, scowling by the door as we tiptoe past.

I stop and gawk at the living room which bears the remnants from last night's revelry. Streamers dangle lazily from the ceiling, some draped over the furniture, others crumpled on the floor. Cluttered on every available surface are empty champagne glasses. Across the room in the floral armchair next to the bay windows, Aunt Marie is snoring softly dressed as a white cat. Sally, dressed as Cleopatra, is curled up next to Sheriff Abe Fuller (who clearly didn't get the memo to wear a costume). Both are passed out. The sound of dishes being cleaned rings out from the kitchen. Mom sings along to Chuck Berry's "Trick or Treat" while she busies herself cleaning. *Of course, Mom would be the first one up and cleaning after a crazy party.*

I drop to my knees and pull out the bottom drawer of the library cabinet. I wince as I reach as far back as I possibly can. My hand sweeps from one end to the other; my heart accelerates. "Uhh…Blue?" I say, panicked. My hand brushes against the back of the drawer, but all I can feel are crystals. "I… think the candle's gone."

"What?!" Blue places his front paws on the open drawer and peeks inside. My fingers bump into something that rolls to the back corner. I nearly dislocate my shoulder reaching for it, but my crawling fingers finally close around it. I whip my arm back, clutching the Black Flame Candle in a vice-like grip, and let out a sigh of relief.

"Never do that again."

Blue and I dash up to my bedroom taking two stairs at a time. I place it under my pillow and remake my bed. With my hands on my hips, I stare at my pillow with no detectable lump. "This seems…"

"Facile? Because it is. But 'tis a folly to stow it anywhere else. Obviously, this isn't a long-term solution, but I will work something out," he assures. He leaps up onto my bed and snuggles down into my pillows. *"Until then, I shall remain here."*

I nod. "If that's the best we've got."

He rolls his deep blue eyes at me. *"Gee, thank you for that passionate vote of confidence."*

After finishing a bit more homework, I join my family downstairs. While Sally and Marie clean up the living room, using their magic of course, Maggie and I scroll through all her pictures and videos from the ball.

"Wait!" I snatch her phone from her hands. "That's Ms. Murphy, my fencing instructor, making out with Mr. Altman from senior seminar!"

"Oh my gosh, that's not even the best photobomb!" Maggie squeals, taking back her phone. We're both still laughing when it's time to help make dinner. Mom, of course, is on the phone with Shannyn who extended her honeymoon in Paris. She must have finally arrived home this morning. Mom keeps giving Maggie and I kisses and squeezes as she strides about the kitchen, putting the finishing touches on her apple cider pork chops, still chatting away with Shannyn.

"Well, it sounds like Shan had a lovely honeymoon," Mom says as we all sit down to eat. Marie is running a bath, and Sally and Abe went back to his place to nurse their wicked hangovers. It feels strange eating with just Mom and Maggie now.

"Duh, it's Paris," Maggie says, helping herself to whipped sweet potato.

Mom shares the details of the party. The house was nearly bursting at the seams with witches from various covens as far away as New York. Past and present Committee members attended, though curiously, Mercy never showed up despite being the one who demanded the party in the first place. But overall, it was deemed a success. Mom seems more than relieved it's over.

Mom then drills into me about my first college party experience, demanding to know if there was any drinking, drugs, or anything she would deem inappropriate. I hesitate, thinking of the three townies that crashed the party and tried to assault me. "Nothing like that happened. In fact, I missed most of it. I had a weird vision and by the time it was over the party was pretty much winding down…"

"Vision of what?" Mom asks as she skewers a carrot.

"Really weird, a party from the 18th century. It didn't make any sense, to be honest."

Mom frowns. "Try writing it down, maybe something will stick out. We can go over it together, if you want."

After dinner, we all engorge ourselves on mom's homemade pumpkin torte dripping in sweet apple glaze while watching a spooky movie in the living room. Mom jumps at just about every scene, using the fleece blanket to block her face.

"Mom, it's House on Haunted Hill, it's in black and white. How are you this jumpy?" Maggie teases. My sister and I cuddle into either side of our mother, knowing that's what Dad would have done.

The next day after school, I race to get ready for my shift at the apothecary. Blue stays vigilant on my bed, guarding the candle under my pillow.

"So, what are we doing tonight?" Maggie asks. "Practice is canceled since it's Halloween. Muhahaha!" She tries to laugh like Dracula, but sounds more like The Count from Sesame Street.

"I work tonight, remember?"

Maggie nods. "Well, invite Zoey afterwards. We should watch an actual scary movie. Nothing in black and white," she says, shooting me a glare.

I chuckle. "I don't think mom's nerves will be able to handle much more." Maggie giggles. "She'll be fine. We'll give her plenty of blankets to hide under. I'm sad we don't get any trick-or-treaters. Sally says Marie buys enough to feed a thousand children, but no one ever ventures out. Other than a few teenage pranksters. Though Sally is looking forward to those," she says darkly with a wicked grin.

I'm not sure what to expect at the shop. Last Friday, we could barely move the aisles were so packed with customers. I'm relieved to find the shop without any pushy tourists gathering outside.

"Ciao, Ragazza," Zoey greets from high up on a ladder, sending elixirs in a levitating dance to the shelves. "These are getting old; Molly and Polly want them discounted in the sales basket up front. Oy! Betty, stay out of that!"

Betty, standing on the counter, retracts her hairless paw from a plastic cauldron overflowing with store bought candy. She narrows her yellow eyes on Zoey and bares her fangs before hopping down and disappearing behind the counter.

I chuckle shaking my head. "Your familiar is…"

"One hairless bitch. But I swear to Minerva, I love that insane cat," Zoey says, jumping off the ladder and dusting off her hands.

I plop down on a stool behind the second register. "What's with the candy?" I pluck a Butterfinger out of the pile and unwrap it.

Zoey opens her mouth to speak just as there's a tepid knock at the door. We both turn our attention to the glass door where a unicorn, ladybug, Batman, and a Transformer all huddle in front of their parents holding out wide open pillowcases. She smiles back at me. "Oh yeah, we get trick-r-treaters here. They're mostly children from the coven, but some Sons and Daughters show up too." She floats the bowl of candy into her arms.

"Zoey!" My eyes dart to the eager children at the door, panicking they might have seen.

Zoey rolls her eyes at me. "It's the one night of year we can get away with shenanigans. The kids are all hopped on sugar the parents are always a little tipsy. Anything they see they chalk it up to a 'trick'," she says with a wink before dashing off to answer the door.

The rest of the evening, we take turns answering the door, cooing at the adorable costumes. I have to elbow Zoey to keep her from grimacing at the witch costumes, especially the ones accessorized with green skin and warts. We keep a tally of the most popular costumes and award the most unique ones with an extra handful of candy. "Another Wednesday Addams," Zoey calls over her shoulder. I make a mark on our note pad.

We yawn in unison, perched on our stools, empty teacups next to a pitcher of spiced apple cider. With a flick of a finger, she turns the sign to closed.

"No sales, but hey, we still got paid," Zoey says. The clock on the wall reads ten-thirty. "So, what's next?" she questions, scooping up Betty off the table. She massages the cat's wide bat-like ears.

"Maggie suggested watching a scary movie, if you're down." I pick up a Jack-o-lantern ready to blow out the small tea candle inside.

"Stop!" Zoey drops Betty and sprints towards me. "What are you doing?" She takes the pumpkin from my hands and places it carefully back in the window. "Ragazza, you're Irish; how do you not know Samhain tradition? You can't blow out the candles of Jack-o-lanterns it's bad luck. You just let them burn out on their own."

I cock a dubious brow. "And risk a fire?" I question playfully.

"My aunts have excellent insurance." She reaches over and switches off the shops light.

"Alright," I say incredulously, taking a step towards the registers. Zoey snatches my arm, gripping me in a death grip. "Stop."

"Now what? Am I supposed to walk backwards through a dark shop?" Zoey shakes her head. Her eyes zero in on Betty. The hairless cat is stiff on the counter, staring off at the shelves towards the back door that's completely painted in shadow.

"Someone's here," Zoey whispers. "More than one."

My entire body clenches, staring at the dark, back of the shop. *Nefari? Committee members?*

There are sounds of several heavy footsteps, and a distinct sound of high heels.

Mercy Bishop steps into the shaft of pale light shining in from the streetlamps. Five men flock behind. None of them look friendly. Even Mercy has lost that 'friendly' air of being our gracious witch leader, the doyenne of the Committee. Her razor-cut, chin-length black bob only adds to her unnerving presence in the dim light.

"Eleanor O'Reilly, step back from Zoey Gallo," she says, her voice dripping venomous authority.

This is it. I've been discovered. Blue! Help me! A trade! We can trade the Black Flame Candle for my life. Something has to be done. This can't be it. Oh my gosh, I'm going to die!

My jaw quivers and my eyes swell with tears. "L-l-listen," I stammer, then hiccup, "you don't have to do this. I have something that might change your mind," I grapple. My phone buzzes in my hand, I see it's Jack calling me. "I doubt it," Mercy says, her lips a fine line, her jaw clenched. "Now step back, or we'll make you!" Mercy descends the platform steps towards us.

The men quickly follow suit.

I take several steps away from Zoey. "I'm so sorry," I cry. Zoey stares at me, wild eyed. "What's going on?"

"Zoey Gallo, you will be coming with us. Now," Mercy commands, her eyes a steely gaze on my friend.

All the blood drains from my face. My phone continues to buzz. Betty arches her back and hisses before sprinting off the counter towards Zoey. A man to Mercy's left stomps on the poor cat's back, stopping her midstride.

"Betty!" Zoey steps forward, only to be stopped by Mercy's outstretched hand.

"Zoey Gallo, you have been accused of being a Nefari. You will come with us, now, to stand trial and be tested. It will be better for everyone if you surrender. If you resist…" A wicked grin spreads across Mercy's face.

"Wait, what?" My eyes dart between Mercy and Zoey. "What are you saying?"

Zoey shakes her head, tears painting her face causing her inky black mascara to run down and drip off her chin. "I know how those trials go. You're worse than the puritans. My parents would attest to that, if they were alive."

My heart pounds in my ears, making me dizzy. *Wait, her parents were Nefari? So, is Zoey a Nefari too, then?* I think of all the hours spent with her; I never detected a thing. No buzzing of a glamour, no contacts in her eyes.

Mercy sighs. "I was merely First Broom back then; you'll have to take that up with my predecessor."

"My dad was just defending my mom from the hunters! You didn't have to destroy them!" she screams.

"There's no excuse for killing humans, Zoey, branding or not. Your parents knew our laws. They chose to kill, so their souls were forfeit. Now yours is too. Hopefully, the two younger Gallo sisters won't follow in your ill-fated footsteps."

"My family aren't Nefari!" Zoey screams. "We're innocent! My sisters aren't evil, they're just children!"

Mercy shows not a drop of empathy. "Of course they are, for now. Your parents didn't become Nefari until after little Fia was born. But we've been investigating you, Zoey, for a while. You've been corrupted, drunk long and deep from the devil's chalice." Mercy rights her shoulders. "Every time I came into this shop, I could feel your glamour trying to hide what you are. The arrogance to think you could hide it from me. Now come with us. You'll be held at City Hall until your sentencing."

Zoey shrinks, staring down at her shoes. "But I didn't do anything…" she cries.

I can barely catch my breath. It was my glamours Mercy was feeling, not Zoey's.

"If I go with you, I'll never see my family again." All the fight in her has vanished.

"Yes, well, think of Anella, or sweet little Fia. No one else has to get hurt if you come quietly." Mercy takes another step towards Zoey, and the men behind her move into a flanking position.

My eyes meet Betty's as she lies injured on the floor. She peers deep into me, pleading.

I'm the one they are after. I can't let them do this, not to my friend. She doesn't deserve this. But what do I do? Just reveal I'm the Nefari and let them take me? Will they just take both of us then? Maybe I should beg. No, they'll never listen. I gaze at my phone; Jack is still calling me. He can probably sense something is wrong. *If he only knew.*

Mercy and the five male witches encircle Zoey. She immediately disappears from my view.

I know what I have to do, and once I do, there is no going back. But I don't have a choice. I don't even have time to consider what it will cost me. My magic is awake inside me. *This is it.*

I ball my fists, resolute, as my heart breaks into a million pieces in my chest.

La Caeli…

CHAPTER TWENTY-SEVEN
No Goodbyes

Everyone in the circle is thrown backward, crashing into the shelves before tumbling to the ground. Zoey crouches down and wraps her arms around her head. I snag her wrist and drag her along to the back of the shop. She uses her free arm to scoop up her injured familiar, then takes off running beside me. Like dominoes, the five bookshelves lining the center of the shop tumble forward, sending elixirs, rare plants, recipe books, and herbal remedies at the assailants.

I race to the back door.

Zoey skids to a halt. "No, this way! The office!" she screams.

I slip into the office alongside her. "Zoey, what are we doing?! We need to run! Now!"

Zoey hands me a broom and takes one for herself. She snatches a tote off the wall, slings the strap over her head and shoulder, placing Betty carefully inside. "There's a secret backdoor in here. Aunt Polly said she used to sneak in boyfriends when she was a teenager." She pulls on a book and the entire wall opens up.

I hurry behind her, gripping the broom for dear life. As soon as we are outside, we hop on the brooms and take flight. We lift as high as we can in the air, hoping the cloak of night will hide us. Neither of us are in a state to correctly perform the invisibility spell right now.

"Where are we going?" Zoey screams against the air whooshing around us. "My house. Then we are leaving town," I holler back, my heart breaking at the thought.

"Then my house? To say goodbye?" Zoey yells, her voice cracking.

I shake my head. "No, we can't. The Committee will be watching your family."

My arms and hands burn against the cold air. We zip over the forest until my home comes into view. The entire place glows against the night. Jack-o-lanterns dot the windows and clutter the veranda. Marie sits in the swinging bench holding a full bowl of candy despite the late hour, hoping maybe a trick-or-treater will venture into the woods and stumble upon the witch house.

My heart is in agony.

Together, we swoop down towards my tower window. I tap on the glass knowing it's locked and I don't want to split my concentration between flying and unlocking. Blue lifts his head, still maintaining his post over the candle. He whips around to the window and squints, then he hops off the bed and gingerly leaps up onto my window seat to swipe at the sliding lock.

The moment the window slides open, Zoey and I tumble in, becoming a tangled heap on the floor. Zoey holds her knee, having smacked on the windowsill on the way in.

"Eleanor, what is the meaning of this! You weren't even invisible! If this is Halloween tomfoolery, I swear…"

I hoist myself up to my feet and immediately begin packing. "No, Blue!

The Committee knows about me!"

"What?!" Blue leaps to his feet. "Zoey and I have to leave, now!"

I toss my suitcase onto my bed and fill it as quickly as I can. I throw open my wardrobe and dig out shoes from the bottom, knocking into the glass bottle of witch's gin. I toss that into my bag. *You never know.*

Feet thunder up the stairs. I don't stop.

My door flies open and Mom rushes inside. "What is going on?"

"I'm leaving. The Committee thought Zoey was a Nefari. I couldn't let them take her, so… I attacked them." I grab the Black Flame Candle from under my pillow, wrap it in one of my fuzzy socks, and place it carefully inside.

Mom helps Zoey to her feet. To both of our surprise, Zoey falls into my mother's arms, sobbing.

Maggie comes running into the bedroom. "Hey, what's going on?" she asks with a knitted brow.

"Maggie, go grab a bunch of your clothes for Zoey. We're leaving Salem.

Tonight," I order, nearly out of breath.

My sister's eyes gloss over. "What are you talking about?"

Mom, still comforting a crying Zoey, turns to Maggie. "Please, grab whatever you can, I can replace it. Please, darling." Tears spill down my mother's cheeks.

Maggie hesitates before tearing herself from the bedroom. Persephone appears in the doorway, as if summoned. "Please get my purse," Mom commands her cat.

Without hesitating, Persephone sprints down the stairs and returns holding mom's black leather wallet. Mom retrieves her credit card and flies it into my open suitcase. Maggie returns with a packed suitcase in hand.

I hug my mother, holding onto her trembling frame. I want to bury myself into her shoulder, inhale her scent of lavender and linen and keep it there forever. When I release her, she tucks away her tears and takes hold of Zoey crushing her in a motherly hug.

"My cat, Betty. She needs help," Zoey whimpers, scooping her beloved familiar from the floor.

Maggie has her arms crossed, her face is red and splotchy. She refuses to look at me.

"I'm sorry," I say, pulling her into a hug anyway.

She resists at first, then crumples into my embrace, releasing a torrent of tears. "I hate them. I hate them all so much!"

I kiss her wet cheek. "I promise we'll see each other again." Maggie falls into our mother's side, sobbing.

Another set of footfalls are racing upstairs.

Mom shoves Maggie behind her, winging out her arms, her face is set with determination.

Sally, out of breath, stumbles into my bedroom. She clutches the door frame as she breathes. "Mercy… she's here… demanding to come… inside." Zoey and I grab our luggage and brooms and race for my open window.

Zoey gazes back at Betty, laying still on my bed.

I straddle my broom and peer over my shoulder at Blue. *"Hurry! We don't have time!"*

Blue looks at the open door then back at me. *"No, I have an idea. They'll take me into custody. I'll 'die' slipping from their prison and they stop searching for you, they'll leave your family alone."*

My stomach drops and my heart stops. "But—"

"I'll find you. No matter where you are, I'll come for you. Now hurry! There's no time! Go!"

The front door slams against the wall.

"Mercy, you don't understand!" Marie screams from downstairs. I feel Mom's invisibility spell cover us. I don't look back.

Zoey and I leap from my window and into the cold night. The dark velvety sky stretches endlessly above us. As we soar away from my home, we approach the city glowing beneath us like a sea of scattered embers.

"Where are we going?" Zoey calls. Her voice is lifeless.

"To Boston. We're meeting some friends at the Logan

airport," I shout back.

We fly as fast as we can from Salem, our brooms slicing through the crisp autumn air. The wind pulls at our clothes, stinging our skin and leaving chills burning across our exposed faces and hands. My heart still races, praying we'll make it to the airport in time.

The sprawling city of Boston glimmers beneath us, a patchwork of haunting lights reflecting off the winding Charles River. Skyscrapers loom below our dangling feet, their windows twinkling like stars against the black sky. In the distance is Logan Airport, shining like a beacon in the night. The wind rattles us, knocking Zoey and I into each other as we keep lowering ourselves, circling above the airport. We exchange a brief glance, the weight of our situation heavy in our eyes knowing we may never return to Salem.

We land on a parking structure roof, abandoning our brooms, and racing toward the departures. I have eight missed calls from Jack and countless text messages. I don't even have time to open them. I take out Silas's card from my pocket and dial.

* * *

Silas meets us at the terminal. There are six others with him; the only one I recognize is Isolde. They're all similarly dressed in yoga pants and sweatpants with long sleeve T's or sweatshirts, dressed for a long flight.

I try to return Silas's smile, but my wind-chapped face aches in every possible way. Zoey stares down at her black boots, her shoulders rolled forward. Silas's broad grin widens as he wraps his arms around me, giving me a tight, bone-cracking hug. "I'm glad you changed your mind." He peers over at Zoey. "And who is this?"

"My friend, Zoey. Zoey Gallo."

Silas tilts his head trying to get a better look at her, but Zoey is bent inward, her chin practically touching her chest. He slides his hand under her chin, forcing her to lift her head. He peers at her eyes, then, filled with ire, slides his stare back to me. "She's not a Nefari, Eleanor."

"I know, but the Committee believes she is. She had no choice, she had to go on the run with me."

He shakes his head at her. "They're hunting non-Nefari now? Just out of suspicion? They're sure getting bold around here." He sighs, then claps us on the shoulder. "Alright, you are *both* welcome to join us. Like I said, I'm glad you changed your mind."

"This is everyone," Silas continues, motioning towards his rag tag team lounging about in airport chairs. Isolde and a man with a beautiful black head of hair and mahogany skin are the only two that wave to us.

"There used to be two more," says a beautiful Asian girl with heavy bangs and high pigtails. "Isabella and Diego were killed in an ambush in Oregon last month." She's maybe a year or two older than me, wearing a neon yellow sweatshirt with Seoul emblazoned across the chest. She yawns and snuggles into a squishy octopus-shaped pillow.

When Silas's phone rings, he stares at the screen a moment before stepping away. The tanned man with a luxurious mane pushes up out of his chair and approaches Zoey and me. He takes my hand, wrapping it in both of his; the skin is warm to the touch.

"I am Youssef Saad, and that beautiful creature is my Alexandra," he says, pointing to a slender black cat curled up on the floor next to a suitcase. Youssef's amber eyes practically glow, like molten gold. He wears a well-worn white T-shirt with "Café Riche" and a Cairo address printed across the chest, layered under a thick, unzipped gray hoodie.

"Welcome," he says, bowing his head to me then to Zoey. "We should be boarding soon." His kind smile slowly falters as he examines Zoey and me. His round eyes are soft as he peers at us. "How old are you both?"

"Seventeen," I answer.

"I turn eighteen in December," Zoey mumbles.

Youssef shakes his head. He places one hand on my shoulder and the other on Zoey's. "You're too young to know this life. I'm twenty-nine, and I am too young," he teases. His eastern accent is subtle, but it adds to his charm. "Let me introduce you to everyone." He gestures to the young woman snoozing on the octopus pillow. "That is Soojin Han, she's been with us for about six months." He leans closer to Zoey, who hasn't looked up from the floor this whole time. "Her eyes are seriously…" he widens his eyes, giving us a wild look. "They are green, but a—" he searches for a word, "neon, you can see them in the dark," he says, wiggling his fingers at us.

Zoey sniffs and wipes her nose on her sleeve.

Youssef motions towards an impossibly tall man staring out the window facing the tarmac with his wrists held behind his back. His pale blonde hair is pulled back in a trim ponytail. He's almost seven feet tall and built like Arnold Schwarzenegger. "That is Markus Van der Laan. He's from Amsterdam, very stoic. Don't take his silence personally. He's been with Silas longer than me. I've only been with Silas for—" he tries to rack his brain thinking.

"Two years," says a stunning, long-limbed black woman. "We were recruited three days apart." Her beautiful braids are pulled up into a knot on the top of her head, and she speaks with a strong African accent. When she stands, her harem pants elongate her already lean form. She wears a thick sweatshirt advertising USA in patriotic red, white, and blue that looks like it was purchased from the gift shop. Her irises are a deep crimson, so deep you could fall into her penetrating gaze.

"I'm Abena Quaye." She retrieves a shiny black snake from the front pocket of her sweatshirt. She holds the snake coiled around her hand up to the light. "And this is Gree," she says. The small snake lifts its head towards Abena, who then gives it a little peck on the head.

"That's her—" Youssef stops for a moment as if searching for the right word, before snapping his fingers, "familiar."

"A snake?" I question confused. "I thought all familiars were cats." Abena shakes her head. "American teenagers…"

Youssef's eyes nearly disappear into his crinkled smile that lifts the apples of his cheeks high on his face. "In North America, nearly all your familiars are cats. In Europe, cat familiars are common, but many are also owls, crows, and ravens. In Egypt, our familiars can be any type of feline or canine, even jackals. Different countries, different cultures, different familiars."

Abena places her snake back into her pocket. "Now, how are you both Nefari?" she dubiously inquires.

I pluck out my contacts and discard them. "I was born this way, but no one else in my family are Nefari, just me," I answer, not bothering to get into Elspeth's history.

Abena looks me up and down with a look of disapproval etched on her face. "Not possible. If you killed someone, just admit. There is no room for lies here. As for me, I'm from Ghana. I killed a preacher man who was raping my little sister." She turns to Zoey. "And you?"

Zoey shakes her head, still staring at the floor.

I wrap my arm around her quivering shoulders. "She isn't a Nefari. She was just mistaken for one because of me. Now we're both on the run from the Committee."

Abena glances at Youssef, but gives us a nod.

Youssef clears his throat. "I'm sure you already know Isolde. She's been with Silas the longest. That is David Marsten, from Manhattan." We look to the man lying on the floor wearing black

Terminator-like sunglasses and using his backpack as a pillow. "He's another who will probably never talk to you, but again, don't take it personally. He's a tortured soul."

Silas returns to the group and claps his hands to get our attention. "Alright troop, the plane is ready. Let's move out."

Everyone gathers their belongings. Isolde gently nudges Soojin awake. I hold Zoey's hand as we follow the line of Nefari to the private plane. Before we climb the steps, we both look over our shoulders, getting one last look at Boston. Inside, everyone spreads out and settles in for the flight.

Zoey and I take two seats next to each other in the front.

"Do you know where we're going?" Zoey asks, finally looking up at me with puffy brown eyes.

I shake my head.

Isolde sits up in a chair across from us. "We're headed to Paris," she says, unfurling a gingham print blanket out over herself.

Zoey mumbles a thank you. She curls up into a ball and stares out the port window. Fresh tears roll down her cheeks.

I gaze down at my fingertips where fingerprints should be. *Will Blue be able to find me? Will I ever see my family again?* I jolt as my phone buzzes again in my pocket. It's another unopened text message from Jack.

I look over at Zoey; she's whispering into her phone, sobbing out her goodbyes to her family. I type out a text to Jack:

The Committee found out about me.
I'm leaving town.
There's a group of Nefari like me. The leader believes there's a way we can cure ourselves.
I'm not sure if I'll be returning to Salem.
Please watch over my family. I love you.

CHAPTER TWENTY-EIGHT
Beware

The plane touches down in Paris around 4:00 p.m. local time. The scent of damp earth and fallen leaves wafts on a gentle breeze. We all climb into a stretch van waiting for us on the tarmac. I stare out the windows as we drive through Paris. Shops and cafes are bustling with Parisians and tourists wrapped in scarves and stylish coats dashing into cozy bistros for warmth. The light of the afternoon begins to soften, casting a golden glow on the historic stone buildings before the sky turns overcast, hinting at the possibility of rain, adding a melancholic mood to the romantic city.

I had hoped to come here with my family one day, or perhaps with my boyfriend or husband. I never dreamed I would be here as a fugitive. I take out my cell phone and try to text my family.

Messaged Failed.

I try again.

Message Failed.

I try texting Jack.

Message Failed.

"Your phone's been turned off," Zoey says flatly, staring forward out the windshield.

I face her, confused.

"My aunts told me last night. Mercy is going to demand our phone records to track us. If our families refuse, they'll be considered hostile and taken into custody. We've been cut off." She sounds like a zombie, like that spark inside her has been snuffed out.

Isolde shifts in her seat, her blonde hair falling behind her shoulders like a silk curtain. "My cousins are vacationing in the States, so they said we are welcome to stay in their Paris home as long as we need. They won't be back until after the new year," she says, effecting a cheerful air. She nuzzles her large orange cat, snoozing in her lap.

I'm unable to return her smile, so I look back out the window instead. The van comes to an abrupt halt outside a sleek apartment building in La Défense, the business district of Paris. Isolde leads us up to the sixth floor. "There's plenty of space, they own the penthouse, so basically the entire top floor," Isolde says as we spill out of the elevator. It's only a few steps from the elevator to the front door.

Everyone disperses the moment we're inside. The living area is an open design with polished concrete and minimalist furnishings giving it a chic urban vibe. Floor-to-ceiling windows flood the space with natural light and offer breathtaking views of the Paris skyline—and if you really squint, even the Eiffel Tower.

Zoey and I get the last room down the hall. Zoey tosses her suitcase onto the twin bed against the wall, the same wall as the bedroom door, leaving me the bed next to the window. The bed has zero give when I sit on it.

"Zoey?"

She says nothing. Just kicks off her shoes and curls into a ball on her bed, her back to me, trembling and probably crying.

I lie down on the other brick of a bed, feeling lifeless, and turn my attention to the window. Paris is undeniably beautiful, but it isn't home. The sleek buildings in La Défense lack the comforting clutter of the old homes in Salem, the kind that creaks when the wind howls. Like my home. But it isn't my home, not anymore. It might not ever be again. I resented being forced to move to Salem. Now I would give anything to be allowed back. To be in my own bed right now, cuddling my familiar. I don't even care that his fur is rough and has a peculiar smell. *How did it come to this?*

Someone pounds on our door. "Eleanor, Zoey. Coven meeting, everyone in the sitting room," Silas shouts through the closed door.

Neither of us move. Sitting up feels impossible. While everyone else slept on the flight, Zoey and I sat awake, her sobbing every ounce of water inside her body, me trembling and saying silent prayers my family will be safe, that Jack won't forget me.

"Let them rest, Sy, they're exhausted. I can fill them in later," Isolde whispers to him on the other side of the door. "Remember

Soojin's first few days? Or David's? They need time." Silas must have agreed, because no more sounds come from outside the door.

Neither of us speak. Zoey's quiet, muted sobs eventually turn to the slow rhythmic breathing of a deep sleep. I stare out the window watching cold shadows grow long in the fading afternoon light. As twilight settles in, the city's glow intensifies. The lights of the Eiffel Tower flicker on in the distance just as the streetlamps below blink to life, one after another after another. Sleep eventually takes me too.

Zoey stays in bed during breakfast, mumbling she isn't hungry. I don't argue with her. "I'm going to find out what we're supposed to do," I say before stepping out.

The chrome and concrete kitchen is a buffet of fresh pastries, fruit with cream, and of course, a kettle of freshly brewed tea. They are still witches, after all.

"Oh, you're up!" Soojin says through a mouth full of buttered croissant. "Oh, my goodness there's so much to tell you!" She pulls my arm towards the table and down into a chair. "Markus and Silas are gone!"

An alarm bell goes off in my head. "Wait, what?"

"They're on a scouting mission," Abena interjects. "They're tracking a Nefari coven, they will be gone maybe a week or two. We are to lay low and wait for them," she says in her no-nonsense kind of way. She rolls her eyes at Soojin. "While they are gone, only senior members may leave the apartment."

"And who are the senior coven members?" I ask, eyeing a tarte tatin. "Basically, everyone but us," Soojin bemoans, crossing one thin leg over the other in a huff. "You know, it's not often we go to Paris."

"You and your friend, Soojin, and David must all stay here," Abena answers, pouring herself a cup of fragrant tea.

"I'm twenty-one, I don't need to be chaperoned," Soojin grouses under her breath.

"It's not about age, Soojin. David is twenty-four and Markus is only twenty-two, yet Markus is a senior whereas David is not. It's about how long you've been here in the coven. You still have several months to go."

Soojin rolls her neon green eyes. The color is electric; Youssef wasn't joking when he said they practically glow.

Abena takes her tea and steps out onto the terrace, closing the glass door behind her.

"Abena Quaye. Ugh. She isn't fun. She has a husband and two

teenage daughters back in…um wherever she's from. She's always so serious," Soojin explains, searching the table for her next pastry.

I nod, staring out the glass window. "It sounds like she's had a tough life."

"We all have," Soojin says, chomping down on an éclair. "My entire family was killed by—what do you guys call it in the States? Witches Committee? Yeah, well, they killed my parents and two older sisters. They even took Mong-Mong, my companion. She's a beautiful oriental Magpie." Her eyes downcast to the table. "I really miss her."

I think of Blue. It's like I'm missing a limb.

"Anyway," she perks up, "do you know your soulmate? Mine hasn't found me yet. I'm dying to know who it is. I'm cool if it's Markus, he's like so," she then says something in Korean. "So hot," she translates for me.

Before I can answer, Soojin continues sharing everyone's background. "Youssef is from Cairo and is super sweet. He and Abena are super close. David is weird. Like, really weird. His eyes are *so* creepy. The colored part, um the iris, they're white, like snow white. So, he just has these black dots, um his pupils. That's why he always wears sunglasses. Don't expect him to be friendly, because he's not. He's from New York. But his parents were *serious* Nefari." She leans close, even though we're alone. "They tried to sacrifice him, but this woman, a witch, super old, lived in Harlem, she rescued him and raised him as her own because her soulmate died in their youth so like she's got no kids. But her name is Bindi Kossi Marsten. She took her soulmate's last name even though they never got a chance to marry. Anyway, he calls the mother goddess 'Faa', because Bindi is from Togo and he follows her traditions. His familiar is a white cat named 'Delilah' but she's back in New York with a friend," she explains, barely taking breaths as she speaks.

"For not being friendly, you sure know a lot about him," I say, picking up another pastry.

She shrugs. "Been here for six and a half months, and that's literally everything I know about him." She continues giving me the rundown of the past six months, the traveling, the adventure, the sacred poisons they use to dispatch Nefari.

"The spell we whisper makes it impossible to detect on an autopsy," she explains, then continues talking a mile a minute. "I call our mother goddess 'Mago'. What about you? Are you of the Norse tradition like Isolde and Markus? They call mother goddess 'Frigg'. I think all of that is so fascinating. Abena worships no one because she's mad at our mother goddess because she feels abandoned. At least, that's what I'm guessing. She doesn't talk about it. I think she has a bad attitude about the whole thing."

By the time she finishes, it's already well past noon. I take some pastries back to the room hoping Zoey will want them. She's still asleep, so I leave them on her bedside table.

Several days pass before Zoey ventures past our bedroom. She still barely eats, and when she does, she mostly just picks at her food leaving it torn to pieces on her plate. We both look haggard and miserable. Our shoulders curl inward, and we both have discolored, puffy bags under our eyes. When I look into the mirror, I don't recognize myself. Zoey looks even worse. She's a waif, a withered whisper of her former self.

"I'm not mad at you," she says one night from her bed. "I just—I miss my sisters and my aunts so much I can hardly stand it."

This is the first time she has really spoken to me beyond "excuse me" or "pass the cream". I try to find something to say, but guilt leaves me tongue-tied.

She rolls over facing the wall again.

I place my hand over my heart, knowing exactly how she feels.

Days bleed into each other. The apartment feels more like a prison of glass and chrome. Zoey eventually starts to warm up to the others. She even cracks a smile occasionally when she is sitting on the couch with Youssef.

Each night, I reach out to Blue hoping he's made it to France, hoping he's kept his promise and found me. There's nothing but silence. Even Elspeth is quiet. One night I reached out to her—out of exhaustion, boredom, and homesickness—only to be met with further, eerie quiet.

One night, Youssef calls us all together. "It's Thanksgiving in America tomorrow, we've got four Yankees with us. Why don't we celebrate?! I've always wanted to attend a real American Thanksgiving." His white smile glows on his charming face, framed by a well-trimmed black beard.

I didn't even realize it was Thanksgiving. We do the best we can with what the Parisian markets have to offer and settle for roast goose instead of turkey and macaroons instead of pie.

"Does it usually take this long?" I ask Isolde late one night as we sit on the sofa overlooking the dazzling city. "Do you think something has happened to Silas and Markus?"

Isolde shakes her head. "No, they've been in contact. Limited, but they've reached out. They're following a pretty big lead.

Something is going to happen soon, they're just working out the finer points so we can strike at the opportune time." She takes a sip of her jasmine tea.

A horrified, manly scream erupts down the hall.

I leap from the couch. "What was that?"

Isolde takes another tentative sip, unfazed by the scream.

I run down the hall, meeting Zoey in the darkened hallway, we both hover outside David's door. Youssef steps out of his own room. "It's okay, it's okay," he assures us.

"What's going on?" Zoey demands.

David releases another blood curdling scream.

Youssef tries to usher us away. "He's suffering, there's nothing we can do."

Zoey stares at him outraged. "What do you mean 'suffering'? And the hell we can't do anything, we need to go in there."

Youssef shakes his head at us. "It's his gift. He can see through dimensions. He sees the souls tormented in Hell, the demons clamoring for life." I stop breathing. I didn't even know that was possible. I had thought Shannyn's gift—the reaper's curse—was bad, but this is truly horrific.

"There's absolutely nothing we can do to help?" I ask.

Youssef shakes his head. "No. We pray to Mother Isis that she will bestow gifts upon him." He turns toward David's closed door and whispers something so quietly you wouldn't know he was speaking if it weren't for his lips moving. He kisses his hand then touches the door. "Goodnight," he says, retiring to his room.

We have only one week left in November and I'm getting more anxious by the minute. I pace the house, desperate to leave. Zoey bides her time reading a few smutty romance novels from Isolde, by the same author our collective aunts devour in their book club.

"It feels like home," Zoey says to me, sitting on the couch in the afternoon light, mere pages from the epilogue.

A buzzing ring echoes through the apartment. Once, twice, and then three times.

Isolde rushes down the hallway, her face etched with worry. "Silas and Markus know the code, and everyone else is home right now. No one should be ringing the buzzer."

"Could it be someone who knows your cousins?" I ask.

She shakes her head. The rest of the group come to the living room. "Be on high alert, everyone. We don't know who this is." We all nod, looking ready to fight if need be. "Eleanor, come with me. Youssef, check the windows. David, feel out if there's a spell against the apartment."

I follow her to the door and she motions for me to lean against the wall, hiding behind the door as she answers it. Isolde takes a nervous breath before tugging the door open, plastering a fake smile across her face.

Through the crack of the door, I see a woman in her fifties, or maybe sixties, it's hard to tell with her scarf wrapped around her head and tied under her chin. Her silver bangs rest against her forehead, and she wears a stylish khaki trench coat.

"Bonjour," Isolde says, nodding at the woman.

"I am Faith Elisse," she says in a heavy French accent. "I must speak with an Eleanor, Eleanor O'Reilly."

Isoldes eyes slide to me, still hidden behind the open apartment door. She hesitates, feeling out the situation, deliberating if she can trust her. Isolde releases an uneasy breath but steps out of the way.

I slip out from behind the door, my heart hammering away. The woman looks me up and down, then holds out her hand for me. Clutched in her hand is a folded piece of paper.

"Shannyn sent me. This is for you." There's a tone of resentment in her voice. "Take it. I have fulfilled my end of the bargain." She shoves the note into my hand, bows her head, and spins on her heel, only to turn back, her eyes bearing into mine. "Penez garde, Eleanor O'Reilly." She then disappears down the hall.

Isolde closes the door as I stare down at the folded note. "Who is Shannyn?" Isolde asks.

"My older sister." I continue to stare at the note. *How could she know I'm here?*

I unfold the note. Isolde steps back, giving me some privacy. "Who was it?" Soojin yells.

Isolde strolls back to the living room, addressing everyone.

I stay rooted in place, unfolding the letter. *What in the hell?* The note makes no sense. It's just weird scribbles and scratches, like someone was trying to sketch an abstract image while riding the tilt-a-whirl.

I rotate the paper, wondering if I'm just looking at it wrong. *Nope. Still doesn't make sense.* I close one eye and hold it away from me, then up to the light in the entryway. *Nothing.* My name is written in tiny penmanship, adjacent to the top left corner of the paper.

I think back on the woman's parting words, grateful I have enough high school French to roughly translate. Something like "beware" or "be careful". *What was she talking about? Maybe I should share the warning with everyone else. But what if she's warning me about one of them?*

I fold the note and place it in my back pocket. Isolde is explaining what happened to the group as I pass them on the way to my room. Climbing up on my bed next to the glass wall, I take out the note and place it against the window, testing if there is any invisible ink that'll be revealed in the sunlight. Nothing happens. I take the note down, placing it on my lap. *My sister is trying to help me and I'm too dumb to figure it out.*

The bedroom door sweeps open. "Silas is back," Zoey says before dashing off again.

I swing my legs off my bed and join the others in the living room.

Silas stands in front of the windows, the setting sun setting the city ablaze behind him, casting his features in shadow as everyone sits, anxiously waiting.

I join Zoey on a stiff ottoman.

"There's no time to properly prepare, the Nefari coven is meeting tonight. We have no choice but to act with very little provision. We tried to hop the earliest train, but we were delayed," Silas pants like he actually ran here from the train station.

"Where are they meeting?" Soojin asks. The playful, jokey girl we've come to know the past month now stares at our leader like a fearsome warrior ready for marching orders.

Silas exchanges an uneasy look with Markus at his side. A fresh cut runs down his face, slicing through the blonde scruff on his large square chin. Silas looks back at the rest of us, meeting our nervous gazes. "Tonight, we leave for the catacombs…"

CHAPTER TWENTY-NINE
Lipstick and Skulls

The crew listens closely as Silas details our plan. When Silas gets to Markus's role in the attack, he gives Abena a pointed look. Abena crosses her arms indignantly and looks to the side.

I glance at Zoey beside me with a questioning look.

Zoey leans close to my ear. "Soojin said Markus killed a guy in a bar fight when he was eighteen. Didn't mean to, total freak accident. But he's kind of shell shocked now and won't use his magic whatsoever."

I frown. "Then what is he doing here? You have to kill Nefari, or you won't be cured," I whisper back.

Zoey shrugs. "He kills them by other non-magical means, plus he wants to help the rest of us. Maybe as some kind of atonement."

I peer across the table at Markus who stands to the right of Silas. His eyes are flat black, almost cartoony, or doll like. They remind me of Elspeth's, although hers are marbled with threads of silver and charcoal; Markus's eyes are a complete abyss.

"Abena thinks he's dead weight and Silas is starting to lose his patience with him," Zoey continues. "Isabella and Diego, an older married couple who joined the group, they died recently and Abena partially blames Markus for not using his magic to protect the coven. Silas thinks he can work with him and eventually coax his magic out."

"Zoey," Silas whips his head in our direction, his tone severe, "do you have something to add to the group or may I continue?"

Zoey shrinks back, embarrassed red splotches creep up her neck and cheeks as she drops her gaze down to the table. "No," she answers quietly.

I grit my teeth. *I wish someone else were in charge.*

Silas turns back to the group. "The assignments are thus: Youssef, you're with Eleanor, David, you will be with Zoey. Isolde with Soojin, Abena with Markus and myself."

I raise my hand, unsure if I'm allowed to just interject. Silas rolls his eyes. "Yes?" he says with an icy tone.

"I don't know what that means. This is our first time assisting, we haven't been filled in on anything. Just that this group is supposedly evil," I say in a tone edging on mockery, "and we have partners, I mean what the hell, Silas? You acted like you wanted us to join you only to be resentful of the fact we're here." I can't keep the days of house arrest and resentment from creeping into my voice.

Silas raises a finger at me, opening his mouth as if about to yell, but Markus steps between us, holding his massive hand out to Silas. "You'll have to excuse Silas's lack of…" He glances at our leader, who runs a hand through his buzz cut, seemingly forgetting he no longer has a full head of hair. "…patience. We've been sleeping in less-than-reputable quarters, surviving skirmishes, and witnessing bloodshed. Our coven has lost too many witches, which is why we started pairing up, taking direct responsibility for one another. These pairings change with each mission. You and Youssef will look out for each other in the catacombs, so you both come back to us." Markus then steps back, allowing Silas to continue.

Silas nods to Markus, a hint of gratitude on his stern face. "These Nefari have a ritual. They drink from 'the devil's chalice'; we've seen it performed a few times now. We will each stand behind them, invisible, and slip the blessed poison into the goblets before they partake. We will not stay to watch them die this time; we must leave immediately. There are always guards posted near the exits, we'll dispatch them later. Any questions?" he asks, clearly not expecting any. He nods, satisfied by our silence. "Dress in black—it'll be easier to escape if your invisibility fails. Rendezvous downstairs in 2300 hours," he says.

Markus adds, "That's military time for 11:00 p.m."

Zoey and I hurry to our bedroom, even though we still have five hours to prepare. Zoey rummages through her things, shaking her head. Nothing feels right for me either. We shouldn't be going to the Paris catacombs… at night…to kill a bunch of evil witches. Why did I ever fear midterms? I wonder what excuse my mother has given the academy. I miss my violin. I miss my room. Hell, I miss doing homework! Most of all, I miss my family. And Jack. Those are holes festering in my heart, cracking, bleeding every time I picture their faces.

Zoey slips into a knitted sweater and tight black jeans and tugs on her battered black boots. She sits on the edge of her bed for a moment, biting her nails and fidgeting. Then pulls out another

Pemberly Royal novel from Isolde's collection: "The Tides of Desire: The Sailor and His Siren."

My heart aches thinking of Sally. She consumed every book written by Pemberly Royal, devouring every salacious, deliciously written page. Mom tried reading a copy once, but when I saw her cheeks burn and her eyes go wide as saucers, she put the book down, reproved her sister, and never returned to it. What I'd give to hear her thoughts now. Or Maggie, making fun of the ridiculous title and reading a saucy page aloud until mom would snatch it and fly it out of reach. If only Shannyn had extended her honeymoon even more, I'd run away from this place, find her and beg her to never let me go. I miss her. I miss them all. My breathing quickens, and I fall back on my bed, coming apart at the seams. I wrap my arms around myself, as I tearlessly sob.

My bed sinks as Zoey curls up behind me and wraps her arm around me. She says nothing, just lets me cry. I'm not sure how long we stay like that, but eventually, I fall asleep. I don't even realize it until there's a soft rap at the door.

"It's time to go," Isolde says sweetly through the closed bedroom door. "I'll see you both downstairs."

Zoey and I both stretch and yawn; her eyes are ringed with red from silently crying into my pillow. The room is dark, save for the faint glow from the city.

Everyone is already waiting outside for us. Silas describes the routes we'll take, each of us paired with a partner. Zoey reluctantly leaves my side and joins David, still wearing his sunglasses despite the dark. She glances up at him nervously.

Youssef grips my shoulder and gives me a thumbs-up, as if we're school buddies on a field trip—not about to commit mass murder. A lump in my throat makes it hard to swallow.

"Eleanor," Silas calls out, "you and Youssef will take a taxi to Café du Rendez-Vous, near Place Denfert-Rochereau in the 14th Arrondissement. Wait until twelve-fifteen, then head to the catacombs. Walk fifteen paces before turning left; that's where we'll meet." He turns to Zoey and David. "You two will rent bikes. You've got the longest route, but no one will be able to take the city bus this late. You'll head to Les Artistes." He continues, assigning the rest of us local landmarks for directions, even mentioning carriage rides for some.

The groups break apart and head in separate directions. Youssef and I, with our rough French, hail a cab and try to explain where we need to go. The driver argues that the café is closed, but we insist. After mumbling some expletives about pushy American tourists, he finally agrees to take us. Once dropped off, and thankfully with enough cash on Youssef to cover the fare, we head toward 1 Avenue du Colonel Henri Rol-Tanguy. Youssef slows down as we near the spot. I look around, unsure if we've arrived. Despite its fame, the catacombs' entrance is underwhelming—housed in a modest stone pavilion that resembles a simple ticket office. A plain, unassuming sign marks the site.

My palms begin to sweat as we approach, my heart racing with every step. Youssef murmurs an incantation in Arabic, unlocking the door. He holds it open, checking to see if anyone notices.

Inside, a narrow spiral staircase leads downward. I grip the handrail, peering over the side. Below is nothing but a black, impenetrable void. Even the staircase disappears into the darkness as it descends.

I hiccup. "Um," hic, "are there no," hic, "lights down there?" hic. Youssef shrugs, peering down the stairs. "I read there's electricity, but they probably shut it off after hours. But fear not." He pulls out a thick, three-wicked candle from his black leather jacket. The wicks ignite instantly, casting an impressive glow. "I'll go first," he says, nodding before starting down the steps.

Together, with me hovering close behind him, we descend the spiral staircase, dropping over sixty feet underground. The stone walls grow colder, the air damp, as we enter the deeper underground world of the catacombs. Youssef reaches the bottom first, holding the candle high as he nods toward the opaque tunnel Silas instructed us to take. I stay close as we follow the dim passageway leading to the ossuary. The hair on my neck stands on end, and goosebumps break across my skin. An oppressive presence presses down on me, as if I'm being watched. Thousands of skulls and weathered bones line the walls in unsettling formations.

I bump into Youssef, my heart hammering in my chest. I knew the catacombs were filled with human remains, but seeing them in person is something else. The sense of being encased in death is overwhelming.

"Can we stop?" I ask, bending over, trying to catch my breath as I hyperventilate.

"We're almost there, Eleanor," Youssef says, pausing with the candle held aloft, illuminating the narrow passage lined with skulls. The dark eye sockets remind me of the bodies on the island. I tug at my turtleneck, feeling suffocated, and not just because we're entombed in bones. There's a malevolent presence—thick in the air, like toxic gas.

"Something is wrong, Youssef. Something is down here. Something evil," I cry, clawing at my turtleneck. I stumble backward, knocking into the skulls, some crumbling under my weight. I leap forward, my coat dusted in bone fragments, a strangled cry escaping my throat as I brush myself off.

Youssef grabs my shoulders, steadying me. "Eleanor, it's okay. We're okay.

The Nefari are gathered here, deep in the tunnels," he whispers, his golden eyes catching the candlelight as they meet mine. "We need to stick to Silas's plan." He takes my hand and plucks the candle from the air with his other. "Stay close, breathe through your mouth," he instructs, demonstrating.

We move deeper into the tunnel, the ground sloping downward. Ahead, several glowing flashlights flicker in the distance. Youssef and I hurry to join the group, where Soojin is making faces in the light of her flashlight.

Silas looks relieved as we approach. "We're just waiting on Zoey and David," he says, rummaging through a black canvas bag slung across his chest. "This is the last of the snakeroot," he adds, distributing small glass vials. "Remember, everyone is in charge of their own invisibility." Markus flashes his silver light at Silas, his mouth open to speak. "Except for you— Abena and I have you covered," Silas assures.

Abena glares at him, arms crossed over her chest.

A bouncing light appears down the tunnel as Zoey and David jog toward us. Zoey clutches the flashlight, while David's eyes, now exposed without sunglasses, make me shudder—his irises blending into the whites of his eyes, pupils like black pinpricks.

"They're meeting in the center of the catacombs," Silas continues. "We'll go in pairs, spaced out. Walk lightly and say your spells now. Make sure we can still see one another when you visualize."

I close my eyes, placing a hand over my racing heart. Blue, why can't you be here with me? No one brought their familiars. Isolde left Mumford, Silas left Machado, and Youssef left Alexandra behind. But Blue would have insisted on coming, making jokes about the bones. I shake my head, trying to focus. I imagine myself walking, turning, even dancing, invisible within these bone-filled walls. My magic surges, and I open my eyes, confident the spell has worked.

Something shiny slithers around Abena's neck. I'm about to

shout, then I realize it's just her familiar, Gree.

With a melancholy sense of reverence, we follow Silas toward the heart of the catacombs. The skulls lining the walls are a stark contrast to the vibrant city above, a haunting reminder of Paris's bloodied history and the fragility of life.

Silas raises a fist, stopping us. He whispers to Markus, who clicks off his flashlight, then signals Soojin, who extinguishes the small flame floating above her hand. The command travels silently down the line, and in moments, we're plunged into darkness.

The sound of breathing becomes deafening as we move forward blindly, knees bumping, hands brushing backs and hips. Every touch feels like skeletal fingers reaching from the walls. I take deep breaths through my mouth, trying to focus, but my mind floods with images of Trixie, Allen, Jack bleeding out, my mother's head. I whimper, bumping into Zoey, who grabs my hand. We squeeze each other's fingers tightly.

Finally, a faint yellow light appears ahead. We move slowly, steps cautious as we approach the gathering of Nefari.

The tunnel opens into a small alcove, where several paths branch off like veins. Torchlight flickers across the neatly stacked bones. The skulls, worn smooth, watch us with their empty eyes, waiting.

The Nefari stand in a circle draped in purple velveteen robes. We spread out, hugging the walls, holding our breath. There are more of them than us, but Silas doesn't seem surprised. He pulls extra vials of poison from his pouch.

Silas closes his eyes and gives a slow, deliberate nod. Each of us steps behind the Nefari in front of us.

Zoey goes pale, and she whips her head at me. In the center of the circle, a girl—no more than fifteen—lies hogtied. She's wearing casual yoga pants and an off-the-shoulder sweater. Duct tape is over her mouth. Her hazel eyes are wide with terror.

I clasp a hand over my mouth to keep myself from screaming.

The Nefari directly ahead of me slowly turns, peering through the darkness of his hood. He stares directly at me.

CHAPTER THIRTY
Eleanor Marks the Spot

The Nefari extends his hand into the empty space between, searching for something unseen. I lean as far away as possible, not breathing, careful to keep my feet still. He cranes his neck, glancing around before turning back to the group.

Oh my gosh. Oh my gosh. Oh my gosh. Blue, what am I going to do?! I can't do this! I can't! He's going to figure out I'm right behind him! Blue, please help me!

I press my hands over my mouth to keep from whimpering.

Thankfully, Silas doesn't notice. He motions for everyone to uncork their vials. We move swiftly, silently, like a choreographed dance. I try not to look at the girl. *We're not going to let her die…right?*

A Nefari steps into the center and retrieves a long, bejeweled dagger. He holds it, high above his head. "Bénis ce rite sacré, salut le Sombre," he shouts, his voice echoing off the bones around us.

"Bénis ce rite sacré, salut le Sombre. Bénis ce rite sacré, salut le Sombre. Bénis ce rite sacré, salut le Sombre," his followers mindlessly chant over and over.

The girl squeezes her eyes shut. She sobs even harder now, her chest heaving up and down, falling into absolute hysterics.

Zoey and I exchange petrified glances, scanning the circle, searching for any sign that we're going to stop this.

The leader brings the dagger down slowly as his coven continues chanting.

This isn't happening. We have to do something, right? We have to. We aren't like them! We can't let this innocent girl die! I won't let it happen!

Just as I'm about to step forward, Zoey does. David snatches her shoulder and pulls her back while Silas shoots her a deadly glare. He slowly shakes his head at her. Zoey looks over at me, pleading.

The leader moves swiftly. He drags the blade across her chest, just below her collarbone. Not deep enough to kill, but enough to produce a bloody gash. The young girl's cry of agony is muted by the duct tape. The leader lets a drop of blood fall from dagger into his cup. The Nefari hold out golden goblets, and the dagger levitates, dripping a few drops of blood into each chalice.

They thrust their chalices into the air.

Silas motions for all of us to empty our elixirs into their cups. The vials float through the air and empty into their cups. Silas then motions for all the elixirs to return to him. He plucks them from the air one by one and returns them to his satchel.

"Nous buvons à toi au nom de le Sombre," the leader cheers. "Nous buvons à toi au nom de le Sombre," the Nefari replies.

My body trembles with anxiety. I'm waiting for them to drink and die so we can get out of here and save that poor girl.

The leader chants something new: "Nous t'offrons cette fille en sacrifice, au nom de le Sombre, Baal, et Mammon!"

My heart stops. I recognize two words from my high school French: "daughter" and "sacrifice." They're going to kill her before they drink from her!

Several of us turn toward Silas. He looks dismayed, his brow furrowed. His lips part, trembling, but then he snaps his jaw shut and lifts his chin. When he opens his violet eyes, they look glossy. He mouths, *We cannot help her. I'm sorry.*

My chest heaves. *No, no, no, no. This can't be right. We can't do nothing.* The blade floats above the girl, the sharp tip aimed at her chest. Zoey shakes her head and tightly squeezes her eyes shut.

The floating dagger, turns directions and shoots like a arrow into the chest of the leader with a startling thump.

The robed followers freeze in stunned silence, then chaos erupts. They scream and point at one another.

"Traître!"

"Nous ne sommes pas seuls!"

"Qui a tué notre cher leader?"

"Il y a quelqu'un ici en bas!"

"Tuez le traître!"

Chalices crash to the ground, hoods are pulled back, and the dagger is ripped from the leader's body by a man with flaming red hair. He waves it accusingly at one of his brethren. The poor girl's bindings are suddenly torn off. She tumbles off the table, crying out for help now that her mouth is free.

The Nefari holding the knife rushes forward ready to strike, but something throws him back into the wall of bones. Several skulls crush into dust behind him as he tumbles to the floor.

"Run!" Silas screams.

Fire and air spells clash, throwing the alcove into chaos.

Zoey and I snatch the girl's arms and hoist her to her feet. With tears painting her cheeks, she thanks us repeatedly in French. She looks at each of us in the eye.

We're visible.

"Go!" I scream. I drag the girl forward and run headfirst down a pitch-black tunnel. Multiple sets of footsteps follow behind me. "Where are we going?" Zoey screams.

I can't answer. I'm gasping for breath, still dragging the girl alongside me. The floor is slanting downward. I try to sense fresh air, hoping for a shift that will lead us to the stairwell, but the air grows thicker with dust and decay.

The girl trips and falls, sending me tumbling down with her. Zoey crashes into us, followed by David and Youssef. We untangle ourselves, crawling away from each other, until my back hits a fragile wall.

A flash of light flickers on, illuminating our huddle. Zoey, the girl, David, and Youssef are all panting, squinting at David's flashlight.

Ghoulish screams echo down the passageways. The blood drains from our faces.

"We need to keep moving," David insists, jumping to his feet. He helps Zoey up, then Youssef and the girl. He turns to me, but I'm already standing. "This place is a labyrinth," Youssef says, panic edging his voice. Sweat drips down his temples.

David shakes his head. "Just keep moving." His eerie white eyes dart around, searching the serpentine pathways.

The calls grow louder, more furious.

"Come on! We've got to go!" David grabs the girl's hand and charges into the shadows.

We run and run and run. Our feet and joints cry out for reprieve, but we push forward. We take random turns, picking left and right without rhyme or reason. At one point, Youssef shouts we are going in circles after recognizing a design made of femurs and tibias. David insists we press forward anyway.

Our sprints slowly give way into jogging, until one by one we collapse in exhaustion desperately trying to catch our breath. I fall to my back, dirt coating my entire body. My chest rises and falls so rapidly, it feels like my ribs might splinter beneath my skin.

Zoey cries, tucking her knees into her chest. "This is hopeless, we're never going to find a way out of here," she wails. Tears form rivers through the dust and dirt on her cheeks and drip off her chin.

Youssef wraps an arm around her trembling shoulders, mumbling reassurances as he gasps for air. David, silent and petrified, stares at the girl, who's sobbing for her parents.

"Wait, Eleanor," Youssef says. He turns to David. "Your light, please."

David tosses him the flashlight and Youssef aims the beam on the wall of skulls above me.

"What?" I manage, feeling like I might vomit.

Youssef's eyes widen. Slowly, everyone crawls closer, gazing at the wall. I scramble into a seated position, scooting away so I can see what they're staring at. My breath catches. Written in bold, scarlet, oily-looking letters is the name "Eleanor" scrawled across two skulls.

I rise on shaky legs, quivering as I move closer to the wall. Running my fingers over the letter "E," I smear it slightly. I rub my fingers together, feeling the substance—it's fresh. I bring it to my nose and inhale. *Honeysuckle.*

Holy shit! I know this smell! La Rouge Parfum by Kilian Hennessy— Shannyn's favorite lipstick, her signature scent and color. I flash back to when my mother was furious that Shannyn had spent fifty dollars on a single tube of lipstick, but she insisted.

My sister has been down here. Recently.

"I need the light," I say, snatching the flashlight from Youssef's hands. I scan the wall, moving the beam up and down, searching for more clues, but find nothing. No arrow. No direction. "Crap," I mutter. *Once again, Shannyn thinks I'm smarter than I am.*

Wait...

"Here, hold this." I toss the light to Zoey. I reach into my back pocket and retrieve the scribbled paper.

Everyone slowly rises to their feet, using the wall for support. David presses too hard, and a skull cracks, causing us all to stumble back in shock. We gather around the paper as Zoey shines the light on it.

"Eleanor, right there," David says, pointing to my name written above some oddly shaped scratches of pen. "Hold on." He takes the paper and compares my name smeared across the skull to my name on the note. "It's a map. We're here," he declares, shoving his finger at my name near the corner of the page. Everyone in unison turns to my name written across the two skulls and back to the paper.

"Okay, but where is the exit?" Zoey asks, looking at us, confused.

"Here," Youssef says, pointing to the bottom right. "See? That's not a scribble, it's an 'E' and an 'X,' then a little arrow out."

David studies the map. "I think I have it." He looks up at me.

"You're going to have a lot of explaining to do when we get back. Like, who the hell gave you a map, why the hell your name is written down here, and what the hell you were thinking. Sabotaging the mission? Silas is going to be furious with you."

Zoey snaps her head up. "She didn't. I did. I wasn't about to let this poor girl die. Sorry, but I'm *not* a Nefari." She tilts her chin up, refusing to back down.

We all jump as the girl lunges at Zoey. She wraps her arms around her as she cries into Zoey's shoulder.

"Thank you! Thank you! You've saved me! You saved my life!" she says in a heavy French accent.

David sighs in an almost growl. "Very well. But you still need to explain all this," he says to me, gesturing about the bone laden tunnel.

"And she will," Youssef interjects, "but we must get moving."

We follow David through endless corridors and turns. The girl keeps a tight hold on Zoey's hand, frequently lifting it to kiss it as we walk. Youssef and I bring up the rear.

"I'm grateful she acted," he admits quietly to me.

"Me too," I say, knowing if Zoey hadn't, I was milliseconds away from doing the same.

"If she hadn't, I would have. Or at least, I would like to think I would have."

Before each turn, David sweeps the flashlight, searching the shadows for hidden threats or sensing magic. Slowly, though, our movements become less cautious—not out of bravery, but sheer exhaustion.

"None of this looks familiar," Zoey moans, dragging her feet along with the rest of us.

David stops at a dead end. Ahead is a stone slab etched with bizarre symbols, framed by skulls and small bones. "I thought this was it," he says, panic creeping into his voice as we stand, seconds from collapsing.

I step forward. "I don't think you're wrong." I point at the top of the curved stone. David shines the flashlight. There, written in lipstick, is an "E" beside an "X," next to what looks like a coincidental design of an "I" and a "T."

"Back up, back up," David orders, stepping back. He closes his eyes and mumbles an incantation. Slowly, the stone slab shifts open. The girl shrieks, probably never having witnessed magic before. The shifting stone reveals an iron ladder reaching up to the ceiling.

We scramble forward and take hold of the ladder, crying out

with relief.

"What about the others?" I ask, voicing the question we'd all been avoiding.

"We follow protocol," Youssef says, feigning confidence.

"Protocol?" Zoey asks.

David nods. "He's right. It's one of Silas's rules. If we ever get split up, we're supposed to rendezvous at the safe house."

"This feels wrong," Zoey whimpers, staring at the ground.

Youssef places a gentle hand on her shoulder. "I know, but if we're the only ones to make it out, we'll come back in daylight to find them. You have my word."

"I'll go first," David says. He climbs to the round tablet just above the top of the ladder. "It's a manhole." He shoves it to the side and hoists himself out then dangles his arm down. The girl is next, then Zoey, myself, and Youssef. Youssef slides the cover back into place as we stumble into a narrow alley between two nightclubs. The pulsating house music clashes from both establishments, a strange contrast to the damp, dusty catacombs below. I've never breathed air this clean and fresh before.

The girl crumbles down next to a dumpster and cries.

"She wants to go home," I translate, grateful for my meager grasp of the language.

"I'll take her to a police station," David says. "You all stay together and head back to the safe house. Remember protocol, take the most roundabout way possible. We never know if we're being followed."

He glances around, then takes off his black wool peacoat and offers it to the young girl. She wraps it around her shoulders as they walk down the alley and disappear around the corner.

We take three separate cabs, each dropping us off at different locations. We walk between buildings, trudging forward, then come out the other side to hail another cab.

By the time we reach the apartment, Youssef punches in the code, and we collapse onto the floor as the steel door shuts behind us.

My entire body screams in pain. Every muscle and tendon trembles from overexertion. I'll be lucky if I can move tomorrow. The adrenaline that fueled me in the catacombs has drained away, leaving me utterly spent.

Something moves in the living room.

The lights flicker on.

We aren't alone.

CHAPTER THIRTY-ONE
Friend Down

Silas, Markus, and Abena step into the overhead light of the entryway. Abena's face glistens with sweat, but otherwise looks perfectly intact in her black hooded sweatshirt and joggers; you would never guess she had been crawling around the catacombs. Silas and Markus both look a little worse for wear. Markus has added a new laceration to his face and a purple mark around his eye which will certainly deepen in color with the passing hours. Knowing he doesn't use magic, all the injuries he sustains are starting to make sense.

Youssef turns onto all fours and struggles onto his feet, still panting. He places a dirty hand on the sleek wall to steady himself. "Are you all that made it?"

Silas's violet eyes tick to each of us, slowly, deliberately, before returning to Youssef. "Yes. Is it just you three? Where is David?"

"He's bringing that girl to the police station so she can be returned to her family," Zoey murmurs.

I don't move. I'm not even sure I can. My exhaustion is nearly tangible. Silas curses under his breath. "You should all shower. There are four bathrooms in this place. Either get cleaned up or make yourselves useful and help with supper." His voice is cold and unfeeling. He marches off to the kitchen, where cupboards are thrown open and dishes clang.

"You three should shower first, you guys are…" Markus trails off.

"I'll shower in the master suite." Abena glares at each of us before storming away.

After a moment, Markus adds, "I'll help Silas with the meal."

"Abena seems pissed," Zoey whispers.

Youssef nods. "Her eyes have permanent specks of dark brown. She's even gone a full day with normal eye color a few times. She's so close to being healed and returning to her family. And we set her back tonight."

I groan as I haul myself to my feet and dust my hands off on my pants. "She'll get more opportunities," I say, trying to assuage my guilt. She's been gone for two years, I've been gone nearly a month and would do anything to get home. I can only just imagine the agony she must be going through.

Youssef shakes his head. "The worse the Nefari, the higher the reward. If you destroy someone truly vile, your redemption is that much greater. I'm not sure if we'll encounter anyone that evil again anytime soon. Still, regret nothing. Abena is a good woman; she didn't want to watch that child die any more than we did. She may not admit it, but she knows it was the right thing to do."

We're silent for a moment, digesting his words.

"Well," Youssef continues, "there are three showers left. Let's get cleaned up so the others can do the same." He bows his head before lumbering down the hallway.

Zoey and I move in silence as we gather our things for the shower. Zoey slips into our bathroom with tears in her eyes. I repeat in my mind what to bring to the bathroom, hoping not to think about tonight's events.

Dust puffs off me as I drop my dirty clothes to the marble floor. I wonder what mom would have done tonight; would she have saved that poor girl, or would she have allowed those who sacrificed so much to finally earn their rewards? *I think…I think mom would tell me no reward is worth the sacrifice of an innocent life.* A dark thought turns my skin cold. *If I was as close to being cured as Abena is, would I still have wanted to save the girl?*

The shower's scalding water burns when it hits my skin. I flip on the steam generator and slide to the floor of the limestone shower. My knees are skinned. I don't even remember falling. My feet are covered in bloodied and open blisters. I close my eyes and lean my head back, reveling in the thought of being swallowed up in the thick cloud of steam, disappearing forever.

I wrap my arms around myself, desperate to be held. Desperate to be home. I imagine Jack. He's painting in class, wowing instructors and students alike. I wonder how Mom is doing. What Maggie is up to, how she dealt with grueling midterms. If Shannyn enjoyed her—wait, Shannyn. How did she know I'd be in the Catacombs? How'd she know we would arrive at that exact spot and need her help to escape? We would still be lost down there without her.

Dressed in striped cotton bottoms and a long-sleeve tee, I amble back down the hall to the dining room. Zoey sits at the far end of the glass table. Her skin is red and raw, like she scrubbed herself with steel wool. Youssef sits a few seats down, gulping back a bottle of water, his thick black hair drips down the back of his neck. Abena is at the head of the table next Zoey, her mouth a firm line as she stares at the table.

Youssef stands as I enter the room. "We have some good news. David has returned, he's in the shower now. He said the girl was left safe at the police station," he informs. "Here, sit, sit." He gestures to an open chair across from him.

Silas speaks in hush tones on his cellphone in the kitchen. Zoey's eyes, despondent and hapless, lift up to him.

"Did he just say something in Italian?" she whispers.

Abena takes a plate from the stack in the center. "You shouldn't be eavesdropping," she chides.

Zoey curls inward and looks down at her lap.

I reach for a plate just as David walks in and sits at the end of the table across from Abena, his sunglasses snug on his face. Markus walks in behind him holding a bag of ice against his face and sits next to me.

"I have something for you," Zoey offers. "For your face, I mean. If you want."

Markus shakes his head, then stops and winces. "No, thank you. If I'm not willing to do magic, I shouldn't benefit from it either."

No one objects. Not because we agree with him, it's just that everyone's had the fight beaten out of them.

No one talks. We just pick at the three-in-the-morning spread: goose liver pâté with baguette slices, remnants of last night's roast chicken and mushy, reheated veggies, brie with fruit and toast points, and copious amounts of wine that David pours generously, filling his glass to the brim. Silas returns to the dining room while slipping his phone into his pocket.

"Isolde and Soojin aren't back yet?"

Youssef shakes his head, David looks at his watch, and Abena scowls. "Is this normal?" Zoey asks, her voice barely above a whisper.

Silas leans on the steel chair in front of him, his forearms resting on the back. "No, it's not," he answers, leveling her with a glare. "And when they return, we will be going over tonight's fiasco and figuring out who exactly is to blame for this."

I set my fork next to my plate. "So, you were prepared to let that innocent girl be sacrificed?" I question.

Silas straightens his back and stares at me with steely resolve.

"Yes."

I shake my head. "Then we are no better than them. If we are willing to let innocent people die to get what we want, are we worth saving? Who the hell are we?"

"Your myopic mentality disgusts me," Silas seethes. "Thanks to one of you, I'm guessing you, Eleanor, a madman got away. That's right, the dagger struck his chest, but didn't kill him. He's alive, alive to rape, kill, and destroy another day." He picks up his chair a few inches off the ground and slams it down.

I shudder at the metallic thwack that reverberates against all the steel and concrete.

There's a knock at the door. It's quiet at first then grows louder.

All the men leap to their feet and rush to the door.

Abena sighs, her expression painfully obvious. *Men*. Her familiar slithers across her shoulders while she gracefully rises to her feet.

Zoey and I just stare at each other, too tired to move, too tired to even think. Yet as we stare at each other, we both know, that's not why we stay seated. There's an unspoken sentiment we both know the other feels. *What good are we?*

The door opens, someone collapses inside, and the door slams shut.

Wailing fills the space, unfettered and unabashed, like a wounded animal.

Youssef gasps. "Soojin! What happened?!"

"Isolde!" she shrieks. "Isolde is dead! They killed her! She's gone!" she screams.

Zoey's mouth falls open, fresh tears spring to her eyes. A solemn silence falls on the apartment; even Soojin's whimpering ceases. Seconds stretch on for what feels like hours.

My mind whirls in disbelief. Isolde was healed. She didn't need to be here anymore. And now she's dead.

"Abena, help her get cleaned up and find out what happened," Silas commands. He marches off and slams his door so hard the frame rattles. No one returns to the dining room. The meal turns cold on the table.

The little I ate turns rancid in my stomach. Everyone drifts about, not speaking, not meeting each other's eye.

I wander onto the terrace and sink into one of the rickety chairs. The soft glow of the city stretches endlessly before me. Paris at four in the morning is impossibly serene. The sleek towers of the business district stand like silent sentinels, twinkling lights reflecting off the glass exterior, indifferent to the world's pain. How can something so breathtaking exist in a world where death, misery, and evil so heavily overshadow the good?

I slump even lower in the chair. Far in the distance, the Eiffel Tower appears faintly in the city's ambient light. Lights keep shining, cars speed down the avenues, people safely snooze in their beds, and all the while, evil just swallowed something so impossibly good…again.

I think of Trixie, a net positive in the world if there ever was one. She was someone who truly left everything she touched better than she found it, someone who *literally* wouldn't hurt a fly. Then there's my dad, who I witnessed opening his wallet for a person in need on more than one occasion. Beautiful, sparkling lights of pure goodness snuffed out. Pointlessly. Needlessly. Evilly. *Good people keep dying while evil lives to fight another day.*

The glass door behind me slides open.

"Eleanor, Silas wants all of us to convene in the living room," Youssef whispers.

I follow him inside. Soojin is wearing a fuzzy onesie with a hood that looks like the head of a teddy bear. Her eyes are swollen and ringed in red making the unnaturally green irises even more striking than usual. Abena sits in the leather armchair, her face impassive. The anger in her is gone; now she just looks empty.

Youssef sits beside Soojin and rubs her back. David paces behind the couch while Markus alone occupies the love seat. Zoey tiptoes into the room and lowers herself next to Markus, careful not to make a single sound. I walk around Silas and take the open seat on the sofa next to Youssef.

Silas stands in front of the large wall mounted television. His feet shoulder width apart, his arms tense, crossed his fit chest. "Now that we are all here," he says through a clenched jaw.

Soojin sniffles. "No, we aren't. Isolde isn't here…"

Silas stares down at his folded arms. "Yes," he agrees with a sneer. "And who do we have to thank for that?" His eyes slowly tick to each and every one of us; he lingers on me an extra moment before moving on.

Zoey shakes like a leaf next to Markus. She's a petite girl, barely five feet; she's typically the smallest no matter where she is, but next to Markus, she's barely more than a whisp. Her jaw quivers as she struggles to admit her guilt to the group.

"That would be me," Youssef says, rising to his feet.

Silas balks. "No."

"He wasn't the only one," David says, pausing mid stride.

"Son of a—" Silas screams a ripping roar, his corded veins lifting under his skin on his throat and forehead.

"Stop," Abena demands. "Her life should never have been in question.

We did not plan properly," she accuses.

"Excuse me?" Silas sneers, posturing over her.

She stands to meet him. They're the same height, but with her braided knot high atop her head, she seems taller, almost regal. She levels him with a stare as menacing as his own. "We've all mastered the air spell. All but one." Her eyes flick to Markus, whose gaze drops to his hands. "We could have broken their necks before they reached for their cups."

He shakes his head. "You know why we don't; it's too risky. We've been foiled too many times when we use force."

"What separates us from Nefari, Silas?" she asks, her voice methodical. He sighs in a growl through his nostrils, peering away from her.

"We are witches, Silas. Made to protect the chosen children. What is the point of a cure if we are no better than the ones we kill?" she says, her accent weaving through her words.

"She's right, man," Markus adds. "If we had executed the plan as it was, the girl would have been killed. It won't count for redemption if we let innocents get killed in the process, I'm sure of it."

Silas shakes his head but doesn't argue. "None of you go rogue again, understood?"

"Then we make a contingency plan. As our leader, I'm sure we can depend on you to handle that." Abena words ring like a challenge before she takes her seat.

Silas ignores it. "We need to bury Mumford. David, I believe it is your turn. Try to dispose of him quietly. There's a dumpster outback." He immediately winces at his own words. Before any of us can react, he quickly interjects, "Familiars are sacred companions, I know, and if it were possible, he would be honored and buried the way he deserves, but it isn't possible. I'm sorry, but it isn't. Everyone pack. We leave in ten hours."

As Silas leaves the room, David waves off Youssef's offer to help with Mumford. A few minutes later, David returns, head hung low and his hands in his pockets. No witch can place another witch's familiar in a trash bag and discard him in a dumpster down the block without feeling shattered by it.

My thoughts turn to Blue. I miss him. Zoey slinks off the loveseat, eyes fixed on the floor. "Youssef," she begins. He lifts his hand, stopping her. "You were just faster. That's all." Soojin rises from the couch and tearfully ambles out towards the terrace, leaving the sliding glass door behind her open. All of us watch as she crumples into the rickety chair I was just in.

"She watched Isolde get murdered," Markus whispers.

"I can't imagine watching someone die," Zoey mumbles quietly. "I can," I whisper, so quietly I almost question if I say it aloud.

Youssef nods towards the balcony. One by one, we trickle out, even Abena. Soojin doesn't react as we gather around her. Abena takes the second open chair. Zoey closes the door behind her and leans against it, as do I. Soojin swipes the back of her hand under each eye and sniffs.

Youssef steps forward, his back to the city. The sky stretching across the city is still basking in the navy blue and indigo of the night, but along the horizon, streaks of lavender and blush begin to creep around the edges. He tries to clear his throat, but struggles. He tugs at the collar of the t-shirt under his unzipped gray hoodie. He blinks and sniffs, and finally shakes his head. He turns away from us and leans his elbows on the railing as he hangs his head. His shoulders tremble.

Markus inches around Abena and stands beside Youssef, patting him on the back with a stiff upper lip. "I knew Isolde for two and a half years, and in that time…" He pauses, smiling as he fiddles with a thick silver band on his middle finger. "She might be the sweetest, most authentic person I've ever met. There was this one time," he chuckles, his eyes turn glassy. "We were held up in this little shithole in Poland. No electricity, so no TV. We'd angered someone on their Witch's Council, so we had to lay low—no taverns or cafeterias."

"I remember that," Youssef says, turning his head towards Markus.

Markus nods, his melancholy smile turning almost joyful. "She decided to put on a puppet show. But no one wanted to give up their socks because we were freezing our asses off. So, she used origami. Well, in the play…" He begins to chuckle, which soon turns into genuine laughter. Even Zoey starts to giggle just watching him struggle to finish his story. "In the play, there's this phoenix who rises from the ashes…" His laughter overpowers him as tears run down his face, a mixture of grief and humor.

"By the end, she'd burned that entire slum to the ground," Abena finishes, shaking her head. "Got a whole new wardrobe out of it," she adds with a rueful shrug.

"She loved hummingbirds," David says. "So much that when we did that run down in Tampa, she got that watercolor tattoo on her foot. She would have gotten more if there had been time." He adjusts his thick black sunglasses, slipping a finger beneath the lens. "They'll always remind me of her." Soojin pulls a little origami bird from the pocket of her onesie pajamas.

She edges to the railing, cupping the little paper bird. The paper bursts into a brilliant flame, but somehow the fire doesn't consume it immediately. Like moths transfixed by the light, we all gather around Soojin.

The small, fiery bird lifts from her cupped hands and drifts into the sky.

Flying farther and farther from us until she disappears beyond the horizon.

CHAPTER THIRTY-TWO
Italy's Salem

"So, we're taking a train to Nice, and then what?" Zoey questions as we pack.

I shake my head. "No idea. Silas isn't exactly communicative."

I do my daily check of the Black Flame Candle, cleverly hidden in my fuzzy sock. Still there. I zip up my suitcase, and the Paris skyline catches my eye again. For just a moment, I forget we're on the run.

"Oy," Zoey calls out as Youssef passes by our door. He halts and steps back into our doorway. "Do you know where we're going?" she asks.

"We're traveling by train to Nice, then a bus to Ventimiglia, then hauling ourselves onto another bus and travel to Triora, where the accommodations will not be nearly as nice as this," he says wide-eyed before stepping away.

Zoey freezes. She runs a hand through her unkempt and slightly grown black pixie. She can almost tuck some locks behind her ears now.

"What is it?" I ask, perching on my bed.

Her eyes tick to me anxiously. "That's my father's hometown." She shakes her head. "I've heard stories, horrible stories. The place is overrun with Nefari, and the Italian Witch's Council, their version of the committee, keeps a very strong presence to combat it." She sits next to me on the bed. "We're basically going into a war zone of witchcraft."

Soojin stomps into our room and flops down on the bed. "Silas wants me to change."

Zoey and I exchange a glance before examining her outfit, assuming she means her attire.

Soojin is dressed in floral-patterned tights with hazard yellow fishnet pantyhose pulled over the first layer. A lavender miniskirt, highlighter green turtleneck with sparkling sequins, and a white, overly fluffy, fur crop coat. She purses her frosted lips in a heavy pout.

A slow creeping smile plays at our lips.

"When I met Silas, I was a fashion student at Seoul National University.

I can't simply 'change'," she grumbles.

Abena strolls into the room, her suitcase in hand, and stares at each of us in turn. She's wearing a crimson cable-knit sweater with a cowl neck beneath a dark brown leather trench coat, wide-legged jeans, and pointed toe boots. Her narrow braids cascade down her back, reaching her slender waist. "You bring too much attention to yourself, and the group. Now hurry, we need to leave soon." Her black snake slithers its head out the sleeve of her trench coat before she turns and leaves.

When we gather at the van, Silas growls to himself at the sight of Soojin's 'reasonable' outfit change. He mutters something under his breath, calling her "Asian Barbie". Soojin is dressed the way Barbie would if she was on the cover of Vogue: pink Hermes palazzo pants, pink peacoat, and baby pink beret with a dazzling broach.

When we board the train, we're forced to scatter to find seats, making Silas nervous. He was hoping our early arrival would secure us a train car to ourselves. Youssef and Abena are crammed amongst a group of tourists taking selfies and shooting videos in their small car. David is wedged between the window and a rather large German family. Markus, Zoey, and I end up squeezing together on one bench across from businessmen who look less-then-enthusiastic to be traveling. Somehow, Soojin and Silas end up side by side.

After the train to Nice, we hop a bus to Sanremo, Italy, then another bus to Triora. My shoulder accidentally bumps into Zoey as the bus jostles us down a winding road. She doesn't notice; she just leans against the window, snoring. As exhausted as I am, I'm too anxious to sleep. I can't even appreciate the Italian hillsides, not with all the questions plaguing my thoughts. I squeeze my eyes closed and try to reach out once more.

Blue, can you hear me? We're heading to Triora. I'm scared. I feel like I'm never going to see you again. Please find me. You won't be the only familiar with us. Silas has his cat, Machado, and Youssef has Alexandra. She's this gorgeous, sleek black cat. Maybe Youssef and I can set you two up. I can't help but smile, wondering what kind of quippy retort he would have made if he were here.

And Abena has a snake named Gree. It's pretty cool. Markus's familiar is an owl, named Oden, but he's back with Markus's family. Same with

David's familiar, Delilah. I wish you could tell me how my family is doing. I wonder if Jack stops by. I hope he doesn't hate me for leaving.

I wait, hoping for a stir in the back of my mind. Some kind of tug on the connection with my familiar. Nothing. I sniff and cough clearing that burning sensation in the back of my throat whenever I need to cry. I release a breath and settle my mind as I reach out telepathically once more.

Elspeth, I have your candle. I try to tempt her, probably irresponsibly. *It's with me in…Europe. Do you still want it?* I can't feel her either. There's a strange open space in the back of my mind, the place where she used to creep about, nagging me. Now it's nothing but an empty shadow. There's a sense of relief in that, like I belong to myself again, but I can't help but wonder where she's gone. It's not like she's tied to Salem; she was killed in Scotland. I button my coat, then dip my chin beneath my scarf. The cold here seeps through the windows, which fog with the breath of passengers while the bus's heater struggles to keep up.

If Elspeth is unreachable, it can't mean anything good. She wouldn't suddenly find her humanity. Is it Blue? Can she not reach me because I'm out of range with my Familiar?

Questions mount with no answers in sight.

The bus emits a loud groan and downshifts, climbing higher into the mountains along a narrow, winding road bordered by steep cliffs and dense forests. The early December twilight hangs heavy in the air, the deep azure sky quickly fading to black as the last traces of daylight vanish behind the peaks.

"Zoey." I nudge her awake, knowing she wouldn't want to miss this.

Her eyes flutter open as she yawns and stretches. "What is it?"

I simply point out the window. The rugged terrain, with its jagged rocks and rolling hills, is covered in patches of crystallized frost. Trees line the road, their silhouettes dark and looming against the fading sky.

The Village of Triora emerges from the shadow of the mountains. Zoey and I both lean towards the window like gawking tourists. Ancient stone buildings faintly shimmer in the soft golden light spilling from windows. Narrow cobbled streets twist up and down the hillside, lit only by the glow of homes and shops. Small groups of locals bundled in thick coats and scarves move leisurely. A few small cars, their headlights dimmed with age, sputter through the village. Occasionally, a moped buzzes by, the rider bracing against the biting wind.

The village is timeless, with its steep alleyways and arched doorways seemingly untouched by the modern world. Perched high on the hill is the ruins of an old castle, a shadowy silhouette against the dimming sky.

The bus groans to an exhausted halt, sounding like it died as soon as it was put in park. Zoey and I are the first ones to exit.

Our little coven huddles under the halo of the station's only streetlamp. Silas zips up his puffy black North Face jacket and tugs his knit beanie lower to cover his ears. "I rented us a house. It wasn't through any normal site, so we'll see how it goes. We'll have to walk, it's less than a quarter mile from here." He grips the straps of his backpack and jerks his head toward a cobbled lane beside the station.

We walk two by two, the narrow roads not allowing for anything more.

David, wearing headphones, bobs his head bringing up the rear.

I whisper the air spell to help me lug my suitcase. The air smells faintly of woodsmoke and damp earth, a little reminder that winter has settled on this isolated mountain town. Despite the cold that nips at our noses and ears, the village bustles with quiet energy as people go about their evening. We nod at passersby, our breath coming out in little white puffs, mingling in the air.

As we meander down the lane, passing by the stone homes, it's easy to forget what year it is. Spotting a local on his phone feels like an anachronism, like catching someone at a renaissance fair breaking character.

"Welcome to the Salem of Italy," Zoey whispers into my ear. I shiver against a chilly breeze. "What do you mean?"

Zoey tugs on the hood of her gray hoodie under her motorcycle jacket. "Triora is famous for their witch trials. They have festivals celebrating it. Maybe, if Silas is in a good mood, we can ask to go to The Museo della Stregoneria; it's a witch museum. My parents went there on a date."

I lift a brow. "I thought you were scared of coming here."

Zoey nods. "Yeah, well, actually being here is different. This is my dad's home," she says, her voice ending mournfully.

"Well, don't ever expect Silas to be in a good mood," I mumble.

We stop in front of a stone house with rectangular windows so dark it's impossible to see into. "Markus, the key is in a lock box, the code is 1580. Now, there are three rooms, bunk beds in each. Abena, you're rooming with Soojin," Silas says while rubbing his hands together.

Neither seem all that thrilled.

"Markus, Youssef, and David, you three will be all together. There's an extra cot in the closet according to the owner. Zoey and Eleanor will have a room, and I'll take the couch. The pantry is supposedly stocked, so find what you can and get to sleep. Abena, you and I will go on a scouting run in the morning. David, you are permitted to leave the house now. Soojin, Zoey, Eleanor, you three stay put."

The air inside the home is cool, albeit musty, mixed with the unmistakable scent of old stone, timber, and aged herbs. Silas finds the light switch, and the yellow lights blink in and out several times before remaining on with a quiet buzz. The rustic interior has low wooden beams stretching across the ceiling, with simple, sturdy wood furnishings and mismatched armchairs scattered throughout the humble room. Uneven terracotta tiles, worn smooth over time, cover the floor.

Everyone breaks off from the huddle. Youssef gets to work on the fireplace, while the rest of the men pull out chairs at the massive dining room, its thick wood resembling the grit and strength of a Viking ship.

"There better be a bathroom in this place, I'm not doing an outhouse again!" Soojin yells as she disappears down a shadowy hall.

Zoey and I abandon our luggage in the entryway and follow Abena into the kitchen. The open pantry is lined with wooden shelves housing the basics: dry pasta, sacks of flour, tins of tomatoes, jars of preserved vegetables, olives, and several bottles of olive oil and vinegar.

Drying herbs hang from the ceiling, their earthy aroma filling the kitchen; rosemary, thyme, and sage, all bundled and tied with twine.

Zoey pops open the small fridge circa 1950. "We've got some milk, eggs, cheeses, dried meat. Nothing that we can make quickly tonight. What I'd give for a greasy burger right now," she mumbles.

My stomach growls. The only thing I've eaten today were a small bag of chips and soda on the train, and that was hours ago. Zoey pulls some dried meat and cheeses from the fridge and fetches some crusty bread from the cupboard, then sets about cobbling together a meal.

Abena and I wordlessly volunteer to rinse the dust off the plates. My eyes naturally drift over the window above the sink. Glaring at me from behind the glass are the crimson eyes of a goat.

The plate I was holding shatters against the floor. The black goat continues to stare.

"Eleanor?" Zoey questions.

Abena looks from me to the window. "What is it?"

The goat's face fades back into the dark. I'm not sure if it disappeared or just stepped out of the light.

Blue! I'm seeing the goat again. My heart throbs like it's trying to beat its way out of my ribs. *How do I even begin to explain this?* "Uh…nothing. Sorry. Thought I saw something," I mumble. "I think I need to lie down for a minute. I'm sorry."

Zoey isn't convinced. "Okay, yeah go find us a place to sleep," she says before cranking black pepper over the olive oil.

I nod and hurry from the room, sprinting up the stairs.

"You and Zoey's room is the last one on the right," Markus calls after me. I close the door to what I can only imagine was originally a closet with a window and throw myself on the bottom bunk. My hands are shaking and I'm starting to hyperventilate. My body feels pressed beneath a stone slab. I curl into a ball and squeeze my eyes shut, trying to block out those crimson eyes and the malicious feeling they pushed on me. It doesn't work.

Blue, what am I supposed to do? I question out of habit, like an amputee trying to move a severed limb.

The door creaks on its hinges.

"I'm sorry about downstairs," I cry to Zoey. "There's something going on. I don't even know how to explain it."

Silence.

"I know, I shouldn't have run off like that. I just got so overwhelmed." Silence.

I open my eyes. The stench of smoke and sulfur prickle at my nostrils.

The lights flicker, then shut off entirely, plunging the room into darkness.

"Eleanor…"

CHAPTER THIRTY-THREE
Grimoires

The voice is smooth like honey, dark like onyx, and as delicious to the ear as sugar is on the tongue. The moment my mind registers the sound, my insides feel slimy. My ears itch from the inside like a million little prickling mosquito bites.

Fear seizes my body. I can't move.

Hooves clomp across the floorboards.

Warm, foul breath grazes the back of my neck. "Who are you?" I ask, my voice trembling.

"I think you know. You've always known. You're drawn to me. They are always drawn to me…"

My mind whirls in terror. *Everything I know about black goats comes only from pop culture, but in every horror movie, the goat is something satanic. But this can't mean… can it? Why the hell would he want to talk to me? I'm a nobody. This can't be happening.*

My rational mind cannot accept that this, the black goat haunting me, could actually be…the Devil.

Even with my back turned, I can feel it smile, a maniacal, ghoulish grin delighting in misery and despair.

I gasp for air. My bones feel heavy, like a suffocating weight is pressing down upon me, as if the very atmosphere itself has thickened with a tangible dread. The room spins around me, breaking apart as the world twists into a cacophony of misery. The shrieks of the damned pierce the air, their voices raw with torment, echoing like the howl of an oncoming storm. My mind is filled with clashing blades from ancient bloody wars, the rage and fury of men slaughtering one another. It's as if every sin, every ounce of hate, every act of violence and betrayal is pouring into me at once—greed, envy, lust, the endless hunger for power and destruction. It swarms inside me, a torrent of evil flowing in my veins like poison.

Oh, Brighid, please! Please help me!

Fingers curl around my windpipe. I claw at my neck. My lips

swell, my eyes feel like they'll pop, my pulse beats just beneath my skin. *He's killing me! Blue, I'm going to die!*

"You will come to me. They all come to me, welcome me in. You will too…"

The door slams shut.

My body writhes on the bed. I blink, fighting for consciousness. My lungs are on fire, screaming inside me, begging for oxygen.

Zoey timidly pokes her head in, creaking the door open. "Hey, Ragazza, are you okay?"

I gasp, shooting up in bed, almost hitting my head on the top bunk as I suck in as much air as my lungs will allow.

Zoey sprints around the bed and falls to her knees at my side. "Whoa, hey, are you okay? Were you choking or something? What's going on?"

I cling to her, tumbling out of my bed, my arms wrapping around her in a tight hug. I'm like a sailor fallen overboard and she's my only line to the ship. Warmth seeps into my shaking body, a soothing balm against the freezing darkness. Zoey breathes into my ear, completely caught off guard. The soft, steady beat of her heart is the only sound that matters right now, the only thing anchoring me back to this world. I cling to her, burying my face into my friend's shoulder, holding onto something, someone undeniably good.

"You're scaring me, Ragazza, what's going on?"

My arms relax around her; I breathe in the scent of rosemary and thyme from her cooking in the kitchen. I feel myself return completely; the terror that had gripped me has passed. I release her, both of us sitting on the floor, I rest my back against the bed frame of the bottom bunk.

"I need to tell you something," I breathe, still trying to adjust to filling my lungs. "You know how I have visions, right?" She nods.

"Well, I've been seeing a black goat."

She stiffens, and for a moment stops breathing.

"It's been happening for a while—it started last year, actually—and it's been getting worse, more vivid. I saw him at the fraternity house, then in the window downstairs in the kitchen—that's why I dropped that plate. And when I was lying here, he actually spoke to me," I say, my words tumbling out so fast I have to stop and catch my breath.

Zoey grips her hands in her lap. "What did it say?"

I try to recall its exact words. "I will come to him…like the others did." Everything he said to me is slipping from my mind.

"So, other witches have seen him, and they went to him, voluntarily," she concludes.

I nod. "I think…there have been many. For a split second, it was like I could…feel them." I recall their agonizing shrieks, and shiver. "Zoey, this feels big. Like *really* big."

Zoey nibbles on her bottom lip. "I wonder…"

"What?"

Her dark brown eyes flick up at me. "If a lot of other witches have experienced what you have, some of them, at least a few, must have written it in their grimoire."

I hang my head back, aggravated. "Yeah, but we aren't in Salem."

"Ahem. Witches didn't *just* live in Salem. Hello, this is the witch capital of Italy," she stresses, giving me a bit of a stink eye.

An idea occurs to me. "Zoey, do you remember when we snuck into the Witch House Museum after hours?"

Zoey grins deviously. "I like where this is going."

"Do you think The Museo della… whatever, would it have any grimoires we could look through?"

"Possibly, but there is only one way to find out," she says in all seriousness.

"Do you know where it is? Our phones don't work, so we can look it up," I complain.

Zoey's face brightens. "No, but on the end table downstairs are all these travel brochures for tourists. I guarantee there's one for the museum."

Our plan takes shape. "So, we wait till everyone is asleep, then we'll sneak out."

Zoey stands by the windows and measures the width. "Okay, I think we can squeeze through. I might need to wear a sports bra though," she says, gazing down C-cup breasts.

"Ha, the one time being flat chested will come in handy," I tease, hoping to quell my rising anxiety.

Zoey retrieves some food from the kitchen, explaining to everyone that I was feeling ill from traveling and was going to just eat in our room. We each dip pieces of crusty bread into the best olive oil I've ever tasted as we review the trifold brochure for the museum.

"Okay, so we're somewhere over here," Zoey says, pointing to the empty space above the left corner of the map. "The museum seems to be at the very center of the village. We could fly, but again, I'm not sure I'm up to making myself invisible to do that. We might just have to walk, and with how winding the streets are it might take a bit."

"I'm fine walking," I say. I take a swig of my Cedrata Tassoni, letting the cool citrus flavor linger on my tongue before swallowing. "When we return to Salem," I say, "we're bringing a case of these."

Zoey emits a melancholy smile. "Yeah, maybe one day."

Thankfully, everyone is exhausted from traveling. By midnight, they're all in bed for the night. We listen carefully at our bedroom door while Silas performs one last sweep of the house before retiring to the living room with his familiar, Machado. In less than twenty minutes, we can hear him snoring.

We lift the latch on our window and push it wide open. We toss our winter coats out the window, letting them flutter to the ground.

The floorboards creak outside our door. We freeze and hold our breath, waiting.

Nothing.

"Let's keep going," Zoey whispers. She levitates, her body parallel to the ground, and pushes the air from her lungs as she carefully squeezes through the window. As soon as she's through the frame, she sucks in breath of cold air.

"Oh my gosh, it's freezing out here!" She crouches on the slopping roof and waits for me, running her hands up and down her arms for warmth.

Just as Zoey did, I levitate and turn on my side so I'm at my thinnest. My body feels skeletal as I slip through the window, never even brushing the frame. Any hint of curves I might have had before Europe have faded into skin and bone.

We grasp each other's hand, mutter the air spell, and leap off the roof, floating like snowflakes to the earth below. The moment our feet touch the ground, we snatch up our jackets and plunge our arms through the sleeves, already chilled from the icy cold seeping up from the ground.

With the map in our hands, we navigate down winding cobbled paths, following the serpentine route between houses. We pass shops selling "witch gear" clearly aimed at tourists, like knit witch hats, frocks, and striped tights.

"Wait, stop," Zoey orders. She stares at the map then looks up, glancing about. "We're here," she says, then points to our right.

The lampposts offer little illumination beyond a three-foot radius, and the stone building with the red tiled roof is identical to every other home and building here in the village.

We glance up and down the street before approaching. It seems we're the only ones out at this late hour. Our breath escapes in white puffs that drift and vanish. Peering through the dimly lit windows, we see a few lights on inside, probably for security. Zoey and I stare at each other in silence, as if daring the other to move or speak first.

My knees wobble as I step forward and silently volunteer to unlock the door. I bend down until I'm eye level with the lock on the door.

Zoey bends down next to me. "You're hopeless with locks. Remember The Witch House? I'm just nervous, so I hesitated."

"I will have you know that I unlocked the graveyard where The Gathering was held."

She playfully rolls her eyes at me. "That was a padlock. Child's play." She places her small hands on either side of the locked handle and closes her eyes. Her lips move as she recites the spell in her mind.

With my ear against the frigid door, I listen for the spring and click. "You got it."

Zoey lightly taps the door above the handle. She places her ear against the door, concentrating on the sound of another lock. Dressed in black, edgy pixie cut, little hands and features perfect for slipping in and out of small crevices, she's perfectly suited for cat burglary.

"Two deadbolts and one chain lock. I could hear the chain rattle when I knocked," she whispers, her face still pressed against the door. Her eyelids fall shut as she mutters another spell. A smile unfurls on her face. "It worked." She springs to her feet. "Now let's just pray they don't have a security system. After you," she says, sweeping out of the way.

The door creaks open, and the museum air, likely kept warm to preserve the historical artifacts, thaws my frost-chapped face. I breathe in the smell of cleaning vinegar and pine. If there are any security systems, they're very well hidden. I take another step forward and lift my arms, waiting to set off any motion sensors. Nothing. I spin around and wave Zoey in.

The walls are covered in murals depicting early villagers, women shackled, crying out as they're being accused of their 'terrible' crime of witchcraft. There are mannequins dressed in period clothing, staring lifelessly. Display cases feature historical artifacts along with detailed explanations for context.

Directly across from us is a brightly lit glass display case. They appear to be ancient books with yellow pages, hand-sewn and uneven.

"Zoey," I call, rushing over.

She joins me hovering over the glass. There are five books, each open to the center. The writing has faded with age. The first has detailed descriptions of spells for a good harvest, nothing helpful. The second is fairly warped by water damage with ink that runs down the page; the words are indecipherable. I move to the middle where Zoey bumps into me after reading the books on the far right. From her interest in the middle book, I assume her first two books were no more helpful than mine. The middle book describes the witch's sacred worship of Minerva.

"Shocker, none of them were magically opened directly to the information we would need," she mutters sarcastically.

I nod. "We'll need to use the air spell to flip the pages," I surmise, not ready to give up quite yet.

Zoey and I both take a far end like before.

I imagine the book closing, painfully slow, then the cover cracking open, careful not to damage the delicate binding. *La Caeli*. The book trembles as it shuts, then quivers open again. The first page is blank, except for a name in the bottom right corner: *Caterina Rossi*.

I turn to Zoey. "These are will all be written in Italian. I can't read Italian."

She inches over to me and, without skipping a beat, reads the contents of the grimoire as I turn the pages. Caterina Rossi's writing is simplistic at first. She describes the birds and insects she sees, how she hates to do chores, and is anxious to receive her powers. She then details how her eldest sister ran away to Rome with the baker's son. Her second sister dies of a fever; her parents suspect demonic forces were involved. I begin to wonder if she's actually a witch until she writes about her exercises with the five branches of magic.

We reach the middle of the book, and my neck and back ache from hunching over the glass. Then, with a quarter of the book left, the writing stops. The rest of the book is blank.

"She might have died," Zoey says.

I cautiously open it to the center like before, and we slide down one and repeat the process, again, and again, until we reach the last book.

"Margherita Barbieri," Zoey reads. "Oof," she says after reading the first page. "She starts this on her seventeenth birthday, a village boy made it for her. She is, um… very…vivacious. She has a crush on basically every boy in the village including…ew, a 'well endowed' priest. At least she's guessing he is." Zoey continues reading and indicates when she's ready for me to turn the page. "Holy cow, get a hobby," she mutters under her breath.

Zoey stops reading aloud; I just flip the pages when needed.

I sigh, glancing at the clock on the wall, we've been here for well over an hour now. I let my upper half lie across the glass, casually flicking my finger every few minutes just so I have something to do.

"Finally," Zoey says.

I jump back to my feet and turn my attention back to the weathered grimoire. I scan the page hoping for any crude, simplistic sketches of a goat. No luck.

"She's nineteen, has kissed every boy in a ten-mile radius, and now fears she'll be a spinster forever. But at least she's done fantasizing about every… single… boy. And I thought modern girls were boy crazy," she mumbles. She places her head in her hands, continuing to read quietly while I return to flipping pages.

"Stop! Stop!" Zoey barks. Her eyes race across the words on the page. "I wast stalked by a black goat in mine dreams. Oft hath I dreams, and visions aplenty. Such fancies didst begin when I wast but seventeen. Yet now, this black goat cometh forth in mine waking hours, as though the veil betwixt dream and reality doth rend asunder. The beast wouldst have me follow, and when I refuse, mine punishment is swift, delivered by the hands of the inquisitors, who wring confessions from the lips of village witches through cruel torment," Zoey reads. "Even when alone, a watchful gaze doth follow me. I can feel thy gaze like unto a knife, pinned to thy back."

This is exactly what we've been searching for, but now as Zoey reads it aloud, I'm afraid of what she'll say. My breathing grows labored as I'm immersed in the young woman's story.

"I am so starv'd. Famine, yet again, plagueth our village, ravaging body and soul. The black goat, thou cursed creature of darkest dream, doth offer me succour. Faint and desperate, mine body weaken'd for want of food, I can no longer resist his call."

Zoey glances at me, then continues reading. "I follow him, though my quill doth tremble at the thought of our doings. I dare not recount them here in full. In the mountains we did commune, and at his bidding, partook of a feast most plentiful." Zoey's breath hitches. She gags, but tarries on. "When dawn's light touch'd mine eyes, I awoke to fur betwixt mine teeth, blood staining both dress and hand. The goat had vanish'd, leaving naught behind save a black candle, its sides bump'd and inscrib'd with markings strange and fell."

I feel the blood in my veins turn to ice. She too had a Black Flame Candle. I think of mine, sitting, like a curse inside my suitcase just waiting to be unleashed.

"It gets worse," Zoey warns. "I return'd home, yet peace eludeth me. Nightmares hound my sleep, and even in waking hours, I am haunted. Strange visions befall me. I am now with child, though no man hath known me. This evil hath wrought itself upon me, an abomination within mine womb. The candle whispereth unto me, urging me to light it. In vision, I see its flame, black as smoke, a darkness which doth devour all light. My belly swells, and with it the villagers' suspicions."

Cold sweat dribbles down my neck. *If this is what the goat did to her, what does it plan to do with me?* I grip the glass case to keep from falling.

"O divine mother, forgive me, for I hath strayed so far beyond thy path. Forgive mine reckless heart, for it is heavy with sin. I must return to the accursed mountain—whose loftiest spires bring a man no closer to heaven—and cast mine body from its precipice. Yet even this, I know, shall grant me no escape. The evil he hath brought down upon us is insatiable, ever feeding, ever hungering, consuming all in its path. The end is nigh. He shall return, and Hell itself shall walk among us, shaping devils from the children of God. Destroying our great purpose. I cannot bear to see it. He is coming. I beg of thee, oh Goddess, have mercy upon my wretched soul. Deliver thou me from mine own undoing. No witch hath the power to stop him…"

My heart is pounding now. "What about the candle? What does it do? Did she take it with her?"

Zoey shakes her head solemnly. "That's her last entry." A lump forms in her throat.

"So, it's like *Rosemary's Baby* or something? She was knocked up by the devil?" Zoey asks with a mixture of confusion and revulsion.

"It may not have been the actual devil. And for all we know, she was mistaken," I argue, desperate to prove Zoey's conclusion wrong. "She was um…pretty…friendly in the village." I bite my lip, disgusted with myself for basically calling this poor deceased witch a slut. "I'm sorry, who knows what it means…"

Neither of us speak as we trudge back to the rental house. Just as before, we fly up to the roof and climb into the window, having accidentally left it open when we left.

The room is an ice box. We both sleep fully clothed, wearing socks on our hands as we shiver beneath the meager blankets.

"Betty would know what to do," Zoey whispers in the dark. "I wish she were here…"

I squeeze my eyes shut, trying to force tears to fall. *Blue! I need you! The goat is so much worse than either of us imagined. Please come!*

I curl up on my side, crying tearlessly while thinking about Margherita, cornered, left with but one choice. *Will I meet the same fate?*

CHAPTER THIRTY-FOUR
Don't Wait

Zoey hops off the top bunk and lands deftly on her feet. "I'm going to scrounge up some breakfast, you want anything?"

I shake my head, still huddled under the blankets on the lower bunk.

Zoey purses her lips, thinking. "Okay, I've made a decision. We're going out and exploring today," she says, gripping her hips.

"And disobey Silas?" I mumble.

Zoey shrugs. "That's right. Look cute, we'll see if someone wants to buy us food."

I don't move. All desire to do anything has withered and died.

She gazes down at me, resolute. "I know what will get you moving," she declares. "I wasn't going to bring this up, because of last night and all, but I changed my mind. I heard Markus and Silas talking last night; they mentioned the date. Today's December twelfth."

I shrug, wondering what that has to do with anything. Then it hits me. "It's your birthday today," I simper then groan as I toss off my blankets and sit up. Zoey relishes her victory with a smug smile.

Soojin lends us her makeup so we can get ready together in the home's only bathroom. Zoey crouches while I balance on my tiptoes so we can both use the oval mirror. Zoey squeals when she spots the charcoal liner and dark shadow, sounding more like her old self than she has in weeks. She applies a cabernet-colored lip stain, then smudges dark makeup around her wide, pixie-like eyes, bringing to life the bold, untamed witch who used to blast punk rock at the apothecary. Her classic mix of edgy and feminine shines through again, like the time she wore a Pink Floyd shirt with a bejeweled Peter Pan collar. I keep pausing my own makeup to glance over at her, watching as each swipe of mascara brings back more of the unapologetic Zoey I remember.

I stare at my reflection, thinking maybe it's time to reclaim my own familiar look. I scrounge through Soojin's makeup bag and spot exactly what I need. I run blue liner along my lower lids, then carefully apply black liquid liner on my top lashes. I finish the look with a few coats of mascara and add a touch of gloss, leaving my lips feeling soft and supple. I shake my hair out of my ponytail allowing my long dark hair to fall freely over my shoulders ending a little past my bust.

"I'm so jealous," Zoey mutters, before sweeping a little highlighter across her tanned cheeks.

I frown at her.

She rolls her doe-eyed brown eyes at me like it should be obvious. "You're tall, you've got the whole 'legs for miles' thing, plus you have a perfect oval face so you can do any hair style; long, short, bangs, no bangs, you can rock it. My face is round, long hair looks terrible on me."

I snort out a scoff. "Zoey, not even. I used to cry because I hated being 5'7". I wanted to be short and petite, like a little fairy. Like my sister Margaret. Besides you rock your look. I wish I could do that makeup, but I'd just look like a raccoon."

"Yeah, but you've got that ethereal beauty. Plus, your natural, lavender eyes are stunning. You really lucked out with a good color," Zoey says.

Our envious faces crack into gleeful giggling. We fall into each other, savoring the moment. Right now, in this bathroom, we aren't condemned witches on the run, fighting to stay alive. We're just teenage girls. I'll never take that for granted again.

As we stand side by side, our old selves have emerged, ready to face whatever comes next.

"Thanks," I say, nudging her.

She winks back at me. "I think we both need this. And if we see that damn goat around town, I say we find a butcher and serve him for dinner."

My heart skips a beat at the mention of it.

We clean up the bathroom, returning all of Soojin's items back to her bag. "Thank Minerva your sister has rad taste," Zoey says, cobbling an outfit together.

While pulling out a pair of high-waisted, dark wash jeans, something else falls from the suitcase, landing with a thud and rolling across the floor. "I got it," Zoey says. She reaches for my fuzzy sock, the sock that conceals the Black Flame Candle.

"Wait!" I say, but I'm too late. Zoey pulls back the sock, revealing the candle beneath.

She examines the lumpy candle with the strange carving scratched into the side. "Weird candle." She sniff it. "Ugh. Don't light this. Smells like rotten eggs." She casually tosses the satanic candle back to me.

I shove it back into my bag and bury it beneath my clothes. "Yeah, no plans on lighting it. Ever," I whisper under my breath.

Zoey points to the window where three black birds are perched outside on the ledge. "Triora is calling. Everything else can wait."

With linked arms, we stroll right out the front door. Machado hisses at us while we pass. Alexandra stares at us, but remains still and silent.

Our first stop is a gift shop, picking up a polaroid camera with my mom's credit card.

Thankfully, with Zoey fluent in Italian, we're able to buy snacks at local street carts and ask for directions to the castle up on the mountain. One elderly woman urges us to visit the village's witch museum. We exchange a grinning look and thank her for the suggestion.

We move about the village like obvious tourists, posing for pictures and trying every food available, like roasted chestnuts, focaccia bread, and panissa. Every time we try to pay, a man or boy leaps in front of us, insisting he would take care of it.

Fortunately, despite how small the village is, we never run into Silas or the other members of the coven. And yet, I still feel a set of intense eyes on me, watching our every step.

Zoey points out a gorgeous stone church with beautiful stained-glass windows. "My parents were married in that church right there." She stares at the Polaroid in her hand as we walk down the path. She sucks in a shaky breath and shoves it into her back pocket.

I wrap my arm around her shoulders. "Hungry?"

"Always."

"Signorina!" a boy calls, surrounded by friends. "Come back, we must speak." His friends laugh and jab him in the shoulder.

Zoey and I giggle, tucking our smiles beneath our scarves as we quicken our pace down the cobbled street to L'Erba Gatta, a restaurant on the corner.

"I think he was ready to propose, Ragazza," Zoey jokes.

The warm establishment makes us shiver as we step inside, nearly hypnotized by the rich aroma of slow-cooked meat and fresh herbs. Zoey points out the now unmistakable earthy aroma of chestnut flour baking in the kitchen.

An older woman wearing a faded gingham printed dress leads us to a table. We aren't sitting more than a few seconds before a waiter approaches our table, a triumphant smile on his face.

"Buonasera signore, cosa desiderate da bere?" he asks. His eyes rake us up and down.

Zoey glances at me, then back to the waiter. "Parli inglese?"

"Yes," he says, in a thick Italian accent. He grins a sparkling white smile at us.

Zoey turns to me. "Mind if I order for us?"

I drop my menu on the table and gesture for her to have at it.

"We'll get a bottle of your Rossese di Dolceacqua," she produces her ID, proudly declaring her eighteenth birthday. "She'll have your Ravioli di Brasato and I'll take your Polenta con Funghi," she says.

I clear my throat, giving her a deadpan stare.

She rolls her eyes at me. "Fine, she'll also have a Cedrata Tassoni," she says, ordering my new favorite soda.

"Make that two," Youssef says, suddenly towering over our table.

The handsome waiter glances at the two of us then Youssef, feeling out our relationship. The waiter nods and steps back from our table.

Zoey and I stare at each other nervously as Youssef pulls out a free chair from a neighboring table.

"It's my birthday," Zoey blurts out.

"It's true," I say, holding up the ID she left on the table.

Youssef's full lips tremble as he fights against a smile. Unable to contain it, he bursts out laughing, shaking his head at us. "I'm not the one you must worry about."

Zoey and I sigh with relief.

We share the photos we took as our drinks arrive at the table. Zoey offers us a sip of her local vintage; we both decline, much to her chagrin. She mutters under her breath that if David were here, he'd join her.

"Hey, you shaved," Zoey says. She skewers a mushroom and devours it with a little moan.

Youssef runs his hand down his freshly shaved cheeks then combs this thick black mustache with his fingers. "I thought it was time."

I raise a brow at him.

He sighs, cutting into his roasted chicken. "She said she prefers mustaches to beards…"

Zoey and I both brighten, once again enjoying our girlish instincts to giggle and beg for further details on this elusive mustache-loving-woman.

"I've been dreaming of her for a while now—yes, yes, I know what that means," he says, holding up his hand keeping us from interrupting. "She's so beautiful. Blonde, covered in dark freckles against her golden skin. I watch her surf, paddling out, she slices down a wave like she is one with the water."

His eyes glaze over, probably imaging this surfing siren, his soulmate. "I think she has a gift with water, the way she can control it. I've seen her save so many creatures of the sea, rising the tide to help a poor beached animal. Last night, I watched her celebrate her thirty-first birthday. I think her familiar is this lizard…a bearded dragon named kook." His voice cracks, and he takes a swig of his drink.

While Youssef describes the soulmate he's yet to meet, I feel the heavy stare of someone nearby. I can't tell who it is, but the weight of it intensifies. The words of Margharita' s grimoire play again in my mind.

"Where is she? Your soulmate?" Zoey asks.

Youssef shrugs, pushing his plate away. "Somewhere on a coast. I'm not really sure. I've never heard her speak, never had any hint at a location."

"Well, describe the beach, the landmarks, vegetation, anything that could pinpoint her location," I urge.

Zoey glances at me, but leans forward, waiting.

Youssef describes different restaurants and surf shops, all of which you would expect in any beach town. He describes the school she teaches at; the elementary school children wear dark blue polo shirts and khaki bottoms. Again, not very helpful.

"There's this one place she goes to frequently," he says, then describes a white sand beach, turquoise water in minute detail. A white lighthouse is perched nearby on a rocky cliff.

Zoey perks up. "Wait. This is probably a long shot…" She digs into her purse, then tosses a soft cover book with worn edges onto the table. On the cover of "Tides of Desire" is a woman, torn dress, wet hair, embracing a man with dark brown hair, blowing in the wind. Behind them on the jagged cliffs stands a white lighthouse.

Youssef snatches the book from the table. "Yes! That's exactly what it looks like. Even that curve to the beach." He flips to the back of the book. "Where is this?"

"New South Wales, Australia. That's Byron Bay," Zoey reveals, her grin practically curling to her eyes.

Youssef's grip on the book tightens, as if the novel itself can transfer him to that exact beach. "Yes, I remember seeing a sign for The Pass, or something like that," he murmurs. "I haven't read this one."

I laugh. "You read the Pemberly Royal books?" My heart stings with thoughts of Sally devouring every new book that hits the shelves. She even threatened the owner of Wicked Good Books, our local bookstore, to set aside a copy for her.

Youssef nods. "Yes, I know. Isolde told me all about them, and I was hooked. Silly pen name, Pemberly Royal. She should go by her real name, Marie Byrne."

My heart skips a beat. Zoey whips around to me with eyes bulging. "Hot damn!"

Aunt Marie—my sweet, adorably clueless, old-fashioned Marie—is the author of those smutty romance novels Sally is obsessed with? I laugh out loud, imagining Marie in her flannel nightgown, typing away at her desk ladened with doilies. There's no way anyone in the family knows. Once again, I wonder what they're doing.

"Perhaps, when I'm no longer Nefari…" Youssef mumbles to himself. I fix him with a serious glare. "No, Youssef, you need to go find her." Zoey glances over at me in surprise.

"We don't know what tomorrow will bring. But if she is your soulmate, you shouldn't wait. Go to her, please, while you still have a chance."

He shakes his head, staring at the faded cover.

"Isolde is dead, Youssef. Any one of us could be next. You need to find her," I insist.

Zoey, who at first appeared dubious, suddenly nods ardently. "I'd give anything to know who my twinned soul is. And if I did know, I'd drop everything and find him. It's who we are."

We lapse into momentary silence.

Our waiter marches out of the kitchen, holding his tray high above his head before sweeping into a low bow, presenting a dense cake with a tea candle perched on top. Castagnaccio, Zoey had called it after I noticed one in the bakery earlier.

The patrons in the restaurant clap along as the waiter sings a sweet but pitchy rendition of happy birthday. Zoey blows out the candle, and when I turn to my right, Youssef has slipped away and disappeared into the crowd.

As we meander back to the rental, our stomachs sag, overstuffed from all the extra food we hadn't ordered but they brought us anyway. One man recognizes us from the restaurant and shouts a happy birthday to Zoey as we hurry along.

"You know, I don't think this is what Silas had in mind when he said not to draw attention to ourselves…" she mumbles to me.

* * *

"You could have blown our entire mission!" Silas shouts, pacing in front of the fireplace. The fire rages each time he screams at us.

Zoey and I sit close together on the stiff couch. Markus and Abena stand stone-faced on either side of Silas. David sits in a nearby rocking chair while Soojin dragged a dining room chair to the sitting room.

"Reckless! Stupid! Immature! This is life or death, and you're acting like children! We just lost Isolde; how many more must die before you two learn?!"

Abena is clearly just as angry as Silas, but her discipline keeps her anger reigned in. Markus, on the other hand, appears torn.

"Do you think you're on vacation?" he yells. He stops, glancing about. "And where the hell is Youssef? He should have been back by now." He checks the smart watch on his wrist.

"He came home," Soojin shares. "I saw him, but then I think I saw him leave with Alexandra again." Her voice is a nervous, high-pitched whisper, worried that speaking up will mean Silas redirects his anger at her now.

Markus uncrosses his arms over his massively muscular chest. "I'll check our room. Maybe he just snuck back in without anyone noticing." He heads up the stairs, taking two at a time.

"I want you both out of my sight. I can't even bear to look at you. You'll both stay in your room until I come for you tomorrow." Silas dismisses us, his jaw trembling with rage.

Zoey and I slink past him towards the stairs.

"Oh, and one more thing." He swivels from the mantle above the fireplace toward us, stopping inches from the first step. "If either of you decides to sneak out again, you will regret it. It's a small village; if we don't find you, I can guarantee the witch's council will, in which case both of you will be destroyed. A fitting punishment for two selfish witches you couldn't care less about the safety of their coven." He waves us off without another word.

We pass Markus on the stairs as he rushes past us.

"Youssef left. All of his belongings are gone. He left a note for Abena," he says, stricken.

"What?!" Silas bellows.

Zoey and I quicken our pace until we reach our room and shut the door. Too nervous to leave the room again, even just to go to the bathroom, we instead wet some towels with the water spell and wipe off our makeup. At my request, Zoey lights a white, long stem candle on the desk so we don't have to fall asleep in pure darkness. I can still recall the sound of clomping hooves across the bedroom floor. We slink into our beds, both gazing at the flickering candle until our eyelids grow heavy.

CHAPTER THIRTY-FIVE
Nefario Streghe

I'm awakened by a whiff of smoke. *Wait, smoke?* The candle we lit before bed is blown out, plunging the room into darkness.

"Zoey?" I timidly call.

She doesn't respond, but I hear the steady rhythm of her breathing.

The floorboards groan, like someone is shifting their weight in our small room. The wall opposite the bunkbeds is just with reach if I really lean and stretch—if something is in here with us, it's close enough to touch. *Whatever the goat wants, I won't follow it this time. There's nothing he can offer me. He promised Margharita a delectable feast and she ended up devouring live woodland creatures. Even if he threatens me, I have to ignore him.*

There's a soft click at the door. The sound is clear, deliberate. The darkness is thick and alive, pressing in on me from every side. My fingers grip the blanket tightly. *Maybe this isn't real. Maybe this is a dream or a vision.*

Light suddenly bursts alive in the room, forcing me to shield my eyes. "What the hell, Ell?" Zoey grumbles. She rolls over and buries her face into the wall.

My eyes struggle to adjust against the sudden brightness. From the bottom bunk, I see the lower halves of two figures standing at the foot of the bed.

Neither of them move.

"W-who's there?" I stammer.

"We mean you no harm. But keep your voice down and do not alert anyone in the house," a male voice orders. There's a ribbon of benevolence in his commanding tone, a stark contrast to the voice of the goat.

I carefully, silently, lean my head out from under the bunk bed. I first notice the woman, short in stature with chestnut hair falling to her shoulders in waves. Her curved hips and full bust are incongruous to her small frame. Her golden eyes glitter under the wreath of her eyelashes.

The man beside her is thin, taller than the woman, perhaps my height, with deeply tanned skin. His eyes, a blue so icy they're nearly white, are ghostly against his dark complexion. He brushes his fingers beneath a long, hawkish nose, staring at me intently, and mumbles something to the woman in Italian. They both look up at the top bunk and freeze. The confidence they carried when they first entered evaporates, replaced with disbelief that hangs thick in the silence. The woman can't tear her eyes from the top bunk; the man, however, directs his attention to me.

"Are you Eleanor Byrne?"

"Kind of." Hic. "My mom's maiden name is Byrne. I'm Eleanor O'Reilly," I answer.

The woman glances at me quickly. "Yes, you look exactly like Will." At the mention of my father's name, I slide out of bed.

Zoey stirs on the top bunk. "Ell?" she asks as she rolls back over. She spots the strangers and shoots upright. "Oh, my Minerva…"

The stranger's eyes glisten. The air in the room shifts, suddenly I feel like an interloper, witnessing something so private, intimate.

Could they really be?

"You're not my parents. They're dead. This isn't possible," Zoey snaps. She crawls backwards until her butt is on her pillow, her back against the wall. The strangers wince as if struck with a club. They again mutter something in Italian to each other, uttered so quietly I'm not even sure Zoey heard it.

A crow lands at the window and pecks at the glass, gaining the man's attention.

"Ombra," the man hisses, his accent thick. He waves it away, but the bird remains, staring into the room. He turns to the woman, "there are two nefario streghe watching the house."

The woman strides closer to the bed causing Zoey to flinch.

"Stop!" Zoey commands.

"Lovey, it's me. There is much to explain, but now is not the time," she says, tears gathering in her gilded eyes. "How many—" she stops, as if searching for the word, "Nefari are in the villa?"

Zoey's jaw trembles with anger. She leaps off the top bunk to her feet. "It's a trick, Ell. Don't tell them anything," Zoey warns. She stands in front of me, going toe to toe with the woman.

Warm tears roll down the woman's cheek and over her soft round chin. "Amore mio, please, we want to help."

I close my eyes, trying to sense the flow of magic in the room. I detect the slight buzz of a glamour. "Zoey," I say. She jumps when

I lightly touch her shoulder. "Reach out and touch her," I bend down, leaning close to her ear, "If you prove they are false, we have enough witches in the house all we would need to do is scream and we'll make them pay."

The bird taps the glass again with its sharp, pointy beak.

"We're running out of time," the man says, hovering by the bedroom door. "Give me your hand," Zoey orders.

Without hesitation, but with confusion gathering on her knitted brow, she offers her left hand. A solitaire diamond glitters on her fourth finger, with rubies on either side, all bound together on a yellow gold band. Zoey seizes the hand and lets her eyes fall closed. Her mouth, at first a hard line, slowly crumbles, turning into a quivering frown.

Her knees wobble. She collapses, but her mother, Beatrice, catches her. They both sink to the floor. Zoey is audibly crying.

"Shhh…" the man says, though his eyes have also glossed with tears. His gaze darts to the closed bedroom door then back at the window, where the crow is perched. He drops to his knees, one arm around the woman. Zoey is draped over her mother's lap.

"Where have you been? Why haven't you come home?" she sobs. "Anella misses you, Fia doesn't even know you."

I fold my arms and look away, wishing there was more space in this tiny room I could give them.

"Amore mio, I promise to explain. But first, how many witches are in this house?"

Zoey just cries, her head resting in Beatrice's lap while her arms are wrapped around her waist. The man, I'm presuming her father, Giovanni, strokes her head.

"There are seven, including us," I answer.

"So, you are Nefari, but The Committee never destroyed you," Zoey sobs. "Why would you come here? Isn't Triora dangerous for you?"

"Do you think you both could steal away for a few hours tomorrow?" Giovanni asks, his eyes shifting to me.

I shake my head. "No, we were just berated for sneaking out today. No way we could sneak out again."

"I know, we saw you both. Happy birthday, love," Beatrice says, her small smile trembles with waves of emotion.

Something creaks in the hall.

"Bea, we must go," he urges, tugging on his wife's elbow. "Zoe, we will be back for you, I promise."

Zoey reluctantly retracts her arms from around her mother. "I still don't understand."

Her mother gently cups her face. "You will."

Giovanni helps his wife to her feet. They press their ear against the door, and Giovanni whispers something in Italian to his wife.

She nods, and they both step out, closing the door behind them.

Zoey is still crouched down on the floor, trembling. I sit beside her, gathering her in my arms and letting her weep on my shoulder. I massage small circles on her back, all the while unable to tear my eyes from the bedroom door.

The crow silently flees from the window.

My stomach turns over, wishing yet again that Blue were here to offer me some advice. *Zoey's parents have been gone a long time, why are they only now making themselves known? They are Nefari, can they be trusted?* I don't voice my concerns with Zoey who's still reeling from the unexpected reunion.

Zoey cries herself to sleep on my lower bunk, curled up next to me. I pray we didn't make a mistake telling them how many of us there are.

* * *

Machado paces outside the house, glancing up at our window ever so often. Soojin threw a fit until finally Silas relented and allowed her to join the scouting mission, leaving David behind to guard us while Machado keeps an eye outside.

Zoey and I offer to prepare lunch.

David, exhausted from a night of screaming torment, lethargically agrees. He continues to lounge on the couch, his Ray-Bans secure on his face.

Zoey elbows my side while we rinse potatoes for her gnocchi. She nods to the window.

Her mother waves at us from the shadows of the pine trees. We crane our necks, peering over at David resting.

"Maybe we can sneak out to them," I whisper.

She shakes her head. "No, I'm done with that." She dries her hands on a rag and marches straight to David, who's fallen asleep on the couch. She touches his shoulder, startling him.

"Zoey?" He scrambles to sit up. "What are you doing?"

She kneels by the couch. "I know I can trust you, David. My parents are outside. They are Nefari on the run. No, I'm not asking for them to join this coven. They need to speak to me. I'm going to let them in. Can you please not tell Silas? He won't understand, all he cares about is curing everyone. Yes, yes, I know that doesn't make him a villain. But I need to this to remain between us, please."

David's brow furrows, but his exact reaction is hard to tell beneath his sunglasses. He itches the dark scruff on the side of his cheek, then nods. "It's got to be quick; Machado is walking the premises. You two lost a lot of trust yesterday."

Zoey doesn't wait. She dashes to the kitchen and out the back door.

"I'm sorry, I know the position we're putting you in," I tell David.

He nods, but keeps his face turned towards the backdoor, watching Zoey greet her parents.

"And you're sure we can trust them?" he asks, dropping his voice low.

I open my mouth to answer just as Zoey and her parents enter the living room. David rises to shake their hand and offers them the sofa. Zoey sits between them, continually keeping a hand on their arm or knee, as if making sure they're really here. David takes a seat in the rocking chair next to the fireplace.

Beatrice and Giovanni gaze at each other before speaking.

"The Nefario know you're here, and they know what you're planning," Giovanni explains. "You all need to leave, *today*."

The blood drains from Zoey's face. "What? No! Not unless you're coming too," she says, leaping up to her feet.

Beatrice waves her daughter down. "We won't be parting. We want you to come with us, both of you," Beatrice stresses.

David stops rocking and leans forward in his chair. "How would the local Nefari know what Silas has planned? He hasn't even shared it with our coven yet."

Giovanni straightens up, as if his honor has been called into question. "Familiars watch the comings and goings of this villa. Triora is a small, isolated mountain village. None of you even bothered with a fascino—err, glamour, as you call it." His words are slightly jumbled, given English is not his native language. "The Nefario knew you were here the moment you stepped off the bus. Your plans aren't the only thing they know."

Beatrice releases a deep breath. "They know one of you has a Black Flame candle," she says, like unto a scolding mother.

David's brow furrows. "I don't know what that is."

"Clearly, you don't have it," Giovanni says, obviously distrustful of David. Zoey slowly turns, peering over her shoulder at me behind her.

"Eleanor…that candle that rolled out of your suitcase…"

Beatrice and Giovanni's eyes dart to one another, inching towards the edge of the sofa.

"Why do you have that?" Beatrice questions. I grind my teeth, glaring at Zoey.

What, Zoey mouths, *they're my parents*.

"Zoey, I need to talk to you for a minute. David, you too." I usher them out of the room and up the stairs. Thankfully, neither Giovanni nor Beatrice object.

David shuts his bedroom door behind us. He takes off his sunglasses, squeezing his eyes shut and pinching the bridge of his nose.

"What the hell?" Zoey snaps.

I grip her shoulders. "I want you to feel your parents when I tell them about the candle. I *need* you to feel what their intentions are. And you have to be honest, Zoey, this is serious."

Zoey's dark brown eyes narrow on me, her jaw clicks shut. "My parents may be Nefari, but they aren't bad people," she growls.

I exhale. "I understand, but they've been gone a long time—" Zoey takes a tense step backward.

"A Nefari could be manipulating them," David pipes up, his white eyes with their pin prick black stare at us. "There are many Nefari in this village. They could know their connection to you, Zoey. They may be under duress."

Zoey nibbles on her bottom lip, her brow heavy.

David tilts his head towards me. "And *why* do *you* possess something so dark that Nefari here in Faa forsaken Italy are now angling for it?"

"It's been in my family for centuries, now it's my turn to protect it," I answer, praying he buys it.

David waves his hand, dismissively. "Okay, let's just—figure this out. First, we need to find out their intentions, and fast. I'm not sure when everyone will be back." He turns to Zoey, and surprisingly, his eyes soften. "If your family proves to be false, I'll have no choice but to act. I'm sorry for that. We've done everything to keep you safe, I hope if it comes to it, you'll still be on our side."

Zoey's eyes bulge when she realizes what he's asking.

I jump in. "But hopefully it won't come to that. You sensed last night they were being honest. They weren't using a glamour, they are *actually* your parents. Let's go talk to them." I sweep open the door, hoping they'll follow. Zoey clenches her jaw and stomps around me, with David a few steps behind.

Beatrice and Giovanni speak in hushed tones that immediately stop once we descend the stairs.

Begrudgingly, Zoey squeezes between her parents who have inched closer together since we left. They make room for her, with her dad wrapping an arm around her shoulders and her mom placing a hand on her knee.

David takes his place in the rocking chair but sits at the very edge, a coiled snake ready to strike. I stand in front of the fireplace and face the room.

I have to avoid Zoey's glare of betrayal, or I'll never get through this. The weight of my secret presses down on my chest like a heavy stone. Even my throat feels parched. I swallow hard, but it does nothing to ease the tightness constricting my voice. "I do have the Black Flame candle," I admit.

Giovanni and Beatrice glance at each from the corner of their eyes. There's a subtle tremor in my fingers as I clasp them together, trying to steady myself. Every instinct in me screams this is a mistake.

Zoey's eyes drift into the distance, and her brows knit.

I'm not the only one who notices. David rises from his chair, predicting her look means the worst. He clenches his hands into fists, ready to fight.

My pulse quickens, fear spreading like wildfire in my veins.

Beatrice dabs at her eye. She stares down at her lap, her bottom lip quivering. "You shouldn't have brought it here."

A chill runs down my spine. "What?"

David straightens up and takes a step forward. "Yeah, and why is that?" His eerie eyes flick about the room, calculating what he can use his magic to throw at them. "Zoey, perhaps you should stand here with us."

Zoey stays rooted in her seat, like she hears nothing. She's deep in thought, sensing out her parents.

Giovanni's eyes narrow on David. "She shouldn't have brought it here because now it'll be that much harder to save everyone," he growls. "Some of you will die."

"Is that a threat?" David snaps, leaning forward.

A knife slides from the wooden block in the kitchen.

"Stop!" Zoey leaps from the couch. Her eyes dart from David to me. "They want to destroy the candle."

David erupts, hurling accusations at her parents. Giovanni leaps to his feet, hurling accusations of his own.

My heart stops. *Is that even possible? Could they really destroy it?* Blue said it was impossible.

"Stop! Stop!" I yell. David and Giovanni—mere seconds from fisticuffs—halt in place, neither backing down but at least postponing the fight to the death. I move around the coffee table and sit down on its edge, facing Beatrice. "You truly think you can destroy it?"

Beatrice's golden eyes are misty as they meet mine. "No. It can't be destroyed."

I look to Zoey, worried she was just caught in a lie. Zoey stares at her mom confused.

Beatrice explains, "I wish more than anything that it were possible, but sadly, it is not."

"But," Giovanni adds, his eyes darting David, "we do have an idea." He's the first to back down and take his seat. "There isn't a record anywhere of a Nefari having the gift of water. The Council here believes it's impossible, that they are too pure in heart."

"With a dirty mind," Zoey mumbles under her breath, hoping to defuse the tension.

I again think of my dear Aunt Marie, water witch and secret author of smutty novels. The corners of my lips twitch, wishing I could give into Zoey's attempt at levity. "So…?" I prod.

"You give us the candle; I take it to my sister Alessia, a powerful water witch. She lives in Taranto, on the coast of the Ionian Sea. She can send it to the bottom of the Calypso Deep; it's the deepest part of the Mediterranean. She will make it her life's mission to guard it, she will make sure *no one*, under torture of death, will be able to retrieve it." He lifts his chin, eyes blazing at me.

My eyes slide to Zoey, who's gripping her father's forearm. I watch as my friend's face softens, her eyes go from frighteningly confused and worried to peaceful and loving.

"He's telling the truth," Zoey says. "My Aunt Alessia is a gifted water witch, she runs a home for children in Taranto. In the city, she's known as 'La Santa Donna', the saintly woman. She can be trusted, Ell."

I nod to her. "Okay, I'll go get it."

Beatrice shakes her head. "No, not yet. Tonight."

"Bea," Giovanni objects.

"Amore, we need to be there tonight. If we don't show, they will know something is wrong."

Giovanni releases a resigned sigh.

"What do you mean?" David questions, his voice still tight.

Giovanni looks up at him. "I'm part of the Nefari coven. The same one your leader Silas plans to murder…"

CHAPTER THIRTY-SIX
What Could Possibly Go Wrong

David thunders, "You son of a—"

Giovanni squares off against David, each goading the other to make the first move.

Zoey leaps onto the coffee table, but even with the added height she's only a few inches higher. "Enough! Both of you, calm down!"

"Honestly, Gio, you could try being a bit more transparent," Beatrice scolds. She turns to David. "We work with the Witch's Council here, what you call the Committee. While they may hate us just for being Nefario, they are willing to work with us if it means we stop those who are truly evil. There are many moles within the Nefario coven of Triora. Gio is one of them. Tonight, the Nefario gather in the castle. Your coven can't kill them. If you do, you will kill many innocent witches trying to end the Nefario terror for good."

David takes a step back, still not convinced, but at least willing to stand down.

Beatrice continues, "There is a network of Nefario covens spread all across Europe. Very sophisticated, and very depraved. Human sacrifice is just the tip of the iceberg. If you kill this coven, all you do is drive the other covens deeper underground. You make them more suspicious, harder to track and harder to stop."

David collapses in the rocking chair. "You don't understand," he says, "Silas is like a dog with a bone, he won't give up so easily."

"But the Nefario know you are here," Gio says. "They have a plan to slaughter you all. You must convince Silas to leave, tonight."

David shakes his head. "I don't think there is anything I can say to him. Especially with Isolde gone, he's desperate to have us all cured as quickly as possible."

"Then you must sabotage his plan, for his own good," Beatrice says.

Giovanni, standing next to her, nods in agreement.

"Ha!" David laughs. "If another mission goes sideways, Silas will truly lose his shit," he says. His eyes flick over to Zoey and me. "I don't know what he would do to Zoey, since she's not an actual Nefari, but Eleanor… he would put her on trial, and probably kill her."

"There will be innocent witches in attendance trying to end this reign of—"

A frantic tapping raps against the dining room window to our right. The crow from last night clicks its beak in a nervous rhythm against the windowpane.

"Bea, we must go, now." Giovanni's tone says there's no time for debate. He turns to me. "Bring the candle tonight. There is a courtyard in the center of the ruins. Beatrice will meet you there."

Giovanni takes his wife's hand and leads her to the back door. At the door, she hesitates, stealing one more look at her daughter before they disappear. The front door swings open. Soojin comes skipping in wearing a cheap-looking sweatshirt with "Triora" emblazoned across the chest beneath a witch riding a broom. "You guys missed out!" she announces.

"It was awesome!"

Markus, Abena, and Silas file inside with far less enthusiasm than Soojin, but clearly satisfied nonetheless. Abena has a reserved smile on her face, as does Markus. Both continue their conversation as they meander to the kitchen, nodding to us as they pass the living room.

Soojin flops down on the sofa. "We went up to the castle! Vincenzo was so hot!"

"And evil as shit," Markus chimes from the kitchen. Soojin shrugs. "Maybe I could change him…" Abena chuckles as she washes her hands at the sink.

Silas shuts the front door and slides his phone into his back pocket.

"I take it today was a success?" David asks, expertly managing a light and conversational tone. He rises from his chair, stretches, and joins the others in the kitchen.

Silas quickly takes a seat across from me on the sofa while I sit on the coffee table. "Yes, you could say that," he says with a twinkle in his eyes. He takes my hands in his, a grin unfolding across his face.

His fingers are rough with callouses. "What's going on?" I ask, leaning away from this sudden affection.

"You, my dear, will be our way in tonight," he says. His purple eyes dazzle with delight.

"What are you talking about?" I gently tug my hands out of his.

He leans forward, his elbows resting on his thighs. "Have you ever wondered why I recruited you?"

My insides twitch nervously.

He chuckles, too delighted to care about my reluctance. "After meeting you in the shop, I looked you up. Youssef did extensive research, Isolde asked around. You took down the Noble Hunters after you were branded. That practically makes you catnip to the Nefari. They seek out branded witches, believing their desire for revenge will lead them to their cause."

I recall the Nefari on the island; they wanted me to join them too. "Not to mention," Silas continues, "you took down the mutual enemy of all witches. They are dying to meet you, even Vincenzo, their de facto leader. He's the big fish we've been after, and he almost never comes to these kinds of gatherings. But he will tonight, if it means he gets to meet you. See, I knew you would come in handy, eventually," he teases in a brotherly fashion as he leans back into the sofa, crossing his ankle over one knee and lacing his fingers behind his head.

"Okay…what does that have to do with tonight?" I question, truly dreading the answer.

He glances at Soojin, who rolls her neon eyes at him. "You will be playing the part of my soulmate tonight. I explained to Vincenzo that my mate had been branded, then showed him what *we* did to the Hunters. Also, I may have taken credit for killing Allen Woods. He was quite impressed, can't wait to meet you, which means for a moment, his guard will be down."

"That's disgusting, I'm seventeen and you're nearly thirty."

Silas rolls his eyes at me, sitting back up. "It's not real, Eleanor. We're not going to consummate our 'relationship' for them. Hell, we aren't even going to kiss. But," his smile slips away, along with the sparkle of excitement in his eyes. "You will go along with this. Everyone else will be joining us later in the evening, while invisible. Zoey," he turns to her seated on the couch, "you'll be sitting this one out. You can work gaining my trust back. Do not leave the villa, is that understood?"

Her mouth springs open, ready to protest, but our eyes meet, and I subtly shake my head. "Fine," she agrees, slumping back with her arms crossed.

"Now, Eleanor, as for killing the rest of the Nefari, you and I won't be involved. Our only focus is Vincenzo," Silas explains. He looks to David sitting with Abena and Markus at the dining room table. "David, Abena has the plans for the dealing with the rest of them, so follow her lead." Silas looks back to me. "You just follow my lead and say as little as possible."

"Wait," I protest, "if Abena and the others can handle all the Nefari, why can't they take care of Vincenzo as well?"

Silas rolls his eyes, clearly unhappy being questioned. "They'll be able to get most of the Nefari, but a few might escape. Vincenzo is the one witch we can't let escape. That's why we'll be on the inside, to make sure that doesn't happen."

David raps his knuckles on the table. "I still don't like it. Do you remember the time we tried to infiltrate that coven in L.A? They caught on to Youssef almost immediately, and Cassidy Michaels paid the price."

Silas shakes his head at him. "This is different. We've got a secret weapon tonight," he says with a sly grin.

Everyone stares at him, waiting for an explanation.

He sighs in a disappointed growl. "Do I really need to spell it out? Eleanor!" He waves at me like I'm on display. "The Huntress of the Noble Hunters. Didn't you hear? She massacred a few of them on some remote island. It made the news, which I was happy to supply them with. While we have the bulk of them focused on her, that's when you'll move into position." He stands, ready to leave the room. "Now, Eleanor, wear something flashy tonight." He strolls towards the hall, only to stop and add, "Make sure it's backless, they need to see that brand of yours." He disappears down the hall and shuts the door. Seconds later, the shower turns on. "Come, Markus and David," Abena says. "We must speak of tonight in private. Soojin, help Eleanor find something appropriate for tonight. We'll give you the details of the plan when you join us." She motions toward the cobblestone courtyard just outside the kitchen door.

Soojin squeals as she jumps to her feet. "I have just the thing! Isolde bought me a bodysuit in Paris! It'll look great on you!"

Zoey stares at me, looking betrayed and pouting.

The thought of taking credit for those ghastly murders on the island makes me sick. My heart aches at the injustice of it, even if it's just for a few hours tonight.

Soojin drags me down the hall towards the bedroom she shares with Abena. She's gushing about something, but I can't pay attention. What am I supposed to do? If I sabotage the mission and Silas finds out, I'm dead. If the Nefari tonight discover the truth about me, I'm dead. But if I don't sabotage tonight, innocent witches will be murdered. And even if I manage to sabotage the plan without Silas or the Nefari figuring it out, how am I supposed to also get the Black Flame Candle to Beatrice?

Soojin pushes me down on the bed as she hovers in front of me. She cocks her head examining me. "Hhmm…Silas was very specific about your look tonight."

I say nothing. How I look is the least of my concerns.

Zoey appears in the doorway. "Eleanor, I need to speak to you."

"You'll have to wait, my art takes time," Soojin replies, seizing my chin and tilting me every which way. "Silas wants smoldering, a temptress, but not the whore of Babylon." She nods to herself thinking.

Zoey perches on the bed across from us, glowering. Every few minutes she mumbles something under her breath.

What does she want from me?! If I don't go along with Silas's plan tonight, there's no way I can pass off the candle. Not to mention, he'll put me on trial like David said and boom, I'm dead. I can't take it anymore! None of this was my idea! I didn't want this!

Soojin applies a thick strip of long black lashes to my own, fluffs and adds to my brows, sweeps a dark violet eyeliner under each eye. "Next, we're gonna borrow a trick from Twiggy," she explains as she draws thin vertical lines under each eye. "Have you heard of her? She was that British model from the 60s. Now that witch had *style*!"

She coats my lips in a matte maroon lipstick, then sweeps a highlighter across my cheeks and nose. My eyes meet Zoey's. I wish now I could read her mind, or that we could communicate telepathically like we do with our familiars. *Is she seriously angry with me that Silas put her on house arrest?*

Soojin gathers my hair into full bun, explaining it needs to be up so my brand is exposed. She claps her tiny hands together with a tight pert smile. "My work here is done! I'm going to go tell Silas!" She spins around and her high pony whips me in the face as she skips out of the room.

I sigh, unable to look at Zoey. I blink several times; the fake lashes are giving my eyelids a workout. "Are you going to tell me why you're pissed with me?"

"Yeah, cause you're Silas's little pet now. So, I guess you're not going to deliver the candle or sabotage whatsoever? You know my parents risked a lot by coming here today." She ends with a petulant huff.

I rush to shut the bedroom door. "Shh! They're going to hear you. I didn't choose this, okay? I don't want this! I'm still going help your parents tonight, however I can."

Zoey turns her head, meeting my desperate gaze. "Promise?" I nod.

She wraps her arms around me, and her fingertips inadvertently brush against the raised omega scar between my shoulder blades. I instinctively wiggle out of her grasp, wincing.

"Sorry," she mumbles. She fixes a glum smile on her face. "Well, at least you look super hot, so there's that," she teases, slugging me in the arm. "Are you worried about being with Silas."

The door creaks open, and Soojin pops her in head in. "He's ready."

* * *

None of this feels real. By order of Vincenzo, Silas parks the rental car halfway up the mountain and we walk the rest of the way. The air is crisp and biting, and I shiver as we walk up the road. Silas snatches my hand and gives it an encouraging squeeze. "We've got this," he whispers.

I can't bear to look at him. Gravel crunches beneath our feet and I lose my footing several times. Silas catches my elbow while I curse Soojin for foisting these high heels upon me.

"I'm okay," I say, taking my arm back. I instinctively pat my coat, ensuring the Black Flame Candle is still secure in the inside breast pocket. All around us, the trees stand resolute, dark and foreboding, their shadows stretching long across the path. I glance around every time I hear a twig snap, or an animal scurry somewhere in the brush.

Another snap.

I stop and whip around while Silas keeps walking. It's too dark now to see much, but I can feel a set of eyes on me. Perhaps more than one. Someone is close. Very. Close.

Silas jogs back to me. "Come along, darling." He wraps his arm around my shoulders and pushes me forward, leaning close. "Whatever you're doing, quit it right now," he growls through clenched teeth.

"I thought I heard something," I reply.

Silas continues to press us forward up the path towards a set of steep stone stairs. "You probably did. They aren't dumb; I'm sure we've been watched since we turned onto the road. Now remember, we're in love and we're evil."

The old stones of Triora castle loom above our heads. A little more than a ruin, its once imposing walls have crumbled, while ivy and other vegetation crawl up its sides, natures efforts to slowly reclaim it. Despite its disrepair, there's an undeniable majesty to it. The hollowed towers, broken battlements, and collapsed archways echo a once formidable fortress. Firelight flickers from within, giving the ruins a haunting glow. Silas falls silent, both of us taking in the eerie sight.

"We better keep moving; *they* are watching," he says, nodding to the towering pine trees behind us. Perched among needled branches is a murder of crows watching us with their beady black eyes. "Familiars," he whispers. He places his hand on the small of my back and pushes me forward.

My heart pounds harder with each step. The candle thumps against my chest, like an ominous drummer boy marching me to certain death. My eyes anxiously dart about, catching fading glimpses of witches peeking from the windows. *Oh Blue, I wish you were here. Or better yet, I wish I was back in Salem.*

Two ominous Nefari stand outside the decaying entrance, sheathed in black robes and raised hoods like medieval monks.

When Silas and I approach the threshold, the two Nefari step to the side, blocking our way.

Sweat prickles across Silas's forehead. He clears his throat and lifts his jaw, eyeing the Nefari in the black robes. "I was invited by Vincenzo himself. We are both expected," he says, pulling me close to him.

"Prove it," one utters in a gravel voice.

Silas's brow momentarily knits. His mouth twitches, then a calmness reclaims his face. He leans close, his lips brushing against my exposed ear. "Take off your coat."

"What?" I hiss back under my breath, holding my coat even tighter around me. "It's freezing up here."

"The brand. They need to see the omega. Do it. Take it off now."

My fingers tremble as I unbutton my coat. The cold stings my skin, like icy hands have wrapped around my ribs and begun to squeeze. I let the coat slide down my arms until it hangs by my waist. The silk bodysuit provides neither warmth nor modesty as the mountain wind cuts through as though I were naked.

I reluctantly pivot so my back is to them. Two sets of hands caress my brand; I flinch as their fingers trace the arch. My teeth rattle, and not just from the cold. I feel stripped of my humanity, just a piece of meat, bait to be used, like a worm on a hook.

"Satisfied, gentlemen? Now if you would take your grubby

paws off my mate, Vincenzo assured me a drink that would change my life." Silas lifts my coat back over my shoulders.

Their eyes follow us as we step through the broken archway. The candle seems to grow heavier in my pocket. An idea comes to me, almost as if Blue were here whispering it to me. I picture a spark, like a firework, small, but painfully hot. *Ne Feerah*.

"Merda! Dannazione!" they curse, leaping back from the archway, shaking out their hands where small whisps of smoke waft up.

I peer over my shoulder at them both. "Don't ever touch me like that again," I threatened.

They continue to curse and blow on their hands, using their magic and the cool air around them to soothe their burns.

"What the hell was that?" Silas says. He takes hold of my elbow and tugs me down the candlelit corridor.

"I'm wicked, remember? Just playing the part. I can't let them get away with manhandling me like that," I growl and rip my arm out of his grasp.

His eyes narrow on me, then drift to the floor. "Fair point." He works on softening his face, trying to slip back into the role of lover and mate. He grips my hand, a saccharine smile playing on his face. "Are you armed?" he whispers through his unnatural grin.

I snort, mostly to myself. "I'm a witch, I'm always armed."

CHAPTER THIRTY-SEVEN
J'accuse

Candles flicker as we walk past. Our shoulders square. Our chins raised.

Everything is beneath us.

Shadows dance across the crumbling stone walls as we enter the main hall, where a gathering of witches has convened. Most have tossed aside their black robes, others wear them open and casual, while a select few have decided to remain hidden under the shadows of their hoods. A bonfire blazes in the center of the room, smoke billowing through the roof that has long-since crumbled away.

A string quartet plays a haunting, ethereal melody that reverberates off the stone, setting a hum in the air. As the room fills, the Nefari greet each other as dear friends, and more passing gazes linger on us. A bead of sweat forms on my brow in spite of the cold. With his hand on the small of my back, Silas guides me deeper into the room.

There must be fifty witches here. They sip from their goblets, cackling and cursing with loud Italian bravado. The female Nefari give me sideways glances and whisper to each other, while the men stare brazenly.

We are so out of our depth.

The music shifts. In the center of the hall, five women let their robes fall to the floor, revealing jewel-encrusted brassieres and beaded skirts. In sinister, snakelike movements they slither, running their hands up and down their bodies, undulating to the spellbinding music. Conversations cease as all eyes are captured by the dancers. They leap and spin, bend and twirl, permeating the crowd in serpentine patterns. A dancer winks at Silas and licks her lips, transfixing him with bright ruby irises.

A hooded Nefari approaches us, and the dancer slinks away, turning her attention to another spectator nearby. The Nefari pulls his hood back, revealing a familiar face.

Giovanni tilts his head, his icy blue eyes glowing in the dim light.

A cruel, lascivious smile unfurls across his face, a smile antithetical to the paternal figure I met before. He looks from me to Silas. "You must be the one Vincenzo is going on about…"

Silas nods once. "Perhaps."

Giovanni takes my hand in his, bestowing a small kiss across my knuckles. "And who is this fine creature?"

I turn my head away, panic swelling in my chest. *This is an act, right? It has to be. This is all just part of it.* There's no doubt the man is a gifted actor, but when was he acting? In the house, or now?

The music has picked up tempo. The dancers now crawl up the walls of the castle like spiders, while the remaining Nefari revel and cavort like animals. Witches watch without shame or hesitation as those around them entwin with one another. They spit their brandy into the fire and cheer as the vapor ignites.

I gasp. A Nefari near us has opened the vein of another witch's inner thigh, while several witches lap up the flowing blood like vampires. The energy here transcends a mere reckless abandon; it is demonic, infecting the very marrow of all who are present. Even the air around me feels toxic. "Sei bellissima," Giovanni says, trying to force me to meet his gaze, but I can't look away. How many of these Nefari are like him? Good witches merely pretending, blending in so they can defeat this evil from within. And if I don't figure out how to stop Abena's plan, and soon, how many of them are going to die tonight? I don't even know what her plan is.

Someone's eyes linger on me from across the room. I know this stare. The malice. The weight. I feel the goat's presence here. And there's a second stare, familiar and heavy.

"I would like to get better acquainted," Giovanni says to Silas, plucking me away from him and tucking me under his own arm.

Silas clenches his fists, then forces them to relax. "You're gonna have to find your own mate, amico," Silas utters disdainfully, reaching for me.

Giovanni shakes his head, sweeping me back. "Perhaps you do not know our ways, *amico*. Here, we share our mates." His voice drips in ice. "You should look around, partake as your desires dictate. I will return your bride to you…" he looks me up and down, feigning hunger, "when we're done."

Silas begins to lunge forward.

Giovanni stands tall, leaning forward at Silas. "Or perhaps you would prefer to speak with Vincenzo? If you cannot abide our ways, it is best if you leave. But I assure you, it won't be quiet." Sparks crackle at the tips of his fingers.

I step between them. "Silas, my dear, it's fine," I say, making my eyes go wide, "Who are we not to partake? Please," I gesture to the table of food near the musicians, "find some enjoyment of your own. I'll return shortly." Silas's nostrils flare, he leans close. "You can't kill him. As soon as I sense Abena, I will get a message to Gree, she'll come for you. Be careful." He begrudgingly steps back and looks to Giovanni. "I warn you, friend. She's feisty."

Giovanni hoists me over his shoulder like I'm a sack of laundry. "I believe I can handle myself." As if I'm completely weightless—which, I guess with his magic, I could be—he casually strolls down the hall. Several Nefari cheer him on, a few even declare they will have me next.

The moment we are swallowed in shadow, he gently sets me back on my feet. I stumble into the partially collapsed wall behind me, regaining my bearings. A crow with a gray body and black wings flutters onto a broken pillar to my right.

"Scusa, sono davvero dispiaciuto, err, I'm so very sorry. I know I behaved badly, please forgive me," Giovanni implores, his eyes wide with humiliation.

The hooded crow squawks at him.

"It's fine," I mumble, my heart slowing down now that I know it was an act.

Giovanni looks to what I assume is his familiar. He nods to it before it flies off. "We must go, Bea is waiting in the courtyard. You brought it, correct?" he says, not daring to call it by its name in a place like this, with so many Nefari around.

I nod.

He snatches my hand, and we take off running down the crumbling corridor without so much as a candle to guide us. I stumble, stubbing my feet into broken marble and fallen pillars. Giovanni doesn't slow in the slightest, continuing to sprint and dragging me along in the process.

I'm out of breath when we reach an open courtyard. The moonlight pierces through the stagnant clouds overhead. The ancient stones beneath my feet are in such broken fragments, the courtyard is more grass than stone.

Giovanni stays close to the castle entrance, glancing over his shoulder into the dark. "Go, go, go," he urges, shooing me with his hands.

Dark trees press close against the edges of the courtyard, their branches sway softly in the breeze, as though whispering secrets to each other. The hooded crow lands silently on the edge of a nearby stone. Its black feathers gleam faintly in the dim light, its beady eyes watching me venture farther out. I hold out my quivering hands, ready for something to burst out of the forest. A troll or a dragon seems fitting, however unlikely.

Out of the darkness of the forest, a rabbit leaps onto the cobbled stones, its fur a striking white with irregular patches of brown. It moves with an eerie calmness, its small paws barely making a sound as it approaches me in the center of the courtyard. Then, it stops. The rabbit locks eyes with me, its gaze unnervingly direct, intelligent in its stillness. Time seems to slow, my breath catching as the cold air freezes between us.

"Beatrice?" I whisper.

The rabbit lifts its head then bows it toward the ground.

"I have it, where should I put it?" I question, glancing about.

The rabbit turns towards the forest, then glances over and nods for me to follow. I do as she bids and follow her to the very edge of the courtyard, where the jagged pieces of stone give way to wild untamed forest.

The rabbit looks directly at the ground in front of her.

I wrap my fingers around the infernal candle; I swear I can feel it pulsate in the palm of my hand as I unsheathe it from my jacket. I hesitantly place it on the ground.

In the blink of an eye, it's gone.

My eyes dart about. The rabbit has disappeared too.

Giovanni rushes up behind me, tossing off his cloak and snagging a winter jacket stowed behind a tree trunk. "Thank you, Eleanor. Bea has it," he says, clasping my hands.

A small black bunny with brown flecks in its fur scampers out of the forest.

I turn back to Giovanni, only to do a double take on this new rabbit. "Zoey?" I whisper.

The bunny sits up on its hind legs, it's little velvety nose wiggles. "She's leaving with us, Eleanor. You should come too," Giovanni pleads. "You're not safe here. Please."

I keep staring at the bunny, knowing Zoey is invisible and close by. Everything inside me screams to go with them. My lower lip trembles.

"I can't," I finally say, my throat burning for tears. "Once Silas figures out we're gone, he'll come for the candle. None of you will be safe if I'm with you. I need to do everything I can to slow them down. But go," I tell him. My eyes survey the woods, wishing Zoey would make herself visible for a last goodbye, but knowing she can't risk it. "I'll miss you. Terribly. But you've got your parents. Please don't stay. You all have to go."

"As do you. There are many paths to escape the castle. Your coven must leave tonight. Not by train or bus, you must fly, as fast as you can."

Giovanni air kisses the sides of my face before vanishing, quite literally, as he sprints into the dense forest.

The crow to my left takes to the sky, arching high above the trees. Its opaque form blends into the satin darkness, and in moments I've lost sight of it.

Music swells from inside the castle, as do the sounds of exotic and sinister revelry. The weight of the candle is lifted, but the dread of having to return to the party and my dwindling coven remains. I scan the impenetrable forest, hoping in vain to see Zoey's little bunny form hopping back to me. Selfishly, a part of me wishes she had stayed.

BOOM!

Fireworks burst overhead, shattering the quiet with flashes of blinding light. The sky is alive in a kaleidoscope of sparkling colors bursting one after another, each faster and louder than the one before. I can feel their detonations in my chest.

Why would the Nefari set off fireworks, drawing attention to our location? They were satanic and hedonistic, but not downright stupid. This doesn't make any sense.

I creep toward the edge of the stone enclosure and peek over the jagged remnants of the crumbling wall. The mountainside below is teeming with people—hundreds of them, their glowing cellphones lighting the way like a modern-day horde storming the castle. It's a surreal scene, as if pulled from an old horror film, except instead of torches and pitchforks, they carry selfie sticks and cellphones, and—*wait, is that a camera crew?*

The villagers are coming, not in anger, but with curious excitement, hooting and hollering into the night.

My pulse quickens, this is no ordinary gathering. Something is very wrong. *Are the Nefari somehow luring them in with a fire show, only to slaughter them once inside?*

The fireworks are unrelenting.

I need to warn Silas. I whip around ready to sprint back inside only for Silas to appear in front of me. He seizes my upper arms, his fingers biting into my skin.

"Did you do this?!" he bellows over the thunderous crack of the fireworks. His eyes dart over the broken terrace courtyard wall, spotting the hundreds of people rushing up the path. Modern beats pulsate through speakers they carry with them.

There's a stare resting on me, assessing, watching from somewhere hidden in the shadows.

I try to wiggle out of his grasp, but he only grips me tighter. "Yeah, I sent out a mass text to the entire village to join us for a party up at the castle. Oh, and spent a million dollars on pyrotechnics," I spit, sarcastically. "Let go of me! You're hurting me!"

The villagers, mostly teenagers and young adults, are mere yards from reaching the castle.

"We need to go! Now! Vincenzo has already fled. Do you have the strength to fly and stay invisible?" he questions, his nostrils flaring with rage. I don't bother answering him. *Oculi Tempe, La Caeli.* In a heartbeat, I'm flying invisible over the mountainside, with fireworks bursting above my head and the mob surging below my feet. I feel a rush of air as Silas flies past me. Together we soar high above the forest peaks, the wind whipping through my hair and clothes, knocking me off course as I don't have a broom to guide me. Silas is forced to wrap one arm around my waist, keeping me on course until we skid across the red tile roof of our villa. We both nearly tumble over the edge, knocking several tiles to the ground. We catch our breath and find our footing, then climb down the side and slip through a window.

David, Markus, Abena, and Soojin are all in the living room. Abena paces the room, her long legs carrying her in heavy strides. Soojin lounges on the sofa while Markus stands at the crackling fireplace, his hands held behind his back as he stares into the flames. David sits at the dining room table, his sunglasses resting in front of him.

Everyone stops when Silas and I stumble down the stairs going as quickly as we can.

Abena rushes to Silas. "We couldn't make it up the path! Sons and Daughters, they are swarming—"

"I know, I know," Silas says cutting her off. "The Nefari fled quickly. I don't know if we were sabotaged, or…" his wild eyes dart back and forth as he grapples for another explanation of why tonight was foiled.

I tiptoe away from him and take a seat in the rocking chair. I wince as the chair creaks beneath my weight.

Machado slinks into the room. His head cocks, peering up at Silas. "What?!" Silas screams. He wheels around on me. "Zoey is gone?!" My stomach tightens and my pulse quickens. I swallow.

Everyone now stares at me, everyone but David.

The air in the room shifts from confusion to suspicion. Gree slithers up Abena's arm and wraps around her narrow shoulders. I look at everyone's incredulous faces until it becomes unbearable, then I stare at my lap. "Soojin..." Silas says through tightly clenched teeth, "go through Eleanor's things, see if the Black Flame candle is amongst her belongings." My head snaps up.

"Shit!" Silas screams, seeing the look on my face. But Soojin still runs upstairs as she was told. Silas grabs a small antique clock from above the fireplace and throws it at the wall across the room. It shatters like confetti.

Soojin hurries back downstairs. "There's no candle."

"Abena," Silas calls, his eyes blazing towards me. "As we discussed."

Abena's crimson eyes slide to me for a moment before darting back to Silas. "Not yet. We must move to a new, safe location. We don't need the dead weight."

Wait, what does she mean, "dead"?

CHAPTER THIRTY-EIGHT
Trial

We had only minutes to pack. Markus and David had even less as they had to stand guard over me while I shoved my things, and anything left over from Zoey, into my luggage.

Soojin left to procure a vehicle for us and asked that we not inquire how she came by it. We drove south for three hours to a little village just outside Naples where Markus secured us two connecting rooms at an inn. I'm not left alone for even a moment. Markus and David follow me everywhere, even to the bathroom; I suppose I should be grateful they at least turn around when I use it.

I curl up on one of the queen size beds in the girls' room while Abena and Soojin are in the living room with Silas, plotting their next moves. Markus shifts in his seat, his arms crossed over his bulging chest as he keeps his flat, black eyes on me, watching every breath, every slight movement I make.

"Do you need to take a leak?" David asks Markus.

Markus frowns.

"Bathroom?"

He nods to David.

David points to the closed bedroom door with his eyes. "Go, I've got this. She isn't going to try anything."

Markus glances at me a moment, then heaves himself onto his feet. He claps David on the shoulder as he hurries to the bathroom.

David peers over his shoulder at the door, waiting. He scoots his chair to the side of my bed, leaning his elbows on the mattress to crane his head close to me. "They're going to use Soojin's gift to find Zoey," he whispers.

I frown. "What do you mean?"

"Soojin. She has a gift, she can see visions. But she's been honing it, and she's powerful. She can now force visions of what she's looking for, exactly what she's looking for. She'll induce a vision to find Zoey, then Silas will stop at nothing to find her and that damned candle. We have to stop her," he says urgently.

I sit up now. "I-I-I don't know how we'd do that."

David runs his hands through his wavy hazelnut locks. "We need something to stop her from having her vision—short of murder, obviously." He hoists himself to his feet so he can now pace about the small room.

I squeeze my eyes shut, resting my forehead on my knees while I think. *Okay, what would Blue say? He'd scold me for not leaving with Zoey when I had the chance. Well spilled milk*, I argue with myself. *Elspeth would suggest we kill everyone, probably myself included for giving the candle away. Hence, why I don't go to her for advice. Okay, Mom, what should I do?* My eyes slide to my suitcase discarded on the floor. *The witch's gin!*

I crawl over to my suitcase and retrieve the glass bottle. "Here, this is witch's gin," I say.

His eyes brighten. "Yes! That's perfect!" He uncorks the bottle and puts it to his nose. "Do you know it's potency? Or rather, do you have faith in the witch who brewed it?"

I lift my chin, meeting his gaze. "Complete faith."

"I shall fill everyone's cups tonight. Then," he stops, and sighs, a nervous but resolute exhale, "I'll leave in the morning."

My brows knit puzzled. "No, what are you saying?"

"I will make certain that candle is buried deep," he whispers. "I'll assist them in any way I can and—" he stops, his brow furrows in thought.

"What?"

He slides his black sunglasses onto his face. "Silas is a determined witch; he will do whatever it takes to help his coven. He's desperate to see all of us healed, and that single-mindedness could put you all in danger, especially Zoey. If he believes she is standing in his way, and he does, he has a vast network of contacts. Drugging Soojin may not be enough. I won't let any harm come to Zoey," he vows.

A sudden warmth fills my chest. "Why, David? Why put yourself at risk?"

His mouth forms a thin, determined line. "I have my reasons."

The floor in the hallway creaks. David sits back in his seat, and I slip back onto the bed just as Markus steps back into the room.

Markus yawns. "If you want some grub, you might want to get out there and grab some. Everyone's foul mood made them ravenous," he says.

David pushes up out of his folding chair. "Do you want

anything?" Just as I'm shaking my head, Markus cuts in.

"Um…this is awkward. Ah, Silas says she's not allowed to eat anything or drink," Markus says with an uncomfortable wince.

David glares at him. "Why?"

Markus's eyes slide to me for a fraction of a second then back to David. "He needs her weak, susceptible to the trial," he whispers to David.

David glances over at me, a look of horror in his features before he's able to suppress them. He shakes his head at Markus then reaches into his pocket and tosses me a Kinder Bueno bar. He leans over the bed toward me. "Be careful. In the test, purity of thought prevails. Remember that. I'll try to reach out when I find our friend." He gives me a little pat on the shoulder before leaving.

I frown, completely puzzled, staring at the door David just went through. *Purity of thought? What does he mean by that?* I unwrap the candy bar and take a tentative bite.

Markus settles in his chair, seemingly content and uncaring that David just blatantly disobeyed Silas's orders.

"So, why did Zoey leave?" Markus asks casually. "I know Silas can be hard, but he means well. He's been through a lot, and he carries a lot of guilt about Isolde."

I shrug. "I don't know. Maybe it's because she's not a Nefari and was sick of being treated like one," I mumble as I lie back down.

Markus chuckles. "That's not it. You may not want to lie to Silas. Your refusal to be honest is why you're under guard in the first place. Zoey may not be a Nefari, but your Committee believes she is one. She won't get far, Soojin will locate her."

Not if David has anything to do with it.

"Wanna make out?" Markus questions.

I whip my head at him. "Are you serious right now?"

Markus grins, tossing his empty plate aside. "What? We're both attractive. It would be fun and pass the time."

"Go make out with Soojin," I growl.

He sighs. "I've tried, but she keeps blowing me off. The last time we made out, I forgot I had gum in my mouth. She got pissed."

I try to find humor in that, but I can't. I know I should be scared, or at the very least worried, about what Silas has in store for me, but all I feel is empty.

There's a knock at the door, then Soojin pokes her head in. "Silas is giving you time to shower, so hurry up," she says then snaps her fingers at me.

"Hey, Soojin," Markus says, flirtatiously.

"Shove it," she says, deadpan.

Markus chuckles and rocks back in the chair.

While I shower, I wonder if David plans on sneaking out of the hotel without telling Silas. Selfishly, I hope not; otherwise, I have a feeling I'll be blamed for his departure as well.

As I walk back from the bathroom, with Soojin nipping at my heels, I try to spot David somewhere, perhaps dosing everyone's drinks. I don't see him anywhere, just Silas half asleep on a pullout sofa and Abena whispering to Gree in her hand.

Thankfully, Markus leaves the room so I'm able to get dressed. I crawl into bed, hoping to pretend to be asleep by the time he comes back. But he never does. Instead, Abena and Soojin saunter in, claiming the bed across from me and turning out the light.

* * *

When I wake up, my head throbs, as if a lead weight is pressing down on my skull. My eyelids are unbearably heavy, each attempt to open them feeling like punishment. The room swims in and out of focus, leaving me disoriented.

What is going on? I try to move my limbs, but they're sluggish and nearly unresponsive. I glance about, trying to gain my bearings. Time feels warped, like I've been out for much longer than usual. I'm not sure what day it is, or even the time of day.

My head rolls to either side. My bed is the only one in the room, and it's small, without sheets. I don't even have a pillow under my head. The room is musty, like a cellar with poor ventilation.

A bare light bulb dangles from the ceiling. I glance down and see I'm still in my pajama shorts and t-shirt. I'm too exhausted to hold my head up any longer, and it falls back to the bed. Something slithers up my bare leg. I flinch and shake as Abena's black snake slithers up my thigh and across my hip bone.

"She's awake," Abena whispers behind the closed door.

The door swings open and Silas carries two folding chairs into the room. He sits backwards in one of the chairs, resting his arms on the back of the chair as he straddles the seat. Abena plops down in the other. Silas stares at me with contempt, his nostrils flared, his jaw clenched.

Abena seems…impassive, but exhausted. Typically, she has a perfect posture that would make any orchestra conductor proud, but today she is hunched over with dark circles under her eyes.

"Do you know where you are?" Silas questions.

I blink several times. My lids are feeling lighter, my brain not so clogged. "No idea," I mutter.

"Are you aware David left?" For a moment, Silas doesn't even seem angry, just heartbroken.

I shake my head, slowly, but it still leaves my vision swimming.

Silas nods dismissively. "He didn't tell us where he was going, but *he* at least said goodbye first. After he left, Soojin's gift for visions suddenly disappeared. She can barely use her magic at all right now. Anything you want to tell us?"

"I've been out," I grumble. "I have no clue what's happened."

Abena clears her throat. "Let's not drag this out. She's weak, we need to do this while she's still malleable."

Silas nods to her once then turns to me. "You have been accused of being false by this coven. You were accused by three people in your coven, a majority suspicion."

I fold my arms over my chest. "Do I get to face my accusers?" Abena looks to Silas and nods.

Silas exhales. "You have been accused by Silas Foster," he places his hand on his chest, "by Soojin Han, and by Markus Van der Laan."

My eyes dart to Abena, shocked she isn't one of my accusers.

She raises a thin black brow, fixing me with a look that says *surprised?* Abena adjusts in her seat, crossing one leg over the other, trying to sit up a little taller. Her braids have been taken out leaving her hair in fluffy curls. *So, not Abena, but Markus, the Nefari who wanted to make out with me last night, or whenever that was.* My eyes meet Abena's. I drop my gaze only to do a double take right back to her. One of her eyes is perfectly dark brown without a hint of scarlet in the iris. Her other eye is a combination of the two warring colors.

"We believe you are working with dark forces. We no longer believe it was Youssef, nor David, nor Zoey who sabotaged our efforts in Paris; it was you. I don't know how it is possible, but we also believe you sent those humans to the castle to either be slaughtered by Nefari or to blow our cover and our plans." His anger steams to the surface, causing his hands to shake. "Vincenzo now has a price on our heads, yours and mine." His breathing is labored with rage. "I wanted to just kill you, let everyone have a shot at ending your life and add it to their tally for redemption. But I was voted down by everyone," he says, almost pouting.

"Silas…" Abena drawls, impatiently.

Silas waves her down. "Yes, yes, but she needs to know the reason for the trial." He turns back to me. "And your last charge, which everyone *including* Abena finds you guilty of, you gave a one Zoey Gallo the Black Flame Candle."

I clench my fists. "That candle has been in my family for centuries. It was my choice to do with it as I please, you had no right to it," I state, glaring at Silas.

Silas shakes his head. "That's where you're wrong. Your family history may have given you a claim to it, but that kind of power is too great for you to be so careless with it. A nuclear explosion is everyone's problem, not just the person who owned it."

"Silas," Abena exclaims quietly, her eyes pointing over to me.

He rolls his eyes nodding. "I'm sorry. Eleanor, you have been told your accusations, the names of your accusers, and by the sacred traditions of witchcraft, will now be held in trial. Abena has spent the last week doing nothing but study the Salem Witch Trials. Hell, she would qualify for a doctorate at this point."

Abena holds up a hand, silencing Silas. "I appreciate the compliment, but I'd rather just begin." Her eyes narrow on me. "I have a rare gift, Eleanor, the same as my mother had and her mother before that. We are called Nufiala, a special kind of judge. We can enter your mind and give you visions indistinguishable from reality. Through this experience, you will be weighed and measured. If you pass your trials, it means your subconscious is innocent, and you will wake up, free to go. However, if your subconscious knows you are guilty, you will fail. The vision will end with your execution, and you will awake here like it had all been a dream. Then your true sentence will be cast. Do you understand?"

I stare at her with knit brows, muddled. "I'm not sure, what does this have to do with the Salem Witch Trials?" I question.

Clip-clop, clip-clop, clip-clop.

The reek of brimstone wafts up my nose. My eyes well with tears that'll never fall. A reflection in the window catches my eye. The black bearded goat stares through the glass, its deep crimson eyes meeting mine.

"Good luck," Abena tells me.

A feral scream claws its way out of my throat, leaving it raw and burning. I fall backward, my feet tumbling over my head as I plummet down a black tunnel like Alice down the rabbit hole. I fall for longer than should be possible, endlessly somersaulting through the darkness.

I crash onto a bed so hard that the wind is knocked out of me, sending a nearby cat skittering away. I gasp for air, but something prevents my lungs from expanding. My heart pounds wildly in my chest.

I sit up, my back cracking in the process. I'm wearing a plain woolen dress, muted gray, with long sleeves and a corset laced absurdly tight. I tug frantically at the laces until they're loose enough to suck in a desperate breath. Tied around my waist is a stained simple apron. My hair is pinned to my head, and a white coif covers my head keeping it all tucked in. The hem of my skirt is painted in a brown ring of dirt and dust.

I swing my legs over the side of the wooden bed frame and wince, glancing down at my feet. My toes are pinched inside leather boots, crudely stitched and impossibly uncomfortable. My bed crunches and rustles as I adjust. Under the dirty, threadbare sheet is a sack stuffed with cornhusks and stretched over sagging rope, crisscrossing under the lumpy excuse for a mattress.

I survey the room, wide-eyed and in disbelief. I'm in a modest, one room home. The walls are rough-hewn timber, the uneven floor is made from wooden planks. The only light source is a small glassless window covered by oiled paper. A simple hearth sits in the center of the room, its stone edges darkened by soot. The smell of freshly baked bread mingles with the stench of smoke and the earthy aroma of dirt and straw from the floors, along with a faint metallic scent from a pail of water or the iron tools resting nearby on a table.

I rise from my bed and pass by the smoldering fire on my way to the door. Inside a clay pot suspended over the fire is a simmering slop of porridge or some other kind of edible muck.

I creak open the door and hesitantly step out into the sunlight. Narrow paths wind between cottages much like my own. The Puritan village is dotted with wooden structures, their roofs steep and their walls darkened by weather. There are no paved roads, only well-worn paths through the dirt. Village men, dressed in dark breeches, coarse linen shirts, and woolen jackets, escort the women by the arm. The women wear dresses nearly identical to mine as they walk along the path or travel by cart.

Children giggle and run about. Little girls lovingly cradle dolls made of cornhusks to their chests while boys chase a wooden hoop down the lane, batting it along with a stick.

The heads of everyone in the village turn to me almost immediately. Some men stare at me with malice in their eyes, while others lick their lips as their eyes rake up and down me. The women whisper to each other behind their hands. One woman points to a crude, rudimentary broom resting against my house near the front door. Another nods to a black cat sitting in my doorway. All I can do is continue staring at everyone, silent and dumbstruck.

Abena said I would be tested in a vision that bends reality. I gulp as her words start to make sense.

I'm in Salem, Massachusetts, in 1692, and I'm about to be accused of witchcraft.

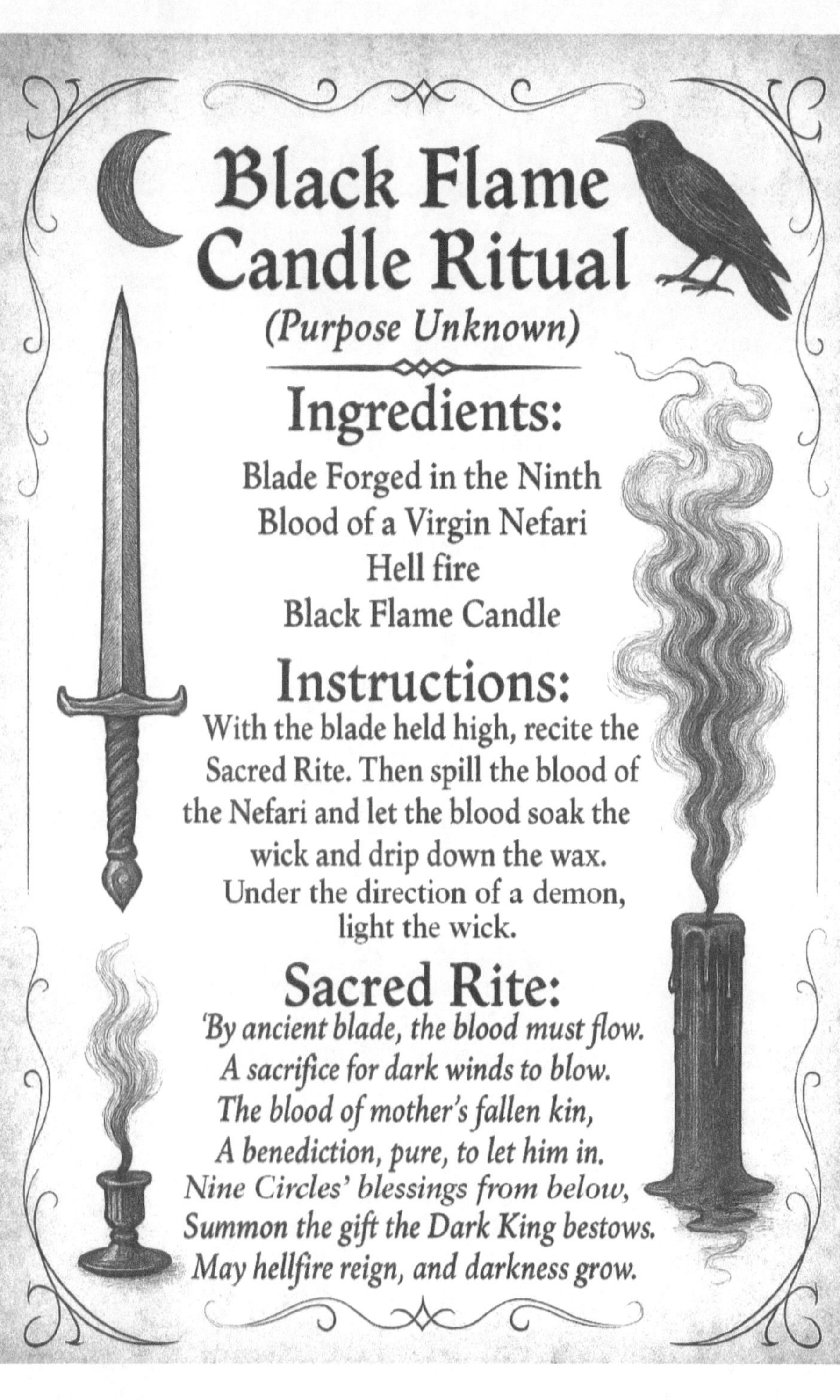

Black Flame
Candle Ritual
(Purpose Unknown)

Ingredients:
Blade Forged in the Ninth
Blood of a Virgin Nefari
Hell fire
Black Flame Candle

Instructions:
With the blade held high, recite the
Sacred Rite. Then spill the blood of
the Nefari and let the blood soak the
wick and drip down the wax.
Under the direction of a demon,
light the wick.

Sacred Rite:
'By ancient blade, the blood must flow.
A sacrifice for dark winds to blow.
The blood of mother's fallen kin,
A benediction, pure, to let him in.
Nine Circles' blessings from below,
Summon the gift the Dark King bestows.
May hellfire reign, and darkness grow.

CHAPTER THIRTY-NINE
Salem 1692

A man wearing a tall buckle hat tips the brim at me as he passes. The apples of his cheeks glow a rosy red as he smiles, then tucks his head down as he continues.

"So, maybe I'm not only a witch but a whore?" I mumble to the cat, idling next to me in the open door.

"Whore is a little strong. Coquette is the more befitting title."

I spin around, my skirts kicking up dust as they swirl about me. My eyes bulge. There at my feet is a velveteen black cat with perfectly leveled ears, straight whiskers, and yellow eyes. *Blue? Is that really you?*

His little feline mouth curls into a smile.

I drop to my knees, scoop my little familiar into my arms. I cuddle him to my chest, tucking his head under my chin as I hold him close. "Oh my gosh, Blue! I've missed you so much!" I cry. "I can't believe you're here! How did Abena know to put you here?! Know what, I don't even care! You're here! That's all that matters!" I keep kissing his small furry head, delirious with relief.

"I assure you the sentiment is mutual; however, let's not call any more attention to ourselves. Please, back inside."

I feel dozens of watchful gazes scrutinize me as I skip back into the house. I close my wonky door that leaves large gaps in the door frame. Not ready to put him down, I continue to cradle him as I sit on the bed. "I'm so glad you're here," I cry again. "Oh Blue, I've missed you so much."

"As have I." He looks about the room, noticing the rickety roof, the hearth in the middle of the room, and the pile of straw in the corner of the small room. Most likely his bed.

"How's my family doing? Have you seen Jack at all? What about Mom, or Maggie? Has Shannyn stopped by? Blue, she helped me in Paris. You wouldn't believe what I've been through. Did she tell Mom and the aunts where I am? Which how did she know?"

Blue continues to survey the tiny hovel. *"Are you having a vision?"*

he muses, as if not even speaking to me.

I shake my head. "No, I'm being put on trial. Silas believes I'm working against them, that I'm an actual Nefarious witch," I explain, still feverishly excited that Blue is here with me. Although, it's strange to see him with the typical yellow eyes of a black cat versus his normal striking blue that I've come to know and love.

"Ha. You must be delirious," Blue derides. *"So that's why I'm here. The judge hasn't included me in her projection. Our connection pulled me in with you, but it was unintentional, hence I'm not exactly to scale. This means I must lay low, I could be thrown out at any minute,"* he says, springing off my bed.

"Please tell me, Blue, how is my family?" I ask, sliding off my bed to the floor.

Blue pauses, hanging his head. *"Helen is beside herself. Margaret is acting out. Marie is forced to travel with the Committee hunting down Nefari. And Sally, well, she's struggling to keep everyone sane. But to answer your question, yes, Shannyn has informed your mother about Paris. She had a vision on her honeymoon of you being murdered. She and Lennox worked with a local witch, an expert of sorts with the catacombs. After some strong cajoling—the details of which aren't entirely known to me—she agreed to help."*

My heart withers in my chest. I picture my mom, crying, collapsing like she did when Dad died. I hold my hand to my heart wishing I could transport back to modern Salem and hold everyone close.

"What about Jack?" I nervously ask.

Blue diverts his eyes. He leaps up onto the table, examining the tools, and sniffs at the pale of water.

"Blue?"

"He came, the night you fled. He spoke to Helen about what was happening, then he left. No one has heard from him since. Have you spoken with Elspeth?" Blue glances over at me.

I shake my head. "I've reached out to both of you since I left." I imagine Jack driving to the house, panicked, only to be informed I left without telling him. *He must have felt so betrayed. If only I could have called and explained.* I wrap my arms around myself, wishing I could weep. *I hope he can forgive me one day. Hell, I'd settle just to see him.*

Blue stops exploring and stares at me. *"You* tried *to reach Elspeth?"* I shrug a shoulder. "I've been really homesick."

"Apparently." Blue sniffs the oil cloth at the window and pads it with his paw.

I rush at Blue gathering him in my arms. "Oh, Blue, I'm just so happy to see you." I snuggle my face into him.

"*Yes, yes, mutual feelings, love is all around and all that. Please put me down now.*"

He strains for patience while I cuddle him close.

I sigh, reluctantly releasing my curmudgeonly, abrasive, wonderful familiar. There's a light rap at my door.

Blue and I share a glance.

"Mistress? Are ye there? Mistress O'Reilly?" a female voice hisses into the crack of the door.

Hesitantly, I tug my door open.

A ruddy-faced woman with soot-smeared cheeks and dirty rags for clothes leans close to my door, her shifty eyes glancing about. She tugs her dirt-stained coif tighter on her head. "Come to the woods, Mistress. there be a full moon tonight." She taps the side of her nose with her forefinger.

"Wench, get thee hence from Mistress O'Reilly!" screams a slender man of short stature from near the apothecary. He's wearing shiny buckle shoes and a tall black hat, waving his arm wildly with a bible tucked under the other. The man hurries down the path towards my house.

"I mean no harm, good sir, none at all," the woman pleads. She cowers, bowing low before shrinking away.

The man is out of breath when he reaches us. He adjusts his hat, then steps between myself and the beggar woman. "Art thou well, Mistress O'Reilly?" he questions, puffing out his chest, glancing back over his shoulder at me. "Stand back, thou wretch!" he yells at the woman, still idling near my house.

"He—"

"*Be quiet! Say nothing,*" Blue commands. "*If a bewitching judge has you under trial, the pain you can feel is very real pain, my dear. Do not bring hell upon us,*" Blue commands.

I snap my mouth shut.

"Aye, aye, sir. Might ye have any coin for a poor soul?" With her head bowed low, she holds her hand out to him, her fingers trembling.

With his shiny black boot, he kicks a clot of dirt at her, sending her skidding away backwards on her hands and feet. "Away with thee, thou foul hag. Out of mine sight!"

"Aye, aye, sir." She scrambles to her feet, ready to flee. That's when I notice her feet are covered with only tattered cloth stained in both blood and dirt.

I grind my teeth, wanting to shove the man from my doorstep

as hard as I can send him.

The man chuckles, placing a sturdy hand on his waist, grinning at me. "Mistress O'Reilly, fair weather be upon us this day."

I cock a brow. *Is he seriously talking about the weather with me?* "Yes, a tried and true classic, and you will *respond in kind!*"

"Um yeah, err aye, it is lovely, isn't it," I mumble back.

He dusts off his britches then takes hold of the lapels of his black coat. "Might I have the honor of escorting thee to the trial?"

My stomach drops. "Trial?"

"Indeed, hast thou not heard? Mistress Bishop standeth accused of witchcraft this day. She hath been held in Ipswich these many months. Surely, thou art aware," he says dubiously. There's a glint in his beady eyes that sit too far apart on his narrow face, making him look like a rodent.

"Oh uh…Aye, aye, I had merely forgotten."

He chuckles, shaking his head at me as he wags his forefinger at me. "Foolish girl, thy sex be fair, but simple." His cheeks bloom a bright red, and he takes a step back from me. "Forgive my bold tongue, I pray thee. I meant no offense."

I roll my eyes. "None taken. Um, aye, let us make haste to the trial," I say, struggling to match his idiolect. I glance down at Blue.

"Eh, not bad."

I reach for the gentleman's arm, only for him to sweep back, flabbergasted. He glances about, then adjusts his hat on his head.

"Were ye about to fall, Mistress? Surely, that must be why ye sought my arm?"

"Um, nay?"

"Oh, my giddy aunt…"

"Ah, of course, Mistress, one of such fine upbringing as thyself would not have reached for my arm without cause," he shouts loudly for the villagers that have stopped to watch the scene that he has caused. "Thou must be feeling ill," he calls loudly "Perhaps faint?" he shouts louder still.

"Eleanor, you're a Puritan, and you're an unmarried woman who just reached for an unmarried man. That isn't done. Keep your hands to yourself, you absolute git."

Aww, you're calling me a git again. I've missed that. "Aye, um, I took but a small stumble just now. I do beg pardon for mine inappropriate conduct."

Blue hangs his head. *"Step right up, ladies and gentlemen, and see the village idiot who's volunteered to be tried and convicted…"*

The gentleman coughs and dusts off his shoulders as he rights himself. "Tis quite well, for thou art of the flesh of Eve, and women oft forget their place. They must be rightly guided, as is known. All is forgiven. Shall we proceed to the trial?"

I step out of my tiny cottage and peer back at Blue sitting in the shadow of my doorway. *Aren't you coming?*

"Eleanor, you're a witch and I'm your familiar, and you're on your way to trial where the charge is witchcraft. You tell me, should your familiar accompany you to such an event?"

I suppose not. But I just got you back.

"I'll remain close enough to hear you. Just remember, anyone can end up on the jury, every interaction can tip the needle toward innocence or guilt."

So, no pressure, then.

I sigh and let the young man escort me along the path. He struts along, being sure to keep a proper distance between us as we make our way down the dusty streets of Salem.

It seems like the entire population is leaving their homes and shops to witness the trial. Men and women parade behind us heading towards the meeting house. Women clutch their aprons, eyeing me with suspicion. The men, though more subtle than the women, steal repeated glances at my bodice while trying to conceal their wandering eyes behind a bible or religious pamphlet.

I exhale, gazing down at my muddy shoes. I read in several different grimoires that the power lust led many a witch to be accused and executed, and not just in Salem. I peer down at my dress that leaves my entire body to imagination.

Standing alone on a plot of land just ahead of us is a three-story house with three triangles on its southern façade that form the roof. "Oh my gosh!" I exclaim. I immediately recognize it, as would any resident of Salem. There before us, standing in all its self-importance, is the Jonathan Corwin House, more affectionately known as The Witch House. The very same house that Zoey and I broke into after hours.

"Mistress, art thou well?" my escort questions. He stares at me in exasperation.

Villagers eye us wearily as they step around us, hurrying on their way to the meeting house.

"Aye, forgive me," I say, staring up at the house, mystified.

"Tis quite well, Mistress. This way now. We must not tarry," he chides, taking several strides to our left following the path that veers around the smithery.

My heart inflates inside my chest as I drift down the path beside him. *Abena is incredible. She's projected all of this into my mind with such stunning detail and accuracy.* My mind whirls with all the other possibilities her gift creates.

Abena could send me back to a time with my dad. I would be able to hug him, laugh with him, hear his laugh! My mom! She could do this for her! Mom could kiss dad and hold his hand again. This is incredible.

"*Perhaps you should scrub that smile off your face, you are about to walk into a trial where a woman will to be sentenced to death…*"

Oh, right. Sorry. You know this is all fake, right?

"*The pain you endure will feel quite real, I assure you…*"

The dirt path leads us to the Salem Village Meetinghouse, a simple wooden building designed for functionality over aesthetics. The structure serves as both their church and their courthouse, which seems fitting for the village. Shuttered windows line the sides of the rectangle building.

The double doors are propped open by two men dressed in the common black wool clothing, which practically seems like the village uniform at this point. They stand stone-faced at their post, eyeing every gawker passing through.

I place the back of my hand under my nose, stifling the smell. *My goodness, Abena, you couldn't have given them deodorant or something?*

Nearly the entire village is crammed together, packed shoulder to shoulder on the long wooden benches lined one right after the other.

"Mistress," the gentleman says with a bow before leaving me to join the men sitting at the front. The women have gathered in the back, claiming the last few benches or standing along the walls, nervously gossiping to one another.

I slip into the last pew, quickly finding myself wedged amongst other female onlookers. I think back on the report I did with Nick Andersen on the witch trials. If this is Bridget Bishop, then Judge Samuel Sewall is presiding. *Wait, Bridget Bishop. Mercy Bishop's ancestor. And the judge's last name is Sewall, as in my old orchestra conductor Ms. Sewall, the one I sent to the hospital?*

Judge Sewall is seated behind a table on a raised platform. His black robes billow as he rises to address the room. His brow is heavy, giving his face a severe, menacing countenance. His booming voice silences the murmuring crowd.

A woman stands before the platform. Her arms are in shackles in front of her, yet two men on either side hold her arms down. Her dark hair is horribly matted, and her dress is saturated with dirt and grime. I can't see her face, but her posture is fearless, even rebellious.

"Bridget Bishop," the judge bellows, "you have been accused

of witchcraft. How do you plead?" he questions with a crooked sneer. It is clear to everyone present that his judgment has already been decided; this is all for show.

"Not guilty!" she declares.

The judge nods, and the first witness is called to the stand.

I struggle to keep the disgust from my face while her accusers recite unconventional behavior that could only be explained by witchcraft, like the audacity for a woman to manage a tavern, her defiant womanly nature, and of course, her audacious red bodice that was surely meant to beguile innocent men and seduce them to the devil. Several men's faces flush a deep crimson as they quickly avert their eyes from their wives, their necks and ears burning with embarrassment.

Other witnesses claim she bewitched a pair of young girls in the village, her unholy specter haunting their nights, striking their bodies with unseen force. Suppressing my scoffs and eye rolls would feel like torture were not for the actual victim of torture standing before me.

Bridget is expected to stand for hours as witnesses are paraded to the front, presenting their "evidence" and hurling their outlandish accusations. At different points, I worry Bridget will faint from exhaustion, but each time she starts to waver, her jailers agonizingly yank her back to attention.

The last witness, a physician, explains a test he would like to demonstrate for the court. He calls for a teenage girl, who upon calling out from the back of the room begins to convulse. The young woman's father and two older brothers have to carry her to the front of the court. The audience winces and gasps watching her flail against her family. The girl pauses just long enough to itch the side of her nose before resuming her seizure.

"Unbelievable," I mutter under my breath.

"*Absolute bollox. But for the love of Brighid, keep those opinions to yourself.*"

They carefully lay the girl down on the floor in front of Bridget. Everyone rises an inch or two from their seat, craning their necks to see. I shift in my seat as well, but I manage a partial view by lowering my head for a line of sight between two men who are now standing.

The jailer to Bridget's right takes her hand and forces it onto the quivering girl's forehead.

The girl's shaking ceases, her limbs relax, and her eyes flutter gently closed.

Everyone in the room gasps. "Witch!"

"Witch!"

The court room erupts in screaming accusations.

Blue, what the heck was that? That didn't come up in my research.

"It certainly should have. She just failed the 'touch test'. Sadly, the evidence was stacked against her from the beginning…"

The judge summarizes the presented evidence to the jury: there was "spectral evidence", witness testimony, a witch's mark (which honestly looked like a cancerous mole to me), and puppets with pins in them found at her home.

The jury takes no time to deliberate. Bridget Bishop is found guilty. Villagers spit on her as she is hauled through the court by the zealous jailers anxious to take her to the gallows. Townspeople follow the macabre parade, bursting through the doors with as much excitement as the town elders will permit them. Women struggle to keep the smile from their mouths.

My "gentleman" escort nods to his friends and companions as they breeze past me.

Air circulates the room for the first time since we arrived, clearing away some of the musty dampness and body odor.

"Well done, son. Thou hast served this village well," the judge says to someone lingering near the jury benches.

"A man of thy standing must seek a goodly and godly woman to take in wedlock," someone else says, almost in jest.

"Aye, is there a woman thou hast set thine eye upon, one to whom thou might consider making a proposal? Surely, her father would not turn away such a match," another juror chimes.

"Jonas, be not so crass!" the judge chides.

"I thank thee," the young man sounds unsure, almost stumbling, "but as of now, there is no such woman."

That voice? Could it really be…?

I'm suddenly paralyzed in the doorway. I clutch my chest, feeling faint as the voice continues. My jaw trembles as I slowly turn. My heart begs for reprieve, hoping, praying that this isn't some kind of cruel trick.

Standing between the judge and another gentleman, the one they call "Jonas", is a young man dressed in fine woolen breeches and a dark cloak around his shoulders. His eyes, green like a stormy sea, flick to mine.

Jack.

CHAPTER FORTY
Guilty?

I linger in the doorway, pretending to be fascinated by the rough-hewn timber. I stretch my arms across the doorframe and cock my head to the side, as if I'm utterly captivated by the craftsmanship.

There's a loud sigh in my head. *"Eleanor, why does it seem like you're trying to mate with the door?"*

Blue? I frown.

"Behind you, child. But don't look, we shouldn't be seen interacting. Remember, they believe cats to be conduits witches use to commune with to the devil."

I steal a quick glance at Jack as they stroll down the aisle. *Could it really be him?*

"Madame," the judge nods at me before marching past. "Mistress," the other gentlemen greet.

Jack's eyes meet mine, only for a second, before looking back at the judge, following him out.

"Is that…?" Blue rises on all fours watching Jack and Judge Samuel Sewall walk out the door.

I rush out onto the stoop. Men and women alike flank the winding dusty paths, whispering of Proctor's Ledge. I spot Jack among the crowd; his golden blonde hair catches the fading sunlight. My body yearns to be held by him. He dons a broad-brimmed, black felt hat, making him blend in as a proper Puritan.

It has to be him. But is he just from my subconscious? Did I put him here?

I follow the villagers promenading through town with righteous fervor that seems more blood thirsty than holy.

I keep a respectable distance, but my eyes never stray from the back of his well-fitted doublet. I'm powerless against the smile that plays at the corners of my lips when I catch a glimpse of his breeches tucked neatly into his stockings.

I can feel Blue trailing behind me on the periphery of the crowd.

He seems so…at ease? Maybe the spell just used the people from my mind to populate the vision.

"I am your familiar, it makes sense I would be dragged in here, but it's highly unlikely your soulmate would be. Tread carefully, Eleanor. Remember, you will be tried and tested, you're going to want the jury on your side."

Jack's graceful movements catch the attention of every woman who passes him. In fact, as he marches a few steps behind Bridget Bishop's jailers, the women of the village—many with their daughters of marrying age—gravitate towards him, their pace quickening to fall in step. They, of course, keep an appropriate distance, heads lowered modestly, but glances are exchanged behind lowered bonnets, while giggles and whispers float through the air.

A girl about my age, her hair pinned tightly beneath her white bonnet giggles to her friend behind her hand. Both staring at Jack's back with deepening blushes.

I quicken my pace to better join the trailing group of women.

"Father saith he shall speak with him concerning marriage," the girl whispers to her friend.

"Not if my father doth speak with him first," her friend simpers in reply. "We hath twice the land, and cattle in abundance."

Her blonde friend crosses her arms indignantly. "But *my* father can offer him a fine apprenticeship in his shop."

Her friend points her nose to the sky. "Well, we shall see on whom his affections lie."

The girls somehow trip and tumble flat on their stomachs, dirt wafting up in a cloud around them.

"Excuse me," I say, quickly stepping around them. Their mothers hurry back and haul them to their feet, wagging their fingers at them.

"Eleanor…"

It wasn't me. I bite down on my lower lip, trying to swallow my smile.

As the sun sinks into the horizon, setting the sky ablaze in peach and pink hues, I take note of my surroundings. *We're on what will become Pope Street. This will eventually become a residential neighborhood. Trixie's parents lived near Pope Street.* I gaze about this impossible scene, surrounded by pious Puritans without an ounce of mercy. *They're really going to put a woman to death Blue.*

"Yes and no. We've haven't traveled to the past, what we're witnessing

is but a very detailed illusion. What happens to Miss Bishop has already happened, and if you do anything to stop it here, you aren't rescuing her in the past, all you'll accomplish is to hasten your own execution. And we would like to avoid that, if possible. Remember, you'll wake up from this, and Silas will know whether the jury found you guilty."

I roll my eyes at him. *Hardly, Blue. He put me in a no-win situation. No one survives a witch trial.*

"Actually, Tituba survived. She was held in prison until Reverend Samuel Parris paid her jail fees. You do have a chance, my dear. So please, don't blow it."

As the villagers advance toward Proctor's Ledge, some whisper whether Bridget will turn into a rabbit and scurry off the scaffold. Two teenage girls titter about the prospect.

"Father, say that be nonsense," says a freckled face girl, narrowing her eyes on her friend walking beside her.

"Does thy father call Reverend Mather a liar?" Her friend folds her arms indignantly.

Mather? As in Vivienne Mather? You've got to be kidding.

I've completely lost sight of Jack. Out of the corner of my eye, I catch a glimpse of the beggar woman from this morning, watching me. Her wild eyes flick toward the woods, then she slips further into the shadows, unnoticed by the crowd. My mind races—the invitation, the reason she sought me out this morning, urging me to come to the woods under the full moon. The decision to follow her gnaws at me.

Being pressed to death like George Burroughs sounds horrific to say the least. But hanging sounds dreadful, too. Or dying from starvation and exposure after being left to rot in prison—that sounds worst of all.

What if this woman can help me somehow.

I slow my pace until I'm at a standstill and the river townspeople have to flow around me. When I feel no one is likely to look back, I gather up my skirts and make a mad dash for the woods. Blue sprints after me.

"What are you doing?!"

I don't want to die Blue. I'm going to avoid the trials all together. They can't force me. I slow my pace as I slip behind the tree line. The forest branches reach out like claws, snagging my dress and scratching at my skin.

Blue catches up with me, his body lean and lithesome, moving in ways I'm not used to seeing. He seems to enjoy the exercise in such a healthy body. I stop, hearing the faint shuffle of footsteps ahead, the beggar moving deeper into the shadows. I push onward, abandoning my white bonnet after a low-hanging branch rips it away. My hair comes undone and cascades down my back.

"Great," Blue sends, leaping over a fallen log. *"Now you look like a harlot."*

I gaze down at myself, suddenly being able to see a line of cleavage where my dress has torn. "Looks like I ripped my bodice too."

"If they give you the option, pick hanging. At least it's quick."

The path leads over fallen and rotted tree trunks. I fight to keep up, though the woman is always just out of reach. My heart pounds as I push through the underbrush. Finally, I stumble into a clearing, the orange glow of a bonfire illuminating several figures gathered around it.

There, at the very edges of the dancing flames, stands the beggar woman. Her hunched form slowly rises into perfect posture. Her limp vanishes, and the rags that hung loose on her body ripple away into typical Puritan attire, a woolen brown dress with an apron tied around a cinched waist. Her grimy face smooths into something sharp and beautiful.

"Come, child!" her voice rings out. "Come hither and gather with this coven about the fire. Fear not, for no harm shall befall thee. Take and partake of our bread and drink, for thou dost appear weary, and worn to the bone." Her back is to me, but her voice is clear as bell. She glances over her shoulder and beckons me with a curled finger.

Everyone's eyes lift, watching me as I emerge from the shadows. Blue nervously joins at my side.

"Thank you," I say as I join their circle.

"My name is Sarah Good. And what be thy name, child?" she asks me while handing me a pewter chalice.

I peer down at the pungent wine. "I'm Eleanor. Eleanor O'Reilly," I answer.

She smiles, her teeth surprisingly white and straight. "'Tis a fair name, Mistress."

A middle-aged woman snatches off her bonnet, stuffing it into the pocket of her apron steps forward. "I propose we flee Salem this very night. We cannot risk another death. Tonight, they take our sister, Bridget. Who shall be next?" Her eyes search the small coven.

Another woman, older, with deep lines running across her forehead steps forward, lifting her cup in the air. "Aye, even the innocent Daughters fall victim. Sarah Osborne was no witch, and yet she is dead. Who else shall pay the price in their thirst for blood?"

As murmuring swells within the group, a man steps forward and removes his hat, exposing his white hair. He appears to be aging poorly, looking far too haggard for a man who can't be more than forty. Then I feel it, a slight buzzing of magic, a glamour. He wants to appear older than he is.

"Silence!" the man yells. "I will hear no more of such dissention. The Committee hath sent us to aid the settlers of this land, to help them thrive and establish themselves. We are here to serve, and if we die, so be it. But I shall return to Brighid with mine head held high, that I vow."

"Enough of this," says a woman with carved cheekbones and full lips. I do double take. The woman is nearly identical to Sariah Burroughs, by sister's new mother-in-law. This is Tituba.

"We must think upon those we serve," Tituba declares. "Do we serve them good by leading them to their deaths, George?"

George? As in George Burroughs? I turn my head to conceal my smile. Little do they know that one day, their descendants will marry, and the first-born son of that union will marry my sister. My chuckle dies inside me when I realize that all of them, everyone but Tituba, will be put to death in a matter of months.

"Yes, I think you should all leave," I call loudly.

"Eleanor, you aren't changing anything. Their counterparts in the real world have been dead for three centuries. You're saving figments of your judge's imagination."

George Burroughs from across the fire from me frowns, raising a brow.

"Who be this child?"

"She is newly arrived in our village," replies a girl around my age. "New or not, she is a witch, and thus she is welcome here," Tituba says, raising her chin and gesturing to the group. "As a sister witch, she hath a voice and a right to speak, Brother George."

George folds his arms in a pout. "Well, I like it not."

"Eleanor, you need to be careful."

Tituba smiles over at him. "Thou dost always wrestle with aught that is new."

"Aye, how long did it take thee to grow accustomed to thine new hat?" a young woman calls over to him.

Sarah Good chuckles, holding her chalice close to her lips. Her eyes suddenly go wide, and she drops the chalice to the ground. "Hush now. They are upon us."

My heart stops. From the corner of my eye, I see

something—faint flickers of light dancing among the trees. The lights grow brighter, torches cutting through the darkness like glowing eyes. Panic spreads through the small coven as the torches emerge from the tree line, surrounding us.

Without warning, George vanishes. A gray rabbit dashes off into the woods while invisible footsteps follow closely behind. My head whips about as each member blinks into thin air, leaving nothing but quick sprinting rabbits in their wake who disappear into the underbrush.

How did they do that so fast?

"Eleanor, the mind spell, do it now."

I try to focus, but I can't hold the image in my head. The men holding the torches close in around me, stealing my ability to concentrate on the spell.

Help me, Blue! What do I do?!

"Stay calm, I'll follow you to the prison. I'll be right behind you, I promise." Blue darts into the trees, his furry black body impossible to see in the dark.

The mob has formed a tight circle around me, close enough to touch. The light from their torches cast dancing shadows across their hateful faces. One of them approaches from the side and roughly seizes my arm. I look up into his eyes. It's Jack.

I gaze at him in confusion. His grip is like iron, his glare cuts through me like an icy wind. My eyes stay on his cold, unfeeling glare, unable to look away. I feel the shackles clink around my wrists, heavy and unforgiving.

"Take heed, men, for she'll cast her spell upon thee with her beauty," one of the men warns loudly. "Women be a cunning lot by nature, and a witch be far worse—more wicked, more tempting. Shield thine eyes and guard thy virtue well."

"Beware, Master Hopkins, I fear this witch hath cast her eye upon thee," an older man warns, placing a heavy hand on Jack's broad shoulder. "Be wary, lest she tempt thee into wickedness. Turn thine eyes from her!"

Jack releases his hold on me, and the other men drag me to a wooden cart and toss me in the back of it.

"To the prison with her! And make haste!" the older man yells. Jack watches me, still holding his torch, his face devoid of emotion, as the cart carries me from the clearing.

The journey to Ipswich is long and grueling. What took minutes in the car now takes hours. The cart rattles over uneven dirt roads, each bump jolting my bones, my wrists chafing against the iron shackles. But what hurts most is the memory of Jack's uncaring glare.

My Jack would never do this. He must be just another projection of the spell. The old man called him, "Master Hopkins." Abena must be using my memory of Jack to create one of the heirs of Matthew Hopkins. Tears well in my eyes. Blue was right, the world is just a vision, but the pain is real. Then, for the first time in my life, I feel a tear spill over my lower eyelid. Just a single tear, but it feels like a cascading dam. My shackles are secured to the side of the cart, so I have to lower my head down to my fingertips. I brush the tear away, leaving a streak across my cheek, and stare at the moisture left on my fingers. More tears begin to flow, creating warm streams down either side of my face. The sensation is strange and foreign, but welcomed. The shock of them nearly steals me from the moment.

The night air is damp and cool. All around us, the forest is alive with the sound of crickets and the occasional howl of some unseen creature.

Blue? Can you hear me? "Yes, I'm close."

I slump back against the brittle straw. The image of Jack's unadulterated hatred of me replays in my mind.

What comes next?

"Well, you'll be imprisoned. They'll perform a series of tests, gather eyewitness accounts.

I'm sure there will be more than enough villagers ready to testify."

I roll my eyes, still glossy from crying. *Yeah, pretty sure my escort today will be one of them.* I sigh, glancing about to see if Jack had left with the others or if he's part of the jailers hauling me to Ipswich to be held until trial. I don't see him. *What if I confess?*

"A myriad of possibilities. Often if a witch confessed, she could be forgiven of her sins and given a lighter sentence, or at the very least spared immediate execution. However, they would still hold you, and perhaps demand that you to testify against your fellow witches."

Not happening. I don't care if this isn't real.

"That's probably wise. If any of your actions are perceived to be dishonorable, that could be used as an admission of guilt."

The cart comes to a sudden halt in front of the jail, a grim, squat building made of stone. My jailer hoists me from the cart and drags me inside. I immediately gag. Nothing in this vision has smelled particularly pleasant, but the prison is even worse than the meetinghouse. The place reeks of mildew, sweat, and a bouquet of other bodily secretions.

They drag my exhausted body down a narrow hallway. The deeper we go, the stronger the stench of unwashed bodies and rotting straw. I'm shoved into a cramped, dimly lit cell, and the jailor slams the metal door shut with a clang that echoes through the corridors. The floor is hard and uneven, and littered with soiled hay. The only window is a little more than a slit near the ceiling, allowing the faintest trickle of moonlight to filter through.

I press my back against the locked door as something scurries beneath a lump of hay. *This feels real. Too real. I need to get out of here.*

"Give me a moment. I'm trying to find a way in." The sound of footsteps echo outside the cell. I freeze.

A small metal window creaks open at the top of the door, revealing a metal grate.

Jack stands, staring at me through the iron bars. He is beautiful—devastatingly so. Even after what happened, I so desperately want to reach out, to stroke his cheek, to feel the smoothness of his skin beneath my fingers, to trace the curve of his lips. I know he's not the real Jack, but right now, I don't care.

"Do you know who I am?" he asks, his voice soft, almost supple.

I swoon, my knees nearly give way as I lean on the door. *Is this a trick? Part of the test? Hell, I don't care anymore.* "Yes," I reply. "You're Jack Woods. You're my soulmate."

His jaw momentarily trembles before he clamps it shut, his eyes searching mine. "Eleanor? Is this really you? Am I dreaming?"

My quivering fingers claw at the door trying to reach him. "I don't know, I don't know if this is real. For all I know you're just a figment of my imagination," I cry.

Jack shakes his head. "I was riding a train and woke up here in Salem. At first, I thought it was a dream, but it all feels too real. I didn't know what to do, so I played along, acted the part. I think I may have stalled Bridget Bishop's death."

Is this really Jack? As in my Jack? How can this be? Maybe this isn't part of the test, instead just some bizarre anomaly.

"Eleanor, what is this place?" Jack asks, glancing about. "Are we actually in 1692? Is that possible?"

I shake my head. "No, this is all a projection, I don't know how you're here. None of this is real. Nothing we do will have any impact on the past. I'm being tried by a witch, it's… a really long story. I'm so sorry I had to leave you. I love you, and miss you," I say through dribbling tears that river down my cheeks and drip off my chin.

"You did what you had to," he says with a stiff upper lip. "But listen, you need to know something. There is a Nefari, a powerful one, that is heading to Ireland. He's searching for something."

My stomach drops. Vincenzo, the leader of the Nefari in Triora. He's going after the other Black Flame Candle, the one with my grandmother in Wicklow. Silas used my real name to get close to him. If Vincenzo knows my name, he knows my family, and thus my grandmother. *Blue, I need to get out of this, now. I need to warn my grandmother. Wait…*

"Jack, how do you know this?" I ask.

There's a cocky twinkle in his eye. "Once your sister shared that you were in Paris, you were fairly easy to track down. There was a group of Nefari after you that had been residing in the catacombs of all places. I alerted the local witches council who took care of them the morning you left for Nice."

"That's why there was never any retaliation. You cleaned up the mess," I utter, mystified.

"I've been traveling with you since you left Paris, keeping my distance, but close enough to keep an eye on you, in case you ever needed me," he continues. "You've been to Triora?" I whisper, recalling the feeling of being watched while Zoey and I were about the town.

Jack nods, then leans his head against the bars that separate us. "I'll be honest, when I arranged for that crowd to storm the castle, I was worried they might get hurt, but I knew you wouldn't let that happen. You would keep them safe, and I you."

The rush of information leaves me feeling faint. I knew in my heart I felt him near. "Jack, I need to get to my grandmother. I have to wake up from this—do you have a knife or something?" I inquire.

Jack disappears as he bends down. "It's small, but sharp," he says, sliding it under the door. He straightens up, placing his hands on either side of the small window in the door. His eyes go wide then dart back and forth. "Eleanor," he exclaims alarmed.

I snatch the knife from the floor and meet him back at the window, clutching the small blade. "What is it?"

"Something is wrong," he says. His chest begins to heave. "I can't feel anything," he quickly realizes. "I'm… I'm fading…" He presses his face against the grate between us. "I'll find you in Irela—" He's suddenly gone, with no trace he was ever there.

"What are your plans with that knife?"

"Abena said this is like a dream. If you die in your dream, you wake up. She didn't explain how much time is passing in the real world, but I can't take the chance that it's a while."

I hold the knife aloft. *Great, here comes the fun part.* I tap my forefinger on the tip of the knife. *This is really going to hurt.* I place the blade, trembling, against my throat. The blade wobbles against my skin as my palm becomes slick from nerves. *Okay, not the throat. Bad idea. Then where? Quick and painless, that's what I want.*

The brachial artery. *I sever that and I'm dead within three minutes.* I roll my arm back to expose the inside of biceps. I take several deep breaths, psyching myself up. I squeeze my eyes shut and make the cut, quick and deep. Warm blood pools into my armpit, down my arm, trickles off my fingertips.

Blue! I reach out to him before I become too woozy to think. *Are you going to keep your promise? I can't do this without you.*

"I'm already in Ireland, my dear. I'll be waiting for you."

I sense myself falling, crashing back into the hay, but feel none of it.

I shoot up in bed, panting. My outstretched fingers grope the mattress.

I'm back in the real world, with Silas and Abena glaring at me.

CHAPTER FORTY-ONE
Empty

Abena leans forward, her elbows on her knees as she releases a deep, aggravated breath through her nose. A flash of frustration ripples across her face. "Killing yourself is not part of the trial. I'm sending you back. Kill yourself again, and I will take that as an admission of guilt."

"Don't bother," Silas barks in the chair next to her. "That was confirmation enough. It's time to end this."

I swing my legs off the side of the bed and leap to my feet, only to stumble back, gripping the bed. I'm still a little wobbly from whatever they gave me. "Silas, you have every right to be suspicious of me. But I swear, I'm not trying to sabotage your mission. I want what you want, what everyone here wants: a chance at redemption. Do you remember when you said the Black Flame Candle is like a nuclear bomb? When it goes off, it's everyone's problem? There's another candle, in Ireland with my grandmother, and it's about to go off if we don't get to it first."

He raises a skeptical, blonde brow, "And the one you gave Zoey?"

I shake my head. "I have every reason to believe it's safe. Zoey and her parents are taking it somewhere Nefari can't reach it. But the candle my grandmother has… its only protection was that no one knew where it is, and now that's gone. If we don't go to her now, then Vincenzo, or hell, any Nefari will get to it first. We have to go, now. Please?"

"I think she's telling the truth," Soojin chimes behind the closed bedroom door. "You should let her go."

Abena and Silas exchange glances, their expressions uncertain.

Silas rises to his feet, looming over me. "If we go, you follow my lead. No mouthing off, no going off on your own. You obey my rules. Break even one, and you'll not be given a trial. You'll just be executed on the spot. Understood."

I nod, feeling like I'm finally getting my bearings back.

Silas nods. "I'll book our flight. We'll fly into Dublin and take a bus to Wicklow."

* * *

The overcrowded bus jostles over the narrow roads between Dublin and Wicklow. The lilting Irish accents of fellow passengers' waft through the air like a comforting song. Silas and the crew are spread out, not wanting to appear to be traveling together. Strangers smile at me and the rest of our scattered coven. Two girls laugh at something one of them shows the other on her phone. My heart tugs for Zoey.

"Wicklow is a quiet place, but full of enchanting stories—if one knows where to look," says the older woman seated next to me.

I keep shifting in my seat, a mixture of emotions bubbling inside me. Ireland has always held a beloved fascination for me. My mother's entire family hails from this green, windswept island. Even my dad's biological grandfather was from Belfast. But we aren't here on a vacation, we're here to rescue my grandmother and protect the Black Flame Candle.

Are Jack and Blue already with her?

A lush sea of green grass surrounds us as the bus rumbles to a stop. Wicklow stands like an old, forgotten village from a dream. The cobbled streets sigh with history, and quaint stone cottages with thatched roofs reach to the sky, as if reaching for the last rays of the setting sun. Shops are modest but bursting with charm, with holly and green garlands draped in the windows and empty window boxes waiting for spring. In the distance, rolling hills stretch out like the folds of an emerald quilt, kissed by the glowing blush of dusk. A cold mist settles across the land like drifting ghosts.

I tighten my coat around myself, feeling the evening temperatures dip. Silas stops under a streetlight and turns to face us. "Everyone stay here. I'm going to go inside and see if anyone knows a Colleen Byrne. If the people on that damned bus are to be believed, everyone knows everyone," he says in a pitiful, high-pitched attempt at an Irish accent.

"Hurry! I'm freezing my ass out here!" Soojin complains, adjusting her puffy, furry earmuffs.

Markus glances about, cool in his heels, wearing only a fleece lined sweatshirt. "I think it's quite nice."

We all wait as Silas enters a nearby pub, its sign swinging lazily in the wind above the red door. The moments tick by as we wait, the damp cold sinking to our bones.

Silas reappears, his face unreadable. "They've never heard of a Colleen Byrne," he says. "We should find some lodging for the night, then figure it out from there."

He looks at me sideways, wondering if I've completely led them astray. *Why does no one know her? Does she go by a different name? What's Silas going to do to me if we can't find her?*

As we turn to leave, a white-haired elderly man hobbles out from the pub's shadow, his gait uneven, but his presence striking. He oddly wears dark sunglasses, despite the nightly hour. His red scarf ruffles behind his shoulder in the breeze. He tips his sunglasses down at us, standing in the halo of the streetlight. My jaw falls, catching sight of his eyes—a metallic gray, like marbled stone.

"Colleen Byrne, ye say? I know of her," the man says. A thick, lyrical accent is woven into his raspy voice. "Follow me, and I'll take ye to her. I'm Emmet O'Dell, by the way."

"I have no idea what he just said," Soojin admits.

We all exchange uncertain glances, but the man is our only lead. Emmet strolls away, leaning on a walking stick as he goes, and we all dutifully fall in line. His sheepdog trots alongside us, tail wagging, as we follow the trail that leads out into a field. Our elderly guide cracks jokes with Abena like they're old friends; she just graciously smiles and nods.

The town vanishes behind us as we're swallowed in mist. I've completely lost my bearings by the time we reach a house nestled deep in the countryside. It's a modest cottage, but respectable, the kind of home that offers comfort and simplicity. The gentle breeze mingles with the bleating of sheep corralled in a nearby fence. With the wave of his hand, Emmet unlocks the gate, and his magic holds it open as we pass through and make our way up the cobbled path. The man knocks on the door.

No one answers.

"Hmm…" he says, peering into the halfmoon window in the door. It's dark inside, impossible to see anything.

After a long moment, he tries the knob. The door creaks open. I subtly elbow my way to the front so I'm the first one to step inside after Emmet. The house is cloaked in shadow, but even in the dim light, I can see touches of warmth and love—quilted throws on the armchairs, shelves lined with mismatched teacups, a cuckoo clock hanging on the wall, and the scent of fresh lavender lingering in the air. It's the kind of home that feels like stepping into a fairytale.

"Colleen? Are ye sitting in the bloody dark, woman?" the man calls, his voice suddenly taut with concern.

Silence.

With a flick of his wrists, the room floods with light. There's still no sign of her, but the air around grows heavier. "I've a bad feelin' about this," he mutters. "I'll be takin' my leave now. Best of luck to ye." With that, he disappears into the night, his dog trotting behind him as they vanish down the road.

My heart races. "Grandma Colleen?" Still nothing.

Everyone else still hovers in the entryway.

The quiet feels oppressive. My footsteps creak on the worn wooden steps as I climb the stairs. A narrow staircase tucked in the corner catches my eye, hidden in shadow. I know that door; it leads to the attic. I slow my pace, surveying the door. It's broken. Barely resting on the frame. Like in my vision.

Are we too late?

The attic is chaos. Cardboard boxes have been thrown about, papers scattered like confetti. The air is thick with dust and silence, as if the room itself has forgotten how to breathe.

I told Mom what I saw, and she said she got a hold of her mother. Did she not leave right away? Did she come back too early? Is she still alive?

"Eleanor," Silas's voice echoes from downstairs, pulling me back to the present. "We're meeting in the living room. We need to talk."

I run my hand along the splintered door frame. "Be right there!" I call. Beneath the attic window is an open trunk. *That's where she kept the candle.* I fall to my knees and sift through loose photos, dried flowers, old bed sheets. My fingers fold as they meet the bottom.

The Black Flame Candle is gone.

I slink back downstairs. *Maybe she got away? She took the candle and ran for it? Mom said she was a powerful witch. But could she fend off a Nefari attack by herself?* I stop on the last step. Markus is seated in a floral armchair, his knees nigh near his chest, too big for the seat. Abena and Soojin rest on the sofa; Soojin is slumped over on the armrest, nearly asleep.

Silas turns to me when I enter the room. "Any sign of your grandma?"

I shake my head.

He squeezes his hand into a fist, his knuckles straining white. "And…the candle?"

My eyes fall to the floor, unable to meet his anxious gaze. "Gone."

"Damnit, Eleanor!"

I open my mouth to defend myself but stop at the sound of clinking glass in the kitchen. Silas starts towards the hall, but I rush around him. "I'll go," I whisper. "If it's my grandmother, she won't use her magic on me. But a stranger walking around her house in the middle of the night..." Surprisingly, Silas doesn't argue.

The floor slopes down towards the kitchen. Sweat breaks out across my brow. I timidly push the door open and click on the light.

Blue crawls out of the sink and stretches on the countertop. *"Slip of the fingers, eh."* He jerks his head at the open window above the sink.

I run to him and bundle him up in my arms, pressing my face into his fur. I inhale his familiar scent of damp earth and my aunts' homemade potpourri. "You're really here!"

"We already had our reunion, remember? Salem? This is a bit over the top, don't you think?" Blue springs from my arms to the floor. *"Everyone is in the next room, yes?* My elation drains away as I remember how desperate our situation is.

"Blue, my grandmother's gone, and so is the candle."

Blue's casts his sapphire eyes down in thought. *"Well, the world is still in one piece. It's not crawling with demons."*

"At least there's that," I mumble.

We amble down the hall and join the others.

Silas stares down at Blue, then grimaces at the mangy sight of him. "We were just saying, Markus and I are going into town in the morning. There's a woman, Clare Wexler from Donegal, she's aware of all the underground witch activity."

"My contact," Markus chimes, smugly.

Silas continues, "but tonight, we rest. In the morning, take an inventory and run to the market." He turns to Abena, "I trust you can obtain what we need."

Abena yawns, Gree looped around her throat. She nods.

Silas looks back at me. "This is your grandmother's house, you should take her room. We'll find places to sleep out here."

We find some leftover shepherd's pie in refrigerator we can reheat for dinner. Nothing in the cupboards or fridge is rotten or stale; she hasn't been gone long. Her shepherd's pie is identical to my mother's.

After dinner, I snuggle under my grandmother's down bedding. Something about this feels ghoulish; technically, I've never met the woman, and she could very well be dead. *I've failed her.*

"Don't busy yourself with that now. You should rest. You know not what tomorrow brings," Blue snuggles close.

"Have you seen Jack?" I whisper in the dark. My eyes lift to the photograph on the nightstand. It's a picture of Grandpa Seamus, Grandma Colleen, and their three daughters. My mother's just a girl, and her giant grin shows off her missing two front teeth. Her eyes disappear in the folds of her cheeks.

"No," he huffs tiredly. *"We didn't arrive together. I arrived here from Venice just this morning,"* he mumbles.

"I woke up just outside of Venice," I murmur. At the time, I didn't know where we were.

"Yes, yes, I've been two steps behind you most of the time. I should have accepted Jack's offer to travel with him. Arrogance be a cat's folly, or however the saying goes…" his voice trails off as he drifts to sleep.

Jack, I could use your help. Please find me soon.

CHAPTER FORTY-TWO
County Wexford

I wake to Abena shaking my shoulder.

"Eleanor," Abena whispers, her voice soft but urgent. "It's already noon. Silas left word, we must prepare for what is coming," she says ominously. She strides out of the room before I can ask what she means. "She's awake now," she calls to someone downstairs. "Apparently some of us believe we're on holiday."

The cold air bites my skin. I sit up and stretch, then I rub my hands together to warm them up. My feet freeze when they hit the floor. Winter has a firm grip on this house.

I shimmy into my jeans and pull a thick cable knit sweater over my t-shirt. Blue is still curled up under the blankets. I kiss the tips of my fingers and lightly pat his head.

While tossing my hair up into a ponytail, I casually scan the walls of the second-floor landing. I pause, my arms slowly fall to my sides. In the daylight, the hallway has transformed into something like an art gallery, where every exhibit is a family memory. Antique frames hang in perfectly uneven rows, each holding a moment of our lives captured in time. Not just of my mother and aunts, but of me and my sisters as well. A photo of my first day of kindergarten, my face beaming with excitement. Maggie, barely five years old, in a tiny soccer uniform kicking her first goal, her wild red ringlets cascading down her tiny shoulders. There are recent photos, too, as recent as Shannyn walking down the aisle, her gown trailing behind her like a river of white amongst strewn rose petals. The realization hits me in the chest like a stone: my grandmother loves us dearly, and her Nefari eyes forced her to witness our lives from afar. How lonely it must have been.

I'm stabbed with guilt, thinking of how hurt I was that I never knew my mom's family, that her own parents didn't come to my father's funeral. I run my hand down the side of an ornate frame with a picture of my parents on their wedding day kissing passionately in front of a stone church.

"I'm sorry," I whisper to the room before hurrying down the stairs.

The soft clinking of porcelain cups greets me as I push the kitchen door open. Soojin stands behind the kitchen table pouring steaming tea into three delicate teacups.

Abena, seated at the weathered table, levitates a cup in front of her and leans over to inhale the steam.

"It's Irish Breakfast Tea," Soojin chimes. "Smells pretty good." She levitates the kettle back to the stove top and the tin of tea back onto an open wooden shelf. Soojin excitedly falls into a chair next to Abena. "Can I tell her? Please?! Please!?" she says, her legs bouncing under the table.

Abena rolls her eyes at Soojin. "Silas left word, we are to go into town—"

"And buy formal dresses! Gowns! Like *fancy* ball gowns!" she squeals, rapidly clapping her small hands together.

I frown, blowing on my tea before taking a sip. "What are you talking about?"

Abena sighs. "Tomorrow night, there is a Christmas Eve ball—"

"A solstice ball!" Soojin interjects again.

"It's on December twenty-*fourth*," Abena snaps. "We're going to attend a Christmas Eve ball." She takes another sip of her tea, eyeing Soojin.

I float some sugar cubes from a glass jar on the counter and drop them in my tea. "Infiltrating a party again, are we?" I ask, dreading the thought of being manhandled again.

"I don't believe so," Abena says. "I actually think we are going as guests. An innocent Nefari is hosting it. I don't think this is a normal mission, it feels more like a recruitment. Our numbers have dwindled, and if we're going to take on someone as dangerous as Vincenzo, we'll need assistance." I nod. "It's weird though, right? Triora was the first we'd ever heard of Vincenzo, and now he's like our archnemesis?"

"So epic," Soojin says with a grin.

Abena dismisses me with a roll of her eyes. The scarlet has greatly dulled. "He has been pulling strings all over Europe, it's even spilling into the states. We were always on his trail, we just never had his name until Triora. You're not in Silas's inner circle, so don't pretend you know everything that's been in motion for some time now…"

I shrink back in my seat, properly scolded. Anytime I express even the slightest distrust in Silas, someone in the coven leaps to defend him. And even if I hadn't been with Abena long enough to know I can trust her, the change in her eyes is enough; the scarlet has receded significantly. She has Silas to thank for that. Maybe one day I'll have him to thank for the change in my eyes.

"Ugh, come on! No fighting, you two! We need to go! Silas is sending a car for us!" Soojin springs from her seat, ready to begin.

* * *

Wicklow's unassuming dress shop is the picture of understated elegance. Its windows are framed with soft white curtains, and its displays filled with delicate gowns that seem to shimmer beneath the warm lighting.

A soft chime of the doorbell rings as Soojin pushes the door open for us. Abena walks through, tall and graceful. I keep glancing about as if my eyes will meet Jack's watching us from a far.

"Thanks," I say, stepping into the warm shop.

A few locals perusing the aisles nearby stop and unabashedly gawk.

Abena's long, beautiful form catches the light as she moves toward the racks, her teeny, intricate braids flowing down her back like a waterfall of midnight. She pulls back her cape coat to more easily browse the dresses packed tight on padded hangers.

"I'm in heaven," Soojin coos. "Don't worry, Eleanor, I'm going to find you something perfect!" She skips off to the front counter questioning the lady about designers, fabrics and accessories. As I watch Soojin, I can't help but recognize how my current life mirrors my old one, Maggie perusing Esmarelda's determined to find us the best costume. *How was that only two months ago?*

I plop on a stiff fabric chair by the door, angled so I can see out the store's front window. I peer up and down the cobble street. Locals hurry past and into pubs for warmth. Parents cart bags of groceries in brown paper bags, hurrying into their cars. My days and weeks have bled into one another since my time on the run. It's Christmas, and I'm finally in Ireland, but without my family. It's strange to think this is the first Christmas without my dad; in fact, it's my first Christmas without any family at all. I'm gripped with unbearable homesickness.

After purchasing our dresses, we step back out into the brisk air of Wicklow. Before I duck into the backseat with Soojin, I glance about once more, wondering if Jack is watching me right now.

"Pleasant day shopping?" Blue asks, deeply sarcastic.

I place my boxed dress on the chair next to the bed. "I suppose," I mutter. "*And pray tell, what are the gowns for?*" Blue questions, leaping out of the bed so that I may make it.

"Silas is taking us to a ball. Hosted by a good Nefari, so he's hoping to do some recruiting while we're there. Apparently, we'll need some back up if we want to kill this Vincenzo character," I murmur, fluffing the pillows and tossing them at the top of the bed.

Blue cocks a dubious gaze at me. "*You don't sound so convinced...*"

I sigh, gazing down at the floral duvet. "I don't know. Silas is so eager to have all of us healed, I'm worried he's too single minded. Like he wouldn't recognize a trap. Though he's been doing this longer than I have. Ugh, I don't know, maybe I'm just missing Jack. He said he was going to be here, but... I guess I'm worried he'll keep his distance."

"*You do realize that is perhaps for the best,*" Blue ventures.

I nod, not wanting to say out loud that he is probably right. "We picked up some things in the market today, hungry?"

"*Do witches fly?*" Blue quips sarcastically as we descend the stairs together. I gaze out the front window at the foot of the stairs. The late December chill clings to the windows, frosting the outlining glass like delicate lace. I dip my head, peering up at the snowcapped cliffs surrounding the valley.

Blue peels off from my side and joins Machado on the sofa while Gree is coiled inside a towel on top of a heater.

Together, Abena, Soojin, and I empty our grocery bags and set about prepping for dinner. The front door opens, a gust of wind blows through with a flurry of snowflakes.

Blue races into the kitchen, his paws skittering across the floor. "*Bloody cold.*"

"Massachusetts is worse," I chime.

"They're back!" Soojin drops the bag of potatoes on the table and skips out into the living room.

"I've got this handled," I say over my shoulder standing at the sink, "if you want to go ask how the trip went."

Abena nods once to me. "I do, I have concerns about this ball tomorrow." The hearth crackles, casting a golden glow over the cozy kitchen. It's strange, I've never been here, but I navigate the home with a weird sense of familiarity. Perhaps it's due to the fact my mother has her kitchen organized identically to her mother's.

The recipe I prepare—a traditional Irish stew—is one I know by a heart, a dish my mom has made countless times having been taught by her mother.

Markus laughs a fully belly laugh while Soojin's giggles from the other room. Silas speaks animatedly, though from this distance I can't make out the specifics.

The heavy iron pot simmers on the stove, filled with tender chunks of lamb, potatoes, onions, and carrots, all slowly stewing in a broth made from Guinness and herbs. I grin to myself, feeling as though I'm honoring my mom with this dinner.

"I won't be coy, but the smell has my mouth watering," Blue sends.

I check on the brown soda bread baking in the oven and carefully brush the top with butter.

From the living room, Abena raises her voice, but in high spirits rather than anger, the laughter from the room rising and falling like the crackling fire.

Silas bursts into the kitchen, his face alight with a mix of relief and elation. "Eleanor!" he says, his voice brimming with urgency. He holds his phone up to his face.

I turn to face him, the wooden spoon continuing to stir on its own. "Your grandmother—she's alive!"

My heart skips a beat.

"I just got word from one of the witches I met with today. Colleen's with a friend, a, um…a Gráinne," he says, pronouncing it like grainy.

"Grawn-ya," I correct as I reclaim my chair.

He shrugs. "Yeah, well, she's with her, and most importantly," his tone drops an octave as he peers into my eyes with a heaviness that makes my stomach knot, "she has the Black Flame Candle. She plans on giving it to Oisín," he says, pronouncing ush-een, "and I know I said that one right because I've been corrected a thousand times today. Oisín Quinn, that's the host of tomorrow's ball."

I'm not sure how to respond.

"Eleanor, this is great news," he says his voice rising as he stares at my incredulous face.

"Yes, of course it is. Sorry, I just—"

"What is it?"

I don't know, Blue. Something feels…off.

"News of Colleen is good. Hopefully you can leave this coven and remain with her. I believe you'll be safer with family."

My heart lifts at the thought. "I'm anxious to go," I mutter to Silas, mustering up a smile.

Silas smiles back at me, the same kind you would give your little sister. "Good! And one other thing. Your familiar stays here, same with Machado. Same with Gree," Silas calls. "Animals are not allowed at the estate. So they all stay here, understood?"

"Methinks the likelihood is slim indeed," Blue sends. *Hop in the truck as soon as we are all inside?* "Agreed."

"Eleanor, understood?" Silas asks again. "Understood."

Everyone filters into the kitchen and drops into chairs about the table. I levitate the ladle filled with stew and fill their bowls while simultaneously sending around a wicker basket of fresh soda bread around. The warmth and levity in the room relieves the tension that's been building in my chest as my mind buzzes with the news of Grandma Colleen.

Silas and Markus crack open a case of Guinness, the bottles clinking together as they toast to the small victory, and the prospect of expanding our humble, little coven.

"Eleanor?" Silas reaches out, offering me a glass bottle of beer.

I shake my head. "No, thank you. I think I'll just have some tea."

I start to rise from my chair, but Silas waves me down. "No, no, allow me, you made the meal. Let me wait on you for a change," he says in bright spirits. He returns with a steaming teacup.

"Thanks," I say. I blow on the nearly boiling liquid and take a sip, detecting coriander, lemon, and possibly orange zest.

Markus slams his empty bottle to the table. Abena rolls her eyes but gives him a tepid applause.

He sways a little in his sweat. "Lightweight," she mutters.

The room starts to settle as Abena and I turn to cleaning the kitchen. The boys hunch over their phones going over maps of Ireland, discussing the finer points of tomorrow's journey to Wexford.

"So, where is this ball?" Soojin says, grabbing a beer. She uses her magic to pop the lid.

Silas grins across the table at her. "Loftus House."

CHAPTER FORTY-THREE
Loftus House

"May I just say you all look lovely this evening," Markus says, holding open the door to the backseat for us.

Soojin stomps her feet at the front door while Abena and I climb into the backseat. She's wearing a narrow column gown, deep plum and smooth as satin. A minimalist number, at least by Soojin's standard, yet refined, with a delicate lace overlay at the bodice, thin shoulder straps, and a chiffon lace peplum at her petite waist.

"You can't make us drive two hours in our dresses, Silas!" Soojin argues for the third time today. "They're going to wrinkle! *Please,* let us get dressed when we get there!"

"Soojin, you're a witch, steam the wrinkles out the moment we arrive," Silas yells back at her. "Now get in."

Earlier this morning, Silas insisted that us girls be made up by professionals and arranged a salon appointment. Our nails were trimmed, buffed, and glossed, Soojin had her long black hair blown out to a glossy curtain, while Abena allowed the team of men to carefully massage oil into her beautiful curls, leaving them soft and shimmering down her shoulders. A young hairdresser pulled my hair into a stylish updo, allowing just a few tendrils to escape.

After the salon, we returned to the cottage to change into the gowns we purchased the day before. Soojin picked out her plum dress, while Abena selected a stunning creation in dark emerald tulle, adorned with delicate floral appliqués. The gown is ethereal, with a fitted bodice that flatters her long frame and off the shoulder sleeves that drape with grace.

I chose a gown in saffron yellow, with a plunging V-neckline, a cinched waist, and a fitted bodice that's slightly ruched at the torso. The skirt flows out into a full A-line silhouette with layers of soft chiffon that swirl with my movements. The fabric has an airy, almost weightless quality. The dress has an open back, with decorative buttons running down the small of my back. With an open back gown and my hair styled up, my brand is brazenly on display, but

Silas doesn't mention it. I wish Jack was going to be there to see me. I can't help but smile, imagining the look on his face when our eyes first meet in the ballroom.

Markus and Silas are dressed in black suits. Markus opted for a black silk bow tie, mumbling something about James Bond as he plays with his cuff link, while Silas wears a skinny black tie that lays flat on his chest.

Abena wraps her bare arms under a thick mink wrap while Soojin dons a flashier, puff coat coated in black feathers. I clip on a wool cloak I found in my grandmother's wardrobe and let it fall closed in the front.

"Couldn't have rented an SUV?" Soojin complains as the women squeeze into the back seat of the sedan.

"Next time, I'll let you find a car on short notice," Silas shoots back.

I spend the two-hour drive ringing my hands, anxious to finally meet the grandmother who has loved me from afar my entire life.

Hopefully Silas won't mind that I'm going to abandon them, I know he's worried about the numbers, but he already has several Nefari ready to enlist.

"Indeed, and seeing how he subjected you to a witch's trial, I doubt you'll be missed, my dear." Blue sends, having snuck into the trunk during all of Soojin's complaining before we left. *"In fact, he might be quite relieved by the news."*

I hope Grandma lets Jack stay with us. If I'm not traveling with Silas anymore, there's no reason for him to stay away. Grandma and I could lie low, avoid the witch's council here, and maybe even invite Mom and everyone out to visit.

"That's quite the rosy picture you're conjuring..." he sends with an air of skepticism in his tone.

Zoey is reunited with her parents, maybe I can be reunited with my family.

The tires crunch on the gravel driveway as the towering silhouette of the mansion looms above us. The Loftus House, dark and gothic against the evening sky, stands like a lone sentinel overlooking the wild landscape of the Hook Peninsula. Its stone walls, weathered by centuries of wind and rain, are imposing, yet the grand windows glow warmly, with a tall white candle dotting each window framed by a hanging wreath.

Markus offers me his hand as I step out of the car, my eyes glued to the massive estate. I can't help but compare it to the Crane Estate where Shannyn was married. Both mansions are perched in isolated areas along the Atlantic coast, and they each share that same imposing presence—sprawling lawns and towering structures that seemed more suited to fairy tales than real life. But while the Crane Estate was decadent, with its perfectly manicured gardens and elegant statues, Loftus House feels… darker. Its three stories are ensnared by dead, half-frozen ivy crawling up its sides, as if nature itself is trying to reclaim it. Gables jut out from the roof, and turrets frame the edges, their shadows long and foreboding.

A valet takes the keys from Silas and putters the car to a designated lot not far from where we stand. Several other vehicles—mostly town cars and sleek limousines—dispose of their perfectly coiffed and poised guests at the front doors. Several men even wear top hats, which they tip and bow to Markus and Silas as we join the flow into the manor.

Despite its intimidating exterior, the front doors are decorated for Christmas. Wreaths of evergreen, pinecones, and holly berries cover the width of the dark wooden doors, with red ribbons tied in perfect bows framing the greenery. Soojin claps and giggles at my side when she spots the twinkling lights wrapped around the pillars and doorway.

The fresh scent of pine and cinnamon waft in the air as we make our way into the grand hall. The high, vaulted ceilings stretch far above, where intricately carved beams support the roof. The walls are paneled in dark oak, polished to reflect the light of the massive chandelier that hangs like a jeweled crown at the center of the room, dripping with crystals that catch the firelight from the nearby hearth. I'm awestruck, not only by the sheer majesty of the place, but also its familiarity. A faint spinning sensation comes over me.

Blue, I know this place. I just—I rack my brain trying to remember. A grand staircase dominates the far side of the room, its banisters carved with intricate Celtic knots.

"From a vision?"

I believe so. Why can't I recall it though?

Guests continue to pour in from the cold, shaking off the winter chill as they discard their fur shawls and overcoats to the attendants stationed at the doors. An Irish string quartet sounds from the corner of the hall, their lively tune filling the space with energy and elegance. Men in tailcoats and white gloves glide about the room offering hors d'oeuvres and champagne flutes on polished silver trays to the gathering guests. Our coven stands huddled in the center of the room.

Silas leans in close to the group. "Let's spread out, explore, make friends, recruit, and enjoy yourselves," he says, his eyes gleaming.

"But remember, we're not just here to celebrate," Markus cuts in. "I heard there is a doctor here that has brought witches back from the dead.

If you can, find him. He would be perfect for our little coven," he says with a grin. He straightens and extends a hand to Soojin. "Fancy a dance in the ballroom?"

Soojin blushes, and together they move toward the ballroom, laughter trailing in their wake. When I turn back to our group, Silas has already disappeared into the crowd.

Abena snags a crystal flute of champagne from a passing server and downs it quickly enough to put it back on the tray before the server continues. "Well, we'd better get to work if we want to find someone powerful enough to make a difference." Her heels click as she strolls away.

I'm left alone in the hall surrounded by witches. The dresses vary in color and style, but the men are all in nearly identical penguin suits; a few have added personal embellishes here and there. But the one thing that remained constant amongst the crowd is their eyes. Every shade in the spectrum is represented, most so vibrant they practically glow.

"Are you also going to be on the lookout for this doctor, or will you hunt for your own Nefari trophy?"

Neither. I'm going to find my grandma. I have a vague recollection of her face, a memory as hazy as the winter fog outside—round cheeks like my mom's, kind eyes with vibrant pink irises, and blonde hair cropped short like the Michelle William's platinum pixie.

My dress sways with each step as I move through the mansion, the skirt brushing against the cool marble floors as I explore each room. The rich fabric whispers softly as I glide past the swirling crowd, my attention turning towards the grand staircase that beckons me from the corner of the room.

The banisters are smooth and cool beneath my fingertips as I follow the broad curve of the staircase to the second floor. The polished timber shimmers like a mirror; the Celtic knots and twisting vines carved into wood look like they might spring to life at any moment.

There's a flash, and suddenly I see the room from a different perspective, like a memory I can't quite place. Watching from the center of the grand hall, I see a girl with mousy features and a nervous demeanor as she's escorted down the stairs. Her gloved hand slides down the polished banister. A smattering of applause.

The fluttering of lace fans. Blushing cheeks. Suitors lining up at the foot of the stairs. Clomping of hooves. Shuddering thunder.

Another flash, and I'm back on the staircase. I grip the banister, nearly toppling over, and suck in a shaky breath.

"Eleanor? Are you alright?"

Yeah, yes, I…I might have had a vision, or maybe had a memory of one? I keep my hand firm on the railing as I struggle to regain my composure. *That was…strange.*

"Just be careful. I'm going to leave this blasted trunk. I'll find you inside."

I nod to myself, even though Blue isn't here to see it. *Just make yourself scarce. Everyone's been drinking for a while now, but they're witches, I'm sure most of their legs are as hollow as Sally's.*

I continue up the staircase, each step creaking faintly underfoot, the sound swallowed by the lofty ceilings above. A nervous flutter fills my chest as I reach the top, and I set about exploring the somber second floor. Heavy wooden doors line the hallway on either side, most of them locked. The few rooms that aren't are silent and dark inside.

Just as I'm about to give up, I notice one door, farther down the hall, is slightly ajar. When I stand still, the faint whisper of voices reaches my ears. My nerves are kicked into high gear.

"Did you find her?"

Possibly. I reach the threshold and press my ear to the door. It's a couple arguing. Definitely not my grandmother. I step back and turn to leave.

"Silas, you liar!" screeches a woman from within. I stop cold in my tracks.

"You promised! I delivered, you traitor! Liar! Liar! Liar!" the woman's voice is frantic.

I tiptoe back to the door.

"No, you clearly misunderstood," Silas responds.

Tilting my head to peek through the crack, I see a girl in a cheap, forest green frock, unbefitting to this party. The dress hangs and bags on her frame in uncomplimentary ways. Her hair is a wild mess of crimped locks, braids, and short tuffs. She's pacing back and forth, all the while keeping her back or shoulder to me. She's ranting, but the words are difficult to discern. I make out bits and pieces. Something about having done everything he asked, what Silas promised in return, an old hag's house, and having her revenge.

Silas, also with his back to me, patiently watches her angry, snarling strides. "I know this is difficult for you, but try to be reasonable," he says in a condescending tone.

She halts and spins to face him. But instead of looking at Silas, her manic eyes meet mine. Those eyes, familiar and horrifying, and the color of orange traffic cones.

The psychotic Nefari from the island. Teran. The door whips open, exposing me.

"Eleanor." Silas's voice is calm and unflustered.

"You!" Teran screams. "You killed them! The whore who hitched herself to a Noble Hunter! *Death* be upon her! You said we could have him, but I'll take her instead!" She lunges towards me from across the sitting room. Then, like running into a wall headfirst, she flies backwards and tumbles across the ground.

I know I should run, but instead I race forward on instinct at the sight of someone falling so suddenly.

Teran's orange eyes are wide, staring into space as blood sputters from her mouth gaping open like a stunned fish. Blood flows freely from her neck where an antique letter opener is wedged deep into her throat.

I clap my hand over my mouth, stumbling backwards as Silas catches me. His worried eyes sweep over me. "Are you alright? She didn't get you, did she? I thought I stopped her before she could cast anything."

"I-I-I she…" I stammer as my brain can't catch up with this sudden change of events.

How did Teran find me here?

"What? The psycho pyro is here?"

Yes. Silas just killed her…

I'm tipsy on my feet. Silas wraps his arm around my waist. Tucking me close, he glides us out of the room, using his magic to shut and lock the door behind us. "You killed her…" I mutter.

Silas tows me down the dark corridor to a divan where he helps me sit. "Take a few breaths. You've lost color in your cheeks."

I draw in several large breaths. In through my nose, out through my mouth. I reach out to my magic, needing to be ready at moment's notice, but it doesn't respond.

"Eleanor? Are you well?"

No, Blue. Something is wrong. I feel…drugged. My magic is a wobbly current inside me, desperately trying to communicate. I think back to when we arrived. Drinks were served in abundance, but I didn't have any. Nor did I eat anything. *I can't describe it, but my magic feels dulled.*

"That is very concerning. Where are you?" *Upstairs with Silas.*

Silas checks his watch. "Why don't you eat something. The

festivities are about to start, and I wouldn't want to appear rude."
Silas hoists me to my feet and his hands wrap around my waist, then
escorts me down the shadowy corridor to the top of the grand
staircase.

I grip the rail with my freehand, frozen to my spot. *Last night,
the tea I ingested…there was that strange aftertaste, bitter and sweet at
the same time. Juniper berries. The witch's gin. This is the first time I've
tried to use my magic since then. That means—*

I'm hit with a horrifying realization. My head slowly turns to
face him. "How did you know my grandmother lived in Wicklow?
I never told you that."

Silas shrugs. "Your clan's name is Byrne; it wasn't hard to go
from there. What's wrong?"

Teran's words now ring clear in my head. "*We did everything
you asked us to do on that island. You promised you would deliver the
Noble Hunter's heir. You vowed we would have his blood. I go to that old
hag's house and get you your damned candle and still no payment! I will
have my revenge!*"

My heart stops.

Silas's eyes glow a deep violet purple. He slowly dips his chin
towards his chest as a menacing smile unfurls across his face. "We
mustn't keep our guests waiting…"

CHAPTER FORTY-FOUR
Sacrifice

Silas holds my hand aloft in a mockingly formal gesture. His grip is firm, the weight of his power unmistakable. Fear courses through me as we begin our descent.

The sight of the gathered crowd below us steals my breath. Gone is the glittering crowd at an elegant ball; the scene before me now is the stuff of nightmares. The guests have added animalistic masks to their resplendent attire—the twisted faces of owls, cats, and rabbits stare back at me through hollow eyes, like followers of a sadistic pagan cult.

Soojin stands among them. She gives me a serene smile before sliding her own rabbit mask into place, the white scruffy fur contrasting with her ebony hair.

"Soojin too?" I gasp.

Silas remains at my side, my hand held in his, clearly not in any hurry. "Of course. When Isolde grew suspicious, Soojin even volunteered to dispatch her. Zoey was next."

"David, Youssef?" I question. *Did I help David leave just so he could track down Zoey and kill her?*

Silas sighs. "No. Youssef was useless, I was already tired of him. Even considered making him our sacrifice. David will always be a sore disappointment, we could have really used him. If only he'd been more malleable."

"What did you expect? You recruited Nefari who wanted redemption," I snap. My eyes scan the crowd for Abena, but she is nowhere to be seen. Her absence from the gathered crowd only deepens the dread settling in my stomach. *Has she joined them, or escaped?* "Was any of this real? Were their eyes really changing?"

Silas gives me a curly grin. "Did I ever tell you my gift with magic? On my seventeenth birthday, I discovered glamours were second nature to me. Not only could I do them on myself with almost no concentration, but on others quite effortlessly as well. And without much detection of magic, especially to those who hope."

"*Eleanor, I seem to be immobile in the ballroom. I'm caught behind the piano.*" *Blue, they're all evil. This was a huge mistake.*

I want to run, to tear my hand from Silas's grip and flee into the darkness, but my legs won't move. It's as if they no longer are my own.

"Come, we still have festivities to partake of," Silas says, giving my hand a little tug and we resume descending the staircase.

When we reach the bottom step, the crowd parts to reveal a tall, somber butler. His steps echo ominously through the hall as he approaches. Atop the silver tray he carries is a black goat's mask, the horns curving wickedly around the face. Silas accepts it with a graceful nod, sliding it into place, and with it, any remaining trace of humanity vanishes beneath. His cold gaze pierces through the goat's eyes.

My chest heaves up and down, as terror grips me tighter with each passing second. The crowd is watching me, waiting with a reverent stillness.

Silas leads us through the hall, his hand never loosening as we pass through the eerie silence of masked faces towards the billiard room. Instead of a collection of gaming tables like before, now there is only one, and what rests upon it sends a wave of terror through my veins.

"Eleanor! Eleanor! Are you there? What's wrong?"

It's the Black Flame Candle. They found it, Blue. I don't know how, but they have it.

The candle's presence seems to suck the air from the room, its black molten wax ominous, waiting like a living entity.

Silas guides me to the center table and removes the candle; then, without a word, he releases my hand. As if on cue, the instant his grip leaves me, the crowd lunges. Hands claw at my shoulders, my arms, my dress. I'm thrown on top of the table with such force it knocks the wind out of me.

I reach out to my magic again, but every time it leaves me even more dazed than before.

I can't use my magic, Blue. This is so much worse than what Mom said would happen.

"They must have altered the witch's gin somehow. Was there any member of this coven who has a gift with earth magic?"

My head lulls about. *I'm... I'm not sure.*

"If not, they were working with powerful magics, perhaps too great to wield properly. There could be a hole; you can fight through this."

I close my eyes and imagine a gale of wind so strong it knocks the guests back against the walls, holding them with such force they tremble. *La Cae*—I can't recall the incantation.

Blue! Blue! What is the air spell?!

"*La Caeli*, hurry!"

I try to summon the spell, but I can't concentrate on what I want my magic to do. My mind is blank, like it's been wiped clean.

Above the clamor of the crowd, Silas's voice booms with triumph. "It is my greatest honor to present to you… our sacrifice!"

Fingers bite into my skin, holding me in place.

He raises the candle high above the crowd until he releases it, letting it float above us all on its own. "As it is decreed from below, blood from a Nefari—one who has been cursed by a branding and has killed a son of creation—must spill upon the holy candle which we wield."

Blue, the candle. He's going to light the candle. We need to stop him.

The crowd roars with anticipation. Their masked faces turn towards me like predators circling their prey. Silas turns to the man beside him; his thick muscled figure is familiar as he towers next to Silas. Markus.

"Markus—err, Asmodeus," Silas says, his voice dripping with a wicked reverence. He offers him a blade with a golden hilt and a blood-red ruby gleaming at its base. "Would you do the honors?"

Asmodeus, I know that name. The demon of lust and vices. He should be in the fourth circle, how did he get out? He must have been summoned…

Asmodeus, once known to me as Markus Van der Laan, tilts his owl mask back exposing his face. His eyes, with those flat black irises, stare down at me with terrifying glee. He grins and runs a thick finger down my sternum causing me to shiver.

"If only I could have a taste of the Mother's angel before she is spent. So beautiful," he says as he strokes my cheek. "Would be such a shame to waste."

I recoil at his touch.

Asmodeus slides the strap of my gown off my shoulder, but Silas snatches his wrist. "Unspoiled flesh is required. The hour is nigh, brother. Time to do the Dark King's will." Silas feigns a polite tone through his clenched jaw.

Asmodeus nods, reluctantly, and accepts the blade held out to him. Silas lets the candle drift from his hand so it hovers between them. Asmodeus raises the blade high into the air and chants:

"By ancient blade, the blood must flow,
A sacrifice for dark winds to blow.
The blood of mother's fallen kin,
A benediction, pure, to let him in.
Nine circles' blessing from below,
Summon the gift the Dark King bestows.
May hell fire reign, and darkness grow."

With the incantation complete, his eyes move from the knife down to mine.

Blue! Blue, this is it! I can't move! What should I do?!

I squeeze my eyes shut, knowing any second that dagger will plunge through my chest. *Mom, I'm so sorry. I was so stupid. I shouldn't have left. It would have been better to surrender to The Committee. Please forgive me. Jack, I love you.*

"Don't you give up! I'm on my way!"

Asmodeus grabs my hand and runs the point of the blade down the length of my middle finger.

I shriek in pain. Blood flows down my finger, dripping off the fingertips and splashing onto the wick of the Black Flame Candle.

The gathered horde awaits with bated breath; the excitement in the room is palpable. They all stare as my warm, crimson blood paints the top of the candle. Asmodeus hands the candle back to Silas.

There is an eerie calm in Silas's eyes behind that goat mask. He raises his hands and the candle floating effortlessly into the air above me. My heart pounds, the sound of my own breathing roars in my ears, my body reacting to the dark magic condensing in the room. I lie helpless, still pinned to the table, my eyes locked on the candle.

The flame ignites.

A flicker of pure black, as dark as onyx, consumes the wick in defiance of the light around it.

There's a collective gasp.

The inscriptions etched around the candle begin to glow, each symbol pulsating with a bright inner fire. Whispers ripple amongst the crowd. Asmodeus steps closer and stares at the wax as the candle slowly swivels.

Blue! Blue! They lit the candle! It's burning! What are we going to do?!

"To open the gates," he squints, "place the babe upon the altar. The child born of both life and death. It'll be swallowed by the beast with seven heads." Silas nods, like he knew what the candle was going to say. "Yes, that's why I brought her. Eleanor's spirit was created in Purgatory by Elspeth McEwen."

Dissenting whispers ripple throughout the room.

Silas senses the shift in the air. "Spill all her blood. Now! If we need to, we'll move her body to Montpelier Hill," he snaps.

Blue, I'm part of the prophecy, I cry out.

"*Yes, I heard it all. I'm here in the room with you. Born of life* and *death?" Yes, what does that mean?*

Asmodeus hesitates, rereading the candle's inscription. He shakes his head to himself. "When Elspeth contacted me in the second circle, she explained how Eleanor was created," he says, trying to decipher the puzzle. "She was trying to resurrect herself, but she created a new spirit instead."

Agitation is rising among the guests.

"*Eleanor, if your spirit was fully formed within Purgatory, you only fit the 'born of death' element. I believe you're just one piece of the prophesy.*"

I repeat Asmodeus's words in my head trying to sort out the double meaning behind them. A child born of death, me. And life. Jack. *Wait…*

A spark ignites in Silas's eyes. "If her spirit was made in Purgatory, then she is death and must have a child with one made in this life!"

Asmodeus's face lights with sheer wicked delight. "Well then, don't mind if I do," he chimes, turning towards me.

I squirm against the hands and magic holding me in place.

Asmodeus moves to climb onto the table, but Silas slams a hand against his chest. "You're a demon, mate. Means you can't create life. Tough break," he says with a supercilious grin. Silas then looks at me with lust in his eyes. Asmodeus growls deep from his chest. "I suppose any will do in a pinch," he snarls. He turns to the woman next to him, snagging her waist and pulling her into him. "What will we do with the wench in the meantime? Nine months is a long time, *mate.*"

Silas shrugs. "I don't know. But look, only half of the inscription is lit. Once she is with child, the rest of the prophesy will be revealed." He grips my hips and pulls me towards him. "Shall we?" he lifts me up.

The glowing chandeliers overhead cut out, and the billiard

room is plunged into darkness. Silas tightens his hold on me. For a moment, there is only darkness and silence, then it's shattered by the bright flash and sharp crack of gunfire. The room erupts into utter chaos.

Screaming. Running. The dull thud of bodies hitting the floor—all blending into one horrific cacophony. For only a split second, Silas's grip loosens in the madness. Summoning all my strength, I give Silas a hard shove and break free. More gunfire and screaming followed by the sounds of whipping gale-like winds.

Balls of fire erupt illuminating the room in a flash before being extinguished. I try to run but trip over a lifeless body on the floor.

I try to move towards the door, but a hand snags my wrist with a brutal grip, yanking me in the opposite direction. I stumble backward, my high heels breaking in the process. The deafening flash of gunfire is relentless. My wrist is released, followed immediately by a muted thud to floor. I'm suddenly seized around my waist and whisked away from the center of the room.

The heavy velvet curtains that frame the massive windows burst into flames, illuminating the nightmare unfolding around me in orange light. Men in black combat gear, knit skull caps, and oil face paint either lie dead on the floor or crouched down in corners firing their weapons. The stench of smoke and gunpowder fills the air as bodies fall, some engulfed in flames. One man screams as he's hurled across the room by an unseen force, his limbs bending into impossible angles before his body crashes to the floor. I freeze as another man's head twists a full one-hundred-eighty degrees, the crack of bone and sinew echo in my skull like a death knell.

The barrage of gunfire has left me nearly deaf, but I just faintly make out the sound of someone screaming my name. I look up to the one holding me.

Jack.

His face is fierce and determined, holding me close. He's dressed in a black sweater with black cargo pants, just like the shooters who crashed the party and are now being picked off one by one.

"Jack," I pant.

The sight of him gives me a momentary reprieve, but terror's grip remains tight. The air hums with dark magic, chaotic and violent. I can feel it tugging at my own power—power that I can't seem to grasp in the haze of the tonic Silas had slipped me the night before.

Jack's hired team of guns are being torn apart; three even break the window and flee. The billiard room doors are blown into shards, letting some of the smoke escape. The bodies of Nefari and the hired gunmen alike litter the floor. In a flurry of panic, Nefari push past us and run from the house. Coughing against the smoke, Jack and I race into the hall. I whip my head around, noticing Soojin fleeing with Blue tucked under her arms. His fur is singed as she darts up the grand staircase.

"No! Soojin!" I dash up to the second level after her. "Eleanor!" Jack calls, sprinting after me.

Soojin races down the hall, stopping at the second to last door and disappearing into the room. I follow her into an opulently decorated bedroom with an ornate fourposter bed poised in the center of the far wall, roped off by velvet rope for viewing purposes only.

Jack and I wheeze out of breath, coughing and gagging after inhaling so much smoke.

Soojin stands gazing out the window with her back to us. Her glowing, neon green eyes reflect off the window. Soojin only giggles, the sound highpitched and maniacal. Her eyes gleam with something wild, something especially dark, as she cradles my cat close. "You really think you stand a chance?" she mocks, her voice dripping with venom. "I killed my entire family. You can't even *use* your magic. Good luck!" she states with a sneer.

My breath comes in shallow, ragged gasps, my heart hammering in my chest as I stare at her cruel reflection. "Why don't you give Jack here," I motion to him, "my cat and we work this out. The two of us. Witch to witch."

"Eleanor, I know I've never credited you with the sharpest of minds, and I apologize, but this move does your brain no credit. Your magic is being suppressed. I'm dead, what the worse she can do?"

Soojin giggles excitedly. "It sounds to me like you're suggesting a game?"

"Sure," I say then cough.

She drops Blue unceremoniously onto the floor. He flumps into oddly angled heap, not moving. "Blue? Are you okay?" I shout to him.

Soojin spins around facing me. "He's a little broken."

"I'll be alright Eleanor, go!"

The freaking place is on fire, we don't know what happens if this form is completely destroyed. So no, I'm not leaving.

Jack moves forward, Soojin watching him like an ant she can squash. "Jack, get behind me," I hiss, but he ignores me. He inches towards Blue, never taking his eyes off Soojin, and scoops him off the floor.

As Jack crosses the room towards me, the rug beneath him violently jerks him off his feet, sending him onto his back with a hard thud. The rug then slides across the floor skidding out the door, carrying Jack and Blue along with it. The bedroom doors slam shut, and a lock turns.

"Eleanor!" Jack screams as he thunders his fists against the door.

"Eleanor! Quick let us in!"

"Eleanor!" Jack's voice laced with panic. The heavy wooden door shakes with every bang of his fist.

Soojin scrunches her face in a saccharine smile, lifting her shoulder up by her head. "Now it can just be us! Let's have some fun!"

She makes a squeezing gesture with her hands, and my windpipe is closed shut. My knees buckle beneath me and I fall onto all fours, gasping for air. My lips throb as a pressure builds behind my eyes. My lungs are set ablaze.

"You know, I never really liked you," she says, circling me. "And you so totally don't deserve to wear Vera Wang by the way. She's just wasted on you." She purposefully steps on my dress.

There's a high-pitched ringing in my ears, and I fully collapse, unable to hold myself up. I claw at my throat, desperate for air. Jack's shouting and pounding on the door now sound miles away.

Soojin sadistically giggles to herself, savoring the torment. She leans down towards me, her hands resting on her knees as she gazes at me, cocking her head to the side. "I made Isolde suffer so badly she begged for death. I'll make you beg too!" she chimes like she's doing me a favor.

The bedroom doors burst open, flying completely out of their hinges. They crash into the opposite wall and tumble to the floor, sending framed pictures to the ground shattering at their sides.

"Think again, bitch."

CHAPTER FORTY-FIVE
A Duel

Abena towers in the doorway, her burgundy eyes locked on Soojin and blazing with fury. Her face and gown are smeared with soot, remnants of the battle ragging below. Jack rushes to me, falling to his knees at my side as I struggle to breath, clawing at my throat. My vision fades in and out. Jack turns me onto my back, desperate to help, panic overtaking his usually calm demeanor.

"Eleanor, it's the mind spell!" Abena yells. "Force yourself to breathe! It's all in your head, child!" She strides toward Soojin, who recoils from her.

I gasp for air, desperately trying to fill my lungs but failing. I try to focus on Abena's words as Jack holds me.

"Breathe, my love. You can do this, please," Jack pleads.

Abena's pulsing magic creates a visible buzz in the air around her. She flicks her wrist, and Soojin is sent flying across the room. Soojin casts a counter spell, spinning in midair and landing gracefully, crouched like a cat. Glass shards from the fallen frames lift into the air, shimmering as they take aim at Abena. Abena raises her hand and the shards halt a mere foot in front of her, then burst into sand. Abena's eyes never leave Soojin.

A sliver of space opens in my throat, and I gulp back my first breath of air in over a minute. My pulsing temples slow as I breathe more and more air into my body.

A man materializes in the room next to Abena, blood trickling down the side of his face. He's dressed in pajamas, a fatal gash across his forehead. He looks hauntingly like Soojin. "Why did you kill me, Soojin?"

Behind him, a woman appears, her throat slit, her nightgown soaked in blood, her face also resembling Soojin's. "Soojin, stop this!" the woman pleads.

Soojin's eyes dart back and forth as two of them shuffle towards her. She screams and bats away at the apparitions, but instead of going right through them like they would a ghost, her fists collide with their chests. Or, at least she thinks they do. Her parents claw at her, chanting her name over and over again.

"I know this isn't real!" Soojin shrieks, swinging wildly. Her movements are erratic, even desperate. She elbows past them, knocking them to the floor as she regains her bearings and the upper hand. Tears streak down her ash painted face.

In the blink of an eye, a splintered plank of wood sails through the air, straight at Soojin. She turns, but too late. The wood pierces her throat, her eyes wide with shock. She crumples to the ground as blood pools beneath her.

Smoke is creeping into the room. Heat is rising, licking at the edges of the room.

"May Hell have you," Abena says as she spits on the floor.

Silas and Asmodeus burst into the room. Their eyes, burning from smoke, lock onto Soojin's bloody, lifeless form.

Without so much as a glance in my direction, Silas's magic lifts me from Jack's arms and tosses me onto the bed like a rag doll. Jack leaps to my defense, but Silas is faster. He lands a vicious punch to Jack's temple, sending him sprawling to the ground.

Abena, still throbbing with magic, sends another blast of wooden splinters at Silas. He deflects them with a wave of his hand, the force of it throwing Abena back against the wall. Asmodeus stands behind him, still not using his magic. Silas thrusts his hand backward, and Abena flies forward through the open doorway. She lands hard in the hallway, but not before she was able to cast a counter spell. The edges of Silas's coat ignite in flames. Silas screams, ripping it off and tossing it to the ground as it ignites in an immediate blaze. Without a glance back, he runs into the hallway, to deal with Abena.

I try to scramble off the bed, but Asmodeus cuts me off. He wags his finger while clucking his tongue. "That would not be wise, now stay down." He shoves me back onto the bed.

Blue, are you okay?

"Yes, but I'm unable to move at the moment. Jack placed me in the room next door.

Now concentrate, Eleanor. Your magic is yours. Use it."

I'm sprawled on the bed, still struggling to catch my breath. Asmodeus stands there, grinning, his eyes flickering up and down my body. "Just a taste won't hurt, will it, Jackie boy?"

Blood trickles down Jack's face from a gash on his forehead. "If you do," he growls, his voice strained, "it'll be the last thing you ever do." Jack forces himself to his feet, wobbly but determined.

He raises his fist, his body tense and ready for a fight.

Asmodeus laughs, a deep, full-bellied sound, matching Jack's stance with ease. Jack moves first, throwing a sharp jab that Asmodeus dodges. Another punch, this one blocked. Asmodeus throws a punch of his own, but Jack's quicker. He ducks under Asmodeus's swing and lands a solid hit to his ribs.

They exchange blows with expert speed and precision. Asmodeus moves with the fury of hell; Jack with a skill earned over years of dedicated training. Jack dodges another hit, his fist finding Asmodeus's jaw with a brutal crack. I watch helplessly from the bed, my mind racing.

Why isn't he using magic? And then it hits me: *he's not a witch at all, he's a demon. He doesn't have magic, that's why he never used it.*

Jack ducks another wild punch and swings upward, landing a blow that sends Asmodeus sprawling to the floor. Blood spurts from his mouth as he lands on his backside. Despite the flood of pain and viscera, a sickening grin spreads across his face.

"Enough of this," Asmodeus growls, wiping the blood from his chin. When he looks at Jack, one of his eyes is swollen shut. "Look at your woman over there. Does she not look divine?"

Jack's eyes dart to me, just for a moment, and Asmodeus seizes the opportunity.

"What would you like to do to her?" Asmodeus purrs, his voice dripping with demonic temptation. Jack's shoulders drop, his jaw going slack, his fists lowering as the demon's words worm their way into his mind.

Jack shakes off his slithering persuasion, lifting his fists in the air, ready to strike.

Asmodeus hauls himself to his feet. "I think you want her, don't you?" Asmodeus presses, his voice taking on a seductive edge.

Demons don't have magic, but they have the power of persuasion over humans.

Jack's eyes flutter, his body trembling as he fights an unseen influence creeping over him. Jack shakes his head violently, squeezing his eyes shut. "Get out of my head!" he screams. Just as Asmodeus lunges for him, Jack throws another punch that connects with Asmodeus's face. Blood bursts from the demon's nose, and he stumbles back against the wall.

Asmodeus laughs, even as he holds his nose, his other hand spread against the wall to steady himself. "You've wanted her for so long, haven't you? You hate yourself for it. Every second you're near her, you want her. Need her. Take her!"

Jack's fists clench, his knuckles white. His mind reels, but his resolve hardens. He charges at Asmodeus, his fists flying again. Asmodeus swings a punch meeting Jack's side, causing him to buckle and gasp for air. Jack's eyes bulge and roll about, he peers over at Asmodeus then sends a powerful kick meeting Asmodeus's knee, bending backwards unnaturally.

Asmodeus tumbles to the ground screaming, clutching his leg. His black eyes blazing at Jack. "Your desperation eats away at you. You've never wanted someone the way you want her. I can feel it. I've heard your thoughts, boy. Have her! Ravage her! She is yours!"

Jack's eyes turn hard, his body spins facing me. Despite the pain and exhaustion from the fight, he crawls up my body. His mouth is hard, urgent against mine, moving with a hungry ferocity. His strong, square hands clamp down hard on my waist, furiously bunching up my skirt.

I push back against his chest. "Jack! Jack stop! This isn't you!" I scream. I close my eyes now desperately trying to call my magic to me. I imagine Jack lifting off me, a breeze separating us, cradling him until he is safely down the hall. *La C—*

Before I can complete the spell, Jack throws himself off me, gripping his head he screams an unbridled cry. He leaps off the bed, throwing himself on Asmodeus. He winds his fists back, pummeling him over and over again. Asmodeus crumples to the floor, his face bloodied to a raw pulp.

Jack's chest heaves up and down as he struggles to catch his breath. With his hands bloodied and bruised, Jack pushes up off the floor and strides over to me.

I slide off the bed and meet him halfway.

"I'm so sorry," he cries. His eyes gloss repentantly. "I don't know what—I'm so—," he grapples for words, still catching his breath.

I cup his face. "It's okay, we need to get Blue and get out here." I grip his hand; he winces but refuses to let go. "We need to see if Abena—" we turn and stop, Silas, bloodied stands in the doorway, his shoulders hunched, his eyes wild.

"She's dead," he answers, his voice husky with exertion. "A great disappointment she wouldn't join, but an honor to kill such a witch. I don't think I've met one more powerful." He steps further into the room.

"Jack, I want you to go to the window and jump," I whisper to him. *He might break his leg, but at least he might live. If he stays, he dies.*

Silas shakes his head. "No, you see, once I kill him, I break your will to live, and you submit yourself to my will and our Dark King."

Images flash through my mind. The Nefari who ran their hands down the scarred brand on my back, delighting at how I flinched beneath their touch. The Nefari on the island, forcing me to see my mother's head. The Noble Hunters branding my back on prom night. An all-consuming need for vengeance swells inside me.

I smile at him darkly. "Then you don't know me. I dispatched those Nefari on the island, wait to you see what I'm going to do to you."

"You see," Silas begins, "You've put in me quite a precarious situation, Eleanor. If I kill you, you'll never produce any offspring, and I won't be able to make an offering to the beast."

"Let him monologue. You attack. Do it!"

"Although, Elspeth claims she can create another spirit in Purgatory. If that's true, I should do with you what I will." He shakes his head. "But that would take another seventeen years, when already nine months feels like asking too much."

"What are you talking about?" Jack interjects.

Silas smiles. "Her child, didn't she tell you? She and I will be expecting soon. I've already taken her for myself."

Jack shakes his head. "No. She wouldn't. Couldn't!" he yells back.

I watch as Silas advances on Jack. Jack is wailing, calling Silas a liar, nearly in tears, and Silas is loving it.

This isn't Jack. Is it an act? It suddenly makes sense. *He's distracting him.*

My gift is with the mind. I close my eyes—the need for vengeance amplifying my magic— and imagine the neurons in his brain communicating across synapses. I picture reaching into his prefrontal cortex, forcing open his parietal and temporal lobes, his mind becoming a playground. I imagine him losing all feeling in his body. *Oculi Tempe*.

Silas flops to the floor like a jellyfish. His legs sprawled out beneath him. His mouth hangs open. His eyes wide, dart about.

"Jack, get Blue and get out of here!" I order, feeling Silas's will battle my own. "Trust me, I'll meet you out in the gardens, go! Hurry!"

Jack hesitates, then looks down at Silas limp as a noodle on the floor.

Jack gives me a quick peck on the cheek before sprinting from the room. Silas's hand begins to twitch, then his arm as well. I try to contain him, but after the first spell, I barely have anything left.

"Don't just paralyze him, kill him." I don't have the strength, Blue.

Silas growls as he heaves himself up to his feet. He waves his hand, throwing the air spell at me knocking me off my feet.

I struggle to lift myself off the warm, unforgiving floor. My limbs tremble, my muscles weak after the spell. Silas lumbers in circles around me like a wounded predator, his shoes softly thudding against the floorboards in a rhythm that heightens my terror. *He's weakened too, but at least he can stand.*

"Don't give in Eleanor! Fight!"

My chest rises and falls in rapid succession, but I will myself to move, to do anything. I have to fight.

While still regaining strength in his magic, Silas resorts to a physical attack and delivers a brutal kick to my side. The sharp crack of bone colliding with bone echoes through my skull. A ragged scream rips from my throat as I curl in on myself, my vision blurring with tears that sink back. My hands claw at the ground, desperate to summon any magic I have left. I imagine pushing Silas backward. *La Caeli.*

Silas stumbles but quickly recovers. "Pitiful," he chides.

I imagine him bursting into flames. *Ne Feerah.*

Silas's pants smoke, but he deflects it with ease. His lips twist into a cruel smirk as he watches me struggle. With just a flick of his wrist, invisible tendrils of power wrap around my neck, hoisting me off the ground. My feet dangle uselessly beneath me as he commands the air to throw me about, smashing my body against the floor, then the wall behind me. Silas tosses me like discarded trash onto the bed. I gasp, barely able to process the fresh wave of agony that ripples through me.

His cold gaze slides to the body of his fallen companion, slumped lifeless on the floor, blood pooling beneath the twisted form. Silas lets out a slow, disappointed sigh, his voice thick with mock regret. "Such a pity," he murmurs, his eyes narrowing as if mourning a lost investment rather than a friend. "He worked so hard to make it back up to the surface. Now, to start all over again."

My fingers graze something sharp beneath me. The glass shards from the shattered window. My heart pounds with a new flicker of hope. Slowly, subtly, I move my hand, gripping the long piece of glass. The jagged edge digs into my palm, but I bite back the pain, slipping it under my thigh.

Silas laughs a loud, condescending laugh that causes him to grip his hips. "Silly girl." He shakes his head at me, then snaps his finger. The glass clutched in my hand zips out from under my leg, slicing my hand in the process. It falls to the floor and shatters, along with any hope I had left.

"You can't give up, Eleanor. Your magic isn't used up; you just need to harness it.

Embrace your nature and call upon the full weight of your magic."

I close my eyes. *Embrace* my *nature.* I tried to use darkness and vengeance, to summon a violent magic that always seemed to come so easy to me, but that isn't *my* nature. That's Elspeth's nature, embedded in me like a sliver, a disease from Purgatory.

Then which part is from me?

I see my father, smiling, teaching me how to paddle out into baby waves in South Beach. My mom and I cooking together. My sisters helping me get ready for prom. Watching TV with the aunts. Learning of Sally's math genius and Marie's secret novels. I think of Jack in the future, standing at the end of an aisle, his smile genuine as I walk up to him holding a bouquet of daisies. My chest swells with love, with tenderness. And with it, a connection to my magic.

A water witch has never become a Nefari. Nefari struggle with it, to cast it, and to counter it…

Uisce.

Silas gurgles, clawing at his throat. He stumbles back as a river flows out his nose and mouth. His eyes are wide and blood red. Steam billows from him as he tries to use the fire spell to quell the flood. His eyes lock on mine trying to call up a spell. His knees buckle, and he collapses to the floor, face down and still.

I dash out of the room, favoring my broken ribs that ache with each step. Just as I enter the corridor, I trip over a body.

Abena.

She groans, blood spilling from her side.

"Abena!" I scramble over to her. "I've got you." Using my last ounce of strength, I utter the air spell and lift her into my arms. I direct us down the grand staircase where fire rapidly consumes the fine wood. Glass bursts out of their frames from the heat.

Outside, the cold hits us with fury. I race us to the nearest parked car and slide Abena into the back seat just as my magic gives out. I tear up my skirt, ripping long strips to wrap around her bleeding abdomen.

Blue, I'm in the parking lot. We need to get Abena to the hospital.

Gravel crunches behind me. I whip around.

My lavender eyes meet a gaze from steady, pink ones. "Colleen," I whisper.

EPILOGUE
War

Thick stubby fingers jab at the phone's interface, patience with modern technology waning greatly. He shoves the device into his coat pocket and steps out into the cold dark night, leaving behind the warmth and frivolity of the packed pub celebrating the New Year.

He blows into his hands as Ireland's damp cold sinks past the wool and down to his dark sinew.

The sleek black town car pulls across the cobbled street, parking under the lamp post.

He checks his watch, a perfectly crafted time piece that needs no modern intervention. *Fifteen minutes late. Typical.* He checks his pocket again, making sure the Black Flame Candle is secure and protected.

The driver steps out of the car and strolls to the back to open the door. A pair of long legs sheathed in those gauzy black stockings women often wear. *With legs like that, she knows what she's doing,* he thinks to himself before entertaining what he would like to do to the owner of such fine limbs. The very thought of a night of carnal glory brings a momentary pain to his cold, dead heart. His brother, Asmodeus, that was more in his wheelhouse, mixing pain and pleasure. The fun he had whispering into Caligula's ear so long ago. He's lost in one of the workhouses of the fourth circle now.

Killed by a human, he'll need to work extra to pay off that debt.

The lanky woman, almost too much so for his taste, steps out, taking the driver's hand with a graceful confidence that seems to come so easy to her sex. Long auburn curls ruffle in the wind. She waits, meeting the man's gaze with a wink and a playful little smirk.

The passenger seated next to her steps out on the other side of the car. He adjusts his long black coat before striding around to the beautiful, wild woman.

Her heels click in a seductive rhythm as she is escorted across the cobble stone. They meet in the middle of the street, where neither lamppost can reach them, and no car would dare hit them.

"Mammon," the man greets. "You're late, Belial," he grouses.

A manicured hand lands on Belial's chest, keeping him from speaking. "I do ask for your pardon, it is my fault entirely," the woman says. Her thin rose painted lips curl in a smile.

"And you are?" Mammon growls. "My name… is Elspeth."

THE END

ACKNOWLEDGEMENTS

First and foremost, I need to recognize and thank my amazing husband, Corey, for all that he has done for this book. To list everything he did to support me could easily fill a tome. My heart is so full. Thank you, thank you, thank you.

My siblings: Chris, Shannon, Ryan, and Meaghan. Thank you for all your love and support. You were the first at book conventions and the last to leave. Thanks for everything. I'm blessed to have you guys.

My rock star publishing team. Your patience, proofing, and polishing helped make this story what it is, my gratitude is infinite.

Piper Davis, Autumn Dickinson, Savannah Friel, and Talia Rodriguez, your enthusiasm and love for this coven and books in general lifted me and helped me more than you know. You ladies are amazing.

Faith Dickinson, thank you for everything. Friends like you are so rare.

ABOUT THE AUTHOR

Kellie O'Neill originally wrote the Daughters of Salem series when she was sixteen years old, and the first edition of Burned was published while she was in high school.

This is the second of a three books in the series which Kellie is looking forward to publishing soon.

In her spare time, Kellie haunts her local bookstore and takes classes on neuropsychology. She currently resides in Texas where she enjoys life as a wife and mother.

www.kellieoneillbooks.com